MW00810010

WE

ARE

WATCHING

WE ARE WATCHING

A NOVEL

ALISON GAYLIN

wm

WILLIAM MORROW
An Imprint of HarperCollins*Publishers*

WE ARE WATCHING. Copyright © 2024 by Alison Gaylin. All rights reserved. Printed in the United States of America. No part of this book may be used or reproduced in any manner whatsoever without written permission except in the case of brief quotations embodied in critical articles and reviews. For information, address HarperCollins Publishers, 195 Broadway, New York, NY 10007.

HarperCollins books may be purchased for educational, business, or sales promotional use. For information, please email the Special Markets Department at SPsales@harpercollins.com.

FIRST EDITION

Designed by Nancy Singer

Library of Congress Cataloging-in-Publication Data has been applied for.

ISBN 978-0-06-327518-8

24 25 26 27 28 LBC 5 4 3 2 1

For Sheldon Gaylin,
my wonderful father-in-law, in loving memory.

Q. If you knew Humanity had three months, three weeks,
three days and three hours left to live, what would you do?

A. Pretend you don't know. Pretend you didn't predict it.
Pretend you and your family didn't cause it. Take your kid
to college.

—the Bronze Lord

We Are Watching. We Are Armed. We Will Triumph.

ONE

It's been the longest day of Meg Russo's life, and it isn't even half over. Her stomach gnaws at her, her hands heavy on the wheel. But when she glances at the clock on the dashboard, she sees that it's a little shy of 11:30 A.M., which means that Meg, her husband, Justin, and their daughter, Lily, have only been on the road for an hour. They've got at least three more hours on the thruway, and then they'll have to contend with the series of veinlike country roads Meg and Justin haven't traversed since their own college days. If they don't hit too much traffic or take a wrong turn, they should be in Ithaca by five, which now feels like some point in a future so distant, Meg is incapable of envisioning it.

Time is strange that way, the past eighteen years zooming by in an instant, all of it leading up to a single day that's already lasted eons. Meg blames the stress of last night, wanting everything to be perfect for their daughter's send-off, which led to thoughts of Lily's first visit home for Thanksgiving break, which in turn made Meg think for the millionth time about how cold their house gets in the fall, and how Lily always complains about it. *New windows,* Meg had thought, lying in bed with her eyes open, envisioning insulated windows to replace those paper-thin sheets of glass, the same windows that were here when she and Justin bought the place twenty years ago—and it was a fixer-upper then. *What if Lily could come home to insulated windows?* Meg mused, still wide awake in the wee hours of the morning. *Will she have changed by then? Will she have grown too sophisticated to get excited over a warmer house?* And so on, until the sky was pink and it was time to wake up and Meg had barely slept at all.

They ate a too-early breakfast of coffee and grocery store bagels, and then they tackled the load-in, which was a pain in more ways than one. They all did their share, Meg, Justin and Lily. But Meg's lower back has been temperamental since she hit her mid-forties, a sad fact that no amount of yoga has been able to fix.

It still burns from lugging all of Lily's dorm room essentials into their Subaru—the filled-to-bursting suitcases and garbage bags and hampers stuffed with towels and bedding and detergents and toiletries; Lily's wireless headphones and laptop, her keyboard and electric bass and guitar and amp and the tangled collection of cables necessitated by all of them; the tubes filled with posters advertising people and things Meg can't wrap her head around Lily's love for: speed-metal bands and experimental-jazz musicians, pro wrestlers from the nineties and Jinkx Monsoon the drag queen. Well, actually, she does like Jinkx Monsoon, who is funny as hell and does a mean Judy Garland impersonation. But beyond that and their mutual desire for a warmer house, Meg and her daughter just don't share much in the way of interests anymore.

She glances at Lily in the rearview, wedged up against the window to make room for her amp and keyboard, as well as a crate full of cables and computer equipment that reminds Meg of the spaceship interior from *Alien*. Lily's profile is so like Justin's—the strong jaw, the soft brow, the regal Roman nose. It's not something that most people notice, since she more obviously resembles Meg, with her dark, curly hair and pale, freckled skin and steel-gray eyes that truly are identical to hers, down to the yellow flecks around the pupil. *She's your mini-me,* Meg's Facebook friends always comment when she posts a picture of her daughter. But it's only genetics, and genetics are shallow. Meg has no idea what's going on behind those eyes. She hasn't for years.

She'll come back again, Justin has said to her, late at night in the quiet of their bedroom. *She's spreading her wings. It's natural. She'll circle back, and we'll be here.*

When Lily was a kid, she was an avid reader who spent nearly as much time in her parents' bookstore, the Secret Garden, as Meg and Justin did themselves. The three of them would devour young adult series together and discuss them over dinner—their own private book club. Lily's bedroom was a library, filled with hardcovers and paperbacks and the advance galleys Meg and Justin would bring home. Fantasies were her favorite. Anything with a dragon in it. She'd read these books in a day, then place them carefully on her shelves, the spines unbent, the pages unfolded, lending them out only to the most trusted friends. Her personal treasures.

But five minutes later, Lily hit age fourteen and abandoned books for music—the bass, of all things, following in the footsteps of the grandfather she barely knew. Dove headfirst into it, same as she'd done with reading. Made it her new passion, because Lily was someone who had passions rather than hobbies. One of the few times he visited, Meg's father caught sight of Lily in the dim light of her bedroom, amp unplugged, headphones on, her fingers a blur as they plucked the thick strings and danced over the frets. *She practices like a boy,* Nathan had said, which had made Meg roll her eyes. (If there was any man on the planet more obliviously sexist than her weed-smoking, antiestablishment, rock musician father, Meg had yet to meet him.)

As a teen, Lily took up other instruments—keyboards, drums (a little). With money she saved from working behind the counter at the Secret Garden, she bought a used electric guitar for the sole purpose of writing songs.

She acquired a new set of friends—boys, mostly, with sullen faces and long, skinny bodies and hair that hung resolutely in their eyes. They were polite; Lily's friends have always been polite. But unlike the squealing, bookish little girls who used to come over for slumber parties, they seemed to prefer music to speaking. After school most days, they would show up at the Russos' house, these hulking boys with their electronic drums and sleek keyboards, guitar cases clutched in their hands like weapons. They'd grab sodas out of the fridge and make a beeline for the converted basement to practice their defiantly uncatchy songs. Music came first for Lily, which made her hard and unreachable in a way that Meg never could have imagined.

Sometimes, Meg would lean against the basement stairwell and watch Lily, curls snaking down her back, those lightning-fast and calloused fingers working of their own accord, head bobbing to rhythms too complicated for Meg to keep up with. It reminded her of when she was a child herself, watching her father in his home recording studio. It made her feel the same way, as though she'd come in contact with a different species, more advanced and slightly hostile.

Meg glances in the rearview mirror, hoping to catch her daughter's eye, but Lily's put on her headphones now. Her eyes are closed.

When are you going to circle back? Make it soon, okay?

"What kind do you want?" Justin says. It takes Meg a little while to remember that twenty seconds ago, before she got lost in this thought spiral, she'd told her husband she was hungry and he'd dug into the floor of the back seat and fished the bag of sandwiches out of the tote they'd packed together this morning. It's why Meg checked the time in the first place—because she's never been so hungry this early in the day.

"Um . . ." Meg says. The truth is, she wants a peanut butter and jelly sandwich, but they just packed one, and since Lily is now vegan, it's the only thing she can eat. Meg tells Justin she'll take a ham and cheese, and he gives her a half, carefully pulling back the wrapping so she can eat and drive at the same time. Her stomach growls. She takes a bite, then shifts into the left lane to get past the tractor trailer in front of them.

"How about you, kiddo?" Justin says. "You want a half sandwich?"

Lily doesn't answer, so he turns around in his seat and says it louder.

"Huh?" She slips off her headphones and opens her eyes. "Oh, sorry. No thanks, Dad. I'm not really hungry yet."

"Too excited to eat?"

Lily blinks at him.

"You know . . . college?"

"Oh," she says. "Yeah. Sure. Mom, please watch the road."

"Hey," Meg says, keeping it light. "I've been driving for thirty years, you know."

"Mom."

Meg exhales hard. "Okay, okay."

"You're going to love it," Justin says. Ithaca is his alma mater. Meg went to Cornell. Lily applied to and was accepted by both, but Ithaca's music program, combined with the scholarship money they offered, made the choice a no-brainer. Meg knows what Justin's thinking—Lily *should* be excited, and nervous. Instead of criticizing Meg's driving, she should be asking the two of them a million questions about what to expect during orientation. But that isn't her way, which Justin knows as well as Meg, even if he doesn't take it as personally.

And so Justin turns to his old standby. "Did I ever tell you the story of how Mom and I met?" he says.

"No, Dad. You haven't." Lily says it like a sigh. Justin has told this story dozens of times since she was a little girl. It's a common refrain at this point—Lily pretending she doesn't know the story, Justin launching in, faux grudgingly, Meg filling in the blanks. As a child, Lily used to nag him to tell it, but these days it's more the other way around.

"Okay, if you insist," Justin says.

In the rearview, Meg sees flashing brights, so she speeds up enough to put some distance between the tractor trailer and herself and slips back into the right lane. She's usually not one to drag her heels in the fast lane, but she's in another world today. Too much on her mind.

Justin, meanwhile, is telling Lily the story yet again, about how both he and Meg were seniors, how she'd taken a filmmaking class at Ithaca for fun, how he noticed "this beautiful English major" right away and tried in vain to get her attention—which he finally earned as a result of winning the "coveted Golden Doorknob Award."

Meg waits. Lily giggles. "What's the Golden Doorknob Award?" she says, just like always. Meg's heart swells.

Not everything changes . . .

"You want to take that one, honey?" Justin says.

Meg smiles. "The Golden Doorknob Award," she says, "is given out once a year to the short film, made by an Ithaca student, featuring the most creative and effective use of a doorknob as murder weapon."

"And Dad won."

"That he did."

Behind Meg, someone blares their horn—a long lean-on that makes her want to jump out of her skin, followed by three short, angry blasts. "What the hell?" she says.

"What was that? Morse code?" Justin says.

"Assholes," Lily says.

Meg thinks she hears the horn again, this time to her left. Her shoulders stiffen. *So many idiots on the road.* "Anyway, I wish you still had that movie, honey. It really was great, Lily."

"I'll find it," Justin says. "I'll find it, and we can screen it at Lily's wedding."

Meg laughs.

The horn blasts again.

"Go away!" Lily says.

Meg turns around. "What?"

"Those guys in the Mazda," Lily says. "They're the ones honking. I thought we lost them."

"Which guys?"

"They've been creeping on me since we got on the thruway."

"Left lane?" Justin says.

"Don't look," Lily replies. "Just ignore them. They were staring at me. Taking pictures. They're gross."

Meg's stomach tightens. "They were harassing you?"

"Not harassing, Mom. Jeez. Why do you have to make it so dramatic?"

"Taking pictures is harassment," Meg says, her fingers tightening on the wheel.

"Why didn't you tell us?" Justin says.

"Because you guys would do what you're doing right now and make it bigger than it is."

Out of the corner of her eye, Meg sees a tan chassis, the glint of a window. A car keeping pace with her own.

"Just drive," Lily says. "They'll go away."

Meg can feel eyes through the driver's side window. The burn of a gaze. She turns and looks. The passenger's face is right up against the Mazda's window. Not even trying to be subtle about it. "That's an adult," Meg says.

"Stop looking at him," Lily says.

The man at the window is at least ten years older than Lily. He's got a buzz cut. Tattoos. He isn't wearing a shirt. The car is a four-door, and there's a similar-looking guy in the window behind him, this one in some kind of tank top or sleeveless T-shirt. Craning their necks to see through the Subaru's windows, watching their car like it's some sporting event on TV. *How dare they? Staring at her like that, like there's nothing wrong with it. Like it's their absolute right to stare.*

Justin says, "What are they? Skinheads?"

"Please, you guys, stop!" Lily says.

Anger bubbles beneath Meg's skin. It roils in her veins. Her hand slips to the window button. She presses it, a blast of cool air ruffling her hair. *"Leave her alone!"* she shouts. *"She's barely eighteen, you perverts!"*

"Mom!"

"Lily's right, honey," Justin says. "Close the window. Keep your eyes on the road. Don't get us in an accident over these lowlifes."

Meg closes her window. Grits her teeth. "Sorry," she says. According to the GPS, there's an exit in another five miles.

Justin says, "Oh, Jesus."

"What?" Meg says. "What?"

"Nothing."

"They're doing it again," Lily says. *"Don't look."*

"Meg, don't engage with these jerks."

"I said not to look. Dad, why won't she listen to me?"

Meg barely hears them. All she can see are the two skinheads at the Mazda's windows, phones raised to their faces. Taking pictures. She opens the window again, the cold air slapping her hair against her face. *"Stop it!"* The words get lost in the wind.

There are more of them in the car. More phones raised. As though her family is a hockey game or a reality show or animals in a zoo. As though they're nothing more than a form of entertainment. "I hate them," Meg whispers.

"Pay attention to the road, Meg," Justin says. "You're swerving all over the place."

"Put those fucking phones down!" Meg shrieks, her anger surprising her. She sounds like her father.

"Mom, stop!"

"Speed up." Justin's voice is calm. The only calm voice in the car. "Don't engage with these lunatics."

Meg's back is stiff. Her throat aches. Her hands tremble on the wheel. "Why won't they stop?"

"Speed up!" Justin says. Meg realizes she's going just under sixty-five miles per hour, keeping perfect pace with the Mazda.

"Mom!"

"Okay," she whispers. "Okay. I'm calm now. I'm sorry." Meg turns back to the road, her foot pressing the accelerator, taking it up to seventy-five, eighty.

The Mazda speeds up too, then pulls ahead of Meg, shifting into her lane. "They're passing us," Justin says. "Thank God."

Meg lifts her foot. The car slows down. The Mazda pulls away.

Lost them, she thinks.

"Finally," Justin says.

"Mom, in the future, can you *please not do that*?"

Meg exhales, the tension starting to ease out of her. "I don't know what got into me," she says.

"Mama Bear." Justin laughs. He pats Meg on the knee. "It's nature."

"It's not funny, Dad. Those guys were psychos and Mom just . . . *Fuck*. That's them."

The Mazda has slowed down. It's right in front of them. Meg can make out two faces pressed against the back window. Bald heads. Phones up. Meg's breathing fails her. A shiver travels down her back, her legs. A raw, primal fear.

It's nature.

The sandwich drops from her hand. It surprises her that she's been holding it the entire time. This stupid ham sandwich. There's lettuce stuck to her shirt. Justin says something she can't hear or doesn't want to hear for the thoughts racing through her head: *This is awful. Something awful is happening.*

One of them moves. The Mazda's rear window opens and he's oozing out of it. Head, shoulders, bare chest. Facing them, the wind in his face. His phone in his hand, a weapon.

"Get down, Lily," Meg says.

"I can't. There's too much stuff."

"Get down," Justin says.

Meg starts to move into the left lane, but a horn blares at her and she swerves back, overcorrecting, her front tires skidding on something, the front bumper swinging too far to the right. "No," she says. "No, no, no . . ."

"Mom, what are you doing!"

"I don't know," Meg says. "I don't know what's happening . . ."

"Okay, okay," Justin says. "Just. Just try and . . . Just . . ."

The car is spinning now. Everything in slow motion. Meg can see every face in every window of every car around them—the old man in the tractor trailer. An angelic-looking kid in a red pickup, his jaw dropped open. The sick fucks in the Mazda. The lights on their phones, that shirtless one half out the window.

Has time slowed because I'm dying? Are we all going to die?

Something's come loose. Something deep within the car. A connection has failed, rendering it useless, and Meg can no longer drive. It's like trying to control a roller skate, the tires rebelling against the steering wheel, just moving, skidding across the thruway and onto the shoulder and over the side. Lily screams.

I'll save you. I'll save you, baby.

"Wait," Justin says. "Please."

The steering wheel is as pointless as a toy.

The car plummets, everything turning, up down, down up. The car on its back, the seat belt cutting into her chest, Meg's arm twisting behind her, bending, the snap of it. She's bleeding. She feels the heat of her own blood running down her arm, slick on her hand. Her face stings, as though she's been attacked by bees. The taste of hot metal in her mouth. A searing pain shoots up her arm, and then it goes numb and still everything spins. Her stomach seizes up. She tries to find Justin, Lily. She calls out their names, but her mouth is full of blood.

"Daddy!"

The car stops and there is nothing but silence. Meg makes herself look at the passenger's seat. It's empty. She remembers Justin pulling the tote bag out of the back seat, unfastening his seat belt to reach it. *No*, she says. But she can't say it. She can't speak for the pain, the blood in her mouth.

Lily is sobbing now.

No. Please, no.

She catches sight of her husband's body on the grass just past the car. The windshield is shattered, and Justin is on his stomach, a constellation of shards around him, glittering. The jeans Meg teases him about. *Too baggy.* Her eyes find the back of his head, the blue-and-white striped shirt she gave him last Christmas. *Brings out your eyes.* She's never seen Justin so thoroughly still.

"Daddy!"

Meg's gaze rests on Justin's motionless arm. His wedding ring. *Must get to him.* She tries to unlock the car with her good arm, her fingers trembling. *Must get . . .* The airbag deploys late, late as everything else in this useless, failing car. The useless, late airbag socks Meg in the face, and she can't get to Justin. She'll never get to Justin. *It isn't fair,* she thinks. *It just isn't fair.*

And all she can hear are her daughter's sobs.

TWO

Three months and three weeks later

December is peak tourist season in Elizabethville. But that really isn't saying much. Compared to NYC weekend destinations like Woodstock, which lies about forty minutes to the east, or historic Rhinebeck, perched all the way across the Hudson River, Elizabethville feels nearly as provincial and undiscovered as it did when Meg was growing up here. To this day, there are three restaurants in town, only one of which has a bar and is open past 8 P.M. There's one family-owned hardware store that also sells snacks, a post office and a modest town hall that most people don't even think about except on Election Day, as it's Elizabethville's one polling place. There's a funeral home and a vintage clothing store, Divine Vintage, owned by Meg's friend Bonnie Claeson, whom she's known since childhood. There's the Lutheran church, which is the largest building in town, followed by the police station and fire department. No synagogue. When Meg was growing up, she had to be driven to the one in Kingston twice a week in order to get bat mitzvahed. That's an hour each way, and it may or may not have played into Meg's decision to marry a non-Jewish man and raise their daughter without any type of organized religion. Elizabethville's library is roughly the size of a double-wide trailer, and most of the books there are either ten-year-old thrillers or children's books. If you want to shop for groceries or fill a prescription, you have to drive twenty minutes to Boiceville. Uber still doesn't exist for Elizabethville's residents, nor does DoorDash. When Lily was little, there wasn't even a cell phone tower.

Still, its popularity has been growing, little by little. An article in the *New York Times* Style section a few years back, coupled with ever-increasing numbers of city dwellers yearning to escape Manhattan, has created a noticeable uptick in out-of-town business, particularly during those prime weeks of the holiday season, when Christmas decorations and regular snowfalls transform this Hudson Valley town into something magical, or at the very least, Instagrammable.

Every so often, some misguided hipster tries to cash in on the magic by opening an overpriced coffee place or an artisanal chocolate boutique on the village green. But those businesses never make it past spring, no matter how quaint they look. The locals just aren't interested. The only fancy out-of-towners to see lasting success in Elizabethville, in fact, were Meg's parents, Nathan and Shira Lerner, who moved up from New York City and launched the Secret Garden here forty years ago. While the store's early traction was credited to Nathan's semi-stardom as the bassist for the prog-rock band Prism, the truth remained that every town needs a bookstore. Meg and Justin knew that when Nathan gifted them the store twenty-three years ago, and they've managed to keep the Secret Garden alive ever since, due in no small part to December holiday sales.

And so on Black Friday—which as all retailers know is the real start of December—Meg reopened the Secret Garden after shuttering it for months. She knew Justin would have wanted her to. Plus, with mounting credit card debt, and monthly payments on the new car on top of the mortgage on her home—not to mention crushing medical bills (their insurance proved even worse than Meg had believed it to be)—she can no longer rely on website orders alone.

To kick things off, she bought ad space in the PennySaver, and posted an announcement on the Secret Garden's Facebook page: *It's No "Secret" That We're Reopening for the Holidays,* followed by the store's hours and a directive to check the space for future events. Hours later, the post had twenty likes, which Meg saw as a very good sign.

During the first few days of the reopening, Meg went over daily sales from her laptop at home, while leaving the in-store operations to her one full-time employee, Sara Beth, and their part-timer, Zach. The plan was for her to start easing back in on December 15, but her daily FaceTimes with Sara Beth made her yearn for the bustle and noise of the store. The normalcy, really.

Lily gets it. Either that, or she wants the house to herself in the mornings. But for whatever reason, she's been encouraging Meg to go in to work. *You and Dad love that store,* she said last night, speaking in the present tense of Justin—who has been dead for more than three and a half months—then throwing out a line Meg knows must have come from her therapist. *Don't deprive yourself of things that bring you joy.*

And so here she is in the Secret Garden, an hour before the 11 A.M. opening time on December 9, sitting at the desk in the little office at the back of the store, behind the children's section, staring at a computer screen she hasn't seen since her husband was alive.

When Meg left home, Lily was still sleeping, and so she sent her a text. Took your advice and went to the store!! She added heart-eye, smiley face and book emojis, which she knows Lily will roll her eyes over, but whatever. Emojis bring Meg joy.

She hears a key slipping into the front door. Hinges creaking. "Sara Beth?" she calls out.

"Magnolia?"

Meg smiles a little. She hasn't gone by her full name since she was a kid, but for some people, old habits die hard. Sara Beth has been working here for thirty-eight years—a Prism fan who made a pilgrimage to the store and never left.

Sara Beth's footsteps quicken. She hurries into the office, her big brown eyes spiked with concern. "You look great, honey," she says. But the eyes say otherwise.

Meg understands. She can barely stand to look at herself in the mirror these days.

"I'm so happy you're here."

Meg pulls herself out of the chair with some difficulty and leans into Sara Beth's familiar, patchouli-and-cigarette-scented embrace. "I've missed you," she says.

All these months later and Meg still feels sore from the accident— her shoulders, her neck. Her right arm, especially. The bone was reset, but like many compound fractures, it'll never completely heal. The arm doesn't have full range of motion, which makes even a hug like this a challenge and, as one of the doctors told her, *the forearm will still ache from time to time.* Meg had found that sort of poignant, the doctor's choice of words. Not *hurt,* but *ache.*

Once they finally separate, Meg eases back down to sitting and Sara Beth slips off her puffer coat and hangs it on the back of the other flimsy chair, a canary-yellow director's chair.

Justin's chair.

Meg wishes she hadn't thought of the chair that way, because her eyes start to blur. This happens all the time. She's fine, and then she's not, and then she's really, really not. She probably should have stuck it out longer in grief counseling, but Meg's never been one for therapy. She hates talking about herself, always has, and now she finds it torturous. She stopped going to counseling after three arduous sessions with this therapist, whose name is Dr. Katie Cody (*With that last name, why not call yourself Katherine or Kat or Kate? Talk about poor judgment . . .*) and who kept insisting Meg discuss not only Justin's death but her mother's, thirty years ago. *Mourning isn't a solo performance. It's a symphony,* she explained. *Each loss plays a part.* Dr. Katie Cody, conductor from hell.

At any rate, Lily still sees Dr. Cody, but Meg does not. And that could be why Lily manages to keep herself together most days, while Meg is still plagued by the type of grief that pounces and incapacitates and consumes without warning. The type that's triggered by something as prosaic as a chair.

Tears stream down Meg's cheeks. Sara Beth hops up and puts her arms around her, and before she knows it, she's clinging to her employee, sobbing. "I'm okay," Meg says, though she knows she's not. "I'm fine, really. Contrary to all appearances . . ."

"I understand, honey."

You don't, Meg wants to say. *You don't understand, because you didn't kill your husband.*

"You know," Sara Beth is saying, "a sales rep called yesterday and asked for Justin and I lost it. I'm not comparing my feelings to yours. Not at all, but you guys are the closest thing to family I have and Justin was so . . . Justin was such a good man."

Meg wishes Sara Beth would stop saying his name. It takes her several long moments to catch her breath and pull away, and when she does, there's a big tear splotch on Sara Beth's India-print blouse, and Meg's whole face is wet. "I'm sorry," she whispers.

"Don't say that." Sara Beth returns to the director's chair. She pulls a packet of tissues out of her coat pocket and hands it to Meg with the type of urgency usually reserved for antidotes or tourniquets. "You have nothing to be sorry about."

Meg opens it gratefully, dabbing at her face, blowing her nose, breathing deeply until finally she can speak. "Did you tell him to call me?"

Sarah Beth blinks at her. "Tell who?"

"The rep."

"Oh," she says. "Yes, I did."

Meg nods. Breathes some more. She can do this. She can talk about books and orders and vendors and customers without thinking, without remembering. She tells Sara Beth that yesterday's sales were good, and Sara Beth says it was probably the most profitable day since the store reopened, "except for Black Friday, obviously," and that as crowded as the store was, at least half a dozen customers had told her they were glad "the rumors weren't true" about the Secret Garden closing for good. "Everybody's been so nice, except for the one jerk yesterday who wouldn't stop taking pictures, even after I pointed at the 'no in-store photography' sign."

Meg rolls her eyes. "I hope you pointed with your middle finger."

"I wanted to. Believe me."

For more than ten years, they've been the bane of her existence—
"savvy shoppers" snapping shots of book covers so they can go home and
buy the books online from bargain sites, or worse yet, picking up their
phones and placing orders right there in the store. "I told him that he and
his algorithm are no longer welcome here," Sara Beth says.

"Good one."

"I thought so. Firm, but also well-informed."

Meg asks how Zach has been doing behind the counter, and Sara
Beth says he's been great. "He's hand-selling the new Kingsolver like
you wouldn't believe."

Zach is a local kid. He's Lily's age, though they never traveled in the
same circles in school, which Meg thinks is kind of a shame. He's talk-
ative and sweet and he loves books and, like Lily, he's taking a gap year.
It would be nice for her daughter to have someone her own age to talk
to, but whenever Meg mentions this to Lily, she says she isn't lonely, that
her *actual friends* will be home for Christmas break soon enough and,
anyway, she's eighteen years old and doesn't need her mother arranging
playdates for her.

Meg says she'll order more of the Kingsolver.

"Maybe you should choose it for book club," Sara Beth says, and
Meg winces. Justin ran the book club. He'd choose the book on the first
and display it in front of the cash register. Meetings were held on the
last Tuesday of the month, via Zoom and in person, and Justin always
led them. Always. The book club was his.

"If we do that, let's let Zach lead the book club." Meg clears her
throat. "We could give it a try this month, anyway. I mean, he clearly
likes the Kingsolver. There'll be fewer people attending, with Christmas
and all. And if he does well with it, we can talk to him about taking the
club over permanently."

"That's a good idea, sweetie." Sara Beth says it in a way that feels borderline patronizing, but Meg doesn't comment. Minutes later, Zach arrives, as if they've conjured him.

"Hey there, Mrs. Russo!"

Meg has never been able to get Zach to address her informally—she suspects he's from a very traditional home, with his short hair and his collared shirts and his perpetual clean shave. Zach looks as though he's grown half a foot since she saw him last, but as the mother of an easily embarrassed child, Meg has the sense not to point that out.

Sara Beth tells Zach he's here early, and he replies that he's here for UPS and Sara Beth says, "Thank God you remembered."

Thank God *is right*. The store receives UPS deliveries a few days a week, but there's no way of knowing whether there will be three boxes of books or thirty. Since the Secret Garden is a small store to begin with, the shelves need to be stocked very quickly and the boxes collapsed and disposed of, simply for there to be enough room for staff and customers to move around. Anything more than a few boxes would have been daunting this close to opening time, especially for a car accident victim with a sort-of bad arm and a septuagenarian who weighs maybe one hundred pounds soaking wet.

Fortunately, Zach is stronger than he looks, which he proves once the UPS truck arrives, with Reggie the deliveryman unloading an estimable fifteen boxes. After helping Reggie bring them all into the store, Zach begins unpacking their contents and stacking them on the floor while Meg stays outside, Sara Beth hovering like a chaperone.

"Uh . . . how are you holding up?" Reggie says. He's a big guy, with the build of a retired linebacker. Meg barely reaches his shoulders. But there's something about the way he asks the question, eyes aimed at the ground, that makes him seem small and boyish. Even a little afraid. Everyone in this town knows everything about each other, and most of them react to tragedy as though it's catching.

"I'm okay," Meg says.

"Your daughter?"

"She deferred college for a year. She's working at Divine Vintage."

"Yeah, I heard . . . Um . . . Is she still playing music?"

"Yep."

"Good. That's . . . that's good." Reggie exhales, and finally looks at Meg, a palpable relief on his face. She half expects him to ask her if he did okay.

"It is good, Reggie. We're both all right."

Reggie says goodbye to Sara Beth, tells Meg he's glad to see the store up and running again, then gets back into his truck, practically peeling away from the curb.

"Well, that was awkward," Meg says, her gaze drifting across the street. A man in a wool cap and a long dark coat leans against the hardware store window, working his phone with one hand. She doesn't think she's seen him before and figures he must be from out of town. It's odd to see strangers out and about this early on a weekday, unless they're at the gas station or at Reese's Diner, which are the only places open before eleven. That's when Meg's store opens. The hardware store hours don't start till noon.

"It's just an adjustment period," Sara Beth says. "By Christmas, Reggie will be complaining about school taxes and telling semi-offensive jokes just to get our reactions, and everything will be back to normal . . ." Sara Beth stops.

Meg looks at her. Sara Beth's cheeks flush red. "I . . . I didn't mean *normal*. I meant . . . God, I'm sorry."

"I get it," Meg says. "Please don't walk on eggshells around me too. I don't think I can take that."

Sara Beth gives her a weak smile. "Reggie means well," she says.

"Everybody means well," Meg replies. "I'm getting kind of tired of it."

Sara Beth pulls a pack of cigarettes out of her coat pocket, slips one out and lights it. Somehow, she knows to hold the pack out to Meg, and somehow Meg takes one, even though she hasn't smoked a cigarette in more than twenty years. She accepts a light from Sara Beth and inhales too deeply, the smoke like hot, toxic liquid in her throat. She coughs, and it turns into a hacking fit. But once she takes another drag, it goes down easier. *Don't deprive yourself of the things that bring you joy,* she thinks, pulling on the cigarette again.

"Speaking of, uh . . . not walking on eggshells," Sara Beth says. "I have to tell you. Your dad called yesterday."

Meg exhales a cloud of smoke. She turns and looks at Sara Beth, but she won't meet her gaze. "He called you?"

She shakes her head. "He called the store. Looking for you."

"Ah."

"He said you've been ghosting him."

"What?"

Sara Beth bends her knee, and carefully extinguishes her cigarette on the heel of her boot. "Well, he didn't say *ghosting*. I couldn't see how he'd know that term, but—"

"I'm not ghosting him," Meg says. "I sent him a letter after the accident. I've also spoken to him on the phone."

"But you haven't returned his calls in weeks," she says.

"Whenever I talk to him, we wind up arguing." Meg squats down and puts her cigarette out on the sidewalk, hanging on to the butt. "I don't have the energy."

The two of them head into the alleyway next to the store and drop their butts in the garbage. Meg hopes Sara Beth will drop the topic as well. But, of course, she doesn't.

"Nathan says he has something he wants to discuss with you," she says. "Something important."

"He can put it in writing. Send me a nice, long letter."

Sara Beth just looks at her.

"Okay, okay. I'll call him later."

"Good girl." She starts to say something else, and Meg says, "If you're going to tell me he means well, don't."

Sara Beth smiles. "I'd never say that."

As they head back in to help Zach shelve the books, Sara Beth stops. She gestures across the street at the hardware store, the man with the dark coat and the wool cap and the phone. "It *is* him."

"What?"

"I thought I recognized that jerk. Keep walking," she says. "Don't look at him."

Try to not look at anything you've been told not to look at, Meg muses. *It's impossible.* She stands next to Sara Beth, the two of them gaping at the man.

"Bargain shopper," Sara Beth whispers.

"The one who was taking pictures?"

Sara Beth nods. "And now he's doing it again. *Like an asshole.*" She says it loudly, but the man stays where he is. Meg takes a closer look at him, the rigid stance, the black cap pulled low, the phone held up like some ugly little mirror. Sara Beth makes a joke about mooning the guy, but Meg barely hears it.

She heads into the store. Meg doesn't follow.

For the first time in months, she finds herself thinking of them. The skinheads in the Mazda. Phones raised like his. The way they'd smiled at her, just before her Impreza skidded. The way they'd stared through their car windows, those glowing eyes of theirs. Rat's eyes, searching for her daughter.

Meg finds herself hating them all over again, their faces, the lenses of their phones—and her whole body tenses up, her bad arm aching. She wants so badly for the crash to be their fault. For what they did to be a crime—*what they made me do, the person they turned me into* . . .

"Stop it!" Meg tells the bargain shopper.

He drops his phone into the pocket of his coat, but his eyes stay trained on Meg, flat and expressionless, as though she's not a person at all, but an image on a screen.

A feeling rushes through her, a terrible rage, fast and hot. Lavalike. *"Stop watching me."*

He doesn't move. Meg takes a step toward the curb, her muscles coiled, a ringing in her ears. An image in her mind—the man's face beneath the sole of her boot.

Push him to the ground. Knock him off his feet. Kick him in the stomach. The head.

She takes another step, and then she's off the curb. The man's eyes widen.

Crush his head.

Meg hears the door opening behind her, Sara Beth's voice. "Magnolia?"

She turns around, and it's as though she's waking from a dream. Sara Beth's face. The concern in her eyes.

What was I just doing? Meg thinks. *What is wrong with me?*

"Are you okay?"

"I'm fine," Meg says quickly. "I'm fine." She heads back into the store, the man across the street staring after her.

THREE

Lily Russo wakes to the dinging of her phone. Her room is very dark, the blackout curtains drawn, and so opening her eyes is no different from closing them. It takes her several moments to get her bearings and figure out exactly where she is.

Lily needs complete darkness in order to fall asleep, which is not a trauma-related thing but the way she's always been. She hated her night-light when she was little, couldn't stand it if the door was open, even a crack. When she was older, she would sneak books under the covers and read them by flashlight until her eyelids would start to get heavy, and then she'd turn the flashlight off, stay under the covers and sink into the velvety, perfect blackness.

Our little vampire, Lily's dad used to call her. She can practically hear him say it, and it makes her smile, but then the remainder of her dreamless sleep melts away, those last fragile specks of it, and she knows where she is and that she'll never hear Dad's voice again.

Her eyes start to burn, her throat doing that terrible thing where it clenches and unclenches and she can't get enough air and it feels as though she's drowning.

Stop.

She sits up in bed with her back straight and breathes through her nose, in and out to the count of ten. Yoga breathing. *In with the positive, out with the negative . . .*

It's something Dr. Cody taught her. A *grief hack,* she called it, probably trying to sound cool. A lot of what Cody says to Lily feels as though she found it by googling "how to talk to teenagers."

A few more rounds of yoga breathing and she no longer wants to cry. Her phone dings again. A reminder. She leans over and switches on the lamp on her nightstand, blinking until her eyes adjust. Then she grabs the phone from its charger. There are two texts on her screen. She swipes the first one away quickly and reads the older one, which she apparently slept through.

Took your advice and went to the store!!

Two exclamation points. Three emojis. That's pretty excessive, even for Mom. Looking at it, Lily feels the way she so often does when she's engaging with her mother—as though she wants to avoid and protect her at the same time.

Dr. Cody always wants to talk about her. Always. *Do you resent your mom?* she asks. *Do you blame her for what happened to your dad? Does she make you feel angry? Sad?* She tells Lily there are no wrong answers to these questions, which may be true. But to Lily's mind, there are wrong *questions*—the kind that lift rocks from your mud-caked mind and turn them over and force you to look at whatever is crawling around beneath, even though there's nothing you can do about those ugly, squirming, spitting creatures. You know you can't kill them. You know they'll stay with you always, outlive you, even. And you know that staring at them— *acknowledging* them, as Cody would say—doesn't do a damn thing other than make you feel disgusted. With your mother. With yourself. With your life. And those are the only questions Cody likes to ask—those terribly, disgustingly *wrong* ones.

It's one of the reasons why Lily canceled her last three appointments, first claiming she had COVID and then, when it felt like she should be testing negative at that point, telling Dr. Cody that her boss, Bonnie, needed some extra help at the vintage store. Lily feels a little guilty, not so much about lying to Cody, but about letting Mom believe that for the past three Fridays from two to three P.M., she was somewhere she wasn't.

Lily texts: Good for you!!

She thinks maybe it looks sarcastic. Mom is supersensitive to sarcasm lately. Lily removes one of the exclamation points before sending it.

The answer arrives quickly.

> Don't worry about getting to Dr. Cody and work. I'll come home for lunch at 1 and you can have the car. Just drop me off at the store, K?

> OK.

> You don't have to pick me up from work either. Sara Beth will give me a ride home. She sends her love, btw.

Lily sighs. She's not sure when her mom went from hating the whole idea of texting to texting lengthy and effusive paragraphs and expecting them in return. But at this point, she'd give up a month's worth of her paychecks to go back to the old days.

> Everything all right? You're so quiet.

Lily rolls her eyes. All good, she types. Just waking up. See you soon!!!

She stares at the screen. Okay, that definitely looks sarcastic because it is. She deletes the second two exclamation points and sends the text.

Mom replies with a hand making the "okay" sign and a winky-face emoji.

Lily gets out of bed. She checks the time. The good news is, she finally has the house to herself. The bad news is, it's just for two hours. She pulls open the curtains and starts to make her bed. She tries to think of nothing besides getting ready for the day, but other thoughts keep intruding, and so after she's done, she stands in the middle of the room and forces herself to do more of Cody's breathing exercises. When those don't work, she lifts her bass from its stand and starts playing one-octave pentatonic scales, major, then minor, then a two-octave minor, then back to the one-octave major until finally, she feels normal again. Or at least close to it.

She sets the bass back on its stand and walks down the hall to the bathroom. And as she walks, she listens. Lily can't help but listen. There's a rhythm to everything, from her footfalls to her breathing to the hum of her electric toothbrush to the groan of the pipes as she showers, the click of a squirrel's claws as it runs across the roof. There's a music to it, a music to everything. Lily's noticed it since it was first pointed out to her, by her grandfather in a letter he sent her when she was a little girl. Grandpa Nate told her that only true artists are able to hear the music, and she used to find it exciting, like being in on a secret. But now, it's just another thing she can't escape.

When she gets out of the shower and dries off, the whole room is full of steam, and she finally feels warm. This house is so old and drafty and every winter, it gets worse.

She throws on her terry-cloth robe and swipes the sleeve over the medicine cabinet mirror. As she combs leave-in conditioner through her hair, Lily examines her reflection: the too-pale skin, the zits on her forehead. She tries to imagine seeing herself through the window of the car, the way those freaks in the Mazda did. What was it about her that made them gape and take pictures? She gets very close to the mirror and looks deep into her own eyes, deep enough to see the truth.

It was you. You saw them first. You stared, and then he turned. The shirtless one. He turned and looked straight at you and you could have looked away. But you didn't. You kept staring, because . . . why? Because you wanted to see what he would do.

Lily remembers his face, pressed against the window of the Mazda as her parents talked about Ithaca orientation and their hotel reservation and whether Lily wanted them to take her and her new roommate out to dinner that night or if they should just, as Dad put it, *head back to the hotel so we can wake up early and skedaddle.* Both of them oblivious, Mom mentioning something about how it was still morning and she was hungry for lunch already . . .

The others in the Mazda joined the shirtless one. They grinned at her and made gestures she didn't understand. Lily had been so ashamed. She wished they would leave her alone. She put her headphones on and closed her eyes, listening to her Spotify. What she remembers now is an old song playing. "Been Caught Stealing" by Jane's Addiction. She remembers listening to the bass line, tapping out the notes on her forearm with her eyes shut tight, willing the Mazda gone forever.

Go away. She had thought it like a prayer. A magic spell. And when she opened her eyes, it seemed to have worked.

She had wished she could sleep the rest of the way to Ithaca. She believed she might be able to, that she'd wake up feeling refreshed, as though she'd done nothing wrong. But then her dad had started talking to her, engaging her in that old story about how he met Mom, and before she knew it, the Mazda was back and she was saying it out loud: *Go away!* And then her mom and dad noticed them and everything started to turn . . .

A tear slips down Lily's cheek. *Stop.*

Lily opens the medicine cabinet. Her bottle of doxycycline is toward the back of the top shelf. She used to take it once a day when she was sixteen and prone to bad breakouts before her periods. But for the past year or so, she hasn't needed it that much. Not that her skin has completely cleared, but the acne's been manageable enough to get her on a lower and less frequent dose. This particular bottle is from her old, stronger prescription and it's been sitting here for months, untouched, unnoticed by her mom. It's a perfect hiding place, really. Lily has to admit, she's proud of herself for recognizing its potential.

Lily opens the bottle and plucks out a roach, removing the lighter from the pocket of her terry-cloth robe and a set of tweezers from the drawer next to the sink.

Before she lights up, she opens the bathroom window. It's even colder than she thought it would be outside, the air a shock as it hits her skin. She holds the tiny roach with the tweezers so as not to burn her fingers and inhales deeply, hungrily, holding the bit of smoke in her lungs, a rare and precious thing.

When she exhales out the window, Lily thinks about Mom, how she hates smoke of any kind and how, the last time Lily allegedly returned from therapy, Lily had thought for sure that Mom had smelled it in her hair.

Lily closes and locks the window, then flushes what's left of the roach, a calm overtaking her, a wonderful numb feeling.

The good news is, I finally have the house to myself.

She remembers her most recent text, which she has yet to reply to.

Lily gets dressed—jeans, plain black T-shirt, a red-and-blue flannel that used to belong to her dad. She checks herself out in the full-length mirror on her closet door, switches the flannel for a fuzzy pink sweater and applies lip gloss and mascara. A little concealer on her forehead. She plays with her damp hair, lays it over one shoulder, then the other, then she smooths it behind both ears. She snaps a selfie and examines it. She doesn't look horrible.

Lily clicks on the text. Carl has never been big on words, and this one's true to form:

Sup

Lily types: Alone for an hour. Wanna come over?

Texting with Carl is a lot easier than texting with her mom. Carl pays no attention to punctuation. He doesn't think about whether or not she's being sarcastic, and even if he does, she doesn't care that much about hurting him.

He texts back: Yep

Lily heads downstairs. About ten minutes later, she hears the music of his tires on her gravel driveway. The sputtering engine of Carl's busted pickup truck.

Last week, they'd sat in his truck for an hour when she was supposed to be at Cody's. They'd shared a joint, a bag of Doritos from the hardware store and a six-pack of hard seltzer (Lily only had one because she didn't want to show up drunk for work). They'd messed around a little, Lily feeling half-hearted about it, because she knew she didn't want to be Carl's girlfriend and she wasn't even sure she liked him as a person. *Better than a poke in the eye* was the thought she had. Somebody had said it on some TV show. She couldn't remember which one, but it pretty well described her opinion of what was happening in Carl's truck.

When they were getting ready to leave, Carl told Lily that he'd heard some weird shit about her mom.

What weird shit? she said, and immediately, she wished she could take the question back. She knew that people in town had been talking about her and her mom. She could feel it in the stares she got at the grocery store, or when she was working behind the counter at Divine Vintage. She knew they were a topic of conversation since the accident, because how could they not be?

People are just lame, Carl said. He'd taken a breath, which made her think he was going to elaborate. But he didn't. *If you hadn't survived that accident, Lily,* he said instead, *I don't know what I'd do.*

Lily opens the front door for Carl, who always looks better in person than he does in her imagination. With most people, it's the opposite. Lily wonders what that means. Carl's blond hair shines in the dull winter sunlight and his eyes are soft and kind. He's even taller than Lily had remembered. Carl is carrying his guitar case in one hand, a plate wrapped in tin foil in the other. "I thought maybe we could jam," he says. "And also, I brought snacks."

Lily thinks maybe she could wind up liking Carl. After all, she's got nothing else to do.

FOUR

Meg's friend Bonnie Claeson shows up at the Secret Garden around noon. "Surprise!" she calls out from the doorway, making everyone inside turn and look.

Bonnie is wearing a long red coat with black velvet trim that matches both her black patent leather boots and freshly dyed black hair, and she's carrying a large box with a red bow that somehow pulls everything together. Bonnie has always been preternaturally fashionable, even in kindergarten. Throughout their lives, she's probably given Meg an entire reference library's worth of clothing advice and more than a dozen makeovers, but they've never quite taken. When it comes to style, you've either got it or you don't. And sadly, Meg doesn't, though she appreciates it in others.

"Well, hello there!" Meg says. She's seen Bonnie many times since the accident, but this still feels like a reunion. She finishes ringing up her customer and asks Zach to take her place at the counter so she can give Bonnie a proper hug.

"Happy first day back!"

Meg holds her tightly, the red wool scratching her face. "Thanks, Bonnie."

Once they finally separate, Bonnie holds out the box. "Brought you a little something."

Tears spring into Meg's eyes. She manages to blink them away, but Bonnie notices. She notices everything.

"It's been a day, huh?" Bonnie says.

Meg nods. "I guess it has," she says. *And it isn't even half over.*

"The beginning of good things." Bonnie gives her a smile that's surely meant to be encouraging. "You deserve good things."

Meg feels as though everyone in the store is watching her, waiting for a response. And even when she looks around and sees that this isn't at all the case, she's still struck by an urge to flee the scene.

"Let's go catch up in my office," Meg says.

Bonnie follows her to the back of the store, past Sara Beth, who is helping a weary-looking young mother navigate the children's section, the two of them whispering so as not to wake the infant twins in her stroller.

Meg closes the door. A tear slips down her cheek.

"Oh, honey," Bonnie says.

Meg shuts her eyes. She swipes the tear away and breathes deeply until finally, she calms down. "It's like standing in the ocean, you know?" she says. "You feel fine, comfortable, even. And then from out of no-where, some big wave slams into you, knocks you over . . . God, I need to stop it with the cheesy analogies. I sound like Dr. Cody."

Bonnie puts a hand on her shoulder. "It's okay," she says softly.

"I don't know," Meg says, her mind traveling back to her encounter an hour ago, her run-in with the bargain shopper. The way she'd stared into his eyes instead of ignoring him. She should have followed Sara Beth back into the store, but she didn't, she couldn't. She wanted to run across the street and push him to the sidewalk and kick him, again and again. She'd yearned to break his ribs, his legs, his teeth. She wanted to kill him, and she nearly did. She nearly ran across the street and beat a man to death for taking her picture. "I don't know who I am anymore, Bonnie."

"You're Lily's mom," Bonnie says. "You're the owner of the coolest store in town, with the possible exception of Divine Vintage. You're my best friend. Should I go on?"

Meg forces a smile. "I don't know that I deserve to be any of those things."

"Meg."

"What?"

"It's your first day back at work."

"So?"

"So . . . tomorrow will be your second day back at work. The next day will be your third."

"And forty-four days from now—"

"It will be your forty-fifth day back."

"Wow. Who needs a calendar?"

"You're a wiseass," Bonnie says. "But you know what I'm saying. These things take time. You've been through something awful. Let yourself go through whatever it is you need to. Let it change you, for god's sakes, because if you stayed the same, there would be something wrong with you." She takes Meg's hands in her own, looks into her eyes. "Do you understand what I'm saying?"

Meg nods.

"Good," she says. "Now open your present."

Meg has a feeling she knows what it is. A few weeks ago, she dropped Lily off at work and noticed a blue velvet duster in the window, the type of glamorous seventies rock star garment that made her think of Debbie Harry partying with Andy Warhol at Studio 54. She hadn't mentioned it to Bonnie. But she had pointed it out to Lily. *God, isn't that gorgeous?* she'd said. And sure enough, when she opens the box, the duster is inside, cushioned by layers of silver tissue paper, mother-of-pearl buttons gleaming. "Oh, Bonnie."

"Don't say 'you shouldn't have.'"

"I wasn't going to." Meg slips it over the gray turtleneck sweater and jeans she wore to work this morning, and though she has no full-length mirror to look into, Meg feels transformed. "You most definitely should have."

"It fits you perfectly," Bonnie says. "And you might not think it, but it really goes with everything."

Meg smiles. "I love it, Bonnie. Thank you." She twirls. She sits down at her desk, pulling the collar up, trying to catch her reflection in the screen of her work computer. "I think I finally get why they call it 'retail therapy,'" she says.

Bonnie smiles. "Took you long enough."

There is a knock at the door.

"You should probably get that," Bonnie says, and when Meg opens the door, she sees Sara Beth and Zach standing there, with a small group behind them that includes Liz Reese, of Reese's Diner, Secret Garden book club members Cora Clark and Patty Johnson, and Pete DeMarco, who owns the hardware store across the street. "Surprise part two!" says Sara Beth. She's holding a round cake with white icing, *Welcome Back!* on top in red cursive letters, a single, lit candle at the center. "We know there's not enough time for a proper party with champagne and all," she says. "But we're all so glad you're back. We couldn't wait."

Meg feels choked up again, this time for better reasons.

"Did you bake this cake, Sara Beth?"

"Yep."

"When?"

"Last night. After you told me you were thinking about coming in."

Meg smiles. She blows out the candle without making a wish—*Are you even supposed to make a wish on a welcome back candle?*—and everybody applauds. Zach pours sparkling water into paper cups and hands them out, Liz Reese raising hers in a toast. "Here's to an inspirational business owner and one tough dame!" Liz, whose sinewy body is riddled with scars and nicks and burns from the kitchen.

"It takes one to know one," Meg says, and Liz laughs, and for a moment, Meg feels like her old self again. Someone with friends and a purpose and a possible future. She thanks everyone and her phone dings: A text from Lily: Good for you!

It takes her a few seconds to remember the context—that it's simply a reply to her earlier note about going to work today and not something with greater meaning—but in that tiny span of time, Meg can actually feel the curtain lifting.

She texts her back quickly. They make plans for the day.

—

The party, such as it is, lasts less than fifteen minutes—which is more than enough for Meg, whose office comfortably houses two or three people. Eight has been a challenge, especially with Liz Reese moving around, cutting the cake, serving people, refilling glasses of water like an over-efficient maître d'. (*You can take the restaurateur out of the restaurant* . . . Meg had quipped at one point.)

With the exception of Cora, a retired teacher, everyone has to go back to their jobs, and Patty is Cora's ride. So that's what they all do, each of them telling Meg how happy they are that she's back, while avoiding the topic of Justin.

The closest anyone comes to mentioning Meg's late husband is when Patty asks if there's going to be a book club selection this month, and even then she keeps her eyes averted.

"You know, I'm glad you asked that." Meg calls out to Zach, who's dutifully taken his slice of cake to the cash register.

"Yeah, Mrs. Russo?"

"Would you want to lead book club this month? I hear you liked the new Kingsolver."

"I'd *love* to." He says it with such enthusiasm, you'd think Meg just offered him a promotion and a raise. If he were Lily, she'd assume he was being sarcastic. But Zach is not Lily by a long shot. During his sophomore year in high school, Zach contracted viral encephalitis and was hospitalized for several months. Between that and the subsequent lockdown, Meg thinks, he spent so much time at home that he never turned skeptical of his elders, the way most kids do. He also became an avid reader. And though Meg suspects he'll go through many changes once he moves out of his parents' home, these setbacks in his social life have made him an ideal employee.

Meg tells Zach to go ahead and post about December's book club pick and meeting on the store's Facebook page, and, after finishing her goodbyes, she moves up to the register to relieve him while he goes back to the office.

"I'm going to put the rest of the cake in a box for you," Sara Beth tells Meg. "Okay?"

"Sure." Meg would normally protest—she doesn't need the extra calories, and since the cake isn't vegan, Lily won't eat any of it. In the past, she'd have donated it to a food pantry. But Meg wants this cake. She wants to eat it for breakfast every morning until it's gone. It's marble with vanilla icing, which was her favorite when she was a kid. Her mother used to make marble cakes for all her birthday parties, sometimes with Sara Beth's help, and each bite of this one is Proust's madeleine to her. Pure memory. Pure comfort.

She's thinking about heading back to the office and cutting herself another slice when Bonnie steps up to the register with the Kingsolver. Meg smiles at her. "You're joining book club?"

She shrugs. "Thinking about it," she says.

Meg rings her up, and they start to say goodbye, Bonnie mentioning that she's late opening Divine Vintage, Meg thinking about Lily, how she's at Bonnie's store most afternoons and how, once a week, it means she's there right after therapy. Bonnie is Lily's godmother, and they've always had what Meg considers an uncomplicated, open and healthy relationship—at least compared to Lily and Meg's. She suspects it's because Bonnie has no children of her own, and so she's never viewed a young person as something to worry about or judge or keep alive.

"Bonnie," Meg says after she hands her the book and the receipt.

"Yes?"

"From what you've seen of Lily . . . is she doing okay?"

"She's a good kid, Meg," she says. "Tough and resilient. And trust me, I hate it when people say 'kids are resilient.' It's usually a way to rationalize doing shitty things to them."

Meg sighs. She looks around the store and lowers her voice. "After my mom died, I overheard Sara Beth saying that to my dad."

"Ugh."

"I know."

"Well, in Lily's case, I'm being honest."

Meg gives Bonnie a quick, tight hug, her thoughts going to her daughter, alone in the room with her headphones on, blackout curtains drawn, shutting out the world. Those short texts of hers, one-word responses over the phone. Yes, she goes to Katie Cody once a week. But are those visits good for her? She's never seemed like someone who would find solace in platitudes about the "symphony of grief." But then again, Meg doesn't know Lily, not really. It is possible to love someone with your entire being without knowing them at all. The other night, she'd heard her playing bass in her bedroom—a solo she recognized as her own father's, from Prism's most famous song, "Pearly Gates." She knocked softly on Lily's door, and asked her when she'd learned it. Lily had replied without looking up, without stopping. *Four years ago,* she said. Four years ago, and Meg had never heard her play it before. "I kind of wish she was going to school next semester, instead of taking the whole year off," Meg says.

"Why?"

"I'd like her to have friends her own age that she can talk to," she says. But that isn't the only reason. There are others that she doesn't want to put words to. But they have to do with wanting to help Lily heal, yet wishing others could do the work. She remembers how Sara Beth had suggested Meg take a year off before college, just as Lily's doing now, so she could get over her mother's death without feeling rushed. *That's the worst idea I've ever heard,* her father had bellowed. At the time, Meg assumed he just wanted her out of the house. But now . . . well, if he did, she can understand it.

"I've tried to get Lily to hang out with Zach," Meg says quietly. "But she's not interested."

"That blond boy seems like a better match for her, though," Bonnie says, "don't you think?"

Meg blinks at her. *Blond boy? What blond boy?* "Um . . ."

"I mean, he makes her laugh at any rate." She leans forward, and speaks very quietly. "No offense to Zach, but I don't think they have the same sense of humor."

Meg forces a smile. "Good point," she says.

"Lily will be fine."

"I hope so."

They say goodbye and Bonnie leaves Meg sitting at the counter, thinking about her daughter's mysterious blond friend. Why hasn't Lily told her about this boy? Why doesn't Lily tell her about anything? Would she have told Justin if he were alive?

She'll circle back, and we'll be here.

Meg's throat clenches up. More people sweep into the store—a couple of bearded men with chains hanging from their belts who look as though they took a Zipcar straight from Brooklyn, a woman holding a cat in a *certified comfort animal* harness. Another woman, wild-eyed, frizzy-haired and wearing an ugly Christmas sweater, who heads straight back to the children's section, shoving the cat and its owner aside.

The store feels small, suffocating. Meg needs another smoke. Her gaze darts around the room and settles on Sara Beth, who's talking to two customers in New Nonfiction. She starts to get up from the register before she realizes that she's literally about to interrupt a potential sale to ask her employee for a cigarette. *I need help.*

Before she can think much more about it, Meg's calling Dr. Katie Cody. She picks up after one ring. *Shouldn't she be busy seeing patients right now?*

Meg says she'd like to make an appointment ASAP, and Cody asks if she's free at nine tomorrow. Meg says, "Sure," and hangs up quickly. It bothers her a little that Cody is available on such short notice—and on a Saturday no less—but it doesn't matter. She's cried twice today and nearly beat a man senseless, plus she's had the oddest feeling, ever since she first walked into the store.

She feels as though someone is watching her.

Meg needs to do anything she can to get past this paranoia, this near-constant anxiety. She needs to feel normal again, even if it means seeing a simile-spouting therapist with no other clients whom, truth be told, she'd rather eat broken glass than have a beer with.

Come to think of it, a beer might help . . .

"Mrs. Russo?"

Meg glances up at Zach standing stiffly in front of her. "Oh, hey," she says. "I didn't see you. Did you finish posting about book club?"

"Yeah," he says quietly, a darkness creeping into his eyes.

"Is something wrong?"

"Kind of."

"What is it?"

"Someone commented on your post. The latest one, about the store reopening. I was going to delete it. I wasn't sure what to do."

"What did they say?"

Zach swallows, his Adam's apple visibly moving. "I think you need to look at it, Mrs. Russo," he says.

FIVE

"I want to know the weird shit you heard about my mom," Lily says to Carl.

He's been at her house for more than an hour and a half, and while they haven't spoken much, everything they've done together has made Lily feel comfortable enough to say it. He's played her a song he wrote called "Bridge to Heaven" that's really more of a guitar solo, but still a good jam. Lily joined him on bass, soloing on her own, taking off on it, *finding joy in it,* Carl recording the whole thing on his phone. Then they played a forty-five-minute version of White Stripes' "Seven Nation Army," Lily getting her old drum kit out of the garage for the occasion. It felt so unexpectedly good, playing with another person. Making actual music. It felt important, almost. As though they were building something together. Lily knows that sounds strange and a little pretentious, even as an unvoiced thought. She'll probably talk about it with Cody this afternoon if she doesn't wind up ditching therapy again.

After they finished the song, they smoked some more of Carl's weed and ate the snacks that he brought, which turned out to be chocolate chip and walnut cookies he'd baked himself, from scratch. They messed around a little, which felt less important than playing songs together or even the idea of Carl baking vegan cookies especially for Lily, but it was still fun.

Lily just hopes that when her mom comes home for lunch, she doesn't smell the weed. She's sprayed Febreze all over the basement, and Carl was understanding enough to help her vacuum to get the smell out of the rug, even though he did point out that marijuana is legal in New York State and healthier than alcohol. *And besides, you're eighteen years old. You can die in a war, you should be able to get high.*

My mom hates smoke, though, Lily had replied. *I don't want to upset her.*

Carl had thought for a while before responding, *I get that,* which is another thing Lily likes about him. He stops and thinks. He considers what's said to him rather than digging in on his own opinion without listening, which is rare for guys. Rare for people in general, to be honest. He *considers,* which, Lily now realizes, is where the word *considerate* comes from. Carl is considerate. And Lily is obviously high.

They're sitting on the couch now, drinking cans of Coke Lily brought down from the kitchen, and when Carl says, "What weird shit?" Lily's been riding this train of thought so hard she forgets, at first, what she said to him.

Carl repeats himself, and then at last she remembers.

"Yeah," she says. "When we were in your truck, you said people were saying weird shit about my mom."

"Oh. I'm sorry about that." Carl swallows some Coke. "I shouldn't have said anything."

"No, you should," Lily says. "I mean, if people are saying things about her, I should know . . . right?"

"I don't know." Carl sets his soda down on the coffee table, making sure to use a coaster. Then he takes Lily's hand in his. It's a surprising gesture and it makes her heart flutter. At least in this moment, holding hands feels more intimate than kissing or even sex, which Lily has only done twice anyway, neither time with Carl.

His hands are strong and rough from working construction jobs with his dad, his fingertips calloused, like Lily's, from playing guitar. She never paid much attention to his hands before because she and Carl have never held hands. In high school, they were just friends who played music together, and barely friends at that. But now she wants to explore Carl's hands, to *read* them. You can tell so much about another person just from the feel of their hands.

"It's out there, Lily," he says. "I'm pretty sure it isn't even worth talking about."

Carl's jaw clenches and unclenches. A delicate vein bulges on his forehead, like a thought trying to escape. Lily wants him to tell her, but at the same time she's scared to know. *It's out there, Lily.* That sentence had actually terrified her. *What could that mean?*

"Who told you this stuff about my mom?" Lily tries. And as she says it, an older memory finds her. Someone saying something awful about her family . . . She hasn't thought of this in years, and probably would have never remembered, if not for Carl's weed . . .

"Just a few guys I met on my last job," Carl is saying. "They're older than us, but not by much. One of them thinks he knows everything because he lived in the city for a couple of years . . ."

But Lily isn't listening. Not really. She's remembering it all now. This mean kid in fourth grade telling her that her dead grandma was burning in hell. *You'll go there too when you die. Your whole family will, because you're Jews and your grandpa plays devil music.*

Lily remembers that she had no idea what he was talking about. She knew her mom was Jewish, but she didn't see why lighting a menorah and getting a few presents on Chanukah meant she couldn't go to heaven like everybody else. And while she didn't know her grandpa that well, she'd heard most of his songs. She called that kid a liar, and he made a cross with his fingers and threw water at her. *Your grandpa used to have a guitar strap that was made from the skin of human babies.*

Who says that? Even in fourth grade, who the fuck says that to another person?

Zach Winters. That was the kid. What a piece of shit he was back then, and even though he acts nice now, even though he works for Lily's mom and puts on a front like he's sensitive and literary and evolved, there are some things you can never walk back, even if you say them when you are nine. *So strange. It took Carl's weed to get me to remember this, like it unlocked something in my brain that I'm meant to remember, and it's a message. A warning . . .*

"Lily?" Carl says.

"Yeah?"

"You spaced out for a little bit."

"I'm sorry," she says.

"No worries."

She glances down at her hands, wrapped around Carl's. "What those guys told you," she says. "Was it . . . Is it mean?"

"No," he says. "Just freaky."

"*Freaky?*"

Carl lets out a heavy sigh. "You really want to know?"

"Yeah. I really do."

"Okay," he says. "I'm guessing you already know that when your mom was fifteen, she wrote this book . . ."

Lily stares at him. Truly, she isn't sure she heard him correctly. "*My* mom? A *book?*"

Carl leans forward. For a long while he gazes back at her, a look on his face she doesn't like—a type of wonderment, mixed with pity. "Oh, Lily. Oh, man," he says. "The book is not the freaky part."

—

So basically, these guys Carl worked his most recent job with—these contractors, whom he claims are "well-versed in conspiracy theory shit"—claim that at fifteen, Lily's mom wrote and published a book called *The Prophesy* that both predicted and caused the end of the world. *They said there are details in there about COVID that nobody would have known about in 1990,* Carl had said. And then it got worse: *These guys said that the people who read your mom's book back then became infected with a demonic curse that got into their systems and like . . . laid the seeds of the real virus.*

Lily gaped at Carl for easily a minute. At first, she thought the story was an elaborate prank. She even made him turn his phone over because she was convinced he was taping her response to show his friends or post online. And, even though she'd seen for herself that his camera wasn't on, Lily was still upset enough to ask Carl to leave her house.

She understands now that she probably overreacted—and that it's not a great idea to start a discussion like that when you're stoned. But she still hasn't answered Carl's R U OK? text, because it's still hard for her to believe that he was telling her the truth.

She's up in the attic now, looking for *The Prophesy*. The way Carl described it, it was the type of epic fantasy Lily was obsessed with in junior high, and yet her mom had never shown her this supposed book, or even bothered mentioning it.

What kind of mother writes a whole novel as a kid that's good enough to get published, and never tells her daughter about it?

After Carl left, Lily had tried googling the book. She wasn't able to find it right away, but that doesn't really mean anything, since, according to Carl, the publishing company went out of business something like thirty years ago.

Where the book would be, if it ever did exist, is in the attic. Lily's mom saves everything.

Lily coughs. It's dusty here, and dark too, just one bare lightbulb illuminating the entire space. When she was a kid, she used to love to explore the attic. It was so interesting to her, seeing all the things her mom had saved and packed into boxes—Lily's very first swimsuit, her baby bracelet, the pink-and-blue hospital blanket from when she was born.

But she hasn't been up here in years. Hasn't even thought about it, though there are plenty of things she remembers: a colorful rolled-up rug, a rack of old coats and Halloween costumes, a row of porcelain dolls in satin dresses that must have belonged to her grandma. The rest is mostly boxes, stacked and labeled in black Sharpie. Lily uses the flashlight on her phone to read the boxes: *WEDDING CHINA, BLANKETS, MATERNITY CLOTHES, WINEGLASSES* . . . all in her mom's rounded handwriting. One of them says *BABY LILY,* which makes her smile. Another says *CHOWDER,* for some reason. No doubt some old inside joke that her parents found hilarious.

She keeps looking, the conversation with Carl replaying in her mind.

I told you it was weird shit, Lily.

I don't believe you. You're messing with me.

I swear I'm not. I don't know how they read your mom's book. Maybe one of their parents bought it when it came out.

And got, like . . . cursed by it?

Hey, I didn't say I believed this stuff.

They told you it caused COVID? This book that my mom supposedly wrote when she was fifteen?

Yeah, and the shit with the weather too. Everything that's been happening this year. Which they say includes the end of the world.

This isn't funny, Carl. You're taping this, aren't you?

I'm not joking, I swear.

Are you taping this?

No.

Show me your phone.

I'm sorry. I shouldn't have even told you. I figured at least you'd know she wrote a book.

I think you should leave.

Carl hadn't fought her. He'd just picked up his guitar case, shoulders slumped. *I'm sorry,* he'd said again. Then he'd trudged up the basement stairs with Lily following close behind, just so she could close and lock the front door behind him.

She feels kind of bad about it now. Locking the door on Carl, of all people, who hadn't wanted to tell her in the first place. Maybe these guys he worked with had made it all up to freak him out.

It's possible. Elizabethville is, for the most part, a boring place to live. When people are bored, they make up stories about each other to entertain themselves. And if they're bored and stupid, they make up stupid stories.

Lily sits down on the floor next to a row of boxes and replies to Carl's text.

I'm fine. Sorry I kicked you out.

It's OK.

He's still typing something. Lily watches the bubbles on her screen for ten seconds. Twenty. This is a lot for Carl, who usually replies in sentences no longer than two words. Lily talks to her screen: "Are you writing a novel too?"

She rolls her eyes at her own dumb joke, her gaze traveling to a cheesy wicker table with a happy face woven into the top. She vaguely remembers Grandpa Nate bringing it over as a Chanukah gift and Mom whispering to Dad, *This is what happens when you do your holiday shopping stoned.* There are two small boxes stacked beneath the table. She glances at the phone again, and Carl's text finally appears.

Are we still friends?

Lily exhales. For a six-foot-two-inch guy with dimples who can play guitar as well as he does, Carl has no game whatsoever—which is actually what she likes most about him.

She replies: yes.

good

Lily moves closer to the happy-face table, taking the phone with her so she can shine the flashlight on the two boxes underneath.

You want to hang out later, types Lily, who has already decided to ditch Cody again.

Carl gives her text a thumbs-up and she smiles. She texts him a time, suggesting they meet where they did last week—the parking lot of their old school.

Then she crouches down and shines the flashlight on the boxes under the wicker table, reading the writing on the top box. Her breath catches, a lump forming in her throat. "Hi, Daddy," she whispers.

Nearly four months after the accident, she still can't talk about her dad in the past tense, because she can't put him there. Not yet. And when things happen like this, she feels like maybe he *is* with her. Maybe . . . She runs her fingertips over the writing on the side of the box, which is not Mom's. It's Dad's.

WUTHERING DOORKNOB

All these years, telling the story of how he and Mom met. All these years, Dad promising Mom he'd find the movie someday, and it would be all the more fun to watch for its long absence.

I'll find it, and we can screen it at Lily's wedding.

Lily closes her eyes. A tear eases down her cheek. Then another. She lifts the box out from under the table. The tape is loose at the top, and as she peels it off, she wants more than anything to believe in signs, in spirits. Inside the box is an old-fashioned roll of film, and, beside it, something that looks like a paperweight. She picks it up, cool and heavy in her hand, and shines her flashlight on it: a tarnished doorknob, glued to a piece of marble, the words GOLDEN DOORKNOB AWARD 1997 inscribed on a small plaque. Lily texts Carl:

Do you know anybody who has an old movie projector?

He puts a thumbs-up on her text, then replies, I think so.

Lily wipes the tears from her face. Her parents had seen Carl a few times in high school when he came to their house to jam. But like most of Lily's music friends, she doubted he'd ever said much of anything to them or vice versa. It's a real shame. She knows that Dad would have liked Carl.

She puts the Golden Doorknob Award back in the box with the roll of film. She closes the lid as best she can.

As she's standing up, the thin beam on her phone hits the box that had been below her dad's under the wicker table. His box slips out of her hands and clatters to the floor.

"Holy shit," she whispers.

Written on the second box—not in her mother's handwriting or her dad's, but in the blockish script she knows from her grandpa's letters—are two words:

Magnolia's Book

Sybil has reopened the House of Horrors.

Tomorrow, she will be back at work.

And back TO work.

On the plus side . . . We know where to find her.

      —the Bronze Lord
        We Are Watching. We Are Armed. We Will Triumph.

SIX

Justin, Meg remembers, had a tell. If he didn't like someone, he would cross his arms over his chest. She first noticed it back in Ithaca, when she'd stop by the bar where he worked as a bouncer on Friday nights and find him trying to talk sense into some drunk. Arms crossed, the drunk was in trouble. In recent years, though, she'd all but forgotten about it. Justin liked most people, especially the ones who came into the bookstore.

But she's reminded of it now in the store's office, where Zach shows her the comment he told her about—the first and only one on Meg's "We're Reopening" announcement.

It's a video of Justin standing next to the cash register, looking nothing like himself. He stares down the camera, eyes narrowed, jaw tensed. And his arms are crossed over his chest.

Meg switches places with Zach. She enlarges the video and plays it again, her throat tightening. That heat behind her eyes. It's an awful, racking feeling, seeing Justin so angry but also so alive.

"It has sound," Zach says.

"Huh?"

"The video."

"Oh." Meg unmutes the video and plays it again. An unseen woman sings to Justin in a reedy, childish voice: *"We are waaaatching. We are armed. We will triiiiumph. You'll pay for your sins."* She sounds like a Manson girl.

"You okay, Mrs. Russo?" Zach says.

Meg's hand trembles on the mouse. She wants to reach through the screen and strangle her, this invisible, singing freak.

You'll pay for your sins.

"I'm fine," she says, but it comes out a whisper.

"Um . . . you sure?"

Meg clears her throat. Slaps a smile on her face. "Completely," she says.

Zach doesn't seem satisfied with that answer. He keeps peering at Meg, as though the room is very dark and she's a book he's trying to read. It makes her uneasy.

"Some people, right?" Meg says. "Justin probably didn't give her a discount."

"Yeah."

"I'll handle this, Zach. Thanks for letting me know."

"No problem," he says.

Meg doesn't like the look in Zach's eyes, the tightness in his smile. He's still frightened, she can tell, and it's the type of fear that's catching. "You want to take a break?" she says.

"Really?"

"You did come in early today, and it's almost lunchtime. Why not go out, get a bite, clear your head a little? Sara Beth and I can hold down the fort."

"Thanks, Mrs. Russo," he says. "I could use it."

Zach leaves the room as though he's just been let out of jail.

—

Why didn't Justin say anything to me about her? Meg stares at his image, frozen on the screen. He told her everything that happened in the store when she wasn't there and she did the same. It was part of their daily routine. Meg wishes he could answer her question. *If you were able to answer. If you were able to look at me . . .*

She longs to watch the video again. She can't stand the sound of the woman's voice, and so she mutes it. What she wants, more than anything, is to see him alive. She plays it again, her fingertips finding the screen the way they used to find his skin. Justin's arms. Justin's face. His soft lips, his beating heart . . . *Stop*.

Meg forces her gaze to the cash register beside him. The book displayed on a stand. The image is blurry but she recognizes the cover. *Haven* by Emma Donoghue.

Haven was Justin's book club pick for August. The video was taken in August. He died August 19.

You'll pay for your sins.

Meg shuts her eyes tight.

"You want me to handle the cash register, honey?" Sara Beth is standing in the doorway.

Meg pushes back from the computer. She opens her eyes. Looks at Sara Beth, not the screen. Evens out her thoughts. "Oh, hi. You scared me."

"Sorry," she says. "Zach said you gave him an early lunch break. He looked . . . um . . . spooked?"

Meg nods. "Some weirdo posted nonsense on our Facebook page," she says. "Not a big deal. I'll block her."

"We sure get 'em here, don't we?" Sara Beth says. "Remember that group of women who called us Satan worshippers because we carried the Harry Potter books?"

Meg squints at her, the memory easing back into her mind. "God, yes. Wow, that was years ago. Lily was in fifth grade . . ."

"I'll never forget that."

Meg nods, recalling more—a truly strange day, these shrieking women dressed in black cotton dresses with starched white collars like Halloween nuns, screaming that it wasn't too late to repent, knocking into customers, trying to pull books off shelves . . . At first, Meg was certain it was a practical joke, actresses paid off by Pete DeMarco or maybe Bonnie. But they kept going. And going. Eventually, Meg had to physically push the women out—not because they were doing any real damage but because they were making children cry. Later, she heard that they were from Rochester, several hours north of Elizabethville. They were part of a group called Mothers for Decency, and they were traveling south, hitting every bookstore in their path. "You know, this video could have been posted by one of them," Meg says. "The content is pretty much the same."

"Really?"

"You want to see?"

"Sure."

Meg plays the video for Sara Beth, with sound this time.

When it's through, Sara Beth keeps watching the screen, her jaw tight. "Bitch," she whispers.

"That about sums it up."

"Honestly. How dare she? We should . . . should have her arrested."

"For a nasty comment on a Facebook page?" Meg smiles at her. "The whole world would be in jail."

"Still," Sara Beth says.

"I know," Meg replies softly. "I know."

"No wonder poor Zach was so out of sorts," Sara Beth says. "He's a sensitive kid to begin with. And that video . . . Justin."

Again, the name stabs her. Meg swallows hard. She reads the name on the commenter's account. Claire Cassadine. "We never found out any of their names, did we? Those Mothers for Decency women?"

Sara Beth shakes her head, and Meg says, "Hmmm," and the two of them stay where they are for a while, Sara Beth tilting her head to one side, watching Meg the way Zach had watched her.

"I'm fine," Meg says. "Really. I am." She knows her face says otherwise—the heat behind it, the brimming tears. But thankfully, Sara Beth doesn't press her.

"I'll take the register," she says. "Let me know if you need anything." Within moments, Sara Beth is gone.

—

Alone again, Meg closes the video and clicks on the name. Claire Cassadine. She opens Claire's Facebook page. She looks it over quickly, skimming for references to Mothers for Decency or *decency* or *motherhood*. She finds nothing of the sort, and so she goes back to the profile pic, against a cover shot of a floppy-eared rabbit wearing a pink collar. Meg clicks on the profile photo and takes in Claire's image. The grim, tight mouth; the frizzy, gray hair, backlit like a halo. The huge, angry blue eyes.

She inhales sharply. *I know her.*

Those wild eyes. That wiry hair. Meg doesn't know Claire Cassadine. Not really. But she's seen her. Today. Storming the children's section, pushing into that woman with the comfort cat. Claire Cassadine was in her store ten minutes ago. And she might very well still be here.

Meg pulls herself up from her desk, away from the computer, out of the office. Her blood burns.

—

The children's section is usually the most popular part of the store, but not now, and for an obvious reason: the woman on the floor.

Claire Cassadine kneels in front of the picture books in her baggy jeans, her Christmas sweater a toxic yellow with winking Rudolphs all over it. *What are you doing?* Meg stares at the back of her head. Her steely hair. Rudolph's angry red nose between her shoulder blades.

Claire leans back on her heels, then lunges forward, removing a book. She peers at the empty space on the shelf, then returns it without looking at it. She takes out another book and does the same thing. Then again. One after the other after the other. It feels ritualistic. Compulsive. Meg glances around the store—at the customers chatting in the aisle, the short line at the cash register, where Sara Beth is stationed. So many of them, stealing glances at the woman.

Meg makes herself say her name, the syllables harsh on her tongue. "Claire Cassadine?"

The woman doesn't turn around.

"Why did you post that video on our page?"

Claire removes a stack of picture books and sets them on the floor. She pushes at the bare wall with her fingers. *"Hello!"* she shouts at it. Pounds the plaster with a fist, then grasps her knees, rocking back and forth. "Ow," she says.

Meg says it again. "Why did you post that video on our page?"

Claire looks up. She turns around slowly, purposefully. "I did it so you'd know," she says in her reedy voice. The voice from the video, singing at Justin. "It's time you knew."

"Knew what?"

"About us." She rises to her feet, and shoves a hand in her pocket. Those high-beam eyes on Meg's face, that tight-lipped witch's grin. For a split second, Meg thinks she's going to pull out a knife or a gun. But no. It's a phone. She taps at it, then holds it up like a prize, the recording light gleaming, aimed at Meg's face. "We are watching."

"We don't allow videotaping in our store," Meg says.

"It's a free country."

Meg smiles into the lens. *Calm. Professional.* "Yes. But this is a business," she says. "And as its owner, I make the rules."

"We know your rules."

"I'm going to have to ask you to leave."

"We don't follow your ruuuules . . ." She sings the words, like she sang to Justin. There's something awful in the purity of her voice, something soulless. Customers stare at her. "Why's that lady singing?" says a little boy. A woman shushes him.

"We know what goes on behind those walls." Claire Cassadine whirls around, the recording light trained on the bookshelves, on Sara Beth behind the counter, returning to Meg. "We know about the secret chamber. We know what you do in there. *We know all about your family.*"

"What is wrong with you?" Sara Beth says. "You're sick."

Meg stares at the phone, a door in her mind creaking open. A memory seeping through the crack.

How old was she then—ten, eleven? Bonnie cornering her in her yard as her mother gardened, telling her what the other kids had been saying about her dad, about her family . . .

She slams it shut. "Get out of my store," she says.

Claire doesn't move. Meg starts to say it again, but then Claire steps forward, knocking into her shoulder. She glides past customers, soaking in their stares, the phone still recording.

When she finally reaches the front door, Claire Cassadine turns, her icy stare locked on Meg. "I have an announcement to make!" Claire says, and the store goes quiet, murmured conversations grinding to a halt. A stillness settles, foreboding and heavy like the eye of a storm.

The phone clasped in her left hand, Claire raises the right one, the thumb pressed to her palm, her four fingers spread. She gazes around the room, making sure she has everyone's attention. Then, slowly, dramatically, she lowers her index finger. *"One down,"* she bellows, wiggling the other fingers. *"Three to go."*

Someone gasps.

"God," Sara Beth says.

But Meg is confused. She hears more gasps before it dawns on her what Claire Cassadine's announcement means. She's talking about Justin, Lily, herself and . . . who else? Meg's father. He used to own this store, which this bitch is old enough to remember. *One down, three to go.* She's talking about Justin's death. About Meg's family. Meg's father. Meg's child.

"You're a monster," says Sara Beth.

Meg hears herself say, "Get the fuck out of my store. *Now.*"

Cassadine leaves, slamming the door behind her. For several seconds, the entire bookstore is awash in silence.

Meg cheeks burn. "Sorry about that," she says. "We're all for freedom of speech here, but . . . Anyway . . . Pardon my French." She forces a laugh and the spell lifts, slightly. Customers talk with one another in hushed tones. Zach slips into the store and approaches the register. Sara Beth speaks to him in a low voice, and he nods, taking over as Sara Beth joins Meg. She places a gentle hand on her shoulder.

"I shouldn't have sworn in front of the customers," Meg says. "There are kids in the store. I don't know what I was thinking."

Sara Beth squeezes Meg's shoulder, as though to assure her she's still here. "No one blames you," she whispers. "She's awful. No one blames you."

—

Back in her office, Meg scrolls through Claire Cassadine's Facebook page. It says she's from Mount Shady, which is only fifteen minutes away, but she and Meg have no friends in common.

Meg sees a montage of pictures Claire posted back in April, of the rabbit from her cover picture, posed next to a purple Easter basket filled with colorful eggs. A single shot of a china teacup that she posted in June and captioned, "Tea for the Twos!" There's one comment from someone named Jeannette with a French bulldog for a profile pic, a series of numbers that must be an inside joke between the two of them: 121222. During the entire month of July, Claire posted only once—a meme of a generic-looking sunset superimposed with the word *Prevail*. There's one comment on this one, also from Jeannette: *Reign or Shine*.

Beyond that, there's very little engagement on Claire's posts. Not one has more than three likes.

Claire Cassadine's most recent post is from August, and it's the only photograph Meg sees that's of another human being: an older woman in a hospital bed, gazing into the lens with the same startling blue eyes as Claire's. The caption: *My heart is breaking. I'll miss you, Mom.*

There are no comments on the post. Only four "care" emojis and one "sad" one.

Meg doesn't want to feel sorry for Claire Cassadine, but she does. In a way, she understands her—the crushing pain, the loneliness. That awful, hopeless feeling, as though you're thrashing around in deep, rough waters, and there is no one to save you, nothing to hold on to. Nothing but teary Facebook emojis, designed so that the people watching you drown don't have to bother thinking up words.

Claire lost her mother in August, around the same time she came into the store and videoed Justin. Meg doesn't want to make excuses for her, but nothing changes a person the way grief does. Nothing warps a mind like losing a loved one, a *needed* one. Meg knows this. She knows it twice over. Why Claire decided to blame Meg's family for her problems, she has no idea. But maybe it has something to do with what Justin said, or didn't say. Or the way he looked at her. Or didn't. Maybe it has nothing to do with anything, other than the bad timing of Claire walking into the Secret Garden at the lowest point in her life.

She returns to the comment. Before deleting the video, she watches again with the sound on. *We are waaatching. We are armed . . .*

Meg listens all the way through. Her eyes widen. "What?" she whispers. She listens again. Then again. One more time to make sure she heard it correctly. Meg gazes at his image. Her husband's stoic face. His crossed arms. She gets it now. Sara Beth's shock and pity. Zach's extreme discomfort.

Justin's silence about the incident.

Meg deletes the video. She sends Claire Cassadine a private message that she's no longer welcome at the Secret Garden Bookstore and blocks her on both the store's account and her own. *That's why you didn't tell me, Justin.*

When she was singing to him, Claire didn't say *your,* as Meg had first thought. She said *her.*

You'll pay for her sins.

"That's why," Meg whispers.

SEVEN

It's the blood that's the problem. Everything else, Nathan Lerner has gotten used to—the tiredness, the loss of appetite, the cough, which he's come to enjoy in a perverse way, the fleeting relief it brings, the purposefulness of it. The blood is different. It serves no purpose but to scare people.

Today, it scared Doris the cleaning lady. Doris comes in once a month to put Nathan's life in order. He likes her because she works fast, leaves early and, most of the time, minds her own business.

This morning, though, Nathan made the mistake of asking Doris if she knew a good way to get bloodstains out of fabric, and when she asked what kind of blood and what kind of fabric, he whiffed it again by showing her his pillowcase from last night. Even though he'd gone at it with the Tide stick like Lady Macbeth, Doris had still stared at the thing as though she'd just happened on a crime scene. *Did that come out of you?* she'd said, her face full of alarm.

Nathan claimed a bloody nose, blaming it on the dry heat in his house, which wasn't a complete lie. Every winter, there's always a few days when he's walking around with Kleenex stuffed up his nostrils. But it wasn't the truth either. The blood on his pillowcase wasn't from a nosebleed but from an especially explosive cough—something that was happening more and more frequently these days.

Doris had recommended a hydrogen peroxide, bar soap and cold-water soak as a prewash, which is what Nathan is doing now, soaking all his bloody pillowcases and handkerchiefs, of which there are quite a few.

Mr. Lerner, I know this is none of my beeswax, Doris had said. *But don't you think maybe you should see a doctor?*

You're right, Nathan had replied with a smile. *It's none of your beeswax.*

Doris had graced him with one of her melodic sighs and accepted her check, Nathan thinking, *Fat chance I'm seeing a doctor.*

Nathan looks at all that cloth in the plastic tub, the traces of blood in the water. He can't remember how long he's supposed to let everything soak, or whether he's been told to wring it out before putting it in the washing machine. He probably should have let Doris do this; she'd offered to. But it was time for her to leave, and he didn't like the way she was looking at him, like he was something to be pitied. *I'm a grown man,* he'd told her. *I can wash a few pillowcases.*

Nathan makes the executive decision to wring everything out, and then throws it in the wash. Doris had recommended the normal cycle, and he chooses, as a grown man, to follow that recommendation. It shouldn't take as long as it does to accomplish all of this, but Nathan has to stop for a lengthy coughing fit.

It could be the smoking. This morning, before Doris arrived, Nathan smoked a bowl of sativa so he could be more social. He'd used the bong, of course. He's been laying off regular pipes and joints since the third week of this cough. But now, he's thinking that he might have to give up inhalants altogether and switch to edibles.

—

Teary and spent, he walks into the kitchen and puts the teapot on the stove. His eyes his collection of homemade teas and goes for echinacea, imported ginger and trumpet mushroom—a blend introduced to him years ago by a friend of Shira's, some lady from Woodstock who was into holistic medicine. The friend (Terry or Gerri or Cherry . . . Nathan's terrible with names) had claimed that the blend improved energy and health. Once the water's boiled and the tea has steeped, Nathan lifts his cup and toasts to both.

The dull winter light streams in through the kitchen window. Nathan finds it unsettling. He bought and renovated Pearly Gates twenty years ago. At the time it was an abandoned inn, with guest bungalows. His family had vacationed in the area when he was young. And though it's certainly changed since then in unexpected ways—contracting and crumbling rather than strengthening and expanding—Nathan believed when he moved here that this combination of familiarity and isolation might make him feel safe at last.

It worked, for a time. But not now. Not for months.

First the so-called accident that killed Justin and then that four-hundred-dollar check and then . . . Suffice it to say that the wolves are braying. He feels watched all the time. He doesn't want to think about what might come next. What *will* come next.

Nathan shuts the curtain.

This illness, whatever it is, scares him a lot less than the wolves. When you're sick, you know what you're getting. You either heal or you die. But the wolves, the witch hunters, they're a different type of enemy. They lie in wait. They can stay dormant for years, then ambush you or, worse yet, your family. It's the way they work. And anything can set them off. It's no coincidence, for instance, that Shira died less than two years after Magnolia's book came out. The doctors had insisted it was an infection from the garden, but doctors are parrots, puppets. Paid tools of the pharmaceutical industry. They know nothing, and they aren't inquisitive, so their minds will never expand. They'll never learn, which is why he doesn't bother with them.

You can grow bacteria anywhere. You can create it in a basement lab. You can rub poisonous chemicals on someone's face towel, spread them on the edge of a fresh razor blade, rim a teacup with them, like salt on a margarita glass. Poisonous chemicals that may mimic MRSA but that are, in reality, powerful beyond a cure.

Shira was never careless in the garden. She was never careless anywhere. Her downfall was not carelessness, but the fact that she saw the good in everyone.

She made friends indiscriminately—customers at the bookstore, mothers from Magnolia's school. She'd invite the mailman in for a cup of coffee when it was cold outside, let strangers into the house to use the phone.

And Justin was just like Shira. Magnolia married a man as kind and trusting as her mother—and look at what happened to him. *Why can't she see the pattern?*

Nathan recalls his last conversation with Magnolia. Five, six weeks ago, it must have been. His own daughter, so uninquisitive, she may as well be a doctor.

It was a loose lug nut, Magnolia had told him over the phone because she hardly ever visits. *When it fell out, I lost control of the tires.*

Who loosened it? Nathan asked.

Nobody.

How do you know that?

Because I'm a normal person.

In other words, she's a sheep.

Lug nuts come loose, Dad, Magnolia had said. *People get in accidents. Things happen for no reason all the time. I know it's comforting to think there's a reason for everything. Some grand conspiracy—*

It isn't comforting at all!

The conversation had ended with a hang-up. It might have been Nathan who slammed the receiver down, but how could anyone blame him? Magnolia understands absolutely nothing.

Did she ever stop and wonder how that lug nut got loose, or why a car full of skinheads appeared out of nowhere, exactly when it did? Magnolia never even mentioned the skinheads, probably because she believes they were irrelevant to the accident.

It was Lily who told Nathan about them, in one of her letters.

She wrote that they had been taking pictures of her with their phones, which makes Nathan think that somehow, she may have been the one to summon the wolves. And he's got a bad feeling as to how she did it. Suffice it to say that Lily's a musician, just like him. She may not have any albums out yet. But these days, unfortunately, you can get famous just from sharing music on the internet.

Nathan makes a note to himself: Once he's able, he'll call his one friend, Leland, and ask him to check the internet. See if Lily has posted any songs. First, though, he needs to calm down.

He takes a sip of hot tea and walks into the den, the mug warm against his hands. The royalty check is still on the coffee table. Still in its envelope, in the exact same spot where he set it down a week ago, after he tried to call Magnolia. He'll never cash it. He'll probably never open the envelope again. He's saving it as evidence. He'll put it in another envelope with Magnolia's name on it, so if anything happens to him now, she will know. Magnolia will finally know that he's been right about everything.

Nathan sits down in his rocking chair and sips the tea. Some rock star. Drinking tea in a creaky old chair, trying not to cough up blood. He wishes he'd brought a glass of water too, because he's parched. This damned dry radiator heat.

Nathan closes his eyes and tunes his thoughts to the grandfather clock in the hallway. *Tick, tick, tick.* Each tick pronounced, reliable, the space between them to the count of two. The clock once belonged to Shira's mother, a highly annoying woman. But it does have a beautiful rhythm.

Tick, tick, tick.

There are rhythms where you least expect them. There is music everywhere. Very few people understand this. But the ones that do, those enlightened ones . . . They know that this music is the only thing in life that you can rely on.

Tick, tick, tick. Time has come today . . .

Nathan's heart keeps time with the ticks, his pulse the bass. That old song in his mind. The Chambers Brothers. He'd love to have written a tune like that, and he could have. He should have. He could have found the beat in this clock, the tune in the growling of his stomach, the wheeze of his chest. *Music everywhere,* he thinks, drifting off, a trill in the living room joining in. A symphony. Or at the very least, a jam.

—

It isn't until the trill cuts off and he hears his own recorded voice that he recognizes it as his ringing phone, an incoming call going to the answering machine.

Let it pick up. Nathan's been getting so many of these junk calls lately. Scammers preying on the elderly. His landline makes him particularly susceptible. Doris has suggested he get a cell phone instead. *How about one of those Jitterbugs, Mr. Lerner? They're easy to work.* But Doris has no concept of surveillance, the danger in it. Nathan would just as soon get a cell phone as go on the internet and sign up for one of those ridiculous MyFace accounts. Honest to God, these people. These trusting, slaughter-ready sheep. Soon, they'll cut out the middleman and attach tracking devices to their heads.

He waits for the message: *Might we interest you in our marketing seminar? You're eligible for a cash reward . . .* He usually picks up the phone when they're mid-pitch and tells them to go fuck themselves, but Nathan doesn't have the energy to do that right now.

He listens for the beep. The message begins. *Hi, Dad.*

Nathan's eyes open. *Finally.*

Fully awake, he struggles to his feet and moves into the other room, fast as he can. He manages to snap up the phone just as Magnolia is saying goodbye.

"I'm here." Moving quickly isn't a great idea on this particular afternoon. Nathan's wheezy. Short of breath. A little lightheaded. He doesn't want Magnolia to notice. He doesn't want her worried about him. What he needs, more than anything, is for her to listen to him. Just this once.

EIGHT

You'll pay for her sins . . . Claire Cassadine's words run through Meg's head, even after she's deleted the video, shut off the computer, left the office. She thinks about them as she helps a customer find a book of short stories, chats with a caller about the availability of large-print books, helps Zach void a credit purchase.

Claire Cassadine, singing to Justin. The look on his face. The anger in it . . . Claire Cassadine waving four fingers in the air. Bending the index finger down. *One down, three to go* . . .

Meg shouldn't be so bothered by one unhinged customer. She's had them before, objecting to books she chooses to carry, books she chooses not to. Railing against the return policy, the prices, even the way the books are arranged. One customer made a rather loud and dramatic point of placing the Bible in the fiction section. Another excoriated Meg for "hiding" the religious titles in the back. You run a business—especially one that involves something as deeply personal as books—you learn very quickly that it takes all kinds.

But still . . .

"What do you think her deal is?" Meg asks Sara Beth. They're alone in the store, a lull in business. Zach's at the post office, mailing out packages.

They've been working in silence, Meg filling online orders from behind the register as Sara Beth shelves the new shipment of books, so the question comes out of the blue. But of course Meg doesn't need to go into specifics. Sara Beth knows whom she's talking about. "Claire Cassadine is sick." Sara Beth says it without turning around. "Don't even think about her."

"It's hard not to," Meg says. "I don't even know which is more upsetting. What she said in the store . . . or what she said to Justin in that video . . ."

"I know," Sara Beth says.

"'You'll pay for her sins.'"

"I know."

"I . . . I heard it wrong the first time."

Sara Beth nods. "If she dares set foot back in here . . . hell, if I catch her looking at our window display, I'm calling the cops."

Meg goes back to the website order she's been working on, but only for a minute. Her pulse thrums in her earlobes, her heart pounding so hard, she feels as though Sara Beth can hear it. It's ridiculous, she knows, the words of one deranged woman upsetting her to this degree. But she can't let it go. The idea that, in a way, Claire Cassadine had been right.

She bums a cigarette from Sara Beth, goes outside and smokes it, the whole time thinking of the drive to Ithaca. Everything she did wrong. All her sins. Asking for the sandwich so Justin had to unfasten his seat belt to get it for her. Overreacting to the jerks in the Mazda, egging them on and making it worse.

Making everything worse.

Most of all, Meg blames herself for the car trouble. Their regular mechanic was full-up for the whole week, and the Impreza was due for an inspection, and so, three days before they were scheduled to move Lily, she'd taken it to a new place. Some garage called Halloway's on Route 28, a good forty minutes from home.

Liz Reese had recommended it. She owns a mint-condition '65 Mustang she's named Clarabelle, and Halloway's is Clarabelle's preferred garage. So Meg took the car. Drove the forty minutes. Got herself a cup of coffee and waited while Justin held down the fort at the Secret Garden.

The mechanic at Halloway's was a guy named Thom with an *h* that he insisted everyone pronounce. He was nice enough, bonding with Meg about her upcoming "empty nester–hood," as he called it (*Our youngest graduates next year. I already booked a cruise.*), and of course praising Liz Reese and her "sweet, classic ride" to the high heavens. But he seemed confused by Meg's Impreza, confessing that he was *still a little thrown by these foreign, computerized vehicles.*

And three days later, one hour into their drive, with Meg swerving all over the thruway, braking and releasing and speeding and slowing down, her attention focused on those creeps and their phones, she lost control of the car. At one point, while the Impreza was spinning midair, Meg had thought of Thom and his suddenly poor choice of words: *a little thrown.*

It was a loose lug nut, Meg found out later. A tiny errant bolt. Her regular mechanic would have caught it. But Meg made a mistake and picked the wrong man for the job and, as a result, she killed her husband.

Justin did pay for my sins, she thinks.

—

"Feel better?" says Sara Beth.

Meg doesn't feel any better, but she does feel calmer, thanks to the smoke. "I guess."

"Good."

Remembering that she has to see Lily in twenty minutes when she goes home for lunch, Meg heads into the bathroom and brushes her teeth, then squirts herself with an old perfume sample she finds in her purse.

"Do I smell like smoke?" she says, once she's through.

She knows Sara Beth is the wrong person to ask. Smokers can't smell smoke, on themselves or on others. She and Justin quit when they started trying for Lily, and it wasn't until they were a couple of weeks into being strict nonsmokers that Meg realized her entire closet stunk like an ashtray.

"No, you're good," Sara Beth says.

Meg winces. "I hope Lily doesn't smell it on me."

"She's not going to care. She understands. You're under a lot of stress."

"I'm still her mom, though," she says. "I have to model good behavior." Strangely, this makes Meg think of her father, who's never been concerned with modeling good behavior. "Shit, I have to call Nathan."

Sara Beth smiles. "He'll be so happy to hear from you."

Meg refrains from rolling her eyes. A Prism fan since she saw them play the Palace in 1972—and the type of otherwise-liberated woman-of-a-certain-age who has a blind spot when it comes to men with creative talent—Sara Beth is more consistent in her support of Nathan than Meg's mother ever was. And that's truly saying something.

Cut your dad a little slack, Sara Beth has always been fond of telling her. *He's wired differently from the rest of us.* Which . . . Well, sure, that's true. But Meg always wondered why "the rest of us" should work to accommodate him. Shouldn't it be the other way around?

Meg was a senior in high school when her mother died from MRSA, which she most likely contracted when she cut herself on a thorn in their rose garden. Mom and especially Dad were distrustful of modern medicine, so by the time they realized she was suffering from something that couldn't be cured with nettles or dandelion tea, it was already too late. The antibiotics wouldn't take. Meg came home from school to a note that read, *Mom's in intensive care,* and days later, her beloved mother was gone. Meg was shell-shocked. That was the only way to describe it—as though a bomb had gone off inside her, turning her heart to ash.

She received no comfort from Nathan. Lost in his own grief, he locked himself in his studio every day, smoking ashtrays full of joints and reciting the Kaddish again and again and again. He grew increasingly paranoid, babbling about religious zealots plotting Shira's death, some secret cabal of anti-Semites who hated rock and roll. *They murdered her!* he'd shout late at night from the other end of the house as Meg tried to get to sleep. Not caring whom he frightened into hours of insomnia. *It's Kennedy all over again!*

Anxiety meds probably would have helped, but Dad claimed they dulled his senses and his ability to make music. Somehow, he managed to level out on his own, but it took months, with Sara Beth managing the store and Meg largely fending for herself at home, counting the days till college.

She wonders what her father wants from her now—probably more reassurance that she's not going to sell the Secret Garden, which, like everything and everyone else in his life, he's only taken an interest in once it was no longer his responsibility.

May as well get this over with.

Meg tells Sara Beth she'll be right back, then she slips outside again to call her dad from the relative privacy of the alleyway.

Nathan doesn't have a cell phone. He's not online. He lives about two and a half hours away in the Catskills, in a remote compound he's named Pearly Gates, after Prism's most famous song. To get in touch with Nathan, you either have to write him a letter and send it to his PO box in the nearest town, Star Lake, or call him on his landline, which is hooked up to the same answering machine he's used since the eighties.

Meg calls. It rings four times. She braces herself for the machine, and reliably it picks up.

Nathan's voice, circa 1985: *We're not here right now.*

Shira's: *But if you leave a message, we'll call you right back!*

In the background, a ten-year-old Meg shouts out, *Wait for the BEEP!*

Thank you, Magnolia! her parents say together.

Meg shuts her eyes and tries to shake it away—the image of her mother, the memory of her laugh . . . *Why keep that answering machine, when you know I'm going to call and I've told you how much it hurts me to hear her?*

It's typical. Meg's father has always put his own feelings before anyone else's. And inanimate objects—his bass collection, his old box of fan mail, the jewelry of Mom's that he refuses to give to Meg or even Lily because he "can't bear to part with it," this stupid answering machine—have always plucked the strings of his heart the hardest.

Meg inhales sharply and blows out air through pursed lips. "Hi, Dad," she says, after the beep.

"Sara Beth told me you wanted me to call you, so . . . I'm calling. Okay, bye."

She's about to hang up, when she hears Nathan's voice. "I'm here," he says.

"Are you okay?"

"Why haven't you called?"

"I'm calling you right now."

"You know what I mean."

Meg says nothing. After she wrote him about Justin's death, Nathan had phoned her, asking if there was anything he could do. He sounded so genuinely distraught that, for a time, Meg felt guilty for writing rather than calling, for not letting him know earlier. That feeling didn't last, though.

"Magnolia," Nathan says now. "The wolves are back."

Meg groans. When her father is especially high and paranoid, he talks in code, like he's the main character in a seventies conspiracy thriller. "I don't know what that means," she says.

Nathan says, "You remember Claude?"

"DuBois?"

"Yes."

"Of course I remember him." Claude DuBois is the lead guitarist of Prism, the band's only other surviving member. He visited a few times when Meg was little and recorded some songs with her dad in his home studio, her mom accompanying them on drums. As Meg remembers, Claude DuBois was soft-spoken and gentle and he had longish red hair, like Floyd Pepper from the Muppets. Meg found him fascinating. "Is Claude all right?"

"He's fine. I mean, I think he is. That isn't the point."

"Okay."

"About a year ago, Claude put some of our songs on one of those computerized con jobs where you can listen to albums on the World Wide Web and screw musicians out of their livelihoods."

"A streaming platform."

"Whatever."

"That's what they're called."

"I don't give a rat's ass what they're called."

She leans against the side of the store, the bricks cold through the back of her coat. "Okay."

"The point is, I didn't expect to see a dime from it, and I was correct. You can get streamed a thousand times, you get a few bucks at the most."

"Right."

"I told Claude he was an idiot to put us on that thing. It's lose-lose unless you're Pink Floyd, and even then—"

"Okay, okay. I get it."

"No, you don't. *You don't understand anything.*"

Meg pulls the phone away from her ear. She wishes she'd asked Sara Beth for another one of her cigarettes.

When she listens again, he's mid-sentence. " . . . just forgot about it. You know? I've got enough money. Claude. He's a schmoe but he means well."

Meg makes a noise that she hopes sounds as though she's been listening.

"So, last week, I get a royalty check from this streaming whatever-the-hell. It's for 'Pearly Gates.'"

"Yeah?"

"It's four hundred dollars."

Meg's eyes widen. "That's . . . that's great."

"Magnolia, that means the song has been streamed more than one hundred thousand times."

Meg says nothing. She can hear her father's shaky breathing, that wheeze to it, like a quivering string. She waits for him to speak.

"You get it? We're not famous enough to get those kinds of numbers. Not for good reasons."

"What do you mean, Dad?"

"I mean that they're *studying* the song, Magnolia. Playing it backward. Putting it through computer programs that can isolate vocals and instruments. Checking it for whatever secret messages they think are in there so they can have ammunition to—"

"Dad . . ."

"I'm scared," he says. "For you. I want you to be careful. I want Lily to be careful."

"Don't worry. We'll be fine."

"You don't know that. Look what happened to Justin."

Meg's stomach drops. She tries to keep her voice calm, steady. "Dad, I told you. That was an accident." *An accident that happened because of me.*

"No, Magnolia. No. They're behind it. These . . . these people . . . *Look at what happened to your mother.*"

Justin used to voice concerns about Nathan. *Are you sure he's okay up there alone?* he would say, after reading one of her father's more rambling letters. *The solitude, all that weed and hash he smokes . . . Plus, he isn't getting any younger. When was the last time he saw a doctor?* Meg would explain that Nathan had always been paranoid, as long as she'd known him. He'd always been self-absorbed and distrustful and mildly self-destructive—not a lethal combination, but one that made him, well, weird. *It's not dementia,* Meg would insist. *It's just the way he is.*

But did that make sense? If someone's been teetering on the edge of a cliff for years, growing older and weaker, doesn't it stand to reason they'll eventually fall off? "Dad?" Meg says. "Are you feeling all right?"

"Don't you dare patronize me."

"Sorry. I just—"

"I'm telling you, it's Kennedy all over again."

She inhales sharply. "Dad?"

"Yes?"

"I was . . . I was thinking. How about if Lily and I come up for Christmas?"

He doesn't reply.

"Or maybe before. I mean . . . I think it would be nice to reconnect as a family. Lily could bring her instruments and you guys could jam. I'll bring food . . ."

"Okay." He says it more readily than Meg thought he would, his voice so tired and soft that it breaks her heart a little. "Just please call before you come. Let me know exactly what time you'll be arriving. I don't respond well to surprise visits."

"Of course, Dad."

"Thank you."

They're both quiet for a few moments, Meg listening to her father's breathing.

She forces a smile. "I don't know if Sara Beth told you or not, but business at the store has been great."

"The customers," he says. "Have they been friendly?"

Meg's face flushes. She shuts her eyes, willing herself not to think of Claire Cassadine. *What a question,* she thinks. "Sure."

Nathan clears his throat, then starts to cough, the air escaping from him in great barking gasps. It's a violent cough, a pot smoker's cough, or so she hopes. *Dad needs to stop smoking. He's getting too old.* "Take good care of your daughter, Magnolia," he says, once he catches his breath. "Hold her close. Keep her safe from this ugly world."

NINE

"I hope you don't have a problem with this," Meg tells Lily, "but we're spending Christmas at Grandpa's."

"Cool," Lily says.

"You sure?" Meg says. "I know it's weird, but I talked to him today and . . . I'm a little worried about him."

"I think it would be fun," Lily says. Then she smiles. There's something odd about the smile, about Lily in general. For one thing, she's being too nice.

They're in the basement. Meg found Lily here alone, but there are telltale signs she's had a visitor. For the first time in months, she's taken her drum set in from the garage. Lily never plays drums solo. Plus, the room is too clean, and reeks of Febreze, and when she first came into the house, Meg spotted two Coke cans in the recycling bin. Not one but two.

Meg hates herself for noticing these things. She doesn't want to be one of those Sherlock Holmes moms, not when her daughter is eighteen years old and, as far as she knows, a reasonably responsible person. If it weren't for the accident, Lily would be five hours away from home at Ithaca, her daily activities—not to mention whatever mistakes she chose to make—a complete mystery. And that's the way it should be. Lily deserves some secrets in her life. Every eighteen-year-old does.

What Meg doesn't understand, though, is why Lily is choosing to hide an entire relationship from her.

Why did Bonnie have to tell me about the blond boy?

"You hungry?" Meg says. "I picked up some pasta salad from Reese's."

"Sure," Lily says. She turns directly toward Meg. There's a smudge of dirt on her forehead. Another on her cheek.

"Maybe you should . . . wash up first?"

"Why?" says Lily. "Do I look dirty?

Meg meets her gaze. "A little. What were you doing? Gardening?"

"It's freezing out."

"That was a joke."

"Oh."

The two of them head upstairs. Lily goes to the bathroom to wash her face while Meg moves about the kitchen, setting out the plastic container of pasta salad, along with a couple of bowls, forks and paper napkins from the pantry. It's a big container. Liz Reese knows how much Meg loves her pasta salad and, "as a fellow business owner," routinely gives her double orders.

Lily opens the fridge. She takes out the pink box Meg brought home and shows it to her. "Cake?"

"They had a party for me at work," Meg says.

"That's nice." Lily tugs at the box string. "So . . . everybody happy you're back?"

Meg flashes yet again on Claire Cassadine. *One down, three to go . . .* "Mostly."

"Huh?"

Meg has no idea why she just said that. It's not as though she has any intention of telling Lily about Claire. "Just . . . you know. Typical annoying customers."

"Ah."

"Oh, honey, that cake isn't vegan."

Lily sighs. She closes the box, reties the string, takes the filter pitcher out of the fridge and pours them both glasses of water before serving herself an enormous helping of pasta salad.

The whole time, Lily's gaze stays trained on Meg, an expression in her eyes that's hard to understand.

"Did you want cake?" Meg says. "I can pick up a vegan one at the bakery in Boiceville later."

"I don't want cake, Mom."

"What is it, then?"

"Nothing."

"Lily . . ."

"I'm fine. Really."

"You don't seem fine."

"Well, I am."

It's true that Justin's death has changed Meg's relationship with her daughter. It's made them a little more reliant on each other, a little more sensitive of each other's feelings. But it hasn't helped them to read each other any better than they used to. It hasn't helped them to communicate. So much of what passes between Meg and Lily are silences, comfortable and otherwise. Sometimes, they'll make it through an entire meal without exchanging any words at all.

Meg scoops some of the pasta salad into her bowl. Lily has already started devouring hers, and by the time Meg sits down, she's consumed nearly half. *Wow. She's hungry today.*

"Why are you worried about Grandpa?" Lily says, once she finally comes up for air.

Meg looks at her. "I don't know," she says. "He's getting older. He lives halfway up a mountain all by himself."

"So, nothing new?"

Meg's impulse is to brush off the question, to lie and say, yes, everything's okay—avoid the topic the way she avoided talking about Claire Cassadine's threats, just to keep things pleasant. But this is family, someone Lily will be seeing in the next couple of weeks if not sooner. It's probably best she go in prepared. "I had a . . . conversation with Grandpa today," she says. "He sounded strange. Paranoid."

Lily sips her water. "He still smokes a lot of weed, right?"

"I'm pretty sure he does," Meg says.

"Well then . . . I mean . . ."

"I know. But this was different. He actually thinks people are after him. Because of his music or . . . because he was almost famous at one point in his life? Apparently a lot of people have downloaded one of his songs."

"'Pearly Gates'?"

Meg nods. "Anyway . . . I don't know. He sounded very agitated. He compared himself to Kennedy, and what scares me about that is, he said the same thing when your grandmother died. He got paranoid back then too."

Lily stares at her. "He compared himself to Kennedy?"

"Yes."

"The president?"

"Well . . . yeah."

"How?"

"He was talking about this situation that he believes he's in. People downloading his song because they mean him harm. He said, 'It's Kennedy all over again.'"

Lily takes another bite of pasta salad. "He could have been talking about a different Kennedy."

"I suppose, but—"

"It's not a totally unusual name."

"But in the context, it was obvious."

"Did you ask him why he said that?"

"No."

"So you don't know, really. You have no idea. You just *assumed* he was talking about the Kennedy assassination and that was good enough for you."

Meg spears some of her pasta salad and chews it carefully, watching Lily. "I'm sensing an attitude."

"Not an attitude," she says. "Just an observation."

"Which is . . ."

"You don't really know Grandpa Nate. You lived with him for years, and he's still a part of your life, but you don't know him." She shakes her head. "It's like Zach."

Meg opens her mouth, then closes it again. "Zach? From the Secret Garden?"

"Yeah, Zach Winters."

"What about him?"

"He was a bully in fourth grade."

Meg blinks at her.

"You love him so much, you think he's such a promising young man or whatever. And I don't know, maybe he's changed since then. But when we were little, he was a bully and an anti-Semite. He threw water at me, and I didn't even remember it until . . . well, it doesn't matter. He did."

"Zach? An anti-Semitic bully? Come on."

"You're going to believe him over me. A kid you've only seen in your own store and only over the past year." Lily shakes her head. "You *don't know him.*"

Meg stares at her for several seconds. "Lily, what is going on with you?"

Lily closes her eyes. She grasps the arms of her chair as though at any moment, it could buck her right off. "You think you know people, but you don't," she says. "You don't know who people were in the past. Even people you love. *Especially people you love.*"

"Zach is not an anti-Semite."

Lily takes a deep breath, lets it out slowly. She opens her eyes again. She seems a little calmer now, but her eyes are slightly bloodshot. *Maybe she is high,* Meg thinks. *Maybe that's where this is coming from.* Honestly, she's never sounded so much like her grandfather, and it's frightening. Meg starts to ask if she has been smoking weed, but Lily cuts her off. "Mom, I just found out today that I don't really know you."

"*What?* Of course you know me."

Lily stands up from her chair. "We'll see." She leaves the kitchen and runs upstairs.

"Lily? Where are you going?"

She hears Lily's heavy footsteps overhead, in her bedroom, then in the hall. "Lily!" she calls out. Lily thumps down the stairs, and when she finally emerges, she's carrying a cardboard box, which she places on a chair with a surprising gentleness.

"What is that?" Meg says, as Lily opens the lid. "What are you doing?"

"You act like Grandpa is too self-absorbed to care about anybody else, but you're wrong. He saved a dozen copies."

"A dozen copies of what?"

"Of this." Lily opens the box. Meg could swear she sees a puff of dust escape as she lifts the lid, like something from an old haunted house cartoon.

"What are you doing?" she asks again, very quietly.

But Meg knows. Even before she reads the side of the box, her father's handwriting. *A dozen copies.* She didn't even know there were a dozen copies left. Her daughter removes a book from the box—the faded cover, the rigid spine—and that feeling washes over her, that odd mixture of pride and shame and dread that the book always gave her. The book she wrote. She reads the script on the cover: *The Prophesy.* The picture—Princess Iyanla standing before the Bronze Lord, holding up the Sword of Truth.

"See? I don't know you, Mom."

Meg can't answer. For quite a while, she can't speak at all.

—

"Where did you find it?" Meg says finally. Her own voice sounds strange to her, asking this irrelevant question. Like a cheater caught in the act.

"In the attic," Lily says.

"What were you doing in the attic?"

"Looking for your book," Lily says. "Why didn't you ever tell me about it?"

Meg sighs heavily. She doesn't know where to begin. How do you explain to your only child why you never told her about what sounds, and feels, like one of the biggest accomplishments of your life? How do you tell her that in your mind, the only book you ever wrote is all tied up in the bad things that followed, and talking about that book only brings them to the surface? How do you say all that without sounding like a liar, or crazy, or both? "I don't know how it got up there," Meg says, more to herself than to Lily. Because she truly doesn't know. If her father gave the box to Justin during one of his solo visits, neither one of them ever mentioned it . . .

Lily is staring at Meg without blinking, her eyes like bare lightbulbs.

"I was fifteen," Meg says quietly. "*The Prophesy* has been out of print for years. Decades."

"So?"

"The publisher doesn't even exist anymore."

"Again . . . so?"

Meg drinks some of her water. *Just tell her. She won't stop until you do.* "There was a contest," she says. "I saw it advertised in some magazine I used to read. *Sassy*, probably . . . Anyway, it was for aspiring writers aged fourteen to eighteen, and the prize was a publishing contract."

"So you saw this contest and you just . . . wrote a book?"

"I'd already written one. A fantasy novel. Like the kind you used to read, only no dragons."

Meg smiles. Lily doesn't.

"Anyway, my book won the contest. I got a deal with this little publisher called Young Readers' Press. They paid me, as I remember, two hundred dollars. And they wound up publishing maybe five hundred copies."

"You were famous."

"No, I wasn't," she says. "They did give me a little media tour, though. I was in the *Elizabethville Courier* and some giveaway magazine in Mount Shady and—"

"The *New York Times*. You were written up in the *New York Times*, Mom."

"It was a tiny little feature. And it was in the Hudson Valley section, not the book review." Meg isn't sure why she's downplaying it as much as she is—maybe because her parents did. Her father, in particular, was concerned about Meg getting "too big for her britches."

There was one time, though, one moment when she and her mother were doing the dishes after dinner and Dad was off in his studio, and Mom turned to her, her whole face glowing. *I loved every word.* It was so strange, so out of the blue. The way she blurted it out, as though it was a secret she'd been holding in for months.

You're the most talented one in the family, Mom had said.

Meg promised her mother she would keep writing. She said it was the one thing that really made her happy—a secret of her own, made truer by the voicing of it. But then Mom died, and with her died all the things that made Meg happy, especially her desire to tell stories. There was a part of Meg that blamed herself for her mother's death—a part that believed she really had grown too big for her britches, and that grief, the way it seemed to shrink her, was the only apt punishment. Meg wound up studying English lit in college, not creative writing as she'd planned. And she never wrote another book.

"It was a fluke, writing a fantasy novel," Meg says to Lily. "I mean, come on. I never even think about it anymore."

"Grandpa Nate does. Or he did, anyway."

Meg laughs at this. She can't help it. As far as she knows, Nathan's never even read *The Prophesy. The genre isn't my cup of tea,* he once explained, which, *God, what a shitty thing to say to anybody, let alone your own child . . .* And yet he saved those copies. Put them in a box, which has somehow found its way into the attic . . . *How?*

Lily takes something else out of the box—a newspaper article, clipped and preserved in a plastic holder. "He saved this too. He pressed it in one of the books."

It's the *New York Times* piece. Longer than Meg remembers, nearly half a page. She looks at the picture of herself, smiling in her old living room, her braces gleaming. Holding up a copy of *The Prophesy.*

Nathan had been against her doing the interview—it was Mom who talked him into it. *We can't put our name out there,* Meg had overheard him tell her. *The wolves,* he'd said. *The wolves.* Even then. Making it all about himself. His paranoia. The barely lingering dust of his fame. And even though Nathan had eventually relented, he'd forbidden the reporter from coming to their home, and so Meg was forced to do the interview in three parts, over the phone. "My mother took this picture," Meg says. She touches the clear plastic. *Photo: Shira Lerner.* "See how happy I look?" Her vision starts to blur.

Meg looks up at her daughter and wishes she hadn't, the threat of tears still in her eyes. One of them escapes, trickling down her cheek. Lily swipes her napkin from the table and hands it to Meg. "I'm sorry, Mom."

"Lily," she says. "Was Grandpa the one who told you about the book?"

She shakes her head. "This friend of mine told me," she says. "His name is Carl. He, um . . . heard about it from some people he was working with."

Meg takes a breath. She dabs at her eyes. "How old is your friend Carl?" Meg says. She's slightly alarmed. She's never met a Carl born after the year 2000.

"He's my age," Lily says. "He was in my class." Her cheeks flush a little. Meg notices this, things adding up in her head.

"Is Carl blond?" she says.

Lily's eyes widen. "How do you know that?"

"Bonnie," Meg says. "She assumed I knew about him."

Lily exhales. "There's nothing to know, Mom," she says. "Bonnie saw me with him once when he dropped me off at work. And . . . Well, maybe I kind of like him now. But I didn't then. Honest."

"I'm glad you have a new friend." Meg tries to smile, to will the tears away. She hates the way her daughter is looking at her. "I'm sorry I didn't tell you about the book," she says.

"That's okay," Lily says. "I'm sorry I didn't tell you about Carl."

"That's okay."

Lily's phone dings. She checks it. "Oh, crap. I'm going to be late for therapy."

Meg hands her the car keys. Lily grabs her backpack, then hurries to the closet to get her coat, Meg's gaze shifting from the book she wrote to the box it came in. Her father's handwriting. "Wait, Lily?"

"Yeah?"

"Where in the attic did you find the box?"

"Under the wicker table."

"What wicker table?"

"The one Grandpa gave us. You know, that ugly one with the happy face on top?"

"Oh," Meg says. "Right."

Lily shouts a goodbye and heads out the door. "I asked your dad to throw out that table," Meg says. "He told me he did."

But Lily is already gone.

TEN

"So you told your mom about me," Carl says.

"Yep."

They're sitting in Carl's truck, in the parking lot behind their old high school. Lily's parked her car in the space right next to his, and it all feels so secretive, like a scene from one of those old conspiracy movies her dad used to love. *Three Days of the Condor. The Parallax View. All the President's Men.* She'd mention that to Carl, but she doubts he's ever heard of any of them. She takes a tiny hit from Carl's vape.

Lily much prefers regular weed-smoking to vaping. Not that it's healthy, but at least joints have been around forever, with entire generations surviving smoking weed in their teens. With vaping, Lily feels like she's always one day away from hearing that it causes instant lung cancer and that everyone who's ever done it once will be dead within the year. But Carl brought this vape, and it's sleek and fancy-looking. *My brother got it from a dispensary in Lennox,* he said in reverent tones, as though he was presenting her with sea emeralds from the city of Atlantis. How could she say no to that?

She hands it to him. "I've been planning on telling her about you for a while," she says. It's kind of a lie, but whatever.

Carl takes a hit and blows out a cumulous cloud. "I hope this doesn't sound weird," he says. "But I'm . . . like . . . flattered."

Lily smiles. *No game at all.*

"How did it come up?"

"When I asked her about the book she wrote, she wanted to know who told me. So I said you. Apparently, Bonnie had already mentioned you to her."

He smiles, his eyes sparkling. "So, like . . ."

"Yeah?"

"Nothing."

Lily gazes out the window. It's not even three o'clock but already the sky is hinting at sunset, the cloudless blue turning orangey pink at the edges like a piece of film that's starting to melt.

Carl hands Lily the vape. She takes another minuscule hit, though she's not sure why. Either it's going to kill you or it's not, right? How much smoke (vapor, whatever) you take in probably doesn't matter. She smokes more. She can feel Carl watching her.

She exhales. "What's up?"

"Okay, so . . . I was thinking," he says. "Winter break's coming up, right?"

"Uh huh." She hands him back the vape.

"That means your friends will be back from school."

Lily nods.

"I mean . . . you're still gonna want me around then, right?" He winces. "Or not. Not's cool too, if you want to, like . . . catch up with them. I just . . . like . . ."

"What are you asking?"

He turns to her, that expression in his eyes. That serious look boys get when they want to kiss you, like they're about to take an oath. "You still want to hang out?" he says.

"Like officially?"

"Yeah."

Lily knows that this is a moment that calls for experience and confidence and the perfect words, but she doesn't have any of those things, even when she hasn't been smoking. And so instead she just kisses him.

"Is that a yes?" he says, once they pull away. "Because, I know I'm not, like, in college or anything and there might be other guys who—"

"Stop," Lily says. "Yes. I do."

"Really?"

"Okay, now I'm starting to get annoyed."

Carl grins at her, but it disappears quickly. "Shit. Cops," he says.

Before the words can even register, something slams against Lily's window, and she hears a man's voice telling her to get out of the truck.

-

Lily opens the door, her hand shaking. Slowly, carefully, she gets out of the truck.

There are two cops, a man and a woman, both with short hair and mirrored sunglasses. The man has a thick, dark mustache, the woman wears frosty pink lipstick, and both are in full uniform, with leather gloves. Their squad car is pulled up behind both the truck and Lily's mom's Subaru, blocking them in, its lights flashing. How did she and Carl not notice them pulling up?

"Lift your hands over your head, miss," says the woman, her lipstick sparkling in the cold sunlight. Thoughts rush through Lily's mind and slam into each other. *Is vaping illegal in New York? Is vaping in a truck illegal? Is the vape illegal because it's from out of state? What did Carl do with the vape?*

Carl's alone in the truck. He can at least throw the thing under the seat and maybe they won't find it. Or maybe it's best he do nothing. Hand it over if they ask for it. Lily doesn't know what to do. She's been pulled over before, but nothing like this. She's never been asked to get out of her car, even when she was driving. She's the passenger. The car is parked. *What is going on?*

Lily's arms shiver. She'd taken her coat off in the truck, and the air cuts through her thin sweater. It must be twenty degrees out here. The female cop pats her down quickly. Then she nods at her partner. Lily wants to look at Carl. She wants to see his face, just to get her breathing back to normal, but she's too scared to do anything but stare straight ahead.

She takes a closer look at the cops. Neither one of them is familiar, which is strange. There are only five police officers in this town. One was a recent graduate of her high school, and between school assemblies and the speeding ticket she got at the end of senior year, she's pretty sure she knows the other four, by sight anyway.

They must be from Mount Shady or Boiceville, she thinks. *Or . . . could they be state troopers? What does a state trooper uniform look like? Do state troopers care about parked cars? We were in a parked car. What did I do wrong?*

"License, please," the woman says.

Lily swallows. "It's in my backpack."

"Where's your backpack?"

"In my car."

"This your car?" The man knocks on the roof of Lily's mom's Crosstrek. "In other words, if I were to check the registration, would your name be on it?"

Lily frowns. She glances at the truck. *Why isn't anybody talking to Carl?*

"Do you need me to repeat the question?" His mustache is so thick, it almost looks fake.

Lily clears her throat. "Yes. I mean, no . . . My mom. It's my mom's car."

"What's your mom's name?" the woman says.

"Meg Russo."

"Keys, please," says Mustache. But Frosty Lips is already peering into the Subaru.

"They're in there." She says it like a joke. "The girl left the keys in the car."

"Because I was right next to it. In my friend's truck."

Frosty Lips yanks open the door to the Subaru, opens the glove compartment. She finds the registration and hands it to the man.

"*Magnolia Lerner* Russo?" Mustache says.

"Yes, sir."

He smirks at her.

"Excuse me!" Carl opens his door. "I'm actually the driver of the truck and—"

"Son, I'm gonna ask you to get back in the car and close the door *now*." *Close the door, Carl.*

After several seconds, he does.

"Can I . . . Officer . . . can I ask what I've done wrong?" Lily says.

The woman smirks at her, those glossy lips gleaming. "You can ask whatever you want to ask."

Mustache moves to the driver's side of her car and opens it. "Can you pop the trunk, please, miss?"

Lily walks to the car on shaky legs, a strong wind biting the back of her neck. *Maybe please is a good sign. Maybe miss is a good sign.* She leans over and pops the trunk, then moves away from her car. She's not sure what to do next.

Frosty Lips is rifling through Lily's backpack. "What's this?" she says.

"What?"

She pulls out a pack of tampons, opens the top. She yanks all of them out and drops them on the pavement.

Why?

Lily's gaze darts from the male cop, poking through her trunk, picking up the projector Carl brought for her, to the female with her backpack, to Carl watching from the truck, the shadow of his face. She finds herself thinking of those old conspiracy movies again. The quick cuts. *The edits are designed to throw you off-balance,* Dad told her once. *Make you feel like you're having a bad dream.*

The woman removes a container of lip gloss from Lily's backpack, an expensive brand she bought online from Sephora with an early Christmas bonus Bonnie had given her two weeks ago. *Don't spend it all on gifts,* Bonnie had said. *Buy yourself something that makes you feel special.* The woman opens the container and peers inside, sniffing the tip of the applicator.

"You know what I'm looking for," she says. "Don't you?"

Actually, I don't, Lily wants to say. But she's smart enough to keep quiet. She's seen enough arrest videos online. She knows things never end well if you're anything other than quiet. Obedient. Her heart throbs. She can feel it in her throat, her ears, her face. Her teeth chatter. Her lips are numb from the cold and she's lost all sensation in her nose, but still, she's sweating. It's pooling under her raised arms, trickling down her rib cage.

Mustache moves over to the truck. Out of the corner of her eye, Lily sees him tapping Carl's window, asking questions in a voice she can't hear. Frosty Lips has found Lily's license now, which she is holding in both gloved hands. "Lily Elizabeth Russo?"

"Yes?"

"Daughter of Magnolia and Justin Russo?"

Lily frowns. "Well, she goes by Meg. And my dad died a few months—"

"I didn't ask that."

"Sorry." Lily's eyes are starting to tear up. Her gaze moves from the woman's face to her badge. She's not wearing a name tag. *Why isn't she wearing a name tag?*

The nameless cop cradles Lily's license in her hands, staring at it as though she expects it to betray its owner. The pinkie finger on one of her gloves is tied in a knot. Lily wonders if she lost the finger shooting someone, killing someone. *Don't cry, don't cry, whatever you do . . .*

"Granddaughter of Nathan Lerner."

"What?"

"Is your grandfather Nathan Lerner?"

"Yes."

"Does he live with you?"

"What? No."

"You live on 2221 Peach Tree Lane."

Mustache joins her. "Lotta twos in that address," he says to his partner. Lily makes a point of looking for his name tag. He doesn't have one either. Isn't that illegal? Lily would ask him about it—she'd ask them both—if she didn't think it would get her arrested or shot or worse.

Mustache gestures at the truck with his head. "The boy's good. Stories match up."

Frosty Lips hands Lily her backpack. "The school is private property," she says. "We could arrest you for trespassing, but we'll let you off with a warning."

Lily stares at her, at her own warped reflection in the mirrored glasses, and the woman's lipsticked mouth, smiling. It isn't illegal for them to be parked here. She knows that. Everybody does.

"Thank you," she says.

"You can both drive out of here in your individual vehicles," the male cop says. "Maybe go find a nice mall to hang at instead." He laughs. Lily doesn't. She can't figure out what the joke is supposed to be. Her tampons are still scattered all over the pavement. Carefully, she crouches down and collects them, putting them back in the box.

As she gets into her car, Frosty Lips gives her a cheesy fake salute. "Drive safe, Lily Elizabeth Russo," she says. "Merry Christmas."

—

Carl tries to help Lily pick everything up, which makes her feel even more humiliated. "Please get back in the truck, Carl."

"What did they say to you?"

"Can we . . . can we talk about this later?"

"Sure," he says. "Should I follow you to work?"

"That sounds good."

He gets back in the truck.

Lily stuffs the box of tampons into her backpack, her face burning.

It isn't until she's behind the wheel and pulling out of the lot that she realizes she's left her coat in Carl's truck. "Great," she whispers. Lily has never been so cold in her life. There's a slick of dried sweat on the back of her neck, and it feels like ice. Her teeth chatter. Her fingertips are blue. She turns the heat all the way up, and sticks her fingers between the slots of the vent until they're warm enough to grasp the wheel. Then, she drives. She doesn't want to think about what just happened to her. She doesn't want to think about anything. She almost puts on Spotify, but she can't deal with words, spoken or sung. Instead, she listens to the heater, the roar of it, like an endless sigh.

—

Lily parks a block away from Divine Vintage, and Carl pulls in behind her. He walks up to her window. He holds up her coat. "You left this," he says.

She gets out of the car and takes it from him and puts it on quickly, zipping it all the way up to her chin.

They start to walk toward the store, neither one of them saying anything, the air leaving their mouths in fine white puffs.

"Are you okay?" Carl says.

"I think so." Lily looks at him. "I don't understand what just happened, Carl."

He shakes his head. Tentatively, he puts his arm around her. She leans in, resting on him.

"Cops are fucked up," Carl says softly.

"True. But that was next-level. Did you notice that neither one of them had name tags? We couldn't report them if we tried."

"We could probably describe them—"

"I don't want to report them," she says. "I just want to forget it ever happened."

"They were probably bored," Carl says. "Saw a couple of kids. Figured we were getting stoned, so they decided to mess with our heads."

Lily looks at him. "Did he take your vape?"

"What?"

"The cop. I saw him talking to you."

"Oh, right. No." Carl moves his hand away.

"Well, that's a relief," Lily says. "So, he just wanted your license?"

"Yeah." Carl stares at the sidewalk, his grip on her shoulder loosening.

"What did he say to you?"

"Huh?"

"The cop. Mustache. He was talking to you. What did he say?"

Carl's arm drops to his side. He turns and meets her gaze but just for a second, a strange look in his eyes, a type of shame. "I don't really want to talk about it, Lily," he says. "Is that okay?"

Lily thinks about Frosty Lips, the sneer in her voice as she asked about her parents, her grandfather. How close she came to bringing Lily to tears, and all she had done was ask simple questions. Carl stares straight ahead, his jaw taut, his eyes glistening, either from the cold or from his thoughts, Lily isn't sure which. She'd like him to put his arm around her again, but at this moment, he seems too frail to lean on.

"Of course it's okay," Lily says.

ELEVEN

"Take the sword, Princess," the Bronze Lord says.

Iyanla tries to do as she's told but the sword is too heavy. She's weak with plague and sicker still from grief. Two years. That's all it's been. Two years of this creeping evil, and she has lost everyone she ever loved.

Gazing down at her mother's lifeless body, she wants nothing more than for the plague to take her too, before the oceans rise and skies heat up and the Great Fires turn the air to clouds of ash, bringing on the Reign of Monsters.

"It is the final month of the Year of Twos," the Bronze Lord says. "You must not ignore The Prophesy."

Lily has yet to come home from work, and so Meg is alone in the house. Back in the converted basement, she's sitting on the couch, reading her own book—one of her father's copies from the box that inexplicably found its way into her attic. Sara Beth dropped her off twenty minutes ago, at the end of a workday that—save the drama of Claire Cassadine—has been reasonably pleasant. But Meg hasn't been around to appreciate it. Not really. This whole afternoon, she's felt distracted, tense. That feeling sneaking up on her, wrapping its tentacles around her. Whispering. *We are watching.*

At one point, while working behind the counter, the sensation of being watched had been so powerful she thought she might scream. And sure enough, she'd looked up to see two strangers at the window, phones raised . . .

May I help you?! She flung the door open and said it like a threat—frightening some young couple who'd simply been taking pictures of the Dickens family Christmas display that Sara Beth had created in the window.

The idea that one crazy customer could do that to her . . . But of course it isn't just Claire Cassadine that's making her feel unbalanced. It's returning to work without Justin. It's eating and breathing and sleeping and doing everything without Justin. It's trying to act as though life can go back to normal when he was her normal. He was her life.

These things take time, Bonnie had said. Dr. Cody had said something similar. And they were both right. But does Meg have that kind of time? Bonnie said that it would be easier forty-five days from now, but she can't even imagine her forty-fifth day back at work, or her third or her second . . .

If only I'd been driving slower. If only I hadn't gotten distracted by those jerks in the Mazda. If only I'd known enough to bring the Impreza to a different mechanic before ever taking it on the road.

Meg silences her thoughts. She closes her eyes and breathes deeply. *You're with me,* she tells Justin in her mind. Because this particular thought has been working for her today. *You'll always be with me.* She thinks it again and again. *You're with me.*

—

Once she's more calmed, Meg tries to go back to reading, but her eyes glaze over after a few more sentences. *Good God, this book is pretentious . . .* Honestly, she thinks Nathan may have had a point. It isn't Meg's cup of tea either. The Great Fires and the plague and all the over-the-top world-building. The Year of Twos (whatever that's supposed to mean). Not to mention these lords she dreamed up, all of them named after the precious metals running through their veins . . .

What the hell was I thinking?

She flips back to the title page, the dedication. *To my parents.*

There's an epigraph too, because all the books she used to read back then, the really good ones, had epigraphs. Meg's epigraph is a few lines from the Prism song "Pearly Gates."

Look to me, to my knowledge, to my fire. In my haste,
I will burn down this garden, steal the fruit for its taste!

She doesn't recall why she chose it. But it was probably for the same reason she dedicated the book to both her parents, not just Mom. The same reason she decided to tell a story like this in the first place, and why she was able to write an entire novel in one month over the summer between eighth grade and freshman year of high school, the plot sweating out of her like a fever.

It was because she'd listened to all of her dad's old songs—the lyrics he wrote about golden-haired queens and fire-breathing dragons and brave knights storming castle gates. She'd seen concert videos of him as a younger man, in muttonchops and flowing medieval hair, dressed in Merlin robes while conjuring complicated riffs out of his bass, pyrotechnics exploding around him and his bandmates like magic spells. It was all to sell albums and tickets, of course. The same dorks who liked progressive rock played Dungeons & Dragons back then, and despite all his eccentricities, Nathan has always been a shrewd businessman. Meg understands that now. But as a child, Meg mistook the sword-and-sorcery act for something her father genuinely cared about. Something she might be able to be a part of if she just put in the effort.

I was trying to get your attention, Dad.

Meg sighs heavily, wearily. For the millionth time, she wishes Justin were around so she could discuss this out loud. She wants to ask him what the box of books was doing in the attic, why he never mentioned it to her, whether Dad had given it to him during one of the solo check-in visits Justin made to the compound on those days when Meg couldn't handle the thought of being in the same room with her father, but still wanted to make sure he was okay.

And if that *is* what happened, had Justin ever opened the box? Had he read the book? In all their years together, she only mentioned *The Prophesy* to him once, back in Ithaca, when they were infatuated and tipsy and playing Two Truths and a Lie. *I published a novel when I was fifteen. I've never been to France. I was a virgin when I met you.* Though Justin had been pretty confident that the virgin part was the lie, he was still surprised that Meg was, as he put it, "an accomplished teen author." She refused to answer too many questions about *The Prophesy*, framing it as a dumb thing she did in high school—as if the one and only book she ever wrote was a shoplifted tube of lipstick or a downed bottle of blackberry brandy.

I don't care, Justin said. *You wrote a novel. I want to read it.*

Nope.

Why not?

First of all, it's out of print, so you can't. Second, it's awful.

But Meg didn't know that for sure. Meg will never know if *The Prophesy* is a good book or an awful one—not just because it truly is not her cup of tea but because it's about a princess whose mother died from a virus, and Meg's own mother had died under similar circumstances less than two years after its publication. How could anyone be objective about a book like that? How could anyone think of it as anything other than bad luck?

Meg's had enough of *The Prophesy*. The open box is on the floor next to her, and she sets it down on top of the other copies. She's about to close the lid again—never to look at it or think about it—when she notices something wedged against the far-right bottom of the box.

Meg pinches it between her fingertips. She tries to lift it out, but it won't budge until she stands up and places both hands on either side of it, bracing it against the side of the box and easing it up inch by inch until finally, it's released. A manila folder, stuffed with what seems like envelopes, several brightly colored rubber bands strung around it to hold its contents in place.

Meg sets the folder down on the coffee table, removing the rubber bands one by one, then turns it over carefully, this collection of relics with its musty, moldy scent.

Nathan has written on the cover of the folder in thick red ink. Meg reads it. "Oh, Dad," she whispers, "why can't you just be normal?" She stares at the words, her father's blockish, angry script, as rash and deliberate as he is.

WOLVES (EVIDENCE!!!)

-

These are the wolves, Meg thinks. *This is the evil, anti-Semitic cabal.*

From what she can see at first glance, it's a folder full of fan mail—or whatever the opposite of fan mail is. Old-school hate mail from people much like Claire Cassadine, lonely individuals looking to blame someone, anyone, for the sad turns their lives have taken. Pathetic souls who listened to "Pearly Gates" one too many times, after one too many acid trips. Ex-fans who took the Merlin act too seriously. One of them even wrote *WARLOCK* in parentheses after Nathan's name on the envelope, as though that might help postal workers ensure it got to the right Nathan Lerner. There aren't that many letters in the folder, maybe a dozen at most. All are addressed to Nathan's old PO box in New York City, which he maintained all the way up until the early aughts, when he sold Meg's childhood home and moved into the wilds of the Catskills.

Meg pulls one out—a pink envelope that was once perfumed and still carries the hint of a scent, with a 1992 postmark from Frankenmuth, Michigan.

She slips out a sheet of crinkly typewriter paper. There's a magazine photo taped to the center—an old shot of Shira and Nathan and a kindergarten-aged Meg taken backstage at a Prism show and published, Meg thinks, in *Creem.* She remembers the show. It was at Madison Square Garden. Prism was opening for Yes. It was very exciting. She can recall the photographer, his British accent. *Smile, love,* he'd told her.

The photo, though. Whoever clipped it saved it for several years. They taped it to this piece of typing paper and drew a big red *X* over Shira's face. Meg looks at the postmark again. December 4, 1992. Nearly three months to the day after her mother died. Underneath the photo someone scrawled *VENGEANCE IS MINE SAYETH THE LORD.*

Take a step back and it's silly. But if you put yourself in Nathan's shoes, so soon after losing her . . . The pain he must have felt. The anger . . .

Meg starts looking through the other letters, which date all the way back to the mid-seventies. She removes the oldest one—a manifesto of sorts, typewritten and single-spaced. She reads the first paragraph:

NATHAN LERNER Warlock: We know what you are doing. We know of the hidden messages you put in your music. We know firsthand the damage caused by your magic spells. By PEARLY GATES. Your bandmates are blind to your SATANIC WAYS but we know about the SECRET RITUALS. We know about the ANIMAL SACRIFICE about the SUICIDE MESSAGES directed to YOUTH so you can make sacrifices of them like you did with the animals. Your deepest wish is to USE THEIR BLOOD. You are unfit to breathe the same air as godly people. We will TRACK YOU DOWN AND MAKE YOU SUFFER.

Again, on one level, it's comical. Thinking that her neurotic father, who has never believed in either heaven or hell, is out there doing secret rituals, sacrificing animals to Satan. On another, it's deeply creepy. On yet another, it's most definitely not "Kennedy all over again." Which is why she isn't going to call Nathan and let him know she's found this. His flair for the dramatic has always extended much too far beyond the stage, and she'd prefer not to get him stirred up again today, especially not with that cough of his.

She removes all the letters from the folder, placing the envelopes side by side on the table, along with the *New York Times* article her father so carefully preserved. She counts them. There are eleven. Six from the seventies and early eighties, the last of that batch from 1982, when Prism broke up and Nathan moved the family to Elizabethville. The other five envelopes, from 1990 to 1993, have red checks on the front, probably made by Nathan. She opens the first of those, a lavender envelope postmarked September 8, 1990. Slips the letter out and reads: *Your spawn wrote a book. Does it have Satanic messages too? Bet it does. I'll make her pay. Vengeance is mine, dirty Jew.* Loopy, feminine writing on unicorn stationery. The biblical line again. *Vengeance is mine*—which might be what led her dad to believe these lunatics were organized.

Hardly an original phrase, though . . . She places the letter back in the envelope, wondering how the writer (someone apparently from Coeur d'Alene, Idaho) found out about *The Prophesy.* But the answer's right in front of her. The *New York Times* article came out on September 1, 1990. It references her father and his band repeatedly. She checks a few more of the early-nineties letters. All brimming with hatred. All mentioning her book. One correspondent speculated that Nathan had ghostwritten it, in an effort to brainwash a new generation of Satanists.

She can hear her father's voice in her mind again, hissing at Mom from the other room, begging her to stand with him in forbidding Meg from doing the interview. *We can't put our name out there. The wolves, Shira! The wolves!*

And then, two years after the *New York Times* article and three months after Shira's death, Nathan goes through his mail to find a photograph of his family, his wife's face x-ed out, a biblical quote about vengeance. Bad timing, yes. But he sees it as so much more than that, Meg knows. To him, it's empirical proof that he's not paranoid. The cabal exists. They did kill Shira. One crank letter from Frankenmuth, Michigan, and it's all the evidence he needs. He must lie low. He must escape.

I've wanted you to have it since your mother died, Nathan told Meg back in 1999, when he gave the Secret Garden to her and Justin as a wedding present. Within the year, he'd sold the family home and moved to the Catskills. *It will be a safer place for you without me there.*

What do you mean, Dad?

If I tell you, you won't believe me, so what's the point?

Meg looks at the envelopes, this little cluster of anonymous letters, all dutifully stamped, with proper postage. *These are the people he's been hiding from all these years.* A handful of obsessives—the type who used to play record albums backward in search of secret messages, the parents who preferred to believe it was rock songs and video games and movies that were brainwashing their children into hating them rather than taking any blame for it themselves. The loners, desperate for a reason to hate those who've shunned them. The kooks.

Meg shakes her head. In some ways, her father is no different from the kooks themselves, letting irrational fear get the best of him, allowing it to make decisions for him, to take over his life. *Why didn't you just show the letters to the police?* Meg thinks. But that's a ridiculous question. Nathan has always feared and distrusted cops, probably more so than his fictional cabal.

She hears a car pulling up in the driveway, the scuff of footsteps on the bluestone path. She checks her watch and sees that it's 6 P.M. Time for Lily to come home from work.

Meg stacks up the envelopes. She starts to put them back in the folder when she sees something inside that she hadn't noticed earlier—a yellowed, faded *New York Post* clipping from June 1980. The headline reads BASSIST INJURED IN AIRPORT ATTACK, and there's a shot of Nathan leaning against a paramedic, his eye swollen shut, blood pouring down the side of his face. "My God," Meg whispers. She reads the caption first and sits back in her chair, the front door opening, Lily calling out, "I'm home!"

The Prism rocker was jumped by three men while waiting in baggage claim at JFK's international terminal.

By the time Lily makes it down to the basement, Meg has read the article.

"Mom? What are you doing?"

Meg's mouth is dry. Her head swims, her gaze stuck to the picture of her father. *So much blood*. The steadying grip of the paramedic. The baggage carousel in the background. When she's finally able to look up at her daughter, her hand remains on the clipping, as though to keep it from fluttering away. "You were right," Meg tells Lily, at last. "It's a different Kennedy."

—

Lily sits down next to Meg, who reads her the *New York Post* article, in which an eyewitness describes three young men "appearing out of nowhere" and "hurling epithets" at Nathan as they punched, kicked and even bit him. By the time security guards had been able to pull the men off of Meg's father, he'd suffered a broken nose, a black eye, multiple broken ribs and damage to his kidneys. "'One of the men, Todd McNally, nineteen, proclaimed to police and bystanders, "We're protecting all of you. Nathan Lerner is evil. He is a follower of Satan,"'" Meg reads.

Lily's eyes go big.

"'Currently at Lenox Hill Hospital, where he is receiving treatment for his injuries,'" she continues, "'the musician released the following statement: "What happened to me at Kennedy was unfortunate. While Prism's upcoming gig at the Bottom Line will have to be postponed, I'm expected to make a full recovery. I am taking some time to rest and be with my family. I'm not pressing charges against my assailants."'"

Meg places the article back on the table, both of them staring at it for a long while, as though if they were to look away, the yellowed newsprint might catch fire and burn down their entire house.

"Why wouldn't he press charges?" Lily says finally.

"I don't know," Meg says.

"He never told you about this?" Lily asks. "Your whole life?"

Meg shakes her head, straining to think back to the long-ago time that the attack happened—her dad returning from the band's European tour, her mom saying something about him tripping over an amp cord. Meg was only four or five years old, and so the memories are hazy.

Nothing she can really grasp on to, other than her mother telling her that children were not allowed in the hospital to visit Daddy, but not to worry, he would be home soon, good as new. "He never said anything about it," Meg says. "Neither one of my parents did."

"They wanted to protect you," Lily says.

And Meg nods, even though she's never felt that from her father— the urge to protect her from anything, his own ugly, self-indulgent moods included. "I guess so."

Lily looks at the table, the folder's contents, neatly stacked. She picks up one of the envelopes, pulls out a letter. She reads it, then puts it back, her expression never changing. "Where did you find all this stuff?"

"In the box you brought down from the attic."

"He stored his old hate mail with your book?"

"Apparently."

"Why?"

"I don't know why Grandpa does anything," Meg says.

"To be fair," Lily says, "you never ask."

Meg can't argue that. As Lily said at lunch, *It's not an attitude, it's an observation.* And it's a correct one.

Meg should know more about her father. And to some degree, it's her fault she doesn't. All these years of avoiding narcissistic Nathan Lerner, his mood swings, his ramblings, his all-too-frequent paranoid spirals and his refusal to hold himself accountable for anything, ever. All these years of tuning him out for the sake of her own sanity, Meg may have missed out on who Nathan really is, what that beating must have done to him, how it may have changed him into the troubled and troubling person she's always known him to be. And now, here he is. Other than Lily, Nathan's the only family she has left.

It's about time, Meg thinks, *that Dad and I had a real conversation.*

TWELVE

For dinner, Lily makes vegan enchiladas from a recipe she found online at work. "You didn't have to go to all that trouble," Mom keeps saying. "We could have ordered out . . ." which annoys Lily a little. *Just say thank you and be done with it. You know?*

And anyway, it isn't trouble. It's therapy. After what she went through with those cops this afternoon, Lily needs to throw herself into a task that makes sense, with a beginning, middle and end. She also needs to do something where she doesn't have to talk to anybody. And cooking dinner, like playing a song, fits that bill. It was all she could do to get her mom to leave the kitchen, to stop fussing around her trying to help, asking her if she was sure she wanted to do this, as though Lily were about to bungee jump off a cliff rather than heat up some black beans. *Why is it so hard to get certain people to leave you alone?*

Lily sighs. She's got everything prepped except the pico de gallo, and she's almost done with that. There's a mound of chopped tomatoes on the cutting board, glistening like jewels and with that summery scent that makes Lily feel as though she's traveled back to the past, to six months ago, helping Dad make salsa for a barbecue. It doesn't even make her sad, just a little wistful. What would Dad say about what happened to her today with those cops? If he were here, would she be able to talk to him about it?

After reading that ancient article about Grandpa Nate, Lily nearly told Mom (*Speaking of people in our family getting abused by strangers . . .*

would have been the lead-in). But at the last minute, she realized that if she were to tell Mom about the cops, she'd have to admit to her that she'd been vaping weed in Carl's truck when she was supposed to be at Dr. Cody's—which would definitely be a bad idea, especially considering it isn't the first time she's done it.

Her other reasons for keeping quiet about it feel more like rationalizations. *Why stress Mom out more than she already is? Nothing happened. I didn't even get a ticket, so why does she need to know? Carl was so traumatized he couldn't even talk to me about it. How would he feel if Mom brought it up to him at some point, months from now? Plus, we both agreed that we don't want to report those cops, and if there's one thing Mom would do, it would be to report those cops.*

Actually, now that she thinks about it, those are all pretty good reasons to stay quiet. And even if they weren't, even if Lily believed her mom would be cool with her ditching therapy to do drugs with a boy (a truly ridiculous thought), she doesn't want to go over it again—not with Mom, not with Carl or Dr. Cody or anyone. She flashes on Frosty Lips, that dead-eyed grin of hers as she watched Lily crouched on the pavement, picking up her scattered tampons. Lily wants to forget she ever felt the way she did at that moment, and if she doesn't talk about it or think about it for long enough, maybe that will eventually happen.

Lily can hear the TV in the den—a breathless reporter describing a volcano that's erupting on the Big Island of Hawaii, destroying people's homes. Her mom switches the channel, and there's another story, about a spike in COVID hospitalizations in New York City, which leads into a commercial for some antianxiety drug. One of its side effects is death.

I feel sorry for you kids, for your generation, Bonnie said at work today. *The world's in such a hurry to end.*

—

After Lily clears the table, Mom tells her she'll do the dishes. "Your work here is done."

"Mom, I don't mind—"

"You cooked a delicious meal," she says. "It's only fair."

Lily protests a little more but Mom isn't having it. "You can go out, you know," Mom says. "Call Carl if you feel like it."

Lily gives her a smile. "Nah."

"You sure?"

Lily nods. She doesn't feel like seeing Carl. Not tonight. She doesn't even feel like letting Mom know that she found *Wuthering Doorknob* in the attic, or that, thanks to Carl, she now has a projector so they can watch it together. What she needs is to be alone, so she can sort out all the thoughts that have been running through her mind. About Grandpa Nate, about those weirdos who worked with Carl, claiming the sword-and-sorcery book her mom wrote had been spiked with a demonic curse that will bring about the end of the world.

And those cops . . .

Frosty Lips, looking at Lily's license, asking if she's Nathan Lerner's granddaughter. Mustache, referring to her mom as *Magnolia Lerner Russo*. The way he'd leaned on those first two names, as though he was talking about someone famous. *Magnolia Lerner*, author of *The Prophesy*.

"It's been a long day," Lily says. "I think I'm going to play some scales and go to bed early."

"If you say so," Mom says.

Lily grabs her backpack from the couch and heads upstairs, the copy of *The Prophesy* that she swiped weighing down the bottom.

—

Lily is nearly halfway through the book when she hears a soft knock at her door. She's been under the covers, reading *The Prophesy* by flashlight, escaping into another world the way she used to as a kid . . . Forget about the predictions Carl's idiot coworkers told him about. There's a plague in the story, sure. Whatever. Lots of books have plagues in them. But there are also orange-eyed monsters with tentacles instead of hands and feet, and lords who have different precious metals running through their veins and a princess who may or may not be strong enough to fulfill her destiny and save the dying planet. Mom's book doesn't predict the future. There aren't *details in it about COVID that nobody could have known in 1990* either. It's just really, really good. It would have been Lily's favorite when she was twelve—if she knew it existed back then. *Why didn't you tell me, Mom?*

Lily hears the doorknob turn and shoves the book beneath her. She comes up from under the covers and turns off her phone's flashlight, resting her head back on the pillow, pretending to be asleep as the door creaks open. She can feel her mother watching her, her eyes adjusting to the darkness. Lily takes a purposefully noisy breath and waits for Mom to close the door. Mom has been doing this every night since they got home from the hospital. Opening Lily's door a few hours after she's gone to bed. Checking in on her to make sure she's breathing, the way you'd do with a baby.

Losing Dad has changed them both in so many ways, and the main one for Mom is this: She no longer trusts in Lily's ability to stay alive.

Lily rolls over on her stomach. Her mom eases the door shut.

Once she hears her heading down the hall to her own room, she slides the book out from under the covers, turns her flashlight back on. Again, she's back on the soon-to-end planet Earth in the Year of Twos, as Princess Iyanla takes Nurse Calyx in to see the ailing queen.

Iyanla's mind vibrates with possibility. "Will you be able to cure my mother?" *she pleads, her eyes brimming with tears. A few of them slide down her cheeks, dampening her mask.*

Lily feels it along with her, that nagging, swirling hope. "Please save the Queen," she whispers. "Come on, Calyx. Save her." Like a twelve-year-old who is willing to believe in princesses and lords and tentacled, plague-spreading monsters. A kid who can commit to the idea that one girl can save her mother, and all of humanity, if she can only find the strength.

For the newbies, here's some required reading. And even if you aren't new to the Truth, it never hurts to brush up on your knowledge.

"In the Year of Twos, the Plague will rise
The Fires and Floods will follow
The ten-fingered and ten-toe'd meet their demise
In the muck of doom to wallow
Find the Princess with the opal eyes
Take her to the hollow
Give her the Stone Sword to hold on high
Slay the tentacle'd Monsters. Time is nigh
Or the end of mankind shall follow."

excerpted from The Prophesy *by Magnolia Lerner,*
Young Readers' Press, 1990

ANY QUESTIONS, NINE-AND-TENS????

—the Bronze Lord
WAW, WAA, WWT

THIRTEEN

When you were a kid, did people say bad things about Grandpa?

At some point during dinner, Lily had asked Meg that question. And while it had been a reasonable thing to ask—given the brutal attack on him that they'd both just read about—Meg had replied, *Not that I remember.* As though she were in a court of law.

The truth was that people *did* say bad things about Nathan. And Meg did remember—she just didn't *want* to. But as she drives alone to her father's compound at seven in the morning, what she wants or doesn't want makes no difference. Memories flood her mind. She can't tamp them down. She has no control. Sixth grade. Or was it seventh? That awful time of life when one day can feel like an eternity. The malignantly bored group of girls and boys who made a sport out of ripping the more sensitive children to shreds. And Magnolia Lerner was sensitive back then. The only Jewish kid in her class, a bookworm with skin that refused to tan and wiry, rebellious hair when most everyone else's was well-behaved and shiny, she was also blessed with a weird first name that came from her mother's favorite Grateful Dead song and a last name that literally meant *nerd*.

She didn't have a chance.

Meg blossomed in high school—or at the very least, she made some friends and learned how to use a flat iron. But during those awkward pubescent years, her only friend was Bonnie. And there's only so much one friend can do.

Bonnie would sit next to Meg on the bus, share her lonely table in the cafeteria. She'd pass her notes in study hall to distract her from the spitballs. Routinely she told the bullies to fuck off, once loud enough to get her sent to the principal's office.

Most important, Bonnie spied on them. And so she was able to tell Meg about the rumors. On Meg's front porch on a Saturday, drinking the lemonade Shira had served them, Bonnie had leaned in close, warning signals in her eyes.

Do you know what they're saying about your dad?

Meg hadn't told her parents what her life had been like for the past several months. Neither one of them knew about the girls who kept "accidentally" tripping her in gym class, the loudly whispered insults in study hall, the spitballs thrown at the back of her head, the cutting laughter on the school bus. They didn't know what she had to contend with at school because if they did, her mother would get upset and call the principal and her dad would take it personally and either way, they'd make the whole thing worse.

But after she heard what she did from Bonnie, Magnolia had to say something. She found her mom outside in the garden and blurted it out: *Is it true that Dad was run out of New York City for being in a Satanic coven? Is that the reason why Prism broke up too? Because they caught Dad doing a ritual where he killed and sacrificed a dog?*

It was the one time her mother was ever angry with her, and it was terrifying. That shadow crossing over her face, the spade dropping to the ground, her right hand drawing back. *Who said that to you? Tell me who said that to you right now, Magnolia, or I swear to God I'll . . .*

Shira never finished the sentence. She checked herself and closed her eyes, her gloved hands clasped over her face. And then, to Meg's horror, she started to cry.

It's not true, Shira told Meg. *It's not true, whoever said it is a terrible liar. Don't ever mention it to your father, it will kill him. It will absolutely destroy him.*

I won't, Meg said, over and over. *I won't, I promise. I won't. Please stop crying, Mom. I won't.*

But still the question nagged at her: *Why would a dumb lie like that destroy him?* It tore at her for years, that garden scene playing back in random snippets, long after the mean kids stopped bullying her, long after she survived her mother's death and grew up and formed a family of her own. It was there, in the back of her mind, right up until last night, when she read about how one of his attackers had called him a follower of Satan. And finally, she understood. It wasn't the smattering of hate mail. It wasn't the rumor at all, but the fact that her father nearly lost his life over it.

Driving west on Route 28, the pink and crimson sunrise bleeding into the sky in front of her, Meg tries to imagine what it must have been like for Mom visiting Dad in the hospital after the attack, seeing him broken apart like that . . .

Another daybreak, one of tens of thousands since that afternoon in the garden, yet still, it's so vivid in her mind, it's as though it just happened.

It was the only time Meg ever saw her mother cry.

—

At eight thirty, Meg pulls off the highway at the exit for Star Lake, a town that, during the golden age of Catskills vacationing, housed a resort called Wellman's, where Nathan and his family used to summer when he was a boy. Star Lake is much smaller and more depressed than it was back then, and Wellman's is now a ruin. It's been like that for decades—an abandoned husk, most of its walls still standing but covered in more than half a century's worth of graffiti and overrun by weeds and mold and decay, nature devouring it slowly. There are many old Catskills resorts in the state that were never bought or even razed to the ground but left to rot, and Wellman's was one of the first to meet this fate. Meg can remember driving there with her parents shortly after the move to Elizabethville, her father's shock at what had happened to the idyllic place where he learned to swim and once heard Duke Ellington play.

Meg was only seven years old at the time, but she can still remember standing back with her mother as Dad wandered the natatorium, circling the rusted-out indoor pool, the tiles overrun with moss, pink chaise longues scattered around like the aftermath of a massacre. (*Where's the Little Mermaid?* Meg had asked, because on the drive there, her mother had tried to pique her flagging interest by insisting that her favorite storybook character summered in the natatorium and loved playing Marco Polo with visiting little girls.)

"My childhood in ruins," Nathan kept muttering, unaware of his family's presence or his wife's well-meaning lie about the Little Mermaid, as Meg clutched her mother's hand, both of them unsure of what to say. Meg was frightened of her father. He was acting so strange, as though he were alone here, talking to himself.

Your dad likes to feel all emotions fully, Mom said. *It's what makes him such a talented musician.*

It wasn't much of a surprise that when Nathan announced his plan to live off the grid, he intended to do it in the Catskills, in a compound that was, at one point, a small inn with additional bungalows, twenty minutes from the ghost of Wellman's. He refurbished the main structure and moved in, transforming two of the bungalows into a recording studio and a guest cottage, while using the other two for storage. No doubt, he hoped to make frequent visits to the ruin, where he could languish in the ivy-covered band shell, feeling his emotions fully.

Meg thinks she remembers how to get to Dad's compound, but she isn't positive. She lets her GPS direct her, following the series of barely plowed roads that leads her away from Star Lake and half a mile up a mountain. She takes these roads slowly, keeping five miles under the speed limit despite her heavy and reliable car, with its four-wheel drive and antilock brakes. The slightest skid, her heart pounds. She hates that feeling, that split-second chance she might lose control.

Meg tries to focus on the scenery—the puffy clouds and blue sky, the snow-flocked evergreens and skeletal maples, twinkling with icicles. It's lovely, really. Like driving through a Christmas card, yet her pulse races. She shivers. According to her car's thermostat, it's just eighteen degrees outside and it's as though she can feel the cold pressing against the driver's side window, trying to break in. She leans into the heated seat, her hands on the wheel. Her forearm throbs, the thick scar stabbing at her, a reminder. A warning.

Be more careful this time, it tells her. *Don't get anyone killed.*

—

As Meg nears Pearly Gates, she tries to remember when she was here last. It's been two years at least. During the height of the pandemic, Justin would stop by once a week to check in on Nathan, to make sure he was doing all right and bringing supplies if he needed them, but Meg always begged off those trips. Phone calls with Dad were difficult enough during that period, the lockdown giving him even more of an excuse to get high and paranoid and angry, spouting off theories about how COVID was some kind of deep state plot, a lab-grown virus designed specifically to pick off the weak and elderly. When Meg dared to disagree, he'd call her ignorant and disrespectful, and yes, she knew he was all alone in that house and not exactly levelheaded to begin with, but she couldn't take it. *Would you like to know how your granddaughter is doing?* she would ask. *Do you care?*

Justin seemed to understand. When he'd return home after a Pearly Gates visit, she'd ask how everything went, and he'd just say fine, knowing that was all she needed to hear; Meg didn't need specifics because the specifics would just piss her off.

Once lockdown ended and Dad was free to run his own errands, Justin's visits became rarer. Nathan came to their house once, ostensibly to drop off Chanukah presents (*God, that awful wicker table*), but Meg never returned the favor, until now.

Meg parks her car and walks up to the main structure, a cold wind ruffling her hair, biting through her thin wool gloves, burning her cheeks, her eyes. Her arm keeps throbbing, a steady reminder that she's broken.

—

Nathan's doorbell is a needlessly loud buzzer that sounds like the wrong answer on a quiz show. And as Meg rings it, she's a little nervous. She knows Nathan told her to call before coming, but she's repeatedly tried from the road, and every time, she's gotten a busy signal.

When there's no answer, she rings the bell again and waits and presses the button one more time until finally she hears footsteps, then Nathan's voice, deep and threatening. *"Who the hell is out there?"*

Meg takes a breath, her heart in her mouth. No one should be this anxiety-ridden over a visit with an aged parent. "It's me, Dad."

A few seconds of silence, and then the voice softens. "Magnolia?"

"Yeah. Hi!"

Slowly, the door opens, and she sees Dad's face first, the sunken cheeks, his eyes dull and watery. He looks exhausted and pale, his long hair wild, a feral creature emerging from hibernation. "I thought you were coming for Christmas."

"I am," she says. "We are. Lily and I. But, uh, I was . . . in the area?"

"Nobody's ever in this area." The door opens more and he steps back. He's wearing a plain black T-shirt, a gray hoodie, plaid flannel pajama pants. His clothes hang on him. Nathan has easily lost more than twenty pounds since she's seen him last, and he was thin to begin with. She thinks about him on the phone yesterday, the coughing fit. Her heart breaks a little. *He's fine,* she tells herself. *He'll outlive us all.* Justin used to say that all the time, she remembers. Then she wishes she hadn't had that thought. *He's outlived Justin.* She swallows hard. It takes her a few moments before she can find her voice. "I tried calling," she says. "But the line was busy."

"I took the phone off the hook."

"Why?"

He opens his mouth, then closes it again, his eyes searching the icy road behind her. "Come in, Magnolia. Jesus. It's freezing outside."

—

Meg steps into the house, taking in the warmth first, then the scent of the place—woodstove and pine needles and marijuana. Same as ever. "You look like hell," Nathan says, in a true case of pot-meet-kettle.

"Thanks, Dad."

Meg follows Nathan into the living room: the floral-print couch she knew as a child, the rope rug her mother made, the old grandfather clock. The credenza behind the couch with the phone on it. That ancient, bulky answering machine. All of it exactly the way she saw it last, so lovingly preserved. Her father's favorite bass is on a stand next to the driftwood coffee table, and there's an enormous glass bong on top, a steaming cup of tea. It's cozy here. Orderly. It puts her a bit more at ease. The man may have let himself go, but he still treats his possessions with care and respect. "Dad," Meg says. "I found some things of yours in my attic and . . . we need to talk."

"About what?"

"Kennedy."

He turns around, eyebrows raised. It's only then that she notices he's been holding a gun. Nathan's gaze follows hers. He sighs. Wearily, he unloads the gun, an intricate process that he nonetheless performs as though he's done it hundreds if not thousands of times. After he removes the rounds from the magazine, he puts them in a small box he produces from his hoodie pocket, and carefully sets the box and gun on the coffee table.

"I should have known I wouldn't need this." He says it quietly, more to himself than to Meg. "The wolves. They would never ring the bell."

—

"Since when have you owned a gun?" Meg asks her father, once they're both sitting down at the kitchen table, hot cups of tea in front of them—something Dad calls his energy blend.

"I've always owned a gun," Dad says.

"What?"

"For the past forty-two years, anyway."

She stares at him. "Since Kennedy."

He nods.

"Why didn't I know you had a gun?" she says. "Why didn't I know about Kennedy?"

"Your mother," he says. "That would be the answer to both of those questions."

Meg takes a sip of her tea. It tastes like cleaning fluid. "Why?"

"She didn't want you to be afraid," he says. "She didn't want you to know that people hated me as much as they did. She only agreed to move out of the city if I promised not to tell you exactly why we had to move. And she was right. Children don't need to know these things."

"What about after she was gone?"

"I still couldn't. Because I knew what she would have wanted if she'd lived."

Meg nods.

"It doesn't matter, though. Nothing matters. Hate breeds hate and that song . . . My song . . ." Nathan starts to cough—a wracking, violent hack, his face going red then purple, his eyes tearing. Meg moves toward him, but he puts a hand up. He pulls a handkerchief out of the pocket of his hoodie and presses it to his mouth until the coughing subsides. "Anyway. After I moved here I bought a few more guns."

"How many?"

"Five." He starts to cough again, but stops. He breathes deeply through his nose. Swallows his tea. He swipes at his wet face with his sleeve.

"Are you okay, Dad?"

"I'm fine," he says. "It's just this fucking radiator heat."

Meg nods. Neither one speaks for several moments. She watches her father, his fingers on the kitchen table, drumming along with the tick of the grandfather clock.

"I just wanted to make music," he says. "Write some good songs. Is that too much to ask?"

"You still can."

"For myself. Sure. Not for others. Not with them out there listening. Interpreting . . ."

"Listen, Dad. I came here because I wanted to tell you I get it, and I wish I'd known earlier. How traumatic that must have been for you . . .'"

"You don't understand."

"I do," she says. "I found the clipping from the *Post*. I saw the picture of you. Your eye. All that blood . . . It's awful."

"It wasn't a good experience."

"You must have been so afraid."

"Being afraid is pointless." He says it very quietly. "Unfortunate things happen, you make adjustments. For yourself. For your family. You moan and complain and then you adapt."

Meg looks at her father: The bloodshot eyes. The gnarled fingers. The plain gold wedding ring he still wears after all these years.

"You saw the folder, then, Magnolia. You found the box of books."

"Yes."

"I gave that box to Justin, you know. I told him to show it all to you when the time felt right, but I should have been more specific. I should have said soon . . . He should have shown you before that accident. Maybe you both could have done something to prevent it."

Meg closes her eyes. *Stop, Dad. Just please. Stop.*

"Did you see the letters from the early nineties? Those monsters, writing what they did about your book? Why did you have to put those words from 'Pearly Gates' in it, Magnolia? I know you meant well, but . . . you could have . . . Anything could stir them up, and you did. You stirred them. They actually believe there's a curse in that song."

"They wrote letters. They never harmed me or you or—"

"We don't know that. Your mother . . ." He doesn't finish the sentence. Meg is grateful for that.

She clears her throat. "Dad, the attack on you was terrible. But that was a onetime thing. And it happened in 1980."

"You still don't understand."

"There were only eleven letters in that folder," Meg says. "Eleven letters in more than twenty years. I know people said bad things about you. They read disgusting meanings into your life's work—"

"Rotten bigots. Anti-Semites. This world is teeming with them. More and more, crawling out from under their rocks."

"But in this case, *in your case, Dad*, how powerful can eleven bigots be?" As she speaks, Meg recalls Claire Cassadine in her store, her reedy voice, the gleam in her eye as she held up her fingers. *One down, three to go.* Just one person, and look at how much power Meg allowed her. She puts her cup down and sits up straighter, her jaw tightening. "Are we going to let a handful of losers scare us into hiding? We're stronger than that. We're both stronger than that."

Nathan sighs heavily. "A handful." He gets up from the kitchen table and walks into the other room. Meg sips more tea and winces. It really is awful. "Where are you going, Dad?" she calls out.

She hears her father's shuffling footsteps, a door opening, something heavy being dragged over the floorboards, a scraping sound.

"Dad?"

"I'm coming," Nathan calls out. "Just wait!"

Meg waits. She takes another sip of tea and looks at her watch, a minute passing. Two. She needs to leave soon. Zach is scheduled to be in early to sign off on the Kingsolvers for book club, but Sara Beth has a morning doctor's appointment, and he isn't experienced enough to open the store alone.

When she glances up, Nathan has made his way back into the kitchen. He's pushing a cardboard box that's tall enough to reach his chest. There are beads of sweat on his forehead. He's straining from the effort.

"What is that?"

Nathan leans against the box for a moment, wheezing. "The folder was just a sample," he says. "I told Justin that. It said it was just to give you an idea of who I've been dealing with . . ." He opens the cardboard box, pulls out a few letters and drops them on the kitchen table. Meg opens one, written on ivory stationery in red ink:

ROT IN HELL, WARLOCK!

Meg's breathing stops. She looks up at him. He tosses another letter in front of her, then another. Meg opens and reads them quickly. Different words, same sentiment. Nathan shoves his hand in the box and pulls out more. Throws them on the table. The box is filled to the brim with hate mail.

"I . . . I didn't know."

"There are two more boxes, just like this one."

Meg gapes at him, at the enormous box. Hundreds of letters, probably thousands, spewing threats and accusations. *No wonder, Dad. No wonder.* Meg says, "You have a reason for wanting to hide."

"That's what I've been trying to tell you." He looks at her with tired eyes. He pulls the handkerchief out of his pocket and dabs his forehead, and Meg stares at the white cotton, the fresh blood spots at the bottom from when he dried his mouth. "You don't know as much about the world as you think you do," Dad says. "It's full of monsters. And when you put your art out there, it feeds them. They attack."

Meg wants to say something. She wants to hug him. But she can't move. "When you owned the store," she says, "did anyone ever come in and threaten you?"

He shakes his head.

"It's happened to me," she says. "Recently. And I think she threatened Justin too. There was a video she posted of him. On our store's website. It was just a few seconds long, but he looked upset. It was from August."

Nathan straightens up, his gaze traveling from Meg to the next room, the living room. She can almost hear the whir of his thoughts.

"It was just one person, Dad," Meg says. "One very lonely and un-balanced woman. God only knows why she singled us out, but she scared me. She knew about Justin's death and she seemed . . . happy about it. It made me so angry. I can only imagine what it's like for you."

Nathan turns and looks at Meg. "Why did it deploy late?"

"What?"

"When you were telling me about your accident. Just after you came home from the hospital. We talked on the phone. You said that the airbag didn't deploy until after the car was stopped."

"I said that? I don't remember."

"Magnolia. That's highly irregular. A loose lug nut. An airbag that doesn't deploy until after the fact. And then this woman comes into your store. Your first day back at work. She pastes a video of Justin on the store's website. And she mentions the accident. *Think, for god's sakes.*"

Meg inhales sharply, her father's eyes on her like lasers, his breathing going shallow. Spiraling, the way he always does. *Big mistake, telling him about Claire.* "I couldn't let you know, because of your mother," he says. "But there's never been anything stopping you from learning about it yourself."

"Not every bad thing is connected, Dad."

Nathan doesn't reply. He leaves the room, returning moments later with the gun and the box of ammo.

"I'm going to show you how to use this." He says it firmly, leaving no room for debate, or even further conversation. "And then, Magnolia, you're going to take it home with you."

FOURTEEN

There's never just one of them. They're like cockroaches, hiding in the dark, feeding, multiplying. The woman who harassed Magnolia in the Secret Garden was not alone in her feelings. She'd gotten them from someone, from somewhere. Nathan would be willing to bet on it. He told his daughter as much when he was showing her how to load the Glock, and for once—for the first time, really—she seemed to accept this fact.

She did say we, Magnolia told him, her fingers trembling on the magazine. *We are watching, we know what goes on behind those walls, we know all about your family. Not I. We.*

Of course she did, he had replied. *Whatever problem she has with us, she didn't come up with it on her own. Not a single one of them has ever had an original thought.*

Nathan's daughter didn't roll her eyes and scoff at him. She didn't act as though it was the marijuana talking or isolation talking or age talking or anything talking other than a fellow human being—which, whether she was just humoring him or not, was quite a development. *If you're right,* she said, *and that's a big if . . . I hope this is the end of it.*

Nathan does too. He hopes that four-hundred-dollar check was some kind of fluke, a mistake on the part of the music platform, and that he's being hypervigilant in giving Magnolia the Glock. He hopes that, as she said, the bad things that keep happening are *not* connected and that a month from now, two months from now, he'll look back on this moment and think, *Perhaps I overreacted.* Nathan didn't say that to

Magnolia, though. He was just glad that his daughter had taken him seriously for once.

It made up for the terrible phone conversation he'd had with Claude at 7 A.M., after a long and sleepless night with the royalty check glowering at him all the way from the coffee table in the living room.

Such a schmoe, Claude. So blind to everything, and with no excuse. Unlike Magnolia, he's always known about the attack at Kennedy. He visited Nathan at the hospital. He saw what they'd done to him, those animals—*he saw the bite marks*—yet he kept saying it was a one-off. A few crackpots, nothing more. Claude, sailing through life under the false impression that the world is filled with good people who mean no harm.

After Prism broke up, Claude quickly found work as a session musician. He toured with a few groups that were, if not stadium-fillers, more successful than Prism. These days, he picks up extra cash playing lead guitar in an Emerson, Lake & Palmer tribute band, and he's enjoyed every minute of it. He's never had a reason to fear doing what he loves. *Did you ever think,* Claude said on the phone, *that all these people may be downloading "Pearly Gates" because they like the song?*

Nathan hung up on him. Then he took the phone off the hook and wrote him a long letter, explaining so many things Claude has never understood: what it was like growing up the son of immigrants, to have been bullied as a kid, targeted and shamed for as long as he could remember based on his looks, his size, his ethnicity—all of it beyond his control. And then he discovered music. He told Claude how, in playing songs, he found control and beauty and peace of mind at last—an escape from the abuse these assholes constantly hurled at him. He told him how he thought being in the band had changed his life for the better—but then it all came back to bite him, figuratively and then literally, when he was forced into being Prism's lyricist.

Nathan is a musician. Period. He never wanted to write lyrics. He told his bandmates that repeatedly, but they wouldn't take no for an answer. *You're the intellectual in the group,* Claude and the others would say, strong-arming him with that dubious compliment. (What exactly did they mean by *intellectual,* anyway?)

Of course, Nathan relented. Prism's songs needed lyrics, and so he put words together that sounded good and complemented the melodies. He didn't care if they made sense, and most of the time, they didn't. Which is why it's so ironic, all this attention paid to the lyrics of "Pearly Gates," this scrutinizing and demonizing—actual *demonizing*—of their author.

He'd love to ask all three of them why he was the only one in the band to release a statement after Kennedy, why none of them publicly came to his defense. But there's only Claude now. Rick, their drummer, OD'd shortly after the band broke up. Tim, the keyboardist, died ten years ago of pancreatic cancer. *It's just you and me left,* Nathan wrote to Claude. *Isn't it time you attempted to understand what I've been through? Isn't it time you apologized for it?*

He'd been planning on ripping up the letter and throwing it in the trash—it had only been a way to vent, after all. But after Magnolia drives away, Nathan feels differently. He feels justified.

He puts the letter in an envelope. Addresses it to Claude DuBois at his home in Boca Raton, Florida, and prepares to drive to the post office to mail it.

Nathan showers. Puts on a sweater, a pair of jeans, sneakers. *When was the last time I combed my hair and wore real clothes?* he wonders, before it hits him that it was most definitely his most recent trip to the post office, a week and a half ago, when he picked up his mail, that royalty check lurking . . .

He thinks he may have even worn the same sweater.

—

Nathan grabs his heavy parka and heads outside and into the garage. He owns two cars, the 2020 Toyota 4Runner that Justin insisted he buy for the harsh Catskills winters, and Missy. Missy is Shira's old car, a Granny

Smith—green 1985 Chevy station wagon with wood siding. Of course Nathan chooses Missy. She may not have four-wheel drive, but she's got new snow tires and she handles nearly as well as she did on the day his wife named her.

It's cold as death outside, but Missy's heater snaps into action, Nathan easing back into the vinyl seat, her engine roaring. Nathan loves these old cars, the way they attack the road with such optimism and vigor. He turns on the radio—the oldies station he always listens to when he drives, the only one Missy's radio can pick up on these lonely roads—and somehow today the music feels brighter.

When Magnolia was growing up, Shira taught her all the important things very early: how to read, how to add and subtract, how to be a kind person. Shira was such a good mother that when he wasn't at work, Nathan often found himself retreating to his home studio, to his music, letting his wife do all the heavy lifting when it came to raising their daughter, for fear that if he tried, he might mess things up. After Shira died, of course, he fell apart. And then, before he knew it, Magnolia was grown up and out of the house.

Today, though. Today, Nathan taught his daughter how to save her own life.

On the radio, Chicago's "Feelin' Stronger Every Day" is playing, a song Shira used to love. He turns it up, remembering how deft Magnolia had become at engaging the slide and loading and unloading the magazine after just a few tries, how steady her aim was by the end of their lesson. How seriously she took it all, how quickly she learned. *Thank you, Dad,* she said, getting into her car with the locked black case. *Thank you for this. Thank you for teaching me.*

Nathan grips the steering wheel, Shira's favorite song blasting. Maybe Claude will read the letter and finally understand. Maybe he'll take "Pearly Gates" down, and the wolves will move on to other targets, other music. Maybe Magnolia will never have the need to open that polymer box.

"Please," Nathan whispers. "Please." It's as close as he's ever gotten to praying.

–

"Hey, Mr. Lerner!" says Leland at the post office. Nathan waves. Leland is in the process of helping a customer, a woman around Nathan's age who can't seem to decide how many stamps she wants to buy. But even though the other clerk is available, Nathan decides to wait. He wants Leland to take care of his letter.

Leland has been working at the Star Lake Post Office as long as Nathan's been living up here, and besides Doris, he's probably the only person Nathan knows well enough to trust. He's over forty, but he's got a cherubic, rosy-cheeked look to him, so that if it weren't for the bushy salt-and-pepper beard, Nathan would think he was in his twenties. He plays guitar as a hobby. Claims to like Prism. Believes that the 1969 Moon landing was staged and shot by Stanley Kubrick, which, to Nathan, shows both a healthy skepticism and an appreciation of good filmmaking.

The other clerk gapes at him. She's a black-haired vixen with tattoos up and down her snow-white arms. Nathan can't remember her name, and he doesn't trust her at all. "Can I help you, sir?" she says.

Nathan starts to politely refuse, but happily the stamp lady leaves and Leland beats her to it. "What can I do for you, Mr. Lerner?"

"I've a letter to send to Florida," Nathan says. "I'd like it to get there quickly."

"You know, we can overnight it, but it's gonna cost big bucks," Leland says. "Between us, we can just put a stamp on it and it'll probably get there Tuesday, same difference."

Nathan smiles. This is why he trusts this guy. "I'll go with the stamp."

"Excellent."

Leland weighs the letter and Nathan pays for its postage. "How's the music going, sir?" Leland says. "Coming out with anything new?"

Nathan shakes his head. "I just play for myself these days." It breaks his heart a little to say that. There was a time when Nathan's greatest dream was to write a hit song, something everybody listened to.

"You play bass, right?" It's the black-haired vixen talking now, and he doesn't like it. It makes Nathan uncomfortable when people know more about him than he does about them.

"Leland has played your music for me," she says. "It's interesting!"

Interesting. The ultimate backhanded compliment. Nathan clears his throat. He's been introduced to her before, he thinks. Bernice, maybe. Beatrice . . . "Thank you."

"You're welcome." She smiles. Her teeth are too white, the way most young people's teeth are these days. Those new permanent dentures they wear. Veneers, they call them, but really they're dentures. You can call a thing whatever you want to; it doesn't change what it is.

"That reminds me, sir," Leland says, "I have that package you called me about."

Belinda (or whatever her name is) gives him a quizzical look. So does Nathan, until Leland subtly taps the breast pocket of his uniform, the smartphone peeking out. Then he remembers. "Ah," he says. "Good."

Leland says, "Bernadette, can you cover for me for a few minutes? Mr. Lerner and I are gonna go out back."

Bernadette. That's it.

"Sure thing," Bernadette says.

Nathan glances around the empty post office, as though he expects spies to be hiding under the counter where you fill out priority mail slips and certified receipts, or amid the packing envelopes stacked in shelves against the wall. Nathan feels watched, the way he always does. But on the other hand, there's something comforting about the respect Leland has shown him. It was only yesterday that Nathan had called the post office, asking his friend if he could check the internet and see if his granddaughter has shared any of her music. Leland didn't ask why, but assured Nathan he'd do it quickly. And here he's made good on his word.

Nathan follows Leland around the counter, past a good-sized room where the larger packages are kept and into a small break room, with a flimsy table and metal folding chairs, a vending machine and a mini fridge.

"Sorry for all the secrecy," Leland says, somewhat sheepishly. "Bernadette and I dated for a little bit, and she's always trying to get in my business."

"I understand," Nathan says. He does. A man's privacy is something to be treasured and respected, much the same as his home. *Violation of privacy, invasion of privacy* . . . There's a reason why those phrases sound as brutal as they do.

"Anyway, I looked up your granddaughter. Lily Russo. I couldn't really find much in the way of social media, not to say she isn't posting under a fake name."

"What about music?"

"Yep, that's what I'm getting to." Leland pulls the smartphone out of his pocket and taps at it. "She doesn't have a YouTube channel or a SoundCloud of her own," he says. "But she played in quite a few bands in high school. Those bands posted on YouTube."

"Yeah?"

"She's really good, but it's not my type of thing. Speed metal mostly."

Nathan nods. He's got some of the music channels on his TV and tries to keep up with the new stuff, but lately he's been wondering why. "I'm torn on speed metal," he says. "It takes talent but it also makes my ears bleed."

"Same," Leland says. "Anyway, Lily hasn't shared any music, by herself or with a band, for more than six months. Probably around the time she got into college."

"Right . . ."

"But then, out of the blue, this guy CarlOnGuitar posts on his YouTube channel. A video of a song he wrote—an instrumental jam called 'Bridge to Heaven,' and it says 'Featuring Lily Russo' on it." He shows Nathan the screen. A frozen image of his granddaughter in the middle of playing, her face hidden in a tangle of hair, her two hands dueling blurs. The only stationary element in the frame is her bass, a cherry-red Fender Mustang, much like the first bass he owned. *She looks like me,* Nathan thinks.

"That's how I found the video," Leland is saying. "Her name's in the title."

Nathan nods.

"Anyway, your granddaughter has a solo on it. I want you to listen, because I think you'll get a kick out of it."

"Okay."

He taps the tiny arrow on the screen and Lily comes to life, her fingers roaming the length of the bass's neck, switching effortlessly from a slap riff to a rich and echoing tone that's nearly cello-like. She's a talent, all right. As good as Nathan was at that age. Maybe better. Most people think of the bass as background, rhythm. But the truth is, it's an incredibly versatile instrument, capable of playing a range of melodies; you just need to be inquisitive enough to find them.

"Chip off the old block, right?" Leland says.

Nathan smiles. There's something magical about genetics—the echo of his gift in someone so young, someone he's ashamed not to know very well. He's written her letters over the years and she's always been good about writing back. But truthfully those exchanges have been too rare, too formal and remote, wrapped up as Nathan has been in his own troubles, his own fears. Magnolia and Sara Beth have always kept him up to speed on what Lily's doing. But not because he asks them to. *I never ask. What's wrong with me?*

"Here it comes," Leland says.

Nathan starts to ask what he's talking about, but then Lily launches into her next refrain, and he no longer needs to.

He stares at the screen, that solo filling his ears, his eyes starting to itch from lack of blinking. "My God," he whispers. "Why?"

It's his own bass solo, note for note, from "Pearly Gates."

When it's over, Nathan looks at Leland, a hard lump in his chest moving up into his throat, his face reddening from it. Leland grins. Clearly he thinks that it's pride, this emotion that's overtaking Nathan, showing in his features.

But it isn't. It's dread.

FIFTEEN

It must have been a nightmare. Lily can't remember much of it—something about tentacles. Teeth. Bells chiming in her ears. Lily sits up in bed, in the pitch-darkness of her room, sweat pouring down her back, her throat raw. *Did I scream in my sleep?*

The bells still chime. It's her phone. *Who the fuck is calling me?* It's only spammers and old people who call Lily on the phone. And not all old people either. Her mom prefers texting.

Lily pats her bedside table, following the sound. She touches the near-empty glass of water she was drinking last night, her clip-on tuner, a small pile of hair ties, ChapStick, the copy of *The Prophesy* that she finished at 4 A.M. *Obviously not ideal bedtime reading . . .* And then she finds it at last, her ringing, glowing phone.

Lily looks at the screen. *Grandpa Nate.* She can't remember the last time he called her. She answers quickly. "Grandpa? Are you okay?"

There's a strange tone to his voice, like a string pulled too tight. "How did you know it was me?"

"Because . . . it says on my screen?"

"Right," he says. "Well, keep it to yourself. Don't tell anybody I called you."

"Why?"

"You can tell your mother if you feel like it."

Lily rubs her eyes. *Am I still dreaming?* She pinches her arm. It hurts. "What's going on?"

Grandpa Nate takes a breath, long and shaky. "Who is Carl on Guitar?"

Lily sits up in bed. "What?"

"Carl on Guitar. He posted a video on the YouTube of a song he wrote. You have a bass solo in it. Who is this Carl? Your boyfriend?"

"Ummm . . ."

"Doesn't matter. Listen, Lily, you're a terrific musician. You play it better than I ever did. But for your own safety, for your mom's, you've got to call Carl on Guitar and tell him to take that video down."

Lily shuts her eyes. She has no idea what Grandpa Nate is talking about, but he's speaking very quickly. It feels as though she has to trap and pin down each word in order to wring sense out of what he is trying to say. "Wait," she says finally. "Carl has a YouTube channel?"

Grandpa Nate sighs dramatically. "Oh, dear Lord."

"Grandpa, I'm still half asleep."

"Well, wake up. It's ten A.M., for chrissakes."

Lily doesn't remember the last time she got up this early. She's starting to resent her grandfather, the way he seems to need the entire world to play by his rules, when his rules are incredibly weird and annoying. Why is he calling her instead of writing a letter like he usually does? Why is he asking about Carl? How does he know about a YouTube channel when he isn't even online?

He's speaking to her slowly now, the way you would to a toddler. It takes Lily a few moments to put aside her irritation and actually listen to what he's saying. ". . . so Carl on Guitar posted a video of a song he wrote. 'Heaven's Gate' or something. Are you familiar with it? It apparently says 'Featuring Lily Russo' in the description, so I'm assuming you are."

"What?"

"How much of that do you want me to repeat?"

"Nothing." Lily is fully awake now, her eyes big, adjusting to the darkness of her room. "It's called 'Bridge to Heaven,'" she says slowly. "He played it for me yesterday, and then we kind of made it into a jam. I knew he videoed it, but I thought it was just for us to watch later. I had no idea he was going to post it."

"Well, it's up there. On the YouTube."

"How do you know, Grandpa?"

"A friend of mine showed me on his phone. Not the whole song. But he did show me your solo, with the riff from 'Pearly Gates.'"

"Oh . . ."

"Don't be mad at your boyfriend. I'm sure he did it with good intentions. Really, you were sensational. But you've gotta ask him to take it down."

Lily swallows hard. She pulls her laptop out from underneath her bed and turns it on, half listening to him. Yes, when she and Carl were stoned and playing together yesterday, Lily re-created her grandfather's solo—she plays it all the time, more than ever since the accident. For some reason, she finds it soothing. *Why did he post it without asking me?*

Maybe Grandpa's confused, she thinks. *Maybe it's something else that somebody posted a long time ago.* Lily clicks the online icon and goes to YouTube and finds the channel. CarlOnGuitar. The avatar is a picture of Carl's Stratocaster. He bought it used and it shows, so he's put stickers all over it to cover up the dings. Same stickers. Same guitar. Same Carl. *Why didn't he tell me he had a YouTube channel?*

She goes to the channel, and immediately she sees the video. *"Bridge to Heaven," Featuring Lily Russo.*

"The thing is," Grandpa says, "there are people out there who, for some reason, think our song is Satanic."

"Devil music," Lily says.

"Yeah, so you've heard that crap."

"Kind of . . . I mean . . . a long time ago. When I was little."

"Who said it? Someone in Elizabethville?"

For several seconds, Lily can't answer him. She's transfixed by the number of views the video has received: More than twenty thousand, and Carl just posted it yesterday. "What the fuck . . ." she whispers. And then she starts to read the comments . . .

"No matter who said it, it goes to my point," Grandpa is saying. "I don't know if your mother told you about it, but I was attacked many years ago by these people. They crawl out from their holes every few years to terrorize me. No one else in my band. Just me and my family, and I think they're doing it now . . ."

She says nothing. Her head feels light, her vision swimmy.

"Lily? Are you still there?"

Lily realizes just now that she's been holding her breath. It comes out of her in a whoosh. *What are these comments supposed to mean?*

"I'll get Carl to take it down, Grandpa," she says. "I'll call him right now. I promise."

—

Lily pushes herself out of bed and switches on her lights, bringing her laptop to her desk, along with her phone. She plugs the laptop into the charger and again, she looks at the video, as though a change of scenery might make it all go away—Carl's post, her name at the top. The views. The comments.

There are more than a hundred comments, all from different accounts: DebInAustin, TruthTeller22, VeganForLife49888, HeavenLeighAngel. Every single one of them says the same thing:

121222

Who are these people? What do those numbers mean? Lily grabs her phone and starts to text Carl, but then she stops and calls him instead. She needs to *hear* him explain. The phone rings several times, then goes to voicemail. She ends the call and texts Carl:

Call me

After she sends the text, she watches the video in its entirety. It's very poor quality. When he taped them yesterday, Carl had set his phone on a music stand, presumably to get both Lily and him in frame. But he's clearly a better musician than he is a cameraperson. It's really only Lily who's visible, with just a sliver of Carl's arm in view, even though 75 percent of the song is Carl playing lead guitar. As a result, the whole thing is boring to watch (excruciating for Lily), which makes the number of views even more baffling.

It's up to 22,000 now. Two thousand additional views in the past five minutes. Lily hates this. She can't stand the idea of people watching her. She's always been shy that way, but since the accident . . . Carl knows. Lily's told him, she's sure. The idea of strangers' eyes on her, like those guys in the Mazda. Capturing her image. Replaying videos. Looking at pictures. Watching. *He knows.* Just a couple of days ago, Carl asked her why she never posts selfies on her Instagram anymore, and she told him the truth. *I know it sounds weird,* she said, and he assured her it didn't. He said he gets it. *You've been through so much, Lily. Of course I understand.*

Lily's phone rings. She sees Carl's name on the screen and picks up fast. "You have a YouTube channel," she says, surprising herself. A million different questions and statements and cuss words were running through her mind when she picked up the phone—yet this is what she decided to go with?

"Uh, yeah. I told you about that."

"No, you didn't."

"Sure I did, Lily. Remember, in my truck, we were talking about our futures? I told you I had that channel but I hadn't posted on it for a while, and you said I should. You said you never know who might be watching?"

Lily doesn't remember that at all, but that doesn't mean it didn't happen. She's never been the best listener when she's stoned. Her mind tends to wander all over the place, analyzing, reflecting, recalling scenes and images and sounds she doesn't want it to, winding its way down rabbit holes, until a whole conversation has gone by and Lily hasn't been around for any of it. "It doesn't even matter," she says. "You posted the video you took of us yesterday without asking first. You put my name on it. Why?"

"What?" Carl says. Then he's silent for several seconds. "Oh, man," he says finally. "I *suck*."

"What are you talking about?"

"I'm sorry, Lily . . . I did do that."

"Why?"

"I was really high, and that solo you did was the best thing I'd ever heard," he says. "I did post it, because you were so, so great. But I thought I took it right down."

Lily swallows hard. "Yeah, well. You didn't."

"I am so sorry," he says. "I'll take it down right now." He says something about getting out his laptop. She hears his keyboard clacking. "If it makes you feel any better," he says, "nobody watches my channel anyway."

She takes a deep breath. She stares at the screen: 24,500 views.

"Holy shit," Carl says.

"You're looking at the views."

"I . . . I don't get it."

"And the comments."

"Has to be bots," Carl says. "Right? Makes no sense."

It's now up to 25,000 views. "Carl, take it down *now*." It comes out harsher than she intended it to.

"That's what I'm doing," Carl says. "I'm sorry."

"It's okay. I didn't mean to snap." There are close to two hundred, identical comments now. Lily grabs a pen and pad from her desk drawer and writes the number down. *121222.*

Carl tells her he's taken the video down, and when Lily refreshes the screen, it's gone. Views and comments and all.

"I shouldn't smoke so much weed," Carl says. "It wrecks my judgment. Makes me do stupid things. I'd never have posted that video if I was sober. I know how much you hate people watching you."

"Just . . . don't do it again."

"I won't."

Lily hangs on for a while, listening to Carl breathing. She stares at the pad of paper. *121222.*

Carl says, "Those numbers in the comments. Do you think it was, like, a code or something?" And Lily's skin jumps. It's as though he's in the room with her, reading over her shoulder.

"I have no idea," Lily says.

"Freaky," Carl says.

"Yeah."

"Yeah."

Carl starts to apologize again, but Lily interrupts him. "You want to hang out later?" She says it not so much because she actually wants to see him, but because she's really anxious to get him off the phone so she can think.

"Sure!" Carl says.

"I'll text you, okay?" Lily ends the call, feeling a little guilty about it.

—

Lily rereads the numbers she copied down. There's something familiar about the sequence, but she can't quite grab on to it. Where has she seen them before? She thinks of phone numbers, addresses, combination locks, zip codes, codes. *Is it a code like Carl said?*

Maybe they don't *look* familiar. Maybe they *sound* familiar.

She says the numbers out loud. "One, two, one, two, two, two." And her heart starts to beat faster, the memory crystallizing.

Lily gets up from her desk and picks up her bass. She starts playing her grandfather's solo from "Pearly Gates," which, in turn, makes her remember the first time she heard the song. She must have been eight or nine years old, and her dad was driving her to day camp, and she heard it on the car's Bluetooth. Back then she only played a little piano, but the bass solo transfixed her. It was like nothing she'd ever heard, and it was beautiful and compelling and a little bit scary. It may have been the first time she ever fell in love, but with an instrument, with a sound. *You know who that is playing the bass?* Dad said. *It's your grandpa.*

How weird is it that Dad was the one to introduce her to that solo, not Mom?

She looks at the numbers again, "Pearly Gates" playing in her mind. The whole song, from the beginning. The opening lyrics. The chorus. The musical bridge. Lead guitar solo. Keyboards. Bass. Grandpa's solo . . .

But no. There's more to the song than that. There's a count-in. Not only did Grandpa write and sing and play a bass solo on the song, he also counted it in on the recording.

At least the way Lily remembers it, Grandpa Nate's count-in voice is fierce but barely audible. Like a demon from a horror movie.

She picks up her phone, searches for the song on her music streaming platform. When she finds it, she puts in her earbuds and plays it from the very beginning, Grandpa's count-in, the pop of the *t*'s into the mic, the urgency of it, ushering in that first power chord . . .

One and two and one and two and two and two I will die for you.

It sounds exactly as she remembered it.

One and two and one and two and two and two . . .

Maybe that was all those comments had meant. Fans of the song, replicating the count-in. But did that many people know "Pearly Gates" well enough to quote the whispered count-in? And if they did, why had they all typed it out in numerals, with no *and*'s, no *I will die for you*?

For the hell of it, Lily googles the number 121222. She finds weight conversions, hexadecimal color codes, modem models . . . Nothing particularly interesting. She thinks about shutting down her laptop, maybe trying to sleep a little more if she possibly can, but she finds herself scrolling instead. A little farther down, she sees town meeting announcements, concert dates, a notice about a Christmas tree lighting— all taking place on December 12. 12/12/22. Which happens to be the day after tomorrow.

She scrolls some more, thinking about how bizarre it is. The whole idea that you can plug anything into a search bar, even a random list of numbers, and find dozens and dozens of entries in response. Were all the commenters on "Bridge to Heaven" referring to the date? Or is there something else that makes 121222 relevant to this specific group of commenters—something that has nothing to do with Lily or Carl or the song they played? Maybe this channel is a meeting spot for them, the numbers some type of code, like Carl said.

She opens another tab, goes to the CarlOnGuitar channel and clicks on his most recent song, posted more than a month ago. It's called "Rubber Bullets," and it's another instrumental, much like "Bridge to Heaven." It has twenty views. No comments. She checks another song, "Rainy Day." Sixteen views. No comments.

So much for that theory.

She closes the tab, Google glaring at her, the numbers in the search bar. She types in *Pearly Gates* after the numbers and presses enter. Basically the same pointless hits, along with some religious websites. She skims over them, until she finds something that catches her eye: a link to a Reddit thread.

She clicks on the link, scrolls through the thread. It's on a subreddit called *What?!* that seems to be about conspiracy theories. And when she gets to the original message—the one that caused the thread to turn up in her search in the first place—she gasps out loud.

How is this happening?

Lily's breathing goes shallow. She grasps at a flickering hope: Maybe she's still asleep. Maybe if she hits herself, or screams loud enough, if she digs her fingernails into the palms of her hands and bites her lip so hard it bleeds, Lily will wake up in her own bed, and Grandpa never will have called her. None of this will be real. *Just a dream, just a bad dream . . .*

Lily rereads the message:

Do you know about 12/12/22, Pearly Gates, The Year of Twos, The Prophesy? If not, go here before it's too late!

"It's real," Lily whispers.

Her hand trembling, she clicks on the link.

SIXTEEN

Meg's father's Glock is unloaded, the rounds safely in their box, and both are locked up in a polymer case on the floor in front of the Crosstrek's passenger's seat. Meg knows how to use a gun now. In teaching her how to load and unload and aim and shoot, Nathan was patient and clear with her in a way she's never known him to be. *Trust your instincts,* he kept saying to her. *Nature gave you instincts for a reason.* But still, Meg is on edge. Not only over the fact that she now has a lethal weapon in her possession, but because, after talking to her father, she feels as though she may need to use it.

Is Nathan's paranoia catching—or is he onto something? While he was teaching her how to shoot, Dad repeatedly mentioned the accident that killed Justin, and maybe that's why, when she was aiming at tin cans behind her father's home—in the area that once housed a small swimming pool for guests of the inn—Meg kept thinking about the missing lug nut, the late-to-deploy airbag, the perfectly timed distraction of the skinheads in the Mazda. Meg thinks about it as she pulls onto Route 28 so carefully, the way she does now, two miles under the speed limit, every nerve in her body stretched to near-breaking. She thinks about how seamlessly all of these elements fit together.

It frightens her, but it's also comforting in a way. Because it absolves Meg of all responsibility in Justin's death. If a group of Nathan's haters really sabotaged her car, then Meg doesn't need to consider all the other things that contributed to the accident: her own over-the-top reaction to the skinheads, her too-early ask for a ham and cheese sandwich, all the speeding up and slowing down she'd done in a 2014 Impreza with more than 200,000 miles on it, not to mention her decision to take it to a garage that clearly specializes in vintage cars, her lack of sleep the previous night . . . Meg could go on and on. But if she were to become a conspiracy theorist, like her father, she wouldn't have to.

A full week. An entire week, Meg's mother had stayed in bed, her body weakening, her fever climbing from MRSA. One whole week, her father feeding her teas that did nothing to cure or even alleviate her symptoms, before she was rushed to the hospital, too late for treatment. It must be so much easier for him to believe that his enemies spiked her coffee with a poison concocted in a basement lab—some powerful blend of chemicals no antibiotic could cure, no matter how early it was administered—and that it was all part of some vast conspiracy, beyond Nathan's control.

Meg had to give her dad some credit. He did have her going there for a little while. He'd even convinced her to arm herself against a bunch of hate-mail writers from the previous century. *Paranoia. The cure for guilt*, Meg thinks. And then her phone rings.

Meg doesn't recognize the number immediately, but she answers anyway.

"Hello, Meg?" Dr. Katie Cody's voice spills out of her Bluetooth. "You had an appointment this morning? At nine?"

"Oh, crap," Meg says. "I'm so sorry. I will pay for it. I just . . . I had a family emergency and it slipped my mind."

"Oh, dear," Dr. Cody says. "Is Lily all right?"

"What? No. Lily's fine. I just . . . I had to visit my father."

"*Oh, thank God*," she says. "I mean, I hope your father's okay, but thank God."

"He's fine."

"Good," she says. "It's just . . . I've been a little worried, to be honest."

"Why?"

"Well, you know . . . Most healthy kids her age get COVID, it lasts five days tops. Two weeks, though. And then a relapse . . ."

"Huh?"

"I'm so sorry. I probably crossed a line in asking you, but after her fourth cancellation . . . And then when you didn't show up . . . It's just. Well . . ."

Meg's grip on the wheel tightens. *Her fourth cancellation.*

"I shouldn't have said anything."

"No." Meg clears her throat. "No. She's . . . Lily was feeling much better this morning. It seems it was a . . . a false positive."

"Oh, what a relief," she says.

"Yes."

"And you don't need to pay for the missed visit. Would you like to reschedule, or—"

"I'll definitely pay. And I need to look at my calendar. I'll call later. Thanks for being so understanding." Meg ends the call.

She turns on the radio. Turns it off again. The heat in the car is starting to get to her, so she turns it down, but before long, she's shivering.

Here she was, thinking she was doing okay with Lily. She thought they might have even had a breakthrough yesterday, the whole conversation about *The Prophesy.* Lily had pressed Meg for answers, and instead of putting her off, Meg had replied honestly, and it had felt like the start of something, a new openness between them.

She's been lying. Lily has been lying to me. For weeks.

Her phone rings again.

The call is from Zach, which seems strange at first, until Meg remembers that he's supposed to be at the store right now, stocking the Kingsolvers and making a display of them for book club.

"Hi, Zach," she says. "Did the books get there?"

Zach doesn't reply.

"Zach? Are you there?"

Meg hears traffic noises, a dog barking, then Reggie's voice. "Tell her, Zach. Come on. *Tell her what happened, man.*"

"What's going on?" Meg says, her injured arm throbbing, the way it always seems to do when she starts to get stressed—a physical reminder of how badly things can go. "Zach?"

"Sorry."

"What did you do?"

"I didn't do anything. I got here. Early. And it was like . . ."

"Tell her," Reggie says.

"I can't."

"Zach."

"Mrs. Russo," he says, the words tumbling out of him, tripping over each other, "please come to the store."

—

Over the phone, Meg had managed to get out of Zach that the Secret Garden had been vandalized, but when she asked him for specifics, he'd said, "I feel uncomfortable talking about it."

Thinking about this as she arrives back in town, Meg can't help but be a little irritated. When she was Zach's age, she would have felt compelled to describe the situation for her boss—no matter how much it pained her—but like most young people today, Zach's feelings come first. *God forbid he should be a little uncomfortable* . . . And over what? Did someone spray-paint a penis on the front door? Did they mess with Sara Beth's hand-crocheted Christmas window display, rearranging Fred Holywell and his family into obscene positions? Meg won't know till she gets there because Zach wouldn't say. She couldn't even convince him to send a picture.

She pulls into her space in the small parking lot behind the Secret Garden. As she gets out of her car, she debates what to do with the polymer case, and decides to put it in her trunk and lock it.

She's not quite ready to take the gun into her place of business, though Pete DeMarco across the street has one. He's kept it under the counter for years. As far as Meg knows, the closest he ever came to using it was one month ago, when he caught a group of drunk teens trying to break into the Secret Garden. Meg's store was shuttered at the time, and Pete was working late when he heard them all the way from across the street, loudly plotting their crime. Pete told Meg that he'd brought the gun across the street, showed it to the teens and scared the piss out of them, literally. It was unloaded, but they had no idea. They scattered, sobbing. He hadn't even needed to unlock the safety.

She smiles a little at that thought, but when she reaches the front of the store, her smile disappears. Her jaw drops. "What the . . ."

The storefront window has been smashed to bits, one of the big, decorative rocks from the town green thrown clean through it, and now lolling on top of Sara Beth's Dickens family Christmas display, cold air rushing in, shattered glass everywhere. *She was so proud of that display . . .* "I'm sorry, Mrs. Russo," says Zach, who is standing in front of the store with Reggie, three boxes of books on the sidewalk between them. Zach is shivering furiously, though it doesn't seem to be from the cold.

"Have you called the police?" Meg asks.

Zach shakes his head.

"I told him to call," Reggie says. "But he wanted you to be here when he did."

"Anything stolen?"

Zach shakes his head again.

"He checked the cash register," says Reggie, who is apparently now acting as Zach's spokesperson. "There was nothing missing. He said the office looks the same. Computer's okay . . ."

"All right," she says. "That's good news. Pete DeMarco chased off some teenagers who were loitering in front of the store about a month ago. I bet it was them."

Zach and Reggie look at each other. Neither one says a word.

"You don't have to stick around, Reggie," Meg says. "I mean, thanks for waiting for me, but you have a job to do. I can take it from here."

He shakes his head.

"Reggie, really, I—"

"I think I should wait," he says, "till you get a look at what's inside."

There's something in Reggie's expression, a caution light in his eyes that makes Meg want to stop talking.

She looks at Zach. He says nothing. It's as though some evil force has stolen his ability to speak.

Meg moves into the store and looks around, Zach and Reggie following. It's freezing in here, the broken window rendering the heating system pointless. She pulls her coat tighter around her, condensation slipping through her lips. Other than the window, though, the front of the store seems untouched. "Where's the damage?" Meg says.

"The children's section," Reggie says.

She nods. *Just one section. I can do this.* She pushes herself to the back of the store, where it's warmer, thankfully.

Meg can feel Zach trailing behind her, while Reggie moves in quickly, practically jogging to catch up, so that when Meg gets to the children's section, he's standing by her side. *Does he expect me to faint?* she thinks, which seems incredibly silly.

But then she sees what Reggie was talking about.

Every book in the children's section has been yanked off its shelf. There are dozens and dozens of them: colorful picture books, chapter books for grade schoolers, dystopian YA tomes, classics like *Little Women* and *A Catcher in the Rye,* the fantasy novels that were Lily's favorites in elementary school and junior high. The books have been piled on each other. Shaped into a sloppy pyramid.

The pyramid is spattered with dried blood. And resting at the top, like the star on a Christmas tree, is a severed, bloody finger.

A Few Truths about the Ritual

It doesn't hurt as much as you believe it will.

You think you need it—that you won't be able to live normally without it—but trust me, your body adjusts to the loss very quickly.

Anything sharp will work—hedge clippers, a small axe, hunting knife. Make sure the blade is sterilized and that the amputation site is numbed.

Toes are easier than fingers. But fingers show true commitment.

—the Bronze Lord
WAW WAA WWT

SEVENTEEN

The link that Lily sees posted on the subreddit leads to a site called 7Park. It's full of porn video clips, violent images, disgusting comments: the lowest pit of digital hell. To Lily, it feels like a malware attack about to happen. She exits the site fast and shuts down her laptop.

But once she gets the courage to restart her computer and looks 7Park up on Wikipedia, Lily learns that, offensive as it may be, the site is safe to visit. It's what's known as an anonymous image board—something like Reddit, only with more photos and videos, no registration, no moderators, no way of knowing a poster's identity, unless they choose to divulge it. There are no screen names (everyone goes by "ANON") and basically no rules. Like Reddit, there are all sorts of normal topics you can post about—sports, music, anime, TV, celebrity gossip, true crime, recipes . . . and also, to paraphrase Wiki, some truly dark and horrible shit. To quote Wiki directly: *Among the spirited political debates and TV spoilers, 7Park has also emerged as a home to hate speech, with three mass shooters posting manifestos on the image board within the past three years, one of them live-streaming his attack on a 7Park subsection.*

Subsections on 7Park, Lily learns, are specific threads within broader topics. And when she returns to the thread the Reddit poster linked to, she sees that the topic is End of the World. The subsection is called TheYearofTwos. She takes a few moments to let that sink in. *The Year of Twos.* A 7Park subsection, named after a plot point in Mom's book.

She holds her breath as she clicks on it, scrolling all the way back to the very first post, dated nearly three years ago.

ANON: I'm retired LE and I was there at the beginning, under deep cover. NATHAN LERNER ("Big Daddy") was a member of an NYC Satanic Coven in the 70s. In exchange for having a hit single (PEARLY GATES) Big Daddy sold his soul and the souls of his family to Satan— and put deadly subliminal messages into the song's lyrics, sparking a suicide wave in the mid-70s. His band—the marginally successful Prism—broke up after he was attacked by True Believers in Kennedy Airport in 1980. (Here's a link to a story about the attack, in the NY Post). After that, he tried to hide. But his teenage daughter MAGNOLIA LERNER ("Sybil") published a book (The Prophesy) in 1990 that contained both the details of the end of the world (The Year of Twos = 2022; Lords/Monsters = deep state politicians, celebs and influencers; Fires, rising oceans, a plague = all obviously happening today) and magic spells that, if read silently or aloud by unwitting young people, could actually speed along the apocalypse. I could go on from here, but best you read The Prophesy (link to entire text in first comment) and see for yourself.

I have no skin in this game, other than my own humanity. I cannot reveal my identity, as this family is powerful (BIG CONNECTIONS) and dangerous (THEY'RE PRACTICING SATANISTS). But I am here to tell you that we MUST get them to repent by 121222 BY ANY MEANS NECESSARY . . . or to quote Sybil, "the ten-finger'd and ten toe'd will meet their demise."

Do not be afraid. Just act. Time is on our side.

The Bronze Lord
We Are Watching. We Are Armed. We Will Triumph.

Lily rereads the page, her head swimming. She opens another tab, googles "LE acronym" just to make sure it means what she thinks it does. *Law enforcement.*

"Jesus," she whispers.

There are hundreds and hundreds of comments after this one, the anonymous posters drastically growing in number as the months and years pass. Many describe themselves as current or former law enforcement or military, health care workers, teachers—upstanding members of their communities, lying low and lying in wait. *Time is on our side.*

Each of the Bronze Lord's posts gets thousands of up-votes and comments. She starts to read some of those comments and her stomach drops. Lily reads more of them and it feels as though she's sinking into quicksand, unable to move, to come up for air. By the time she's halfway through the entire subsection, she has forgotten how to breathe.

—

Lily can't stop trembling. She stands up and stretches, pacing in circles around her room. But still, she feels that chill, same as she did after the accident. It snakes into your muscles and invades your bones until your insides feel colder than your outsides. Your organs are shivering and you're trapped in your own, too-tight skin and nothing is working the way it's supposed to.

It's shock. One of the paramedics had explained that to her after the crash as Lily pulled the blanket around her shoulders, unable to get warm, but in this case it makes more sense in a way. Obviously, Lily isn't as traumatized as she was after the accident, which set the trauma bar pretty fucking high. But she is shocked. Literally. Through and through.

Within the past hour, Lily has learned that there's an entire cult out there, made up of people who hate her and her family. Lily has seen their messages, their memes. The videos they've made, photoshopping and deep-faking her parents and her grandpa and even Lily herself into ritualistic scenes so depraved, so disgusting, she can't even think about them without wanting to throw up.

And odds are, this cult has been around much longer than 7Park has existed. Longer than social media and maybe even the internet. Though the Bronze Lord seems to have created this subsection a few years ago, many of the photos posted on it are much older than that.

One post featured a bunch of stalker pics of Lily and her mom, the two of them involved in an intense conversation at the Elizabethville Municipal Playground. It had included a caption: *"I hate people, Mommy. I want them all dead."* *"Don't worry, honey. In ten years, the plague will kill them all!"* The municipal playground was torn down eight years ago. And in the picture, Lily looks about six.

They've been watching her family. Taking pictures and videos without their knowledge and whispering theories about them. Maybe for as long as Lily's been alive.

It's real. You aren't dreaming. This is really happening.

Looking back, she can now recall a string of incidents that she tried to tell herself were normal, part of being a girl, though her gut said otherwise. The many, many times strange men stared at her in a way that made her feel uneasy. That boy at her friend Emma's party last year whom nobody knew, watching Lily from across the room for what felt like hours. (*What a creep,* Lily had said, laughing it off, turning away . . . But there was something in the intensity of his gaze, the laser focus of it.) The old lady in the beat-up Volkswagen parked outside her school when she was in fifth grade, mouthing curse words at her from behind the wheel. The phone calls her family used to get when they still had a landline, her dad slamming the receiver down. *It's the breather again.* That weird middle-aged couple who came into Divine Vintage just a week ago and asked Lily her name but didn't buy anything, didn't even browse. Those asshole cops in her school parking lot *(Is your grandfather Nathan Lerner?).* The skinheads in the Mazda. Taking her picture.

Grandpa Nate isn't paranoid. He's right. There really are people after him, after all of them. Lily clicks on one of the posts, a dry, instructional video on how to chop off your own finger. ("Don't perish on 12/12 with the rest of the ten-finger'd, ten-toe'd," a robotic-sounding voiceover says, quoting the phrase from Mom's book. "Join the powerful ranks of the Nine-and-Tens and immunize yourself of the Lerner curse.") It makes Lily think of Frosty Lips yet again, her glove tied in a knot to accommodate her missing pinkie finger . . . (*Toes are easier,* the Bronze Lord said in one post. *But fingers show true commitment.*)

These strange, deeply unhappy people, banding together and targeting Lily and her family, stalking them. Planning ways to hurt them. *We must make them repent or die,* so many of them say. Because of a story told by a fifteen-year-old girl back in 1990 that happened to have a few coincidences in it, these people truly believe that the Lerner-Russos of Elizabethville, New York, have the power to end the world.

This is insane.

It might even be funny if there weren't hundreds of them. If so many, the Bronze Lord included, didn't claim to be members of law enforcement or the military and if several of them hadn't posted photos and videos of machetes, guns, hunting knives . . . If those posters and others hadn't created animated scenes in which Lily stabs her grandfather to death or puts a gun in her mother's mouth and pulls the trigger. If it wasn't 2022, "The Year of Twos" from Mom's book. And if December 12, which the Nine-and-Tens seem to think is doomsday, wasn't two days away.

Lily stands up. She backs away from the computer and collapses to the floor, putting her head between her knees, drawing breath in gasps. Lily feels like Princess Iyanla from Mom's book—doomed Princess Iyanla, who needs to stab an army of monsters with poisonous tentacles, one by one and through the heart, in order to save the world.

I cannot let the monsters get to me, Lily tells herself. *I cannot let the monsters break my resolve.* It's a line from *The Prophesy.*

A few more breaths and she's up on her feet—not calmer so much as able to function without hyperventilating, which is as much of an improvement as she can hope for. She goes to her desk and grabs her phone. She sees a text from Mom, from 7 A.M.

Running out to take care of a few things. Took car. 🚗

Lily calls her mother. She doesn't know how she's going to explain this without sounding like she's completely lost her mind, but hopefully, Mom will at least try to understand without judging or meaningfully asking her if she's "mentioned this to Dr. Cody."

The call goes to voicemail, which is interesting. Meg always picks up for Lily, no matter what she's doing. Lily debates whether to leave a message or not. *You never know who's listening,* she thinks. It's something Grandpa would say. But as it turns out, Grandpa has a clearer vision of the world than anyone else in their family.

She leaves a quick, vague message for Mom, telling her to call her back when she can; it's important. Then she brings her laptop downstairs, attaches it to the printer in the den, goes back to 7Park and prints out the Bronze Lord's original message, plus ten pages' worth of additional messages, comments and photographs—a sort of "greatest hits" of the YearofTwos subsection. She writes out a letter to Grandpa, telling him everything she's learned this morning. Lily's hoping that his friend who showed him the video of her bass solo can also show him 7Park. That way, Grandpa can get the full effect, the deep-fake videos . . . Maybe he shouldn't see those, though.

Lily puts all the papers in a manila envelope. She addresses it to Grandpa Nate's PO box in Star Lake, and by the time the envelope is sealed, she feels calmer, clearer. Not that sending a letter is going to solve everything—but for Lily, it makes a big difference, taking some form of action.

She wants to overnight it to Grandpa so that he can get it by Monday and it isn't until she's searching around the house for the keys that she remembers: Mom took the car.

She needs a car. So much going on, it's hard for Lily to corral her thoughts, but she does know one thing. There are very, very few people she can tell about this.

She checks the time on her phone. It's after eleven. Her mom has to be at work now, so she calls the store. The call goes right to voicemail. She tries her mom's cell phone again, but no luck there either. She doesn't leave a message this time. *Calm, calm, calm,* she tells herself, and then his image pops into her mind: The one truly calming person she knows who's still alive.

She texts Carl: Can I borrow your truck?

He answers immediately. Sure. When?

Is now okay?

Yeah. Why?

Lily sighs. *Why do people always have to ask why?* Not that she blames him. If he wanted to borrow her car all of a sudden, she'd ask why too. I have to go to the post office. And I wanted to stop by the bookstore. Make sure my mom is okay. "Ugh," Lily whispers. Why did she just type that?

What happened to your mom?

Lily winces. She went out to run some errands, and I haven't been able to get hold of her. I'm sure she's just busy at the store.

But Carl replies before she can send it: I'll bring it over. I just have to find my shoes.

Lily puts a thumbs-up on Carl's text.

As Lily heads to the bathroom to get showered, she remembers that Carl's truck is a stick shift, which may be a problem. Dad taught her how to drive stick, but that was a long time ago. She doesn't have a lot of practice.

Maybe she'll see if Carl can drive. The thought of having company cheers her up a little, and so after she's out of the shower, she texts Carl again:

I actually don't have a lot of practice driving stick. Can you drive?

Carl immediately puts a thumbs-up on her text. Lily smiles. No matter what happens between the two of them in the long run, she's glad that Carl is a part of her life at this moment in time.

After she's dressed, Lily slips the letter to Grandpa Nate into her backpack and it all comes flooding back again: the Nine-and-Tens. An entire cult full of strangers, many of whom have been watching her and her family for years. *Are they watching me now? Are there people in town who are involved? People I know?* Lily remembers what Carl said to her just yesterday, the "weird shit" people were saying about her mom. And a thought pops into her mind. She texts him:

Those guys on your construction job who told you about my mom's book. Was either of them missing a finger?

She's about to hit send, but then she rereads the text and deletes it. If you're going to ask a question as weird as that one, it seems best to do it in person.

EIGHTEEN

It's the severed finger that complicates everything. If it was just the rock through the window and the books pulled from the shelves, local police would have handled it themselves. One of two Elizabethville cops explains this to Meg as they stand outside the store, waiting for the state police to gather evidence. "We know how to deal with vandals. Bored kids. Weekenders who've had a few too many Long Island Iced Teas at Sue's," he says. "But that finger. Who knows where it came from or how it got in there? It's a body part. It could also be evidence of a violent attack or even a murder. You know what I'm saying?"

Meg does know what he's saying. In fact, she's a little confused as to why this cop, whose name is Grady, thinks he has to say it in the first place, let alone explain it to her so thoroughly. She suspects that it's because Grady's as spooked as Zach and she are (not to mention Reggie, who cut out as soon as the first police cars arrived), but unlike Zach and Meg, he's one of those people who feels the need to fill uncomfortable silences with the sound of his own voice. It also could be an ego thing. Grady's much younger partner—a tall, athletic camp counselor type named Peele—is showing the state police contingent around the crime scene, the detective in charge having personally selected him for the job.

Meg realizes Zach hasn't said anything for a long time. She glances at him, sitting on the curb, his knees pressed against his chest with a look in his eyes as though he's just been kicked in the stomach but is trying to be stoic about it. For a few seconds, Meg sees Lily in his place—Lily after the car accident, shivering within the folds of the trauma blanket. "Are you okay?" she asks him.

He looks up at her. "Yeah. It's just . . . It's not the way I expected this morning to go." He gives her a weak smile. She feels like hugging him, poor Zach, so excited at the thought of taking over book club, signing off on the Kingsolver shipment. He'd even made a new sign to put up next to the cash register. It's lying on the sidewalk next to him, like a forgotten, passed-out friend.

"*Demon Copperhead*, huh?" Grady says.

Zach looks at him. So does Meg.

"I saw the boxes. You ordered a bunch of copies."

"For book club," Meg says.

"Kind of a weird title. Don't you think?"

"It's Barbara Kingsolver," Zach says.

Grady gives him a blank look.

"It's based on *David Copperfield*. By Charles Dickens?"

Another blank look. Clearly, Officer Grady doesn't do a lot of reading. Zach's cheeks redden.

"It's gotten wonderful reviews," Meg says.

Grady's beady gaze travels from Meg to Zach and back again. Meg knows him, though he doesn't realize this. Shaved head. Shiny pink skin. Puffy eyes and cheeks and a neatly trimmed ginger beard, creating an overall look that somehow reminds her of a fantail goldfish. She didn't recognize him at first because the beard is new. But Grady is definitely the same cop who pulled her over five years ago, for running a red light that was clearly yellow. When she protested, Grady had told her she should keep her mind on the road rather than her grocery list—whatever the hell that was supposed to mean. At any rate, she fought it in court and won, mainly because Grady couldn't be bothered to show up that day.

"*Demon Copperhead*," Grady says now. "Creepy title."

"It's a great book," Meg says. "Beats the hell out of a grocery list."

He frowns, but there's no flicker of recognition, which Meg finds disappointing. "I'm just saying," Grady says. "The title of the book and the . . . uh . . . severed finger."

"What?" Meg says.

"I mean, maybe the book club choice provoked the intruder. *Demon.* And all. Maybe the person was reacting to the Satanism."

Good Lord, what an idiot. Meg glances at Zach, expecting an eye roll. But he doesn't seem to notice her. He's staring at his hands, moving his ten fingers as though he's never seen them before. "It's not because of that book," he says quietly.

Meg puts a hand on Zach's shoulder. He flinches, and she pulls away. Meg's thinking Zach should get home to his family or maybe a doctor, take a mental health day, as soon as the cops give them the all clear. He doesn't look well at all.

She's watching Zach, that slumped back, those wiggling fingers, when her phone rings. She looks at the screen. *Lily.* Meg declines the call. For the first time ever, Meg lets Lily go to voicemail. Lily, who's been lying to her for weeks about therapy. She can't deal with Lily right now.

"Your daughter?" says Grady, who has apparently been peering over her shoulder at her phone's screen.

How does he know I have a daughter named Lily? Meg glares at Grady. He stares back at her. This continues for several seconds, like some ridiculous game of chicken where neither player knows what they want the other to do first.

"My brother-in-law is a contractor," Grady says finally. "Remind me and I'll give you his number before I leave."

"Huh?"

"For the window. He can fix it for you."

"Oh. Thanks." Meg had completely forgotten about the broken window.

—

The bookstore door pushes open and a few of the state cops leave. One carries a case that isn't unlike the polymer one that Meg's father put the Glock and ammo in before giving it to her. *Evidence*, Meg thinks, as she watches them get into two of the squad cars and pull away from the curb. She'd guess that the case is refrigerated, and that finger is packed inside it. The state detective—a steely, conservatively dressed woman named Bell—told her they'd need to run it through both missing person and criminal databases in order to determine whether it most likely belonged to the person who broke into the store, or to a victim of that person. *What do you think, though?* Meg had asked the detective.

I try not to think too much, Bell had said, *until I have all the facts.*

Across the street, Pete DeMarco is standing in front of his hardware store, watching the police leave. Meg catches his eye and waves at him. He waves back, and it feels like he's thrown her a life preserver. *A friendly face.* "Everything okay over there?" he calls out.

Meg shrugs her shoulders.

"Let me know if you need anything."

"I will," Meg says.

Again, the door creaks open behind her. It's the other Elizabethville cop, Peele. He's very young, probably three or four years older than Lily. Meg thinks he might look familiar though not in the same way as Grady; he never pulled her over. It would make sense, though, if she knew him from somewhere. This is a very small town. Nearly every full-time resident and even many of the part-timers look somewhat familiar to business owners like Meg.

"How's it going in there, Officer Peele?" Meg says.

"You can call me Charlie, ma'am." He tips his hat at her, a gesture that would have looked sarcastic on someone like Grady. "And it's going okay, really. They've photographed everything, collected blood samples. You guys should be able to open up again later today—or, whenever you get the window fixed, I guess. "

He looks at Zach, who is still contemplating his fingers. "You okay, buddy?"

Zach's hands drop to his lap. He looks up at Charlie as though he's waking from a dream. "Yeah. I'm okay."

"You wanna come in with me? Detective Bell wants to ask you a few questions."

"Should I come too?" Meg says.

Charlie shakes his head. "You're next, though, ma'am."

Silently, Zach stands up. He stares straight ahead as he walks into the store, his back rigid as a tin soldier's.

After Zach closes the door behind him, Meg looks at the young officer. "This is going to sound like a weird question," she says. "But where do you personally think the finger came from?"

"Um. Well . . . "

"I mean, do you think the people or person who broke in . . . whoever they are . . . committed an act of violence in town somewhere and . . . you know . . . brought the spoils into the store?"

"The spoils?" Grady says.

She ignores him. "Do you think there's someone out there in need of medical attention?"

"Well," Charlie says. "I mean, if someone had been attacked and mutilated in town, we'd know about it."

"That's right," Grady says. "And we don't know about it."

"You want to know what I think?" Charlie says. "I feel like it was done in your store. Amputation, first aid, all of it."

He casts a quick look at Grady, as though he's worried he may have overstepped his bounds. "You agree with me, right, Officer Grady?"

"I didn't get a very close look," Grady says.

"Come on in," he says. "I can show you guys."

Meg's store doesn't look the same. With the bloodstained children's books bagged and taken away for evidence testing, the section is mostly just empty, brightly colored shelves, while the rest of the space looks pretty ransacked, as though it's been violated a second time, just from the inspection. Looking around, Meg finds herself thinking more about all the work that needs to be done in order to reopen the place than what was done to it and why. A defense mechanism, she figures. It's weirdly comforting.

Charlie ushers Meg and Grady to the children's section, where he points at the floor in front of the empty bookshelves on the farthest wall. There's a stain there that Meg hadn't noticed earlier—a thick, rust-red streak. "That wasn't here before you got vandalized, right?" he asks her.

"No."

"Okay, Officer Grady has been at this a lot longer than me, so he should tell me if I'm wrong, but look." Charlie shines his flashlight on the small stretch of floor that lies between the bloodstain and the pile of books. "See that?" he says, moving the beam along a series of deep red droplets. "There's one here, and here, and here." He looks at Grady, as if giving him a cue.

"Looks like the finger got cut off right there, next to the bookshelves after they were emptied." Grady says it as though he was figuring this out for himself for the first time, unprompted by anyone.

"That makes a lot of sense," Charlie says.

Interesting dynamic between these two. Charlie doing all the thinking, then working twice as hard to make Grady believe it was him that came up with it all. In a way, they remind Meg of her parents.

"So," Grady says. "They walked the digit over to the book pile. Placed it where it could be seen."

The digit. Meg tries not to roll her eyes.

"Spot-on." Charlie gives Grady an imploring look. "And, since there's no blood anywhere else in the store, maybe they did the first aid right here."

"Maybe."

"You think he cut off his own finger, right?" Charlie says. "Doesn't it look like he did?"

Charlie presses on. "I think, in this specific case," he says to Grady, "we're talking about people who don't care about cleaning up after themselves, right?"

"Right."

"But, see, there's no sign of a struggle. I mean, other than the kids' section and the window, the place looked pretty untouched before the state police got here. If someone had been, uh . . . mutilated against their will, wouldn't there be more things knocked over and broken?"

Charlie points to a bookshelf that's come loose, one end of it hanging. Meg hadn't noticed that before. "Looks like the only struggle here was between someone and the wall." He straightens up and turns to Grady. "Right, sir?"

"Yep. Exactly. Good job."

"Thanks!"

"What do you mean?" Meg says. But then she sees it, a series of dents in the plaster. They look as though they've been made with a hammer or a mallet.

Meg's breath leaves her for a moment, images flashing through her mind. Claire Cassadine yesterday morning, removing a book, pressing against the plaster, pounding on the wall with her fist. Claire Cassadine, her hand held high above her head as everyone in the store gaped at her. Claire Cassadine, bending the index finger down. *One down, three to go . . .*

Claire Cassadine, bending the index finger down.

Zach walks out of the office, Detective Bell behind him in her trench coat and sensible shoes. She speaks directly to Charlie, as though Grady were still outside and Meg wasn't even in the room. "You guys can go ahead with your investigation. Canvass the neighborhood. See if anybody has security camera footage. Ms. Russo—"

"Detective Bell," Meg says. "Officers. I think I know who did this."

NINETEEN

Carl is late. He shows up at Lily's house full of excuses about his dad taking his truck to meet a potential client for an estimate and how he didn't know about it until he left the house and saw the empty driveway and then he couldn't find his phone and when he did, it wasn't charged and blah, blah, blah. Lily doesn't care. She just wants him to stop talking so she can ask him the question she's wanted to ask him for what feels like centuries. "It's fine," she says, interrupting Carl's monologue. "It's fine."

"Are you sure?"

"Yes."

"Because I'd be pissed at me if I were you."

They're standing just inside the front door, and Carl has been talking ever since she let him in, which is weird. Like Lily, he normally isn't that much of a talker. She thinks he's thrown out more words within the past five minutes than he has in the last week. "It's fine, Carl," she says firmly.

He exhales.

"Can I ask you something, though?"

"Yeah. Sure."

"Those guys you worked that construction job with," she says. "The ones who told you about my mom's book."

"Yeah?"

"Were either of them missing a finger?"

He blinks at her.

"I get that it's a weird question."

He inhales sharply. "How did you know about that?"

"So you're saying yes."

He nods. "One of them was missing a middle finger. Hunting accident, he said. I asked how he could work without it, and he said it was easy. He barely noticed anymore."

"Wow."

"Do you . . . have you met these guys or something?"

"No," Lily says.

Carl stares at her. "Then . . . I mean . . . how do you know about the finger?"

Lily looks at Carl for a long while, taking in his face—the confused smile, the worry in his eyes. She owes him the truth. At least that's what she tells herself, because she wants to believe that telling Carl about the Nine-and-Tens before she's able to speak to her mom about them is both selfless and necessary. But Lily isn't selfless. Not at all. She just doesn't want to be alone in this knowledge for a minute longer.

"Lily? Are you okay?" Carl says.

"No," she says. "I'm really not." She brings him into the living room. Sits him down on the couch. And tells him everything.

—

"That cop who hassled us. The woman. She was missing a finger."

It's the first thing Carl says after Lily finishes, and she sees this as proof that she made the right choice.

"I know," she says. "I thought of that too."

"So if some random cop in our shitty little town believes this stuff about you, and those two guys I met on my last job . . ."

"Anybody can be a follower. Anybody we come in contact with."

"Yeah . . . I guess we can check fingers."

"It won't mean much. Some of them cut off their toes. Some haven't performed the ritual yet."

"The ritual?"

Lily nods. "That's what they call it. They even have videos on the image board showing how to cut off a finger or a toe safely and without too much pain."

"Jesus."

"Do you want to see it? The image board, I mean."

"Not really."

Lily heads into the den and grabs her laptop, TheYearofTwos still on the screen. She carries it to the couch where Carl is sitting and places it in front of him, on the coffee table. "I'm going to finish getting ready and grab the letter I need to send," she says. "If you change your mind and want to look at it while I'm gone, feel free."

As Lily runs upstairs, her heart is a little lighter. She's still fucked up, scared and doomed, but at least now she has someone who shares those feelings. In her room, Lily looks out the window and sees a few drifting snowflakes and switches her sweater for a heavier one. She puts on her boots and examines herself in the full-length mirror. *Weird,* she thinks. She looks the same as she did an hour ago, when she believed that the worst thing that could happen to her already did happen—and while she'd carry the grief with her always, the terror of that day was fading, and slowly but steadily, her life was returning to something close to normal.

I know the truth now. I should look different.

She grabs her backpack and makes sure that her wallet is in it, along with the letter addressed to Grandpa Nate. As she hurries downstairs, she calls out "I'm ready!" But there's no response.

"Carl?"

Still nothing. *Did he use the opportunity to escape?*

When she gets to the living room, Lily finds Carl exactly where he was earlier, sitting on the couch, the laptop open in front of him.

"Carl," she says again, "are you okay?"

He points to the screen. "Look at this, Lily," he says. "Isn't that your mom's store?"

She moves next to him. "Oh my God," she whispers.

The picture was posted less than an hour ago.

Lily stares at the pile of children's books, stacked in front of the shelves she helped her dad paint when she was little. She gapes at the severed finger at the top of the pile, the blood caked beneath it, dripping onto the book covers. She reads the caption, from yet another ANON: *Had me some FUN last night!*

The post has a hundred up-votes. Lily can't form the words to describe what she's feeling.

—

Lily and Carl are in his truck, and Carl is driving. Neither one of them has said a word since the living room. Carl's radio is turned off, and the windows are closed, the only sound the squeak of his windshield wipers dusting away the falling snow.

"What the actual fuck," Lily says, just to prove she's still able to speak.

"I'm sure she's fine," Carl says.

"Huh?"

"I'm sure your mom is fine."

Carl doesn't sound sure at all, and this terrifies Lily. She hadn't even considered the idea that her mom might be in danger. But now all she can think of is the fact that a couple of hours ago, she called Mom and had to leave a voicemail, and she hasn't heard from her since. "Carl, do you think . . ." She's trembling. She can't finish the sentence.

They're in town, a few blocks from the Secret Garden. It's very quiet, the streets empty, a couple of old ladies holding on to each other, struggling with the icy sidewalk. The snow is falling harder, and the sky is that type of dirty winter gray that's caught between day and night.

Carl parks by the hardware store. "Shit," he says. "I was thinking maybe it was just photoshopped or something."

He's turned away from Lily, staring at the bookstore. She has to crane her neck to see around him.

"Oh . . ." Lily says.

One of the Secret Garden's two display windows has been broken, a large sheet of cardboard taped in its place. Lily never believed the picture on TheYearofTwos was photoshopped, and so unlike Carl, she finds it comforting that somebody has already started fixing things up at the store. Probably Mom. That cardboard looks like her handiwork, and it would explain why she was too busy to call Lily back. At least, that's what Lily's choosing to tell herself right now. *Please let her be okay. Please let her be okay . . .*

Carl and Lily get out of the car and race across the street, the prayer running through Lily's mind the entire time. *Please not Mom too.*

The *Closed* sign is out, but Lily tries the door anyway. It's locked. She starts knocking, but then she hears someone calling out her name from the alley next to the store, and recognizes the voice immediately, just as she catches a whiff of cigarette smoke.

"Sara Beth?"

She's standing in the alleyway in her hooded parka, smoking a cigarette next to Zach Winters. Zach is smoking too, which surprises Lily. She never figured him for the type.

"Is Lily's mom okay?" Carl says it before Lily can.

"She's fine," Sara Beth says.

Lily exhales hard, condensation pouring out of her mouth, mingling with their smoke. It's only then that she realizes just how worried she's been. Once the tension inside her lets up, her muscles relax and she's suddenly freezing, the cold air biting her face, her teeth chattering, snowflakes burning the top of her head. Lily zips up her coat, pulls her hood around her face. "Is she here?"

"She's with the police," Sara Beth says. "You know, we had some . . . some vandalism other than the window."

"Yeah, we know," Carl says. "We saw it."

"You did?" Zach breathes out a cloud of smoke, his gaze pinned on Carl. "How?"

Carl starts to answer, but Lily interrupts him. "Somebody posted about it on Facebook," she says.

"Boy, news travels fast, doesn't it?" Sara Beth says it lightly, but there's tension around her mouth, a weariness in her eyes. "Why would somebody do such a thing?"

Lily wants to tell her, but she can't. Not with Zach standing right there. She keeps thinking about what he said to her in fourth grade—and how similar it was, on a very basic level, to what the Nine-and-Tens are spreading about her family today.

Lily's gaze settles on Zach's hands. One is holding the cigarette. The other is at his side. He isn't wearing gloves. She starts counting his fingers. She can't believe she's doing this.

"People get things in their heads, I guess," Carl says.

"They do." Zach says it between his teeth. "People do get things in their heads." But Lily can't tell which people he means, or what things he has in mind.

"You've been through it lately, haven't you, Zach honey?" Sara Beth says it apologetically, as though Zach is a sullen five-year-old. *He's usually much more cheerful* . . . She waits for him to answer. When he doesn't, she turns to Lily. "Zach was the one to find it."

Lily's eyebrows shoot up. Zach has all his fingers, but that doesn't mean anything. The Nine-and-Tens are a group. Group members help each other. If he found the finger, doesn't that open up the possibility that he helped someone put it there? "You found it?"

He nods. Takes another drag off his cigarette.

"How scary that must have been," Lily says.

"Zach opened the store," Sara Beth says. "We had a shipment for book club, and so he was there early."

"I bet you couldn't dial 911 soon enough," Carl says.

Zach shakes his head.

"I'm sorry," Sara Beth says. "I didn't get your name."

"This is my friend Carl," Lily says.

"Me and Zach know each other." Carl smiles.

Zach doesn't. He won't look at him. Carl moves closer. He and Zach are the same height, but somehow Carl looms over him.

"Dude," Carl says. "You didn't call 911?"

"I called Mrs. Russo."

"Why?"

"Because it's *her store*."

"Technically, it was Reggie who called her, right, Zach?" Sara Beth says. "Reggie just left." She looks at Lily. "He dropped by a little while ago to see how Zach was doing. He said he's never seen anyone so traumatized, and I can understand. If I'd been the one to find it—a human finger, my God—I'm quite sure I'd be in intensive care right now."

Lily looks at Zach, his face reddening, his eyes burning holes into the sidewalk.

"So you waited to call 911?" Carl says. "Because it isn't your store?"

Lily gives Carl a sharp look. *Ease up*, she thinks. *Read the room.*

Carl shrugs at her elaborately, annoyingly.

Sara Beth puffs on her cigarette. She turns to Carl. "How do you and Zach know each other?"

"School," Carl says. "But we also went to camp together."

Zach says nothing.

Lily glances at Sara Beth, who is watching Zach warily, as though he may explode any minute.

"Hey, Zach?" says Carl. "Can I ask you something?"

Zach levels his gaze at him, his eyes dull, flat stones.

"Carl," Lily says.

"Promise you won't take offense," Carl says. "I'm only asking because I really want to help Lily and her mom."

Lily opens her mouth, then closes it again. She actually wants to hear the question.

Zach takes a long drag off his cigarette and exhales through his nose. "Ask away," he says.

"The finger," Carl says. "Do you think that could have been done by someone in your friend group?"

Lily's eyes widen.

"What are you talking about?" Sara Beth says.

"It wasn't someone in my *friend group*." Zach says it to the sidewalk.

"You sure about that? Because I get it. If one of my friends was involved in shit like that, I'd have waited to call the cops too."

"I just said—"

"So, like, look, if you know who did it—"

"I don't fucking know who did it."

"Zach." Sara Beth turns to him, puts a hand on his shoulder and speaks in a tone so low, Lily can barely hear it. "You should go home, sweetie. Get some rest. Mrs. Russo won't mind, I promise."

Carl tells Lily he's going to head back to the truck. "Sorry about that," he says awkwardly.

Carl turns to leave, and Lily tells him she'll be there in a second. "I have to run to the post office. I'll be back, though. Can you tell my mom I need to talk to her?"

"Of course," Sara Beth says. But Lily's eyes are on Zach. When he pulls away from Sara Beth and takes another pull off his cigarette, she notices that his hand is trembling. He's shivering. *He's traumatized. You know what that's like. Don't presume things about him, like people are presuming things about your family.*

"Hey, Zach?" Lily says.

"Yeah?"

"I hope you feel better."

"Thanks, Lily," he says. He looks up at her with something new in his eyes—something soft and sad, like an apology.

—

"I'm glad your mom is okay," Carl says, once they're both in the truck and headed for the post office.

Lily exhales hard. "Listen, Carl, I know you meant well," she says. "But . . . back there with Zach. That wasn't cool."

"I know and I'm sorry," he says. "But . . . I mean . . ."

"What?"

"Look," he says. "We're on limited time. One-two-one-two is the day after tomorrow, and you saw what the Bronze Lord said. 'By any means necessary.' I swear I don't have any beef with Zach. I feel sorry for him, honestly. But if we're going to start rooting these people out before it's too late, we have to think about who's likely to be a member. Which means we can't afford to be all woke about mental health issues."

Lily looks at him. "What are you talking about?"

Carl makes a left on Route 28, and immediately the truck skids, lights flashing on the dashboard. Lily's heart pounds. She grips her seat with both hands, her seat belt tight at her chest. *No, no, no. Not again, not again.* She shuts her eyes, that heat under the lids, that awful, powerless feeling.

"Don't worry," Carl says. "We'll be fine. My dad taught me how to do this."

Lily opens her eyes as Carl steers into the skid, his shoulders relaxed, his features smooth and calm. In control. After a second or a minute or maybe a year, the truck rights itself. Carl smiles. "Whew!"

Lily's breath exits her lungs in a whoosh. "You're a good driver," she says.

"I'm just used to this truck." He gives her a smile. It makes her feel safe.

Lily nearly tells Carl, *You're also a good person.* But she doesn't. That would be overkill. All he did was not crash the truck. It isn't as though he rescued her from a burning building. "My dad told me that too," she says. "About steering into skids."

"I wish I could have known him," Carl says.

She watches his face, the calm glow of his eyes. "Me too."

The post office is on their left. Lily's worried it might be closed already—it's Saturday, after all—but when she checks the time on her phone, she sees they still have more than half an hour. Carl pulls into the icy parking lot. He offers to go inside with Lily, but she says no, she won't be long. So he parks in a space close to the door, and waits in the truck while Lily sprints inside.

—

There are no customers in the post office. No one working here either, seemingly. It feels like one of those old science fiction movies where an entire population gets killed off, and all that's left are the empty, open buildings.

Lily rings the bell at the counter. After about a minute, a clerk emerges, an older guy with a buzz cut and dull, sleepy eyes. It's very cold in here, and his postal uniform has short sleeves, but this guy doesn't seem to mind, same way he doesn't mind the sound of the fluorescent lights, that incessant, flat hum.

Lily asks if she can send the letter to Grandpa Nate priority, and he nods. He grabs his rubber stamp, but then he glances up at her again, his eyes lingering on her face in a way that makes her uncomfortable. "Hey . . . aren't you that girl?" he says.

Her stomach drops.

"You're the girl that got in the accident?"

She tries to smile. "That's me."

He goes back to work, Lily watching his hands.

"I saw about it somewhere. Online, I think," he says. "I'm real sorry. Love your parents' bookstore."

"Thanks."

Lily finds a tattoo on his wrist—a *2* in fancy script. Her breathing catches.

He slips a label out of the drawer and affixes it to the front. "You and your mom holding up okay?"

"What do you mean?"

"Sorry, none of my business," he says. "I feel bad for you guys is all."

"We're doing okay. I mean, it's hard but . . ." Lily has been counting

his fingers, and now she finds herself staring at one of them—the ring
finger on the left hand, multiple Band-Aids wrapped around it from the
knuckle to the tip to form a thick, pink cap.

She grabs the envelope back.

"Something wrong?" He smiles. *Why is he smiling?*

"I, uh, forgot something I wanted to include with the letter," Lily
says. "I'll . . . I'll be back later." She shoves the envelope in her coat
pocket and runs outside, thinking, *I'll never be back. Never.*

TWENTY

"Her name is Claire Cassadine," Meg tells Detective Leanne Bell. "She lives in Mount Shady."

As she says it, Sara Beth slips into the store behind them, takes in the damage and more or less screams. "What is going on?" she says. "What happened to my Christmas display?"

Zach tells her he'll fill her in, and the two of them go outside, presumably so Sara Beth can smoke. Meg thinks she could use a cigarette too, but obviously, that will have to wait.

Detective Bell asks Meg why she believes Claire Cassadine was behind the break-in, and Meg tells her the whole story, from the Facebook comment through yesterday's altercation, with Grady and Charlie listening. And for her part, Bell seems to take her seriously.

"Were there any witnesses?" Bell says. "Anyone who saw her pounding on the walls, making that threat—what was it?"

"'One down, three to go,'" Meg says. "And yes, there were at least ten people in my store at the time, including my two employees, who saw this woman lose it."

"Interesting."

"Why?" Meg says.

"Because Zach Winters never mentioned this woman."

Meg blinks at her. "Oh, that's right," she says. "Zach wasn't in. He'd seen her comment on our Facebook post."

"The video of your husband."

"Yes," Meg says. "And he seemed so upset by it . . . I thought he could use a break."

Bell nods slowly. "He didn't mention the comment either."

"Probably blocked it out of his mind," Meg says. "God knows *I* tried to."

"You said she was taunting your husband in the video," the detective says. "What exactly did she say?"

Meg clears her throat. "'You will pay for her sins.'"

"Meaning . . ."

"Mine. My sins."

"And you've never met her before yesterday," Bell says.

"Not that I can remember." Meg clears her throat again. "But right after she made this video, my family was in a car accident. My husband . . . didn't make it."

"How long exactly?"

"A couple of days at most."

Bell nods slowly, a look crossing her face—not so much sympathy as pity.

"That must have been difficult for you, ma'am." Charlie looks at Bell. "Everybody in town knows about the car crash," he says. "Happened on the thruway. The Russos were taking their daughter to college."

Grady says nothing.

Meg pulls her coat closer, the chill in the room pushing at her, biting her skin. She needs to have that window fixed. She needs this place to be warm again. "It was difficult for me," Meg says, answering Charlie's question. The image floods her mind, Justin lying face down on the grass, windshield shards all around him. The blood on his arms, the back of his striped shirt, in his beautiful, thick hair. There had been so much blood, yet at the time, she hadn't registered it. All she could see was the wedding ring on his finger and the strange stillness of his body. A tear streams down Meg's cheek. She swats it away.

"Is the comment still up?" Bell says.

Meg shakes her head. "I deleted it and blocked her."

"Have you had any experiences like this before?" Bell says. "Other customers who've acted out or threatened you?"

"Not like that," Meg says. "We've had rude customers but not . . ."

Grady is shaking his big goldfish head.

Meg looks at him.

"Officer Grady?" Bell says.

"As I was telling Ms. Russo earlier, it could be about that demon book." It's exhausting, not being able to tell this guy off. "People get emotional about that kind of thing."

"Demon book?" Bell says.

"*Demon Copperhead* by Barbara Kingsolver," Meg says. "It's our book club selection."

Bell rolls her eyes, which Meg is grateful for. She pulls her phone out of her purse and records her voice. "Claire Cassadine," she says. Then she spells out the name. "Mount Shady."

"Are you going to talk to her?" Meg says.

Bell gives her a slight nod.

Meg exhales. "Thank you."

"Have you checked the Facebook page since this morning?"

Meg says she hasn't, but she wouldn't expect there'd be any more comments. "I blocked her yesterday," she explains.

"Let's have another look," Bell says. "She could have created a new profile and posted something else."

Meg nods, the cold air crawling under her collar, snaking down her back. "I have to post a new announcement anyway," she says, "about the store being closed for repairs."

—

The back office is much warmer than the rest of the store, especially once Meg closes the door. Because she doesn't want to forget, Meg asks Grady for his brother-in-law's number. As annoying as she finds the guy, she also knows how hard it is to find a contractor on short notice, especially around the holidays. And she wants the window fixed. She wants Sara Beth's Christmas display back up and the store open and filled with friendly customers, and Claire Cassadine, all nine fingers of her, in jail or in treatment somewhere very far away. She wants things back to normal—as normal as they can be. And step one in that process is fixing the window.

Grady texts the information to Meg's phone. She glances at the name: *Willis Baus.* It looks familiar, but she's not sure why. "He's afford-able, honest and he does great work," Grady says. Meg thinks Grady probably gets a finder's fee from his brother-in-law, but she doesn't care.

Meg sits down at her desk, Detective Bell and the two officers stand-ing behind her. She calls up the store's Facebook page, her post about the reopening up top. She scrolls down. There are three new comments on it. One from Cora from book club: *Saw the broken window. Everything okay?* One from Patty: *Anything we can do to help?* And one from someone named Jeannette, with a French bulldog for a profile pic. Meg inhales sharply. "That's Claire Cassadine's friend," she says, tapping the screen.

"What does that mean?" Detective Bell says, reading the comment.

"I don't know," Meg says. "But she posted something similar on Claire's page."

At Bell's request, Meg takes a screenshot of the comment and emails it to her. She hands her a business card and leaves, along with Grady and Peele, assuring Meg that she'll be in touch once they find anything out.

After they've gone, Meg sits at her desk for a few moments, reading Jeannette's comment again and again, as though it were a song lyric or a line of poetry with a meaning she can't quite grasp.

121222. Get ready.

TWENTY-ONE

The next town over from Elizabethville is Mount Shady, and when she gets back in the truck, Lily asks Carl if he can take her to that post office instead.

"Sure," he says. "How come you didn't mail it from our post office, though?"

"Nobody was in there. I rang the bell a bunch of times." Lily doesn't want to lie to Carl—but at this point, she feels as though she has to. She doesn't want him storming into the post office and firing questions at that clerk like he did with Zach. Not before she's had a chance to send the letter to Grandpa Nate and tell her mom what's going on.

"That's annoying," Carl says. "Isn't the whole thing with postal workers that they're supposed to go to work even if the weather's bad?"

Lily shrugs. "Maybe he was on break or something."

"Yeah. Maybe."

Carl starts up the car. They drive in silence for a while, Lily thinking about the postal clerk. His bandaged finger. His *2* tattoo. Two details about a complete stranger that she never would have noticed a few hours ago. And the way he'd recognized her. Her family . . . *You and your mom holding up okay?*

Lily shudders. *You and your mom . . .*

Carl asks Lily if she wants to listen to music, and it's almost as if he's read her mind. She needs something to drown out these thoughts.

"Sure," Lily says.

There's no Bluetooth in Carl's truck, and no Sirius on its ancient radio. He turns it on and finds the station with the strongest signal, the classic rock station. Her dad used to listen to it all the time. Pearl Jam is playing, and in her mind, she's five years old again and strapped into her car seat with her dad behind the wheel, loudly singing along with Eddie Vedder, making her laugh.

A tear slips down Lily's cheek. She turns toward the window, her forehead pressed against the cool glass.

"You okay?" Carl says.

"I miss him." She doesn't say any more than that, and Carl doesn't ask her to. He puts a hand on Lily's shoulder, just long enough for her to feel the weight of it, the warmth. Then he goes back to driving, his eyes on the windshield, on the heavy, falling snow.

—

The snow starts to let up as they near Mount Shady. The classic rock station is getting crackly, and so Carl messes with the dial for a while—football commentary, news, a pop song Lily used to find annoying when she was twelve. When he gets to the overemotional preacher having a breakdown about the end times, he gives up. "This radio sucks," he says. Lily feels bad about asking him to drive all this distance in the snow just to mail a letter and tells him so.

"It's not just any letter," he says.

Lily nods, remembering Carl's urgency after questioning Zach. *We're on limited time,* he'd explained. Which was true. But he'd also mentioned feeling sorry for Zach, and mental health issues, and that was where he'd lost her . . .

"Carl?"

"Yeah?"

"You asked Zach if someone in his friend group left the finger in my mom's store."

"I'm sorry about that," he says quietly. "I mean, thinking about it now, it probably was a little harsh."

"No," Lily says. "I was just wondering what you meant. What friend group?"

Carl exhales hard. "I was talking about the other people," he says. "You know . . . from when he was in the hospital."

"You mean, when he got encephalitis?"

"Oh. Shit. You don't know . . ."

"What?"

"Okay," he says. "Okay." Carl is quiet for a few moments, his grip tight on the steering wheel, a pained look on his face, as though he's trying to pull together his thoughts but they aren't cooperating. "What's it called when your family puts you in a mental hospital against your will? You know what I'm talking about. It happened to Kanye."

She stares at him. *"What?"*

"A 5150. That's it."

"Zach was in a mental hospital?"

He nods.

"Why?"

"He had a total breakdown at summer camp. Thought one of the counselors was possessed by the devil and tried to stab him."

"What?"

"I mean, it was a Swiss Army knife. It's not like we had serious weapons at camp, and the counselor didn't get hurt. But still, you know . . . Basically, Zach lost his shit."

"Who told you this?"

"I was there."

"You were *there*? You saw it?"

The snow has stopped completely now. Carl speeds up, the engine revving. Lily sees a billboard announcing a new restaurant in Mount Shady called Betty's. *Just one mile to good eatin'!* Just after the billboard is the town's exit. Carl takes it, and then makes a left, and once he's nearing Main Street, where the post office is, he speaks.

"No, I didn't actually see it," he says. "But I was at camp at the same time. And kids were talking about it. And then all of a sudden, he left camp. It was like he just . . . disappeared."

Lily remembers Zach's face when Carl mentioned they'd been at camp together. The downcast eyes. The shame.

"In morning meeting, the camp director said he'd gone home sick," Carl says. "And really, when you think about it, it wasn't like he was lying when he said that. He *was* sick. He *did* go to a hospital. By the end of the summer, most of us who were there knew about it, but we were told to keep quiet. And his parents definitely talked to Principal Bailey, because he told everybody the same thing. That he'd been hospitalized for encephalitis."

She stares at him. "Principal Bailey made an announcement about it over the PA."

"I know."

"Everybody signed a big card for him," she says. "Bailey's secretary had it at her desk."

"I know," he says again.

Lily stares out the window at Main Street. Snow-caked and empty. She's been to Mount Shady before. It makes Elizabethville look as big as New York City. She wonders if anybody here is a Year of Twos believer, because she feels watched, hunted. Eyes aimed at her from within the darkened buildings.

"Anyway, that's why I said what I did to Zach," Carl is saying. "He found the finger. He was the first to see all that blood. Sara Beth told us about that and I thought . . . not that he did it himself, but that people he knows might have done it. People from the mental institution who believe all that stuff about your family."

Lily nods. "He said something weird to me when we were little kids," she says. "About my family going to hell."

"Really?"

"Yeah, I just remembered it yesterday."

He turns to her. "The thing is, he didn't call the cops, Lily."

She looks at him.

"Zach found that finger. He saw that blood, that . . . pyramid thing made from books. And he called your mom. He waited for her to show up. It was like he wanted her to see it."

Lily swallows hard. It makes sense. "You shouldn't have said that to Zach, Carl."

"What?"

"About his friend group."

"Why?"

"Because," Lily says, "if he's with the Nine-and-Tens, he'll know you've found them out. And that you're on our side. He'll tell them. Or post about it. You'll become a target too."

Carl pulls up to the curb. Lily sees the post office to her right, next to Clark's Drugs, but she doesn't get out. She just looks at him.

"I don't care about that." He gives her a smile. "Obviously."

"Carl."

"I mean it," he says. "We just need to figure out what we're going to do. We've got a day and a half. And your mom doesn't even know yet."

"But you don't have to—"

"Mail your letter, Lily," he says. "Please."

Lily gets out of the truck and walks into the post office, that feeling stronger now that she's out in the open, that sense of eyes all over her, of awful, crawling stares.

—

This post office is empty too, save for the clerk behind the counter. She's an older woman, curt and kind of snippy, which Lily finds weirdly comforting. She sends the letter to Grandpa priority express mail, and the clerk assures her in a flat voice that it will get there tomorrow, on Sunday. She asks Lily nothing about herself, except whether she wants to pay with cash or a credit card. Lily pays in cash, the clerk barely looking at her as she takes it.

When Lily leaves, though, she feels it again—the watching. Her skin prickles from it, her heart starts to race. *Fight or flight,* she guesses. The same way a deer must feel when it hears the sound of a bow tensing.

On impulse, Lily spins around to her right. And she sees her immediately, standing in the glass doorway of Clark's Drugs. She has frizzy gray hair and wears one of those ugly Christmas sweaters under an employee's smock. She's staring at Lily through the glass. Lily stares back, but the woman doesn't move. Doesn't smile. Doesn't wave. She reaches her hand into the pocket of her smock and pulls something out. A phone. Lily doesn't wait to see what she's going to do with it. She runs for the truck and throws the door open, bending in two as she slips inside and closes it, curling into herself.

"What's wrong?" Carl says. "You're shaking."

Lily makes sure the door is locked. She puts her back to the passenger's side window and covers her face with her hands and shuts her eyes tight. "Just go," she tells him. "Please."

Carl pulls away from the curb. He drives fast, slowing down only when they pass a police car that's going in the opposite direction. "We'll talk to your mom," he says. "We'll come up with a plan. Don't worry."

Lily says nothing. She keeps her head down, her hands covering her face. She stays that way for most of the ride home.

TWENTY-TWO

"They can both go to hell," Sara Beth says. She's talking about Claire Cassadine and her friend Jeannette. "Nothing better to do than harass people."

"I don't know that it's technically harassment on Jeannette's part," Meg says. "It's not like there were direct insults or threats in her comment. I don't even know what it means, do you?"

Sara Beth pauses for a moment. "Sometimes a comment can be offensive for its timing."

"That's true, I guess."

They're at the front of the store, reshelving the books that the cops left in piles on the floor, while waiting for Grady's contractor brother-in-law to arrive and measure the window.

"I told you I spoke to Lily outside, right?" Sara Beth says as she drags the step stool over to the set of shelves she's working on.

Meg nods. She never returned Lily's call from a couple of hours ago, and now, a part of her feels silly punishing her daughter for not going to a therapist whom Meg has been avoiding herself. Yes, Lily lied to her. And yes, that hurt. But kids lie to their parents. It happens. And as it turns out, there are far worse violations . . .

"What did Lily say?"

"She had a quick errand to run but wanted me to tell you she'd be back," Sara Beth says. "If I'm going to be entirely honest, I was more focused on Zach."

"Yeah? Why?"

She puts a few more books on the shelf. "He was acting strange. Hostile. I'm glad he went home." Sara Beth shelves the last book she's been holding, then gets off the step stool and grabs another armload from the floor. "He needs rest."

Meg watches her, an image in her mind—Zach hiding in the corner of the store, silently staring at his wiggling fingers. She hears herself say, "He was giving me the creeps." Immediately, she feels bad about it.

"Me too," Sara Beth says. But still, Meg's disappointed in herself, judging this poor kid—who spent a whole year out of school with a brain disease—over the way he reacted to yet another traumatic experience.

"At any rate, Lily wanted me to tell you that she needs to talk to you," Sara Beth says.

"Did she say what about?"

Sara Beth shakes her head and goes back to the shelves. "We'll find out, I guess."

Meg notices a spray of dried blood on the floor, right next to her shoes. She realizes she's standing in the exact spot where the pyramid used to be. She takes a few steps back, breathing deeply until she feels like herself again. "I'm not looking forward to telling Lily about this," Meg says.

"Actually, she knows what happened," Sara Beth says. "The break-in, the finger . . . She says she saw a picture of it."

Meg's eyes widen. *She waits till now to tell me that?* "What? Where?"

"Facebook."

"But . . . the cops were here. They bagged up everything. Who would have had a chance to post a picture on Facebook? And who would want to?"

Sara Beth turns from the shelf and peers at her for a long while. "Both very good questions," she says.

Even though she doesn't want to, Meg finds herself thinking of Zach again.

—

Willis Baus shows up within half an hour—just like he promised over the phone. He seems like a good contractor and, from what she can tell, a decent person.

He measures the window and gives Meg an estimate, which winds up being quite reasonable. He even resets the broken bookshelf for free, treating the wood with Gorilla Glue and using a hammer from his tool chest to tap the freed nails back into the plaster. "It won't take long to get the new glass," he says when he's done. "If everything goes the way I think it will, I should have it fixed by tomorrow at the latest."

"Best news I've heard all day," Meg says. "Granted, that's not saying much."

Baus gives her a wince of a smile. "I hear you." He's the physical opposite of his brother-in-law Grady, wiry and energetic, more minnow than fantail. He walks with a limp and wears a thick orthopedic shoe, but if he and Grady were in a race—marathon or sprint, it doesn't matter—her money would be on Baus. "You mind if I say something personal, Mrs. Russo?"

Meg steadies herself. Sara Beth is back in the office, writing up the "Closed for Repairs" Facebook post, and, for a brief moment, she considers calling her out here for support. "Sure," she says.

"My wife and I love your store," Baus says. "We've both come to book club quite a few times, and I can't begin to tell you how sorry we are about your husband. He was . . . He was a very special guy."

Meg swallows hard. Just yesterday, she told Sara Beth she was getting tired of everyone's condolences, but that feels like such a long time ago—when she'd never heard the name Claire Cassadine and she didn't feel under attack, only sad and adrift.

Back then, Meg honestly believed that no one hated her or her family. Now, she has this crazy woman to contend with, and, quite possibly, her friend Jeannette. "Thank you," she says. "That means a lot."

A silence passes between them. Meg feels the heat of fresh tears on her face.

Baus reaches in his pocket and pulls out a packet of Kleenex, which he hands to Meg.

"It's okay," he says as Meg dabs at her eyes. "I've been there too. I—"

He's interrupted by a scream. Sara Beth's scream. Meg rushes to the back of the store and into the office to her sitting at the desk, her hands frozen on the keyboard. "What's wrong?" Meg says. "What happened?"

Sara Beth turns, her eyes huge and unblinking. "I just refreshed the screen," she says.

—

There are 124 comments on Meg's post about the store reopening, all from different accounts. Names she's never heard. Profile pictures she's never seen. But every comment is the same: *121222*.

"What does this mean?" Sara Beth says. "Who are all these people?"

"I don't know," Meg says quietly. "I'm thinking they may all be Claire."

Baus excuses himself quickly, telling Meg he'll be back to fix the window. "Thanks again, Willis." Meg says it without looking at him. Who could blame him for wanting to leave?

She grabs her purse from the back of the desk chair, where Sara Beth still sits, frozen. Goes into the pockets and fishes out Leanne Bell's business card. Asks Sara Beth if she can get up for a second, screengrabs all the comments and emails them to Detective Bell. It makes her feel good, as though she's taking action. Fighting back. *You can't bully me, Claire.*

Meg is about to call Bell and give her a heads-up about the email, but the detective calls her first. She shows Sara Beth her name on her screen.

"Now, that is impressive," Sara Beth says.

Meg answers her phone. "You got it?"

"Pardon?" Bell asks.

"The screengrab," she says. "All the new comments on the Facebook post. I just emailed it."

Bell exhales. "No, Ms. Russo. I didn't get it."

"Oh, well, you'll see," she says. "It's pretty scary, but you can see what this woman is capable of."

Bell is quiet for several seconds. Meg can hear voices in the background. The roar of an engine. She realizes she's probably on speakerphone or Bluetooth, her voice emanating throughout a car.

"Hello?" Meg says.

"I'm here, Ms. Russo," she says. "I was calling to let you know that Officers Peele, Grady and I spoke to Claire Cassadine."

"And?" Meg says. "Was she missing a finger?"

"No," Bell says. "She also has an alibi for last night."

"She does?"

"Ms. Cassadine works at Clark's Drugs in Mount Shady, and she was there, with a couple of coworkers, doing inventory till midnight. Her boss backed her up on this. Plus, he says he gave her a ride home. She has glaucoma and can't drive in the dark."

"Did she . . . did she give you any other leads?"

"No, ma'am," she says. "I'm heading back upstate. Detectives Peele and Grady will let you know about the forensics results. If you think of anyone else who might have done this, don't hesitate to let them know."

It isn't lost on her. *Them* rather than *me*. "Claire has this friend, Jeannette," Meg starts to say. But Bell has already hung up.

Meg puts the phone into her back pocket, aware that Sara Beth is watching her, and she feels a little dizzy—the way you do when you come off an amusement park ride, and everything is off-kilter and strange and makes you sick.

"Well," Sara Beth says. "What happened?"

"It wasn't her," she says.

"What?"

"Claire Cassadine has an alibi for last night."

Sara Beth stares at Meg for a long time. "Well, who did it, then?" she says. "Jeannette? One of those . . . those commenters?"

"Detective Bell doesn't know," Meg says. "She says they're looking into it."

Outside the store, she hears the squeal of tires. Sara Beth turns toward the sound, and so does Meg. *Was that Claire? Jeannette?* At this point everything feels intentional, even the sound of a car trying to navigate the snow, the whole world the way her father sees it, full of malice, directed her way. *How can he live like this? How can I?*

"Who else would have done that disgusting thing?" Sara Beth says. "I'm trying to think why . . ."

"You know what?" Meg says. "Maybe there is no *why.*"

Sara Beth looks at her.

"Maybe it was a deranged stranger, someone on drugs, and the Secret Garden was the first store they saw. Maybe those numbers in the comments are the result of some computer virus, and maybe lots of Facebook pages are getting them, and maybe we just need to focus on getting the window fixed and the store opened and living our lives."

"Do you believe that?" Sara Beth says.

"I'm going to try to," she says. "And unless we get some answers soon, which doesn't seem likely, I suggest you do too."

Sara Beth's face breaks into a smile. "You know who you sound like?"

Meg shakes her head.

"Your mom," she says. "You sound just like your mom."

And Meg finds herself smiling too, Mom's spirit in the room with them, alive in her. Mom, who worked so hard to protect Dad from his own crippling fears and was actually able to do it, for a time. "Let's just move on," Meg says.

"Agreed," Sara Beth says, just as Meg's phone vibrates in her back pocket—a short, sharp blast, like an electric shock. She pulls it out and looks at the screen.

It's a text from Lily: Please come home. It is very important.

—

Meg texts Lily that she'll be right there, and leaves Sara Beth at the store to wait for Willis Baus. As she heads out to her car, she keeps thinking about Lily's text. The word *please*. The complete, punctuated sentences. It doesn't sound like her daughter, and she finds herself spiraling again, imagining a kidnapper with a gun to Lily's head, a knife to her fingers. Claire Cassadine, on the loose. Angrier than ever after being questioned by the cops. Or worse yet, her friend Jeannette, with the French bulldog profile pic. Jeannette, who is not necessarily named Jeannette and could be anyone, anywhere, male or female. *Anyone can create a Facebook account.*

Once she's got the car started, she taps Lily's number into her phone. "I'm sorry I didn't call you back this morning," Meg says.

"Mom," Lily says. "Are you on your way?"

Meg lets out a gust of breath. It's good to hear Lily's voice. *It's really you. You're alive.* "Yes," she says.

"Okay. See you soon."

"Is everything all right?"

Lily says, "I don't feel right talking on the phone about this."

"Lily?"

"I'll explain everything once you get here, Mom. Please."

—

There's a truck in Meg's driveway, a beat-up-looking old rust-orange pickup with peeling paint and, once she gets closer to it, suspicious-looking equipment in the bed—a few roles of duct tape, a tarp, a toolbox. A coiled-up length of rope. Either a contractor or a killer, and Meg isn't having any work done on the house.

Meg remembers Lily over the phone, the tremor in her voice as she spoke. *I'll explain everything once you get here . . .*

"No . . ." The word floats out of her mouth. She doesn't know what type of vehicle Claire Cassadine drives, or what the mysterious Jeannette might drive or what had made Lily say, *I don't feel right talking on the phone about this.*

She remembers the gun. *I have a gun. I know how to use it.* She hurries back to her car and pops the trunk, her eyes finding the polymer case, her father's instructions running through her head. *Keep your fingers behind the grip as you release the slide . . .*

"Mom?"

Meg whirls around. Lily's standing just outside the front door, a tall blond boy next to her.

Meg's shoulders drop. Lily doesn't seem afraid of him.

"What are you doing?" Lily says.

"Just . . . nothing." She locks the trunk.

Lily frowns.

Meg looks at the boy. He's wearing a flannel shirt and jeans, and he looks like he could have stepped out of one of those old Abercrombie & Fitch ads. Aside from that, though, his face is familiar. The peachy skin. The dimples. He's been at her house before, one of the boys who used to play music with Lily. "You must be Carl," she says.

He gives her a bright smile. He seems flattered. "Nice to meet you, Mrs. Russo."

Lily looks mortified, which Meg finds strangely comforting. *Some things never change, no matter what . . .* But there's no eye roll. No *Mom, please . . .* And Lily's blush fades in an instant.

"Come on inside, Mom," she says, that tremor returning to her voice. "Carl and I need to show you something."

TWENTY-THREE

As is usually the case with Mom, she insists on talking first. "Is this about Claire Cassadine?" She says it once they're in the house, before she even takes her coat off, launching into a story that begins with a five-second video of Dad looking angry and twists into most of what Lily knows already—only it's about one woman. One weirdo yelling Nine-and-Tens slogans in the bookstore. *Big fat fucking deal.*

Throughout the monologue, Carl listens and nods with an infuriating patience, while Lily keeps trying to interrupt Mom, to tell her that Claire Cassadine—whoever she is—is not that important, as she's one of many. *Many.* But then something Mom says makes her stop, and listen. "The cops say that it can't be Claire who left the finger," Mom says, "because she was working past midnight at Clark's Drugs last night, doing inventory—"

"Clark's Drugs?" says Lily.

Mom frowns at her. "Yes?"

"In Mount Shady?"

"Yes."

"What does she look like?"

"Wild, frizzy gray hair, pale blue eyes. When she came in, she was wearing one of those ugly Christmas sweaters . . . "

Lily stares at her, well aware of the color draining from her own face. *The smock over the Christmas sweater. Those pale eyes, cutting through the glass door.*

"What's wrong?" Carl says.

"I saw her," says Lily. "I was leaving the post office. She tried to take a picture of me with her phone."

"You saw Claire Cassadine?" Mom says.

"The post office is right next to Clark's Drugs. I came out and . . . I saw her watching me."

"You didn't tell me that," Carl says.

"I was too scared," Lily says. "I just wanted it all to go away."

Mom is staring at them both. "What are you talking about?"

Lily hears herself say it: "They're everywhere." The words hang in the air. A solid, separate presence in the room.

"Who's everywhere?" Mom says. She sounds frightened. And she doesn't even know.

Lily has already set up the laptop on the coffee table, the latest post on 7Park open on the screen. It's a video that Carl and Lily have just watched. *Just show her. Tell her. The sooner the better.*

"Show her, Lily," Carl says.

Lily asks her mom to sit on the couch. She turns the laptop toward her and tells her to watch.

"Who's Sybil?" Mom says, reading the subject line.

"Just watch, Mom."

Lily clicks on the video. A woman steps off the curb in front of the Secret Garden. She wears a heavy red coat. Her face is a blur, but in a few seconds, it comes into focus. It's Mom—an unhinged version of her, spittle flying from her mouth, her eyes wild. A knife gleams in her hand. *"Stop watching me!"* she shrieks. *"I'll slit your throat and feed you to the demon!"*

Mom's jaw drops open. "What . . . what is this? Who did this?"

"The board is anonymous," Carl says.

Lily gives him flat eyes. She knows he's trying to be helpful, but could he be any more beside the point?

"That isn't me," Mom is saying now. "I mean, it is but . . . There was . . . A man was outside the hardware store taking my picture and I told him to stop. I said, 'Stop watching me.' But I didn't say that second part. I . . . I didn't have a knife. My face . . . I didn't . . . That isn't me."

"It doesn't matter, Mom." Lily says it as calmly as she can, as though an even vocal tone could soothe the terror her mother must be feeling. "They have their own reality."

"Who?" Mom says. Her voice quavers. *She's going to lose it,* Lily thinks. And who could blame her? *"Who are they?"* Mom practically screams it.

Lily puts her arm around her mother. She's shivering. *Shock.* She pulls Mom closer, trying to keep her warm. Carl runs to the kitchen, returning moments later with a glass of water. Mom takes it. She brings it to her lips with two trembling hands, and says it again, calmer now, once she's drained the glass. "Who are they?"

Lily takes a breath. "It's a group, Mom," she says quietly. "An online group. They're called the Nine-and-Tens. And they hate us."

—

Once Mom is more relaxed, Lily tells her everything. She explains it all chronologically, starting with Grandpa's call this morning and the comments Lily saw on Carl's YouTube post. (*What did the comments say?* Mom says, her voice stretched thin to the point of breaking, and when Lily tells her about the numbers, she goes strangely silent.) Carl explains how he quickly took the video down, and then Lily shows Mom the Wikipedia entry about 7Park, which she reads quickly, looking up at Lily when she's done.

"The YearofTwos is the image board, and it's where they meet," Lily says. "They spread ideas and fake videos and rumors and bizarre theories—all about us."

"Why us?"

"I don't know," Lily says. "They've made up this whole narrative, and some of it is about Grandpa's music, and some of it is about your book."

"My book . . ."

Lily tells her about the Bronze Lord. Then she scrolls back to his very first post and gives the laptop to Mom, who reads it in absolute silence.

Mom scrolls through some of the comments, a sentence escaping her lips. "My father's been right all along." She says it like she's alone in the room.

"About what, Mrs. Russo?" Carl says.

"The wolves," Mom says, her eyes focused on Lily. "He's right about the wolves."

—

"The Year of Twos," Mom says. "What does that mean?"

"Well, it's from your book," Carl says.

Lily sighs. "She knows that, Carl," she says. Then she looks at Mom. "It's also this year. 2022. They all believe that you, like . . . foretold this year in your book. COVID, all the weather stuff . . . They think it's the end of the world, and you predicted it."

"Along with your dad," Carl says. "He cast the spells to make it all come true, and the people reading the book contracted the curse and spread it . . ."

"That's *crazy*. I was a kid. I was making things up."

"Reality didn't do you any favors, though," Carl says.

Lily and her mom look at him.

"I mean . . . so much of the stuff you wrote did wind up coming true." He clears his throat. "Sorry."

"Carl," Lily says sharply. "Do you have any idea how many books have plagues in them?"

"Yeah, but . . . never mind."

Mom's gaze travels between the two of them, her eyes huge and helpless and strangely ashamed. "I feel like I should read these posts," she says. "As many as I can. On my own."

Lily nods. "Can I get you something? More water? Food? I could make sandwiches . . ."

"That sounds good, honey," Mom says, though Lily is relatively sure it's just to shoo her and Carl out of the room.

As they head for the kitchen, Lily hears her mother whispering something, and she turns and looks at her: Mom trying to make sense of what she's reading, her eyes catching the glow of the screen. "'One and two and one and two and two and two . . .'"

—

"What if we just repent?" Lily says.

She and Carl are at the kitchen counter, Carl spreading vegan mayonnaise on pieces of bread, then stacking them with Daiya cheese as Lily slices a tomato.

"What do you mean?" Carl says.

"You know," Lily says. "They keep saying that we have to repent or die by the twelfth, right? So what if we post a video on YearofTwos of me and my mom. Maybe my grandpa too. We apologize to everyone for the curse. We say we repent, we've found the right path. Whatever bullshit they want us to say. All is forgiven. We move on."

Lily lays the tomato slices on top of the cheese. She waits for Carl to answer. He doesn't say anything for a long time.

"Carl?"

He clears his throat. "You know that isn't what they mean by repent, right?"

Carl adds the final slices of bread to the sandwiches and cuts them all in half.

Lily watches him. "What do they mean, then?" she says.

"You didn't see the post? The Bronze Lord's definition?"

She shakes her head. "No. What is it?"

Carl winces. "You should read it yourself, Lily."

"Come on. You can tell me."

Carl puts one of the sandwiches on a plate and hands it to Lily. "You want to bring that to your mom? I don't know if she wants a soda or juice or anything, but—"

"Carl," Lily says. "What is the Bronze Lord's definition?"

Carl has put the other two sandwiches on plates, and for a long time, he just stands there with them, one in each hand. He stares Lily in the eyes. Carl's eyes are a deep green and right now they remind Lily of a pond after a storm, like something has been stirred up within them. "I'm sorry, Lily," he says. "I don't feel comfortable telling you."

Lily nods slowly.

"Just read it on the laptop when your mom is done," he says. "You can do a search for 'Bronze Lord' and 'repent.' It will turn up."

"Okay," she says quietly, hopelessly. "Maybe my mom will think of something we can do."

"Yeah," Carl says.

She heads out of the kitchen, Carl taking his plate and following her. "I made sandwiches, Mom!" she calls out and they move toward the living room. "I can get you something to drink too if you . . ."

She looks around. The living room is empty.

"Where did she go?" Carl says.

"*Mom?*"

"Mrs. Russo?"

Lily calls out her name two more times before she and Carl see the piece of notebook paper next to the computer:

Stay put! Be back soon. I have an idea.

For the curse to be lifted and the world to be saved by 121222, the demons must either repent—or die violently on film at the hands of the true believers.

We all know this.

But there seems to be some confusion as to what "repenting" means.

Here is what it means:

The demon offspring must kill the parent.

WHY: Although this family has ALL achieved demon status, the dark power gets weaker with each generation.

(Big Daddy > Sybil > Spawn)

If the world is to be saved, the weaker demon must lift the sword and drive it through the heart of the stronger.

Clear enough for you?

—the Bronze Lord
WAW, WAA, WWT

TWENTY-FOUR

Dad is right, Meg thinks. He's always been right. The world really is out to get him and his family. It's been going on for years. Decades. They were able to escape to Elizabethville once he sacrificed his music career for their safety, but then Meg published *The Prophesy* and it all started up again, this witch hunt—a literal *witch hunt*—worse than before and with added material.

Why did I have to write that book?

Lily and Carl go into the kitchen to make sandwiches, leaving Meg alone with TheYearofTwos, this new and inescapable reality. But it isn't new, not truly. The only thing that's new is her awareness of it, which may be too late. *December 12, 2022.*

"One and two and one and two and two and two." She says it again, Dad's count-in to "Pearly Gates," as though saying the words aloud will rob them of their ridiculous power. *What is wrong with these people?* She reads post after post, the slurs hurled at Meg, Justin, Nathan, even Lily. A link to an article in the *Elizabethville Courier* about the accident, followed by a rush of gleeful comments: *GREAT NEWS; Finally!; Too bad it couldn't have been all of them; One down, three to go!!!!!* Meg pauses on that last comment, remembering what her father said about not a single one of them having an original thought.

She continues scrolling, her gut clenching up. The pictures of her family, snapped when she believed they were alone. The lies about them: Meg predicting and causing COVID, her father's curses, Satanic rituals conducted within a hidden room behind the Secret Garden's children's section, sacrifices of animals and babies to ensure the plague would come to pass . . .

Meg recalls Claire Cassadine removing books and pounding on the wall, trying to find this imaginary room.

Meg watches a doctored video of herself, her head atop some other woman's body—a taller woman in a black hooded robe, this demonic alter-Meg standing in front of lit torches, blood smeared across her opened mouth, dripping down her chin, her eyes red and glowing. Bleeding words float across the screen: *SHE'LL KILL US ALL!*

Meg stops the video, her breathing shallow, ineffective. She presses play on what another poster claims is found footage of her father from the seventies, but she's only able to make it through a few seconds.

Dear God . . .

She goes back to the posts by the Bronze Lord, the originator of all of this, too cowardly to reveal his real name. *The Bronze Lord.* How horribly ironic. The character Meg imagined, the villain of her book—creating bad fiction about *her.*

Who is he? Who are all of these people, chopping off their own fingers and toes? Urging each other to kill Meg and her family before the world comes to an end, *unless they repent in the preordained way . . .* The more she reads, the more suffocated Meg feels, their sickness worming into her mind.

"What the fuck is wrong with you?" she whispers to the screen.

From outside the house, she thinks she can hear the school bus passing, the way it always does at this time of day. She listens for the *pffft* of air brakes, the cautionary beep as the stop signs unfold and the doors open, kids rushing out like prison escapees. She hears nothing, though. It takes her a few moments to remember that it's a Saturday. No school bus.

But still she thinks about it. How she's been keeping time by those air brakes for years and years. Waiting for Lily to come home. And so were they. *So were they.*

One of the Nine-and-Tens posted a picture of Lily from when she was around fourteen. It had been snapped from outside the school bus window with a telephoto lens, Lily leaning her head against the glass, lost in thought, believing no one was watching her. Believing she was safe. And beneath the photo, the anonymous poster had written: *Too weak to hold the sword.*

—

Meg can hear Lily and Carl's muffled voices emanating from the kitchen, the clatter of plates. They are talking very quietly. Meg can't make out any words. She's up to one of the most recent posts, a picture taken in her store: the severed finger atop the pile of children's books. This must have been what Lily was talking about when she told Sara Beth she saw the picture online. Meg rereads the caption. *Had me some FUN last night!*

It was posted less than two hours ago, and it's already racked up 145 up-votes. And so many comments . . .

Welcome to the LIVING!

You've saved yourself from their CURSE. Any pain you felt is worth it, brother (or sister)!

Wish I could see Sybil's face when she checks out that display!

I hope she gets scared to death. Literally.

She has damn good reason to be scared LOL

WE WILL TRIUMPH

Fuck her and her disgusting family! Now they know who their dealing with.

Did you find the secret room? Were you able to save any children?

OP here. Found the room but it was empty! SAW THE ALTAR. IT WAS
CAKED IN DRIED BLOOD!

"Liar!" Meg hisses the word, as though the anonymous poster is
standing in front of her.

Meg imagines all of them, these cultists, these zombies. She imagines an army of them with their faces covered, their bodies covered,
every distinguishable part of them hidden from view . . . except for their
disfigured hands and feet.

Their disfigured hands and feet.

In Meg's mind, her father tells her yet again to trust her instincts,
and it's a lit fuse, snaking backward through this awful day, through
all of these awful months, to three days before the accident, talking to
Thom Halloway at Halloway's Garage, making conversation while he
filled out the paperwork, moving on from Liz Reese and the stunning
Clarabelle to Meg's own life, her only daughter leaving home in just
three short days. *We're going to hit the road just after sunrise,* she said. *It's a
really long drive from Elizabethville, and that way, we can take our time. See
some sights. I love road trips, don't you?* Meg, nattering on like a complete
ass, revealing the date and time of their trip, their starting place as well
as their destination. Thom Halloway, filling out the paperwork, Meg
trying not to stare at Thom's left hand. The missing ring finger.

Nature gave you instincts for a reason.

Meg picks up her phone and calls Liz, who answers fast. "Hey,
sweetie," she says. "I was just thinking about you. I saw the broken window. You okay?"

"I'm fine," Meg says.

"Who was it, teenagers?" Liz says. "I fuckin' hate teenagers. So
bored and entitled. No offense to your lovely daughter."

"None taken."

"Come on in later," Liz says. "I'll set you up with some apple pie. We can talk more . . ."

Meg can hear the sizzle of a grill, the hum of customers in the background. Liz does her own cooking with minimal assistance, so Meg knows enough to keep it short. "Sure, Liz," she says. "Can I just ask you a quick question?"

"Of course," Liz says.

"How well do you know Thom Halloway?"

There's a short pause, Liz shouting *"Order up!"* before she gets back to the phone. "The mechanic?" she says.

"Yes."

"You mean . . . personally?"

"Yes."

"Not much, to be honest," she says. "All we talk about is Clarabelle. He knows *her* like the back of his hand."

Which hand? Meg nearly says it aloud.

"What's that, honey?"

Meg realizes she *did* say it.

"Oh, nothing," Meg says. "I'll stop by later. Looking forward to that pie!"

Liz tosses off a distracted goodbye. Meg ends the call. She needs to pull herself together. Figure things out, find out how much of who they are is talk and ritual and how much is . . . *My God, is Dad right about what happened to Justin?*

She grabs a piece of paper out of her purse and scribbles a quick note to Lily and Carl. *Stay put! Be back soon. I have an idea.* She can't be more specific than that until she knows for sure. And even then, even if it is true . . . How would she tell Lily?

Meg puts on her coat, grabs her phone and her bag and hurries out to her car.

—

Outside at his compound while teaching Meg how to shoot, Dad had said, *You need to trust your instincts more.* He'd said it not in regard to Meg's aim or handling of the gun, but when, after a lot of needling, she admitted to having a bad feeling about Thom, about the garage in general. *Only because it was a new garage,* Meg had said. *He was nice. Liz Reese loves him. They do good business. He did not sabotage my car.*

To which Dad had replied, *Nature gave you instincts for a reason.*

Would he be proud of her now, parked outside Halloway's Garage in her Crosstrek, reading its hand-painted sign for the first time since the inspection?

She's come to talk to Thom. To tell him about the accident that killed Justin and gauge his reaction. But he isn't here. The garage is closed, according to the sign in the window of the darkened office.

It doesn't matter. What matters to Meg now is the cluster of cars parked in the small service lot, just behind the garage. She noticed them when she first came in—a baby-blue Cadillac, a golden Dodge Dart, a bulbous black Studebaker that easily dates back to the fifties, some kind of K-car from the eighties, white, with red and blue racing stripes—all of them bright and interesting and vintage, except for one.

She starts up her car and pulls closer to the lot, her gaze stuck to the other car, the modern standout. The compact.

A tiny part of Meg's brain tells her not to be ridiculous. *Stop jumping to conclusions. Stop acting like Dad. There are a million cars like this one on the road. You see them every day . . .*

She's now close enough to see the logo on the back. Her instincts are correct. It's a tan Mazda. Just like the one the skinheads were driving.

Meg pulls a pen out of her purse. She digs around for something to write on and finds an old receipt. After taking down the Mazda's license plate number, Meg carefully folds it up and slips it into her wallet. She could have taken a picture of the plate, but she's wary of having that type of evidence on her phone. (Evidence of what, she's not yet sure.)

As she moves to turn the ignition, there's a light knock on the driver's side window. Meg screams inside, but she makes a point of turning slowly. She prepares herself to calmly say Thom's name.

It isn't Thom who knocked, though. It's a woman in a puffy parka, a black wool beanie pulled down to her eyes, a black KN95 mask concealing the lower part of her face. She looks like a ninja.

Meg opens her window.

"I'm sorry, we're closed," the woman says from behind the mask.

"That's all right," Meg replies. "Is Thom around?"

The woman's eyes narrow. They start to water, Meg thinks from the cold. "He's in the hospital," she says. Muffled by the mask. "I'm not sure when he'll be back."

"Oh . . . I'm sorry."

She adjusts the mask with a dainty, gloveless hand, and Meg stares at it.

"You were here a few months ago, weren't you?" the woman says.

"Yes."

"I remember . . . We don't normally do much with the foreign cars. Your name is Meg, isn't it? Magnolia Russo?"

Magnolia.

"Would you like me to give Thom a message? I'm his wife. Diane."

"Just . . . tell him I hope he feels better."

"I know he will."

"Excuse me?"

"In a few days, he'll be cured." She taps her mask and crosses her fingers . . . which makes the gap between the middle finger and pinkie all the more obvious. "I know it."

Meg forces a smile. She starts up her car. As she leaves the parking lot, she can see Diane Halloway waving at her in her rearview mirror with that same dainty, gloveless hand. She's missing her ring finger. Just like her husband. Diane waves and waves as though she knows Meg is watching her. *In a few days, he'll be cured,* she'd said. Like a true believer.

As Meg reaches the road, Diane yanks off her mask and stares after her car. She's beaming.

—

Once she's nearly home, Meg pulls into a gas station, where she grabs her purse, takes out her wallet and finds the receipt with the Mazda's license plate number. Both Charlie's and Grady's business cards are in her wallet too. She calls Charlie. He picks up quickly. "Officer Peele." Over the phone, he sounds older and more serious than he does in person.

She takes a breath before she greets him and speaks as calmly as possible. "Hi, Charlie. It's Meg Russo."

"Ms. Russo!" he says. "You must be psychic."

"*What?*"

"Uh . . . I was just going to call you?"

Meg exhales hard. *Calm down.* "Oh."

"I think we might have a lead on who broke into your store."

"Really?"

"Yes. I mean . . . innocent until proven guilty and all that. But I checked with all the area hospitals, and I found out they had a patient in the emergency room at Benedictine at about four in the morning with a missing finger. The chief surgeon told me this person was drunk and bleeding profusely and claimed to have cut it off with gardening shears. Normally when there's an accident involving a severed digit, the person brings it with them to be reattached. This patient didn't, though."

Meg stares at the screen—all those anonymous posts. "Did you get the person's name?"

"Yeah," Charlie says. "I'm going to question him this afternoon."

"Him?"

"Yes, ma'am. His name is Eric Henderson. Does that ring a bell?"

Meg's stomach drops. "No," Meg says. "The name isn't familiar."

Somehow, she finds this more frightening than if it were. Eric Henderson, a man who hates Meg enough to have disfigured himself in order to prove it, is a stranger. And there are so many of them out there. Planning, plotting. Their deadline looming.

"You sure?" Charlie says. "He's white, twenty-seven years old? Six-foot-four?"

"I don't know him."

"I believe you." Charlie says it quickly, soothingly. "There's no reason why you would. He's not from around here."

"Where is he from?"

"Cleveland," Charlie says. "He's staying at some motel on Route 28. No idea where he got the gardening shears."

Meg takes a breath and lets it out, making a whistling sound. "I don't know anybody from Cleveland," she says.

"Me neither," Charlie says.

"Sorry I snapped. It's just . . . been a tough day."

"I know," he says. "I was there for some of it."

Charlie seems like a nice kid. But is anyone the way they seem to be? All those people on the image board, claiming to be cops . . .

"Ms. Russo?"

You can't trust anyone.

"Hello? Ma'am?"

"Yeah?"

"Is there anything I can do for you?"

"Why are you asking?"

"Well . . . you called."

"Oh, right," Meg says. "Listen, I know this probably isn't kosher, but I've . . . I mean like I said, I've been . . . going through things, and I was wondering if you could do me a favor."

There's a pause on the other end of the line, Charlie trying to figure out what to say next.

Meg presses on. "For the past week, a tan Mazda has been parking in my employee lot and, uh . . . I'd just like to find out who it belongs to."

"You want me to run the plate?" Charlie says. He actually sounds relieved. *God only knows what he thought I was going to ask him.*

"If it's not too much trouble," Meg says.

"It isn't," Charlie says. "It's easy. And I know you've been through a lot between this and . . . and the accident . . . My condolences, by the way. I don't think I ever got a chance to say that."

"Thank you, Charlie."

"Just don't tell anybody I did it for you, though," he says. "I could get in trouble."

"I won't," she says. "So long as you don't tell anybody I asked."

"Deal."

She reads him the plate number, and he tells her he'll run it as soon as he can. "I'll get back to you, okay? Your cell number still the best way to reach you?"

"Yes."

"By the way, did I tell you that I went to high school with your daughter?"

"No, you didn't. Did you know her?"

"Not really. I graduated four years ahead of her. But I knew who she was. Everybody did."

Meg's shoulders tense up. *"Why?"*

"Well . . . I mean . . . She's a kick-ass musician, ma'am. Excuse my language."

Meg exhales. "She is, isn't she?"

"She'll be famous someday. I'd bet on it."

Meg's gaze stays on the scrawled license plate number, her thoughts returning to what Lily told her: Nathan's call to her this morning, the footage of her on YouTube, performing his "Pearly Gates" solo. The comments. *One and two and one and two and two and two . . .*

They've got a little more than one day.

"Lily already is famous," Meg says quietly.

TWENTY-FIVE

Nathan slowly lifts his arms, the Beretta 92FS in his grip, his eyes fixed on the first of three cans he's placed alongside each other on the garden wall behind his home. He remembers the manual safety and disengages it, picturing his enemy's face on the first can as he bends his knees and pulls the trigger. Nathan says his enemy's name out loud. "Todd McNally." The sweet resistance of that first pull, the delay of the fire. It's what Nathan likes about the Beretta. A safety feature, yes, but it also makes that initial shot feel as though you've worked for it. *Todd McNally.* The can explodes.

He aims at the next can. "Christopher Lindstrom." He shoots, hits his target. Then the next. "Mitchell Rowley." Boom. Another one down. All three of the animals who attacked him at Kennedy. So many cans he's named after them. Every target practice, this fleeting satisfaction.

He reengages the safety and plops down on the garden's lone bench, which is wrought iron and so heavy, it feels as though it's got roots. It came with the property when he bought it, a spot where couples staying at the inn could bask in the sun and pose for pictures. A place to keep their towels while taking a dip. Nathan's had the swimming pool drained, filled with cement and covered with patio tiles. (Pools aren't worth the upkeep they require.) But he has never even attempted to move this bench. Fixed in the same place for more than a century, this piece of metal has weathered the seasons with far more fortitude than Nathan himself, who, at the moment, is spent.

After just three shots, his head is light, his limbs weak and rubbery. The bench is deeply uncomfortable and coated in ice, the cold pressing through his jeans and long underwear. But even so, Nathan could easily drift to sleep right here amid the falling snowflakes, the weather no match for his own torpor. He imagines closing his eyes and allowing the frost to cover him, icicles weaving through his hair, crusting his thick eyebrows and wispy beard until he's frozen to the bone, a part of the bench, anchored here forever.

The thought appeals more than it probably should.

It makes Nathan sad that his energy level is this low. Really, it doesn't seem so long ago that he could jam for hours in a smoke-filled club, head thrown back and legs akimbo, the thrum of his bass fueling him, animating him. Nathan Lerner, Demon God of Rhythm, in his flowing velvet cape, girls screaming and throwing their bras at the stage . . .

Oh, all right. Fine. That last part is an embellishment. Even at the height of their fame, Prism was not what you'd call heartthrob material. Their fan base was 90 percent male, most all of them bookish and undersexed and pissed off at the world. Nathan didn't mind. He was bookish and pissed off himself, and as he'd been with Shira since senior year of high school, he had no need for groupies.

But he did want to please the crowd. He wanted to be a rock star. And the guys who came to their shows expected so much out of Prism. Out of *him.* Nathan just wanted the band to take off, that's all. He wanted success like everyone does, and so he went a little dark. He acted out a persona in order to please his fans. Demon God. The Warlock. It was just a character—less dangerous than Ozzy's. No bats were harmed in its creation. Yet he's been punished for years. Decades. And not just him but everyone he's ever loved . . .

Nathan closes his eyes, the chill pressing into his bones. Why is it that he can't even reminisce about the good old days without guilt ambushing him?

It's that YouTube video. Lily said that she would tell CarlOnGuitar to take it down, but has the damage already been done? He feels the same way now as he did when Magnolia announced she'd won that book contest. Terrified. And ashamed of himself. *I've ruined their lives.*

He feels that nagging tickle in his throat, and starts to cough, a faint rasp maturing into a bark, a hacking. Nathan tastes copper in his mouth and he wants to bargain with his body. *Stop. Please. I'll do anything. Just stop.* He leans over and grasps his knees and forces himself to breathe as slowly and deeply as he can. He spits blood onto the ground and tries to look away from it, a splash of red against the fallen snow.

The sun is starting to set already, the sky turning purplish gray at 4 P.M. He really does hate this time of year, when daylight lasts five minutes. Such a joke that as a boy, he used to think of the Catskills as some magical summery place when really, summer is the shortest season here, and it just keeps getting shorter with each passing year.

Nathan had planned on setting up more cans and going at them with another gun, the Ruger probably, but he nixes that idea. He's had enough target practice for the day. Nathan swipes his mouth with his bare hand and looks at it. No blood. That's something, at least. He picks up the Beretta and starts toward his house.

—

As soon as he gets inside, Nathan hears the phone ringing. He sets his gun down on the coffee table and lets the machine pick up, humming the rhythm track to "Smoke on the Water," anything to drown out those ghostly voices: Shira, Magnolia and himself, young and happy. Unaware of what would happen within the next five years. He's thinking Magnolia may be right about retiring the answering machine, when he hears Magnolia in real time, her adult voice, leaving a message.

"Can you call me please, Dad? As soon as you can? I wanted to ask you about . . . something. It's important . . ."

Nathan fights his own body to get to the phone in time. "Magnolia," he says, grabbing the receiver just as she's about to hang up. He's winded, as though he's just run a race. He also feels like crying.

"Dad? Are you okay?"

He finds the nearest chair. Collapses into it, a single tear running down the side of his face. "That's relative," he says.

"You're good, though, right? Nothing's happened?"

"No, no. I'm fine."

"Great. Listen, I can't talk long because I've left Lily and her friend Carl at the house and I know they're probably worried about me," she says. "But I think you may be right about what happened to Justin."

Nathan wipes the tear from his cheek, his shoulders tensing up. "You do?"

"Yes, and I'm sorry for . . . for being so dismissive of you. Not just about that but about everything. Well, almost everything . . ."

"Magnolia, are you okay?"

"That's relative." She laughs. It sounds forced. "What I'm saying is, your fears are justified. There really are people after us."

Nathan's heart pounds. He shushes her. "Don't say things like that over the phone," he says. Something that would normally produce an exasperated sigh.

"You're right," she says, her voice quavering. "Anyway I was . . . I was just kidding. You know how I kid."

Nathan's breath catches in his throat. He's growing genuinely frightened.

"Dad, I want to visit," Magnolia says. "With Lily and maybe Carl. Tonight or tomorrow. I can't give you an exact time. We'll be leaving our phones behind, so you won't be able to contact us. Is that all right with you?"

Nathan pauses for a very long time. So many questions run through his mind: *When? Why? Does this have anything to do with Lily playing my solo on the YouTube?* But he's afraid to voice them into Magnolia's cell phone. He also wants to promise her that whatever and whoever it is she's running from, he'll protect her. He'll protect Lily. He won't let them down like he has in the past. *I'll give up my life if I have to.* He wants her to know this. "That's fine," he says instead. "Any time."

"Thank you."

Nathan feels another coughing fit coming on, but he closes his eyes, using all the strength within him to ward it off. "Magnolia," he says quietly. "I'm sorry. For everything."

There's no answer. Nathan says his daughter's name again two more times before he realizes that she hung up after thanking him. She's no longer on the line.

—

The girls are going to need food, Nathan thinks. He walks into the kitchen and checks the fridge. There isn't much in there. Half a loaf of bread. An untouched strawberry rhubarb pie Doris brought over for him when she was here last. A head of lettuce, some rice and beans he fixed last night but fell asleep before even tasting it. A carton of milk. A bag of onions. The thing is, Nathan rarely eats anymore, which is the reason Doris brought him the pie. *I hope you don't mind my saying, Mr. Lerner. You're much too thin. With all that marijuana you smoke, you'd think you'd get the munchies, but no, huh? This oughta fix you up.*

Nathan figures he should stock up on a few things so the girls won't starve. There's a grocery store near Wellman's. Not a great selection, but the place is close—walking distance, if the weather were better and Nathan were healthier. He'll have to drive, though. He grabs his coat.

As he looks through the junk drawer in the kitchen for the right set of keys, he remembers a review the band received in the *Village Voice* around 1979. It had been in the back of the paper, and short, probably a hundred words at the most. But it made Nathan so proud—a review of a show he'd especially enjoyed playing, at the Bottom Line. And in the *Voice*, no less. His favorite paper. His parents' favorite paper. Nathan had been so pleased that he clipped the review and wrapped it in a special plastic so it wouldn't yellow, Shira ribbing him at all the care he was taking. *You'd think it was a priceless relic,* she'd said, giggling. *Or really expensive grass!* But Nathan couldn't even laugh, the review was that meaningful to him, the way it singled him out. In one sentence in particular: *Nathan Lerner plays the bass like a man possessed—a rock-and-roll Beelzebub shooting sparks from his fingers and stealing your soul.*

He recited that sentence, out loud and in his head, so many times back then that even today, it's committed to memory. *Rock-and-roll Beelzebub.* Ridiculous. But Nathan had been so flattered that he'd leaned into it, throwing devil horns at fans when he performed, switching his black guitar strap for a shiny red one. For a time, he even wore makeup, drawing a pentagram on his forehead in Shira's red lip liner. Silly stuff, honestly, an attempt at showmanship that he'd put an end to relatively quickly after too much teasing from his bandmates. *The warlock cape is fine, Nate,* Claude had said. *But you've got to stop drawing on yourself. I looked at you last night, I almost lost it in the middle of my solo.*

The wolves weren't laughing, though. A Jew with a pentagram etched on his face confirmed their worst fears, and rumors spread that Nathan's best song—his one and only close-to-a-hit—was infused with a curse.

And here's the truth: It was. *It is.* "Pearly Gates" is cursed. Only what those idiots still fail to grasp is that they were the ones to curse it, and the one to suffer most has been Nathan's daughter, a born storyteller who never wrote another book after *The Prophesy.* Magnolia lost her mother, her creative passion and later, the love of her life. Because of that song. Because of the wolves. But really because of Nathan.

Is Lily headed down that same path? Nathan thinks about how he told her to take her bass solo off the YouTube. The urgency with which he'd asked her to hide her astounding talent and succumb to the wolves, just as he had done with Magnolia.

I can't let it happen again. I won't.

Nathan opens his front door. He steps back. It's snowing much harder now. Like it's being emptied out of buckets. The grocery store can wait until it lets up. For now, Nathan thinks, he'll load the Ruger. He has the energy for more target practice, even in heavy snow.

TWENTY-SIX

After ending the call with her father, Meg feels a little calmer; she always does once she has some sort of plan in place, even if it's something as shaky and tentative as the one she's devised: escaping to her father's, going off the grid and waiting out the storm until the thirteenth arrives. As she nears Elizabethville, Meg is able to call Lily, though she knows enough not to reveal her suspicions about the Halloways, the Mazda parked in their garage's service lot, Diane and Tom's missing fingers.

Right now, all of those things could still be coincidence. And dim to dark as that possibility may be, Meg wants with all her heart to believe that they are. She wants for Lily to believe that as well. It's bad enough knowing these people exist, and they're everywhere. To know for a fact that they caused Justin's death . . . Meg can't think about what that would mean. And she doesn't want Lily considering the possibility.

Meg calls Lily's cell phone. Lily answers fast, her voice floating out of Meg's Bluetooth. "Mom? Are you all right?"

Meg can hear Carl in the background, asking the same question: *Is she okay?* It makes her feel good, knowing her child is not alone. "I'm fine," Meg tells Lily, adding that she's got some important things to discuss in person, and that, in the meantime, Lily should have Carl drive her to work. "You'll be safe with Bonnie," she explains. "But please don't tell her anything."

"Why? I mean . . . maybe she can help."

"Honey, it's not that I don't trust her. I just feel like she may inadvertently tell the wrong person."

"She wouldn't do that."

"How do you know?" Meg sighs heavily. She hadn't meant to say it so loudly. "Look, anybody we tell is a potential leak. Not Bonnie. But people could be in her store, or listening in somehow and—"

"Okay, okay. I get it, Mom."

"I feel like this shouldn't leave our little circle."

"I understand," Lily says. "It won't."

"Thank you."

"But . . . Mom?"

"Yes?"

"Why can't you give me a ride to work? Are you far away?"

Meg gazes out of her window as she passes the sign: *Welcome to Elizabethville.* The town she and Lily both grew up in, postcard-pretty thanks to the recent snowfall, Christmas lights twinkling on the storefronts, the bare little tree in the middle of the green, awaiting its lighting, a few feet away from the massive divot created by the missing rock launched through her storefront window.

We grew up here, and they were watching . . .

"I'm close," Meg says as she pulls into the parking lot of Reese's Diner. "But I need to take care of something."

—

"How about that apple pie you promised?" Meg says to Liz Reese.

Liz is alone at the counter, drinking a cup of coffee. Meg knew she would be. She calls four-to-five her "lull hour." Her waitresses change shifts at four, with Liz handling stragglers while getting ready for the dinner rush, which usually lasts from five till seven. The diner closes at eight.

Five years ago, Liz opened the place up at nine one night, so that Justin could throw Meg a surprise dinner for their twentieth anniversary. Liz had played the role of maître d', donning a bow tie with her customary black T-shirt and jeans, a black blazer hiding the oven burns and scars on her arms, white gloves covering her battered hands, half her pinkie finger missing from what she's always claimed was a blender accident. She'd served them fine wine and chateaubriand and called them *Madame et Monsieur.* At the time, Liz had been living here for nearly two years and had become fast friends with Meg because she was in her store so often, feeding her romance novel addiction. (*To be one of those Regency ladies,* she'd swoon, when Meg would slip her an advance galley of the latest Julia Quinn. *To live in that world rather than this freakin' dystopia.*)

"You got it, doll," Liz says. She sets her coffee cup down on the counter and slips into the kitchen as Meg removes her coat and takes the center stool—the same one she always sits in when she comes here alone, Liz leaning over the counter, refilling Meg's coffee, the two of them discussing their businesses and sharing town gossip, Liz bemoaning her less-than-romance-novel-worthy dating life. *You got one of the good ones, honey. One of the very, very few good ones.* She used to say that all the time.

Meg hates the thoughts that are running through her mind.

Liz returns with a slice of apple pie, heated up the way Meg likes it, a slice of cheddar cheese on top. She pours her a cup of coffee without asking if she wants one, and tops off her own cup too—they both take it black—and slides onto the stool next to Meg's, the way she always does. Liz lifts her cup to her lips. Meg stares at that stub of a finger.

"So," Liz says, "did you ever find out who beat the crap out of your store?"

Meg nods. "Somebody named Eric Henderson."

"Who?"

"Exactly." Meg takes a bite of her pie. It's delicious as always. She sips her coffee. "He's a complete stranger. From Cleveland, apparently."

"Cleveland."

"Yeah."

"And he's a grown man?"

"Yes."

"I figured it must be teenagers."

"I know. You told me that on the phone. You hate them."

"No offense to—"

"Lily. I know. You said that too." Meg sips more of her coffee. The conversation feels strange to her, as though Liz is reading from a script. It's a feeling she's had throughout her life, with other friends she thought she knew . . . that slight rip in the fabric, the trust turning, going sour. *She's not who I thought she was. All this time, playing a part.*

Meg has always believed in her ability to read people, but this has happened to her more than once, this odd sense that makes her pull away slightly, then scold herself for it.

In the past, Meg told herself she was being unfair, believing that people were trying to get close to her for "wrong reasons" she couldn't name. She attributed it to insecurity, paranoia—flaws within herself that have been there since childhood . . . But maybe, as Dad said, Meg should have trusted her instincts. She never felt that way with Bonnie. Or Justin. Not even once.

Maybe the reason has always been the same, and it has to do with their *flaws.* Their *paranoia.* Their *lunacy. Not mine. Maybe I can name that reason now . . .*

"Don't you like the pie, honey?" Liz says.

"I love it." Meg takes another bite. From reading the image board, Meg knows that the Nine-and-Tens believe that her death must be both violent and filmed to break the curse. And so, even if her suspicions about Liz prove correct, she isn't afraid of getting poisoned. "I was just wondering about something."

"What's that?"

"We know each other pretty well," Meg says.

"True that."

"But I don't know why you moved here."

"Sure you do. I told you. I owned that little Mexican cantina out in Bakersfield, California. My ex got it in the divorce. I picked up all my stuff, loaded it into Clarabelle and came here. Diner was up for sale. The rest is history." She beams at Meg the way she always does when she tells this story, as though she's gotten the monologue right and expects a gold star.

Meg drinks her coffee and watches her friend of seven years. Nine fingers grasping her coffee cup, the twitching mouth as she takes a sip. "Why *here*, though?" Meg says. "You have no family in Elizabethville or anywhere in New York State. No old friends. There are diners for sale all over the country."

Liz blinks at her, and Meg thinks she sees it, a hardness behind her eyes, the slipping of the mask. "I love a town with a great bookstore," she says.

Meg gives her a fake smile. "Good one," she says.

"I mean it."

"Sure you do."

"Meg?"

"Yes?"

"Why did you ask me about Thom Halloway?"

Meg's stomach clenches up. She takes another swallow of coffee, but that just makes it worse. She puts the cup down and looks into Liz's pale eyes, her snakelike stare. Her bad arm throbs. She holds it close to her stomach.

"Because three days after he inspected my car," Meg says, "it had mechanical issues that killed my husband."

Liz opens her mouth, but says nothing.

Meg stands up, her face burning. She hadn't expected to say that, but in a way she's glad she did. She pulls a twenty-dollar bill from her wallet and sets it on the counter. "Thank you for the pie," she says.

"Thom's sick now." Liz says it through her teeth. "The damn plague. You know that, right?"

Meg tries to say *I'm sorry* or *I hope he feels better* or something appropriate, but she can't. Liz called it *the plague.* She can't say another word to her.

She turns and leaves the diner. Maybe she's wrong. Maybe she's reading into things when she shouldn't be. Maybe Liz has never heard of the Nine-and-Tens and neither has Thom, and this is all something she'll have to apologize for later on. Meg wants that to be true. *Please let that be true.* Lots of people call COVID *the plague.* Not just the Nine-and-Tens.

Just as she reaches the door, Liz hisses out a word. It sounds like *repent.* Meg whirls around. "What?" she says.

Liz is standing now. She smiles at Meg with unblinking eyes. "I just said, 'Merry Christmas,' honey."

—

As Meg starts up the car, her phone rings. She waits until she's out of the diner's parking lot to answer, as though Liz Reese has secret recording equipment there. *She might,* Meg thinks. It dawns on her that, at this point, she's fully crossed over. Her thought process now mirrors her father's.

Once she's on the road, Meg answers the phone, the town green looming before her. That divot, like an amputated limb.

"Hi, Mrs. Russo." For a second, she thinks it's Zach, and almost asks him how he's feeling. But it isn't him. It's the young cop, Charlie Peele. "I'm just calling because I ran that plate for you."

"Oh . . ." Meg says. Such a short time ago, and she'd nearly forgotten asking him. Time has been working so strangely—speeding up, then slowing to a crawl. Today feels like a minute and a year, all at once.

"Yeah, so I can tell you who the car's registered to," Charlie is saying, "but if you want my two cents, I'd just have it towed rather than talking to him about it. That type of confrontation never goes the way you want it to."

It takes Meg a little while to remember the story she told Charlie when she asked him to run the plate. "I'll take that into consideration," she says. "So, what was the name?"

"Hold on a sec." Meg hears a rustling of papers, then Charlie talking to somebody. Another man's muffled voice. When he comes back, he speaks much more quietly. "My boss," he says. "Thank gosh he didn't hear."

Thank gosh?

"Remember, mum's the word on this."

"Got it."

"Okay, the name on the registration is Todd McNally."

Meg's jaw drops. "Todd McNally," she repeats.

"Sound familiar?"

She coughs. "No."

"Probably for the best."

"Yeah, I'll just have it towed." Meg thanks Charlie and hangs up quickly.

Todd McNally.

The name slithers through her mind, materializing like a ghost, then becoming palpable, visible.

"'Todd McNally, 19.'" She says it out loud as it appears in her thoughts. *Todd McNally, 19,* in newsprint and behind protective plastic covering. Todd McNally, 19, calling Dad "a follower of Satan," in that old *New York Post* story, Dad's bleeding, swollen face in the accompanying picture.

TWENTY-SEVEN

Lily gets a text from Mom. It arrives after Carl has dropped her off at Divine Vintage and just after he's kissed her goodbye, which is something new for them—they've kissed, sure, but not goodbye. That's different, somehow. It's more of a formal commitment.

Lily still feels the kiss as she walks through the front door. She wonders if Bonnie saw it happen and if she did, whether she'll ask her about it—and if she does, what should Lily say? *He's my boy-friend? Should I use that word?* She's realizing how nice it is to have thoughts like these—normal teenage thoughts about a boy, that combination of excitement and embarrassment and what's-going-to-happen—when her phone chimes with the text from Mom. She pushes open the door and reads it once she's inside, and those thoughts dissolve.

Don't go to Reese's

Lily's stomach drops. *Back to reality.* She isn't sure why Mom doesn't want her going to her favorite diner, but she knows there has to be a good reason—one that involves the online cult—which makes her feel even worse.

She texts back: OK

Mom replies: Where are you

Just got to work

Good

Lily puts a thumbs-up on Mom's text. There's no reply. She misses the days when Mom sent long, punctuated texts. She misses the exclamation points. The emojis. Lily starts to get choked up, but takes a long, steadying breath. *I'm not going to cry over emojis. I'm not a fucking baby.*

"Hey, are you okay?" Bonnie says. She's standing behind the counter, wearing a silky black seventies blouse with sunflowers all over it, a yellow band in her black hair and bright red lipstick, a pile of cashmere sweaters in front of her that she's in the process of folding. The sight of Bonnie cheers Lily a little, all those bright colors she always wears and how effortlessly she fits in with the décor of this store—the purple velvet couch and the big gilded mirror and the two sparkling chandeliers, all of which Lily finds magical. Plus there's the very simple fact that she's Bonnie.

Lily wants to tell her godmother why she isn't okay, but she remembers what Mom said about keeping the information about the Nine-and-Tens within "our little circle." And so she stops herself, her heart sinking. How tiny that circle is. How helpless and alone she feels outside of it. *Why can't I tell Bonnie?* She still doesn't get it. "I'm okay," Lily says. "Why do you ask?"

"I just heard about what happened at your mom's store," Bonnie says.

"Oh," Lily says. "Right. That was this morning." It doesn't surprise Lily that Bonnie just heard about it. Divine Vintage is always the last to know town gossip because of its location. While most of the businesses, including Mom's, are on Main Street, with the heaviest foot traffic around the town green, Divine is all the way at the other end of Main on a quiet, mostly residential cross street called Summer Lane that gets hardly any foot traffic at all. To put things in perspective, the only other business on Summer Lane is Weir's Funeral Home, which handled Dad's cremation.

"I can't believe your mom didn't call and tell me," Bonnie says. She looks genuinely hurt. Lily feels bad for her. She'd be hurt too.

"I don't think she's had time," Lily says, "with the police there and everything. She didn't even tell *me* until hours after it happened."

Bonnie nods. Even though it's the truth, Lily isn't sure she believes her. She takes off her coat and hangs it on the brass rack next to the door. Then she moves behind the counter and starts helping Bonnie fold the cashmere sweaters.

"Thanks," Bonnie says.

"No problem," says Lily, who is glad to have something to do with her hands.

Bonnie is quiet for a long time. Lily glances at her, and sees that she's just standing there, her soft gaze on the sweater she seems no longer capable of folding. "A human finger," she says.

"I know."

"I don't understand why."

"Me neither," Lily says. Not a lie. She *knows* why, but she doesn't *understand*.

"It feels like the cult."

Lily freezes. She stares at Bonnie. "What?"

"It feels like the occult," she says. "You know . . . like an occult ritual."

"Oh." With shaking hands, Lily goes back to folding her sweater. "I've been stressed out today," she says quietly. "Hearing things wrong."

Bonnie nods. "If you want to talk, you know I'm here."

"About what?" Lily says.

"You know."

Lily stares at her.

"I mean . . . Look. It didn't happen that long ago."

Lily exhales—a massive sigh. She knows Bonnie well enough to understand that by *it,* she means nothing other than the accident.

"Almost four months," Lily says.

"Not even," Bonnie says.

It's the way they often talk, in shorthand, half reading each other's minds. They've known each other since Lily was preverbal, Bonnie having spent more time with Lily as a baby than Grandpa Nate—her only other family, since Dad's parents died before she was born. Two only children have one baby, that baby finds family anywhere she can, and Lily has found it in Bonnie. She's her godmother, but she's so much more than that, and now Lily can't tell her this thing. This awful, life-or-death thing that's isolating her more than ever. *Why, Mom?*

"How did you find out?" Lily says. "About the finger, I mean. Did Sara Beth call?"

She shakes her head. "Liz Reese."

Lily stares at her, her heart suddenly pounding.

"I went to grab a coffee and she told me . . . Lily? What's wrong?"

Lily hears herself say, "Don't talk to her."

"What? Why?"

"I don't . . . I don't know."

Bonnie says nothing. Lily can feel her gaze on her.

"Should I just talk to your mom?" Bonnie says, after a long while. "I feel like there's something you aren't telling me, and that's all right. But is it okay if I ask her what's going on?"

Lily nods, her face growing redder, hotter, tears springing into her eyes. She tries to go back to folding, but a memory worms its way into her brain—of being very young and small and in the old municipal playground, her mom and Bonnie chatting on one of the benches while Lily tried to follow a group of bigger kids, running to keep up, her little legs refusing to cooperate. Lily took a wrong step and sailed off her feet. The kids didn't even care enough to turn around—that was the first thing that hurt her. The second was feeling as though a giant had plucked her off the ground, raised her high in the air and dropped her. She remembers it so well: the mixture of shock and pain that was the impact, the unbearable sting of her scraped-up legs, the sight of her own blood on the hard white path, which had made the scrapes hurt so much more. She even remembers that silence, the sucking in of air just before she started to scream. It's all rushing back, as if it's happening again.

It had been Bonnie who pulled Lily to her feet. Bonnie who saved her. She's sure that both Bonnie and Mom ran to her at the same time, but her godmother had gotten there first, and it had been Bonnie's neck she buried her head in, Bonnie's lavender shampoo she inhaled.

Lily can remember looking up as her terror subsided, peering past Bonnie's shoulder at Mom rushing toward them, kneeling down, asking where it hurt.

And she can remember a man in a hoodie, standing by the playground gate. Raising a camera to take a picture.

They've always been watching.

Lily feels Bonnie's arms around her now, because she's crying. Not just a few tears but great, gasping sobs, racking her shoulders, her chest; that panicky feeling, as though she'll never be able to catch her breath. She burrows her head into Bonnie's neck, same as she did back then, feeling just as frightened.

"It's okay," Bonnie says. "Everything's going to be okay." She says it over and over until Lily is able to breathe regularly. It takes a long time.

"I need to talk to you," Lily says, her face drenched from her own tears. The decision made. "I need to tell you something. In private. Nobody else can know."

Bonnie doesn't ask for details. She simply walks over to the door and locks it. Puts the *Closed* sign in the window and moves back to Lily, her gaze on her, warm and familiar and comforting. "I'm here," she says quietly. She grabs a box of Kleenex from behind the counter and hands it to Lily.

"Thank you." Lily grabs a wad of tissues out of the box and holds it to her wet face, wiping away some of the tears as she collapses onto the purple velvet couch. Bonnie sits beside her, and waits.

"Can you say it one more time?" Lily says.

Bonnie doesn't need to ask her what she means. It's the way they are. It's how they communicate. It's been that way between them forever. "Everything's going to be okay," Bonnie says.

And Lily tells her everything.

—

"My God," Bonnie says, once Lily is through. She doesn't say anything more for a very long time.

"It's a lot, I know," Lily says.

"Are they meeting on other platforms, or just this one image board? Are there YouTube videos? Reddit posts?"

"I don't know," Lily says.

"I mean . . . the image board alone. That's . . . how many?"

"Seems like hundreds at least," Lily says. "Maybe more."

"And they come from everywhere."

"Yes," Lily says. "But there are a lot of them here."

"In Elizabethville?"

"Yes," Lily says. "I think because of the twelfth coming up, there are some who've made, like . . . pilgrimages."

"There have been a lot of new customers," Bonnie says carefully. "People I've never seen before."

"I figured it was because of the holidays. Weekenders."

"Same, but—"

"I know. When you think about it . . ."

"That couple who was in the store last week," Bonnie says. "That gray-haired man and the woman in the camel-hair coat. She asked your name and then they both left."

"Yes," Lily says. "I remember them."

"That teenage boy standing outside the window yesterday. Taking pictures with his phone."

"Yeah," Lily says.

"And Liz Reese?"

"Maybe," Lily says. "I don't know details. Yet." She thinks of the cops in her high school parking lot, the postal worker with the *2* tattoo and Zach Winters, the way he glared at Carl and how, polite as he was to Lily, he consistently avoided her gaze. "I think that there are a lot of them who have been here for years."

Bonnie folds her arms over her chest. She tilts her head to one side, as though she's readjusting her thoughts. "What are we going to do?" she says.

Lily smiles—her first real smile in forever. She's glad she told Bonnie. That *we* is worth more to her than anything.

"I think Mom has a plan. She told me to go to work, that I'd be safe with you, and she'd tell me about it in person, later."

"You guys need to lay low until after the twelfth," Bonnie says. It's one of those sentences that seems to make sense, but has less and less meaning as it hangs in the air.

"It's really hard to hide," Lily says, "when you don't know who you're hiding from."

Outside the window a siren blares. Bonnie and Lily freeze, waiting for it to pass. "A lot of them are cops," Lily says. "Or at least they claim to be."

"What about the FBI?" Bonnie says. "Can you contact them?"

Lily just looks at her.

"Right. Like they're gonna come rushing to your rescue over some weird online posts. People cutting off their own fingers and toes."

Another cop car whizzes by, its siren shrieking. Lily cringes, waiting for it to pass. "I mean . . . yeah. We might convince some honest FBI person, if we can find one, that they're dangerous, over time. But the thing is, we've basically got one day."

Bonnie looks at her for a long while. "I have weapons," she says finally.

"What?"

"Knives," she says. "My dad used to collect them. He left them to me and my brother, and I have a dagger from the 1890s. Also a samurai sword . . ."

"I didn't know that."

"Why would I tell you? They freak me out."

"I'm sure."

"But anyway, I have them. They're in a safe. At my house."

"Bonnie, I don't . . . I don't know that I could . . ."

"Not you. God, Lily. *Me.* I'll come over. Protect you guys."

Lily swallows hard. "Have you ever used the knives?"

"No," Bonnie says.

"See? I don't want you to—"

"But the thing is, Lily, I've never *had* to use them." She smiles at her, a warm smile. Bonnie's I-can-do-anything smile. It makes Lily feel safe, almost.

Another siren shoots past. Then another.

Lily looks at Bonnie. "What is going on out there?"

Bonnie shakes her head. One more siren passes, the two of them staring at each other for a moment that feels weighted, like something out of a bad dream, when you suddenly can't speak and the walls start closing in.

"It sounds like the end of the world out there," Lily says.

"You want to put the 'back in fifteen minutes' note on the door so we can go out and check on it?"

"Yeah," Lily says. "Yeah, I do."

TWENTY-EIGHT

It could be a different Todd McNally, Meg thinks. She knows she's grasping at straws, and if it *were* a different Todd McNally who owned the horribly familiar-looking car she saw parked at Halloway's, it would be one hell of a coincidence. But on the other hand, the Todd McNally who terrorized Dad in baggage claim would be in his early sixties at this point. None of those skinheads were even close to that age.

She'll look him up, Meg decides. She'll look up Todd McNally on Facebook, because most people in their early sixties are on Facebook. She'll do it at the store, in her office, after she deals with Willis Baus.

She's been thinking about Baus since she left Reese's. Willis Baus, the contractor. Recommended by that otherwise-unhelpful cop Grady with the same enthusiasm Liz Reese had shown while hyping the living daylights out of Halloway's Garage. Willis Baus, with his fair estimate and his ready smile and his declaration that he'd have the window fixed by tomorrow at the latest. Tomorrow. The eleventh. The day the Nine-and-Tens see as their last chance.

I can't begin to tell you how sorry we are about your husband, he'd told her. Willis Baus, who looks familiar to Meg and walks with a limp and wears the type of orthopedic shoe one would wear, say . . . if one happened to be missing a big toe.

Meg parks her car in the small lot behind the Secret Garden. She unlocks the back door and jogs past the office, through the empty children's section, to the front of the store, her left side stabbing at her, her head light from hunger and thirst and from everything else she's been through today, her bad arm aching down to the marrow.

Sara Beth is standing by the window talking to Baus and a kid who must be his assistant, a boy a few years older than Lily with clear blue eyes and blond curls and round, rosy cheeks, like a Botticelli cherub. They're both wearing gloves, the new pane of glass propped up against the front door. The boy has his arms crossed over his chest. Willis is leaning against the wall.

"He's doing all right," Sara Beth is saying to Willis. "I'm worried about the cough, though . . ."

She stops talking when she sees Meg. Baus turns to face her, and Meg's gaze shoots from his face to his right foot, that clunky black shoe. She makes a point of staring at it. "Hey, thanks for everything." She says it quietly, coldly. "But I think we're going to go with another contractor."

"What?" It's Sara Beth who says it. "Honey, Willis and Emmet were just about to fit the glass."

"I'll pay you for the day," Meg says. "But I'd be more comfortable going with someone else."

"I'm sorry, ma'am," Baus says. "You mind my asking why?"

She keeps staring at the foot. "We have different belief systems," she says. Pointedly.

"Magnolia, are you all right?" Sara Beth says.

"I'm fine."

"Are you sure?" She turns to Baus. "It's been a difficult day, as you know." She looks at Meg, an infuriating expression on her face—that same blend of protectiveness and pity as when she was talking about Zach Winters. "How about you go home and take a rest? I can close up. We'll have a new window tomorrow. I'll set up my Dickens display again. Everything will be good as new."

Meg's gaze moves from Baus to Sara Beth, their identical hopeful smiles. It almost feels like gaslighting, and it makes her wonder about

Sara Beth, who came up here nearly forty years ago on a pilgrimage to her parents' bookstore and never left. *Were you really a Prism fan? Is that why you stayed and insinuated yourself into my family?*

"I'm fine," Meg says. "I am seeing things very clearly, actually." She stares at Baus. "I can write you a check. Or Venmo. Your choice."

"You . . . you don't have to pay me," he says. "Maybe just reimburse me for the glass—"

"Check or Venmo?"

"Um . . . Check's fine."

Meg walks over to the cash register. Pulls the company checks from the drawer and writes out one for a hundred dollars over the estimate Baus gave them, as he and Emmet and Sara Beth speak to each other in urgent whispers too low for her to hear. By the time she's done signing her name, Meg is fuming. She hands Baus the check. He takes it.

She hears herself say, "You lost that toe for nothing."

"*Magnolia,*" Sara Beth says.

"Excuse me?" Baus says.

Emmet stares at Meg as though she's just sprouted horns.

"You'll see. Whether I'm alive or dead, the world will go on and things will be just as shitty as ever, and you won't feel special or saved. Just stupid. *You're all stupid.*"

Willis Baus stares at Meg for a full minute. Then he hands the check to Sara Beth, who looks stunned. Paralyzed.

"Keep your money," Baus tells Meg. "We'll come back for the glass when you aren't here."

"She's not like this," Sara Beth says. "I've known her since she was a little girl, and she's not . . . She isn't . . ."

Baus glances at his assistant, who is watching Meg with enormous, incredulous eyes.

"Let's go, Emmet."

He turns and leaves. Emmet starts to collect the tools, his hands shaking visibly. As he turns to go, he looks at Meg. "You . . . like . . . You should have more respect for our troops."

After they're both gone, Meg looks at Sara Beth. "What was he talking about?"

"You know."

"No, I don't."

"Willis Baus is a war hero," she says quietly. "Don't you remember? Had to be about ten years ago. They had a ceremony for him on the green."

Meg's eyes widen. Baus's name sounded familiar, and that was why. She remembers now.

"Why did you say that to him?" Sara Beth says softly. "What were you thinking?"

Meg says nothing. She walks back to her office and closes the door. She turns on the computer, calls up the website for the *Elizabethville Courier* and searches the archives for "Willis Baus." Moments later, an article turns up from June 2014, titled *Local Hero Honored*. In one picture, an even thinner Willis Baus stands next to the town supervisor, framed commendation in one hand, the other resting on a metal cane. In a different picture, he's in full uniform, embracing his wife. She reads the caption:

In physical therapy for a severely injured foot, part of which was lost in an IED explosion in Afghanistan, Lt. Baus says, "I'm just grateful to be back in Elizabethville, with the people I love most."

Meg tilts her head back, tears forming in her eyes. For a few awful moments, she considers the possibility that this day could have been some kind of lengthy, grief-induced hallucination—the severed finger, Lily and Carl showing her the YearofTwos image board, Halloway's Garage . . . Liz Reese, Meg's close friend of seven years, the word oozing through her teeth: *Repent*. Maybe she never said it. Maybe none of it ever happened. Maybe Meg has simply followed in her father's footsteps, causing the death of the love of her life by making a series of bad decisions . . . and going insane as a result.

No. Meg lifts her head. She changes tabs and taps at the keyboard until 7Park comes up. She finds TheYearofTwos and scrolls through the posts, skimming them, trying her best to ignore the images. They exist. These lunatics are real. She didn't imagine them. Odd that she finds this comforting, if only for a few seconds before her heart starts to race.

Calm, calm, calm.

Meg closes the tab. She shuts her eyes and takes a few deep breaths, repeating the word in her mind until the panic subsides. *Calm, calm . . . You've got a gun. You know how to use it. Stay calm and you will win.*

She hears a soft knock on the door. Sara Beth's voice. "Are you all right, Magnolia?"

"Yes," she says. "I'm sorry about . . . I don't know what I was thinking."

"I understand," Sara Beth says. "It's been an awful day. And grief can do things to your mind. If you need anything . . ."

"Thank you."

Once she hears Sara Beth's retreating footsteps, Meg sends Lily a text: Don't go to Reese's.

The old Lily would have asked why, and put up a fight. The new Lily simply responds, OK.

Meg asks if she's at work yet, and Lily says she is and Meg breathes a sigh of relief. *We're a team, now,* Meg thinks. *We can fight them.* But first, she needs to know the truth.

Meg goes to Facebook and types the name Todd McNally into the profile search bar.

There are many possibilities, but Meg rules out the ones who are too young, too old and/or not from the United States. She winds up narrowing it down to three Todd McNallys, two of them sixty and the other sixty-one. She clicks on the sixty-one-year-old's page. He's from Liberty, New York. A graduate of SUNY Cortland. He's married. And his wife's name is Karen Halloway. *Halloway.*

That explains it, Meg thinks. *The Mazda owner's wife is related to Thom Halloway. That's why the car was there. His name happens to be Todd McNally.*

Could that really be possible? Could Thom have just missed the loose lug nut, the late-deploying airbag? Could Justin's death have truly been an accident? Meg gapes at the screen, her gaze traveling across the page to the most recent post. It's nearly a year old, from February:

> We're so sorry to share the news that after bravely battling COVID, our beloved father Todd McNally has passed away . . .

There's more information, about McNally's lifelong love of the New York Rangers, the years he spent as a proud volunteer firefighter, how he was rarely seen without his golden retriever Daisy and how he and Karen loved doting on their two-year-old grandson and spending time at their new vacation home in South Carolina when Todd wasn't busy running his landscaping business. The post describes Todd McNally as a devoted husband and father and "the type of friend who'd give you the shirt off his back," his children clearly making a convincing case for him to be let into heaven. There is no mention of a four-decade-old assault on a rock musician in Kennedy airport.

There's an accompanying picture of Todd McNally and his family. It's not of much use to Meg, because she doesn't know what McNally looks like. The only picture in the *Post* article had been the one of her father. No mug shots, as Dad never pressed charges.

She looks at the picture anyway: Todd McNally, with Karen and the authors of this post—their three grown children, Becca, Lauren and Trey. In the photo, they're all on the beach at sunset, all in bathing suits, the women in cover-ups. Meg enlarges it. She stops breathing, a terrible feeling moving through her body. Something worse than dread.

She knows Trey McNally. She would know Trey McNally even if he had a shirt on and she couldn't see the tattoos across his chest. She'd know the shaved head, and the narrow jaw and most of all the grin, the same grin he wore on the thruway in August, when he and his friends held up their phones to take Lily's picture.

—

Meg falls apart, half screaming, half sobbing. She hears the door opening and feels Sara Beth's arms around her, and she doesn't resist. She leans into Sara Beth, trusting her because she has to. Because she's known Sara Beth for nearly her whole life, and she's never been anything but kind to her, and if it turns out she's one of them, the way Liz Reese most definitely is, Meg doesn't think she'll be able to handle it.

"What's wrong?" Sara Beth says. "Is it the people on your screen? Who are these people, honey? What's going on?"

Meg wants to tell her, but she can't catch her breath. This emotion coursing through her—this mixture of shock and grief and rage—is so powerful, she feels as though it might burst through her skin. She's spinning from it, spinning like she was in the car before it all stopped. Everything stopped. Justin perfectly still on the grass, windshield shards all around him, the blood in his hair. *Justin's death wasn't an accident. It was the result of a coordinated attack.*

"Breathe, Magnolia," Sara Beth says. "Just breathe."

We were all targets. They were trying to film our deaths. Meg inhales as deeply as she can, her body trembling, vibrating. She takes a breath in. Lets it out as slowly as she can. Does it again. Then once more.

"That's it," Sara Beth says. "That's it."

She asks Meg if she wants some water. Meg half nods. She's aware of Sara Beth moving to the mini fridge, taking out a bottle of water and opening it and handing it to her. Meg gulps from the bottle. It makes her think about Lily. Lily telling her she really shouldn't buy those six-packs of water for the store. How they're bad for the environment, and if she was concerned about Lily's future, she'd buy a filter pitcher like the one they have at home. *It's selfish, Mom. Stop putting your convenience over my generation's health.* Such an irrelevant thing to think about, but it calms her down for some strange reason. The idea of Lily being Lily. Meg's breathing is easier now. She finishes the bottle of water and Sara Beth pulls away, and Meg looks up at her, the confusion on her face. *I have to explain*, Meg thinks. *I owe it to her.* And so she does. Kind of.

"That's one of the skinheads I told you about. The ones from the accident," Meg says, tapping the screen.

"Oh my God," Sara Beth whispers. "How did you find him?"

"His name is Trey McNally. He's the son of Todd."

Sara Beth gasps audibly.

"You know who Todd McNally is?"

"From Kennedy," she whispers. "One of those awful boys . . ."

"He's gone now. But his son . . ."

Outside the store, Meg hears the screech of a police siren moving closer.

"He was there. On the road. Taking pictures . . ." Another siren joins the first, a wailing Greek chorus. Meg waits for them to pass, but they don't.

Sara Beth says something, but Meg can't hear her. Meg asks her to repeat it, and she says it again. Something about Dad. How worried he's been lately.

"He's right!" Meg shouts. "Dad is right. There are people out there who . . . believe strange things. And they're after our family. They've always been after us."

Sara Beth speaks again, but there are even more sirens now. They're so loud, Meg can't hear herself think.

"What's going on out there?" she yells. "Do you think there's a fire?"

The sirens stop.

Meg and Sara Beth stare at each other.

Meg steps closer to the door. She hears a garbled voice, someone talking through a megaphone. Sara Beth moves out of the office, and Meg follows her through the alcove, into the children's section. The voice is coming from just outside the front of the building.

Fire at the hardware store, Meg thinks, her mind spinning, flipping back to Pete DeMarco, scaring those teenagers with the gun. What if the teens were Nine-and-Tens? What if they set a fire to get back at him?

Please let it just be a tripped alarm.

Sara Beth keeps moving toward the front of the store. Meg stops for a moment and inhales deeply through her nose. *If the hardware store was on fire, wouldn't I be able to smell it from here?*

She would. Of course she would, with nothing but a sheet of cardboard protecting the inside of her store from the elements. Meg inhales again. She smells nothing more than books and plaster.

Sara Beth stops at the front of the store. "It's us," she says. "Magnolia. It's us."

Meg doesn't know what she means. Not at first.

-

Once Meg is past the children's section, everything shifts into focus: the line of uniforms outside the good window, plastic shields, bulletproof vests and helmets, tear gas canisters and guns—a battalion of armed, oversized insects.

Sara Beth raises her hands over her head. She looks tiny and timid. "What the fuck is happening?" she whispers.

"It's okay," Meg says. "Deep breaths. Everything's going to be fine. Somebody made a mistake, that's all. They called the cops, apparently. Everything will be okay."

Sara Beth's arms quiver. She turns to Meg, her bright eyes on her face. "Are you sure it's a mistake?" she says.

"Hands in the air!" the cop with the megaphone says. "Brown sweater. I'm talking to you."

Meg left her coat in the office. She's wearing a brown sweater. Her pulse races. Sweat trickles down her rib cage, her back. She slowly raises her hands. The brown sweater she chose to wear this morning has been through the laundry too many times and creeps up her torso when she lifts her arms, exposing her belly. It makes her think of all those poor people on that cop reality show Justin used to watch in college, so many of them half naked for their arrests, which in a way was even more humiliating than getting cuffed and charged on national TV. *If they'd only known ahead of time so they could put some more clothes on,* Meg used to think. She hated that show.

"Stay facing forward," the megaphone says. "Do not turn. No movements."

"God," Sara Beth whispers.

"We didn't do anything," Meg says.

"Doesn't matter to them. The fucking fuzz," she says. "Ask your dad. He knows. He hates them for good reason."

"Walk out of the building. Onto the sidewalk," the megaphone says. Sara Beth moves toward the door on wobbly legs, her breathing wheezy.

"It's okay," Meg says quietly as she starts to follow. "Don't worry."

"No!" the megaphone shouts.

Sara Beth lets go of the door handle and steps back.

"Brown sweater. You come out! Keep your hands in the air. Move slowly. Ma'am, you can stay where you are."

As Meg walks toward the door, she can hear Sara Beth whispering to herself. *"Don't hurt her. Please don't let them hurt her."*

"Make sure we can see your hands!" the megaphone roars.

Meg keeps her hands in the air. It feels like a bad dream and it feels like the car accident. Every movement is amplified; every footstep, every breath with an echo to it; the world around her in slow motion; people standing outside their storefronts. Pastor John from the Lutheran church. Pete DeMarco, gaping from his doorway, just like the man yesterday— the one Meg had thought of as the bargain shopper.

"Please don't let them hurt her. Please. Not now."

"Brown sweater, exit the building!"

Her hands still raised, Meg pushes open the door with her hip, breathing deeply, conjuring Justin in her mind. *You're with me. You'll always be with me.* It doesn't work as well now. Now that she knows he was murdered, the setup intended for all of them. *One down, three to go . . .* A gust of wind slaps Meg's face, the cold pushing through her thin sweater.

"Get on your knees," says a woman's voice. "Clasp your hands behind the back of your head."

She does as she's told.

Gloved hands seize her by the collarbones and someone pushes her down, the sidewalk smacking the side of her face, burning cold against her exposed stomach, a heavy knee at the small of her back. Her poor aching back. The knee grinds into it. Someone grasps her bad arm.

Somewhere above or behind her, Meg can hear Sara Beth. "You must stop this. Please. This is an honest woman. A widow."

Meg finds her voice. "I don't understand." She says it into the pavement. She tries to sound calm. It feels necessary to sound calm. Gloved hands frisk her, Sara Beth watching, the whole neighborhood watching, her body overtaken by a feeling beyond fear, beyond shame. Pete across the street. That piece of shit Liz Reese. They can see her right now. Everyone can see what is happening to her.

"Somebody please tell me what is going on," she says very quietly, Sara Beth still shouting at the cops, and then a girl's voice, her daughter's voice.

I don't want her to see this.

Meg catches a glimpse of Lily's sneakers on the pavement, Lily rushing up to the cops, Bonnie struggling to keep up with her in her red platform boots.

"Let her go! Get off of her! Let my mother go!"

And through it all, she's aware of the policewoman's hands on her, the voice at the back of her neck, low and dry. Just above a whisper. *"Stay still,"* she says, her breath on Meg's skin. *"Stay still."*

TWENTY-NINE

Nathan is able to get off several more rounds with the Ruger before he starts to feel tired again. And the whole time, he doesn't cough up blood. He doesn't cough at all, in fact, which he attributes to the fact that he now has a purpose: preparing for the girls' arrival.

The snow's let up now, finally, so he can go to the grocery store. From one of Lily's letters, he remembers that she is a vegan, which to Nathan means she has a healthy distrust of the meat and dairy industries. But it also means that while he's got plenty of rice and beans, he should stock up on vegetables and other legumes. He hopes she doesn't want anything fancy. Star Lake's only grocery store is very small and old-fashioned, owned by the same Hassidic Jewish family that used to own Wellman's. He's not sure how many of those lab-generated meat substitutes they stock, or even if they're aware of the products' existence. If Lily were kosher, Nathan would be set. Vegan . . . not so much.

He showers and changes clothes and makes up a grocery list before he remembers that Magnolia had mentioned that Lily's friend Carl might be joining them. *CarlOnGuitar*. He checks his watch and calls Leland to ask how long he'll be at the post office.

"Till five," he replies. "We're doing extended Saturday hours through the holiday season."

"Great."

"You got Christmas cards to mail?"

Nathan clears his throat. "I . . . uh . . . I just want to look at your YouTube again."

He can hear the smile in Leland's voice. "You want to see your granddaughter ripping out your solo one more time, huh?" he says. "Don't blame you, sir. It's awesome."

Nathan thanks him and hangs up without bothering to correct him, but the real reason why he wants to see the YouTube is to get a look at Carl.

He doesn't like the idea of a stranger coming to his house, but he is glad that in whatever it is they're facing right now, Lily and Magnolia have an ally, a knight—a young man willing to fight for them.

He thinks about that as he grabs his keys and heads outside to take Missy on the road. He thinks about it as he cleans the snow off Missy's hood and windshield and climbs inside, turning the ignition. Switching on the defroster. Gunning her engine and backing all the way down the long driveway and pulling out onto the road.

Missy revs up to sixty miles per hour very quickly, big American gas guzzler that she is, with Nathan still trying to picture this young man Carl. What type of person he must be. Escorting Lily and Magnolia to his home. Unafraid of any danger involved. A knight. A protector. A muscular ally. Call him sexist—and his daughter has called him that many times—but every young woman needs a knight, whether Magnolia wants to believe that or not.

Nathan's on the road now, the sky dark at just 4:30. He's thinking about Justin, how he'd trusted in him from the moment he first met him—*someone to protect Magnolia from the wolves.* And his instincts, as always, proved correct. Justin protected Magnolia for years, decades, the two of them taking the bookstore off his hands and raising a daughter of their own in safety and peace, not a word from the wolves until . . . well, until they got him.

They got Justin.

Nathan remembers one of the last times he saw his son-in-law face-to-face. It had been one of Justin's regular visits to Pearly Gates, and instead of discussing films and politics like he usually did—an obvious attempt on Justin's part to keep Nathan aware of the outside world—he'd brought up something strange that had happened at the Secret Garden. A woman had shown up three days in a row, when there were no customers in the store, and Justin was alone behind the counter. She'd sung to him. Mocked him. Videotaped him with her smartphone. Each time telling him it was a shame he married the demon Sybil because that meant he'd die violently on tape, along with his wife and daughter. *You'll die for her sins, but your deaths will save the world.* Justin had ignored her the first time, kicked her out of the store the second. The third time, he'd told the cops, who detained this woman briefly before suggesting he file a restraining order. But he didn't have to. She didn't return. It had been well over a month. *Somehow, her absence bothers me more,* Justin told Nathan during that visit. *I keep looking for her. I want to hurt her before she hurts us.*

Nathan had told Justin he understood, deeply. And then he'd shown him why: The three boxes of hate mail. The article about what happened at Kennedy. He'd given him a small selection of their letters, along with all the copies he had of Magnolia's book, and Justin had listened to him in a way that his daughter never had, without judgment or pity. *You believe me,* Nathan said.

Of course I do, Justin replied.

What a feeling that is. Another person, believing you.

Days later, Justin had called Nathan to tell him he'd read and loved *The Prophesy.* Nathan, who has never been able to make it beyond the epigraph, asked Justin if he'd told Magnolia. He said he was still looking for the right time.

Months later, Justin called Nathan again. *The woman was back today,* he said. Four days later, he died in the accident.

Nathan's throat tightens. He doesn't want to cry, but this is the problem with growing old. Everything is so hard to control. Tears, blood, piss . . . Every bodily fluid is close to the surface, threatening to escape at any given moment, as though it's running out of time. Besides Shira's death, Nathan can't remember crying as an adult man before he turned seventy. But now he's behind the wheel of a car, traveling on icy roads, sobbing for Justin and for Shira and for his parents, for his three brothers and for his two bandmates—for everyone who's gone, all of them better people than him. He cries and cries until the tears subside and he's able to see the road again.

At least it happened while he was alone. At least it didn't get him into an accident. At least it was only tears that relentlessly flowed out of him and not blood or piss.

Nathan hears the growl of an engine. His gaze darts to his rearview. *Another car.* He isn't sure how long it's been there, lost as he's been in his own weakness. But what he does know is that it's too close, especially when he's driving at this high a speed. He takes it down to seventy, then sixty, the tailgater slowing along with him. It's like choreography.

He reaches a bend in the road and winds quickly around it, making a right turn at the flashing red light without using his blinker. The vehicle behind him does the same, riding Missy's bumper the entire time. He glances in the mirror again. It's a black SUV with tinted windows. He can't see the driver, and because he's so close, Nathan can't read the license plate. Nathan's chest pulls at him. He coughs into his hand and wipes the blood spatter on Missy's pristine leather seat.

I'm going to die the way Justin did. Nathan's thoughts are running away with him, his fears. He's thinking of the girls and Carl, heading up his way. He wants to save them in the way that he couldn't save Shira. *What a terrible knight I was. Letting the wolves get her . . .*

Nathan winces, a mixture of physical and emotional pain, a sickness that's debilitating and all-encompassing.

Nathan takes his third turn of the drive—a left, which leads him in the wrong direction. This time, the SUV doesn't follow. He doesn't feel relieved so much as surprised. He draws a long shaky breath. "I'm alive," he whispers.

He keeps driving until he can safely make a three-point turn, and heads to Star Lake. He listens to the rhythmic crunch of his wheels on the road, the music of it, and tries to shake the ghosts from his mind.

—

About five hundred feet ahead of him, Nathan sees the *Welcome to Star Lake* sign. Once he reaches it, he makes a quick left, drives a few more blocks, and at last, he's reached his first destination. He parks his car in one of the many free spaces in the post office parking lot and zips up his down jacket, pulling the collar up against his ears as he slams the truck shut and jogs up to the front door, the cold cutting into his poor, worn-out lungs.

Leland is standing behind the counter. "Hey, Mr. Lerner," he says, patting his pocket, just like he did this morning. "You ready to hear your little prodigy again?"

"Sure, and I'd also like to watch some more of that YouTube station, Leland," he says. "That okay with you? You have time?"

"Sure thing," Leland says. "They're called channels, though, Mr. Lerner. Just FYI."

Leland glances around the room. At the table against the far wall, there's a woman marking up a large package. At the counter, a burly guy in a parka is flirting with Bernadette. No one seems to notice that Nathan is even here except for Leland.

"Let's get ourselves some privacy," Leland says.

Nathan joins Leland behind the counter and follows him past the stacks of new mail to the narrow hallway that leads to the "employees only" area, back to the break room, the same spot where he'd watched Lily earlier.

Leland pulls his phone out of his pocket and starts playing with it. "Oops, looks like the video of your granddaughter was taken down," he says. "I wonder why. She was so great."

"That's all right," Nathan says. "Can you just show me some video of Carl? OnGuitar? It doesn't matter which song."

"Sure?" Leland says it like a question.

"I'd just like to see who my granddaughter is associating with."

"Oh, sure. Of course." He messes with the phone. "Here's something called 'Rubber Bullets,'" he says, setting the phone down on the table in front of Nathan and tapping the play arrow on the screen.

The boy starts in. Nathan notices his fingering first, which is fine. Pedestrian. Nothing to write home about. The sound is not distinctive. He's playing a basic blues riff that he's trying to pass off as a song he wrote himself. Nathan's not impressed, which is actually good news. It means Lily isn't blinded by Carl's musicianship—she's with him for different reasons. "Can you make the picture bigger, Leland?" Nathan says.

Leland places his thumb and index finger on the screen and stretches out the image. Leland looks at Carl's face. He's blond. That's all Nathan can see of him, the way he's turned to the side, his hair flopping onto his profile.

Nathan watches until the boy stops playing and finally looks up from his instrument and into the camera. He smiles. "Thank you very much," he says.

Nathan stares at Carl's face, his pulse racing. *Those swamp-green eyes. That voice. No. It's just my mind. Signals crossing.*

"You okay, sir?" Leland says.

"Yeah, yeah. I'm fine."

"Okay, good. Because I have something to tell you."

"You do?"

"I was going to call you about it, but you got to me first. And I felt weird bringing it up over the phone when you sounded so happy."

Nathan's heart starts to pound. "What is it, Leland?"

"I know you told me to let you know about suspicious packages."

"I . . . I received a package?"

He nods slowly. "It got here this afternoon, and I put it out back because . . . um."

"Yes?"

"It has an odor."

Nathan stares at him.

"I didn't want to tell you about it over the phone. I . . . I mean . . . I can just throw it out."

"This was addressed to me?"

"Yes."

"From where?"

"No return address. But the postmark is New York City. You want to take a look?"

Nathan nods. He has to. It's always better to face things. To know.

Leland removes two masks from his shirt pocket. He puts one on himself, and hands one to Nathan. "Because . . . you know . . . the smell. I'm really not sure what it is. It could be anything. A toxin?" He gives him a look of genuine concern. "I don't want you to get hurt."

Nathan takes the mask and puts it on. He's more moved by Leland's gesture than he should be. His eyes well up. He hopes Leland doesn't notice, but he can't help it. It's been such a strange day. Signals crossing. CarlOnGuitar. Those eyes of his. The voice . . . The past and present tangling up together, polluting his brain. Nathan hasn't smoked any weed in more than twelve hours. Maybe that's the reason. Too much real-world. Not enough buffer. Or maybe that's not it and his mind is going and there's absolutely nothing he can do about it. . . .

"I understand," Nathan says as they reach the small back room, and Leland leans down to pick up a package, Nate's name written at the top in thick, rounded script. Nathan looks for the postmark. He doesn't see it. He breathes in. There is an odor, but it's different from what he expected. It's faint and cloying, with a faux freshness to it, like baby shampoo.

Leland produces something from his back pocket, a box cutter.

As he starts slicing into the package, Nathan sees that Leland is missing most of the index finger on his left hand. He's never noticed that before. "Ouch," he says.

"I know, right?"

"When did that happen?"

"Pretty recently," he says, still intent on the box.

"How?"

"Lawn mower accident."

Nathan stares at him for several seconds. "Really?"

"Yep."

"But it's winter, Leland," Nathan says. "There are no lawns to mow."

Leland looks up at him, his eyes dark moons above the pale blue mask. "Yeah, well." He picks up the package, box cutter grasped firmly in his bad hand. "The smell's getting worse. We gotta open it outside."

He stands up and heads toward another set of doors, pulling a jacket off a hook on the wall and putting it on. As he does, Nathan stares at the sweat stains on the back of his uniform. "I mean, these crappy masks can only do so much," Leland says. He turns around. Gives Nathan a meaningful look. "They didn't save my older brother from the plague."

Nathan keeps following. He's not sure why. Is he that lonely? Or is he that unwilling to be wrong? Either way, he understands that following Leland outside is a dumb idea. And when he's in that soundless, walled-in alley behind the post office, the cold air freezing the sweat at the back of his neck, Nathan isn't surprised to see the package on the pavement, Leland rushing toward him with his eyes blazing, his curly hair slick with sweat, the box cutter raised like a weapon of war.

Nathan's not surprised at all. He's just disappointed.

THIRTY

"Stay where you are, Lily!" Mom says it from the pavement. "Stay with Bonnie!"

Lily's face is damp and warm—tears on her cheeks, though she doesn't recall crying. She leans against Bonnie and tries to catch her breath. It comes out in aching gasps. Everyone on Main Street is on the sidewalk outside their businesses, the world's saddest and most foreboding block party. Lily's gaze moves from one familiar face to the next: Mr. DeMarco standing outside his hardware store. Mr. Frank, who used to be the janitor at her school and now works at the gas station. Pastor John. Liz Reese, who stares right back at Lily, shaking her head slowly, her mouth a straight line. *Don't go to Reese's,* Mom had said. And Lily is beginning to see why. While she's only a few feet away, Mrs. Reese doesn't even take a step toward Bonnie and Lily, which seems very weird. She's been Mom's friend for years. "She's not right," Mrs. Reese says in her raspy smoker's voice, to Lily or to Bonnie, or to herself. Lily doesn't know which. "There's something wrong with her. She's not right." Those wire-thin lips. The wrinkles around them, like someone scored her with a fork. Lily's gaze travels down her arm. To the missing finger she's known about for years, barely noticing it beyond Liz Reese's ability to work around it, to cook delicious food without it, as though she never needed it in the first place. She stares directly at Lily and speaks so quietly, Lily needs to half read her lips. "She'll kill us all," Liz Reese says. "If you don't stop her."

"Meg?" Bonnie says.

Finally, the cop lets Mom stand up. Lily watches them speaking for a few moments, the cop doing most of the talking, Mom nodding, her arms crossed over her chest. Neither one of them smiles.

Finally, the cop breaks off the chat and heads toward her car along with the rest of the police, everyone sliding into their cars, like the whole thing was a drill. Lily scans the group for Frosty Lips or Mustache, but sees neither one of them.

"Lily?" Mom says.

"Mom." She chokes out the word. "I'm so happy you're . . . you're okay."

She takes off toward her. But as the lead cop moves to her car, Lily finds herself stopping to look at her, the brim of her hat pulled low over a face that's all hard angles. Lily drops her gaze and strains for a glimpse of the cop's fingers. She wants to count them, but her hands are shoved into the pockets of her uniform jacket. To Lily, it looks awkward. Purposeful.

—

"It was a swatting. Do you know what that is?" Mom says it to Lily after the crowd outside has dispersed and they're both back in the Secret Garden with Bonnie and Sara Beth, all of them with their coats still on, stomping their feet and rubbing their hands together to warm themselves.

It annoys Lily a little, the way Mom says it—that forced calm, as though she's trying to protect her. But then it occurs to her that her mom could be putting on the act for Sara Beth and Bonnie.

"I know what a swatting is, Mom," Lily says.

"I don't," says Sara Beth.

"Me neither," says Bonnie.

"It's when somebody anonymously tips off the police, claiming there's, like . . . a hostage situation, and they get them to send a whole team over," Lily says. "But it's a lie."

"Why would somebody do that?" Bonnie says.

"To freak the person out," Lily says. "To scare them. Maybe worse.

Like, if one of those cops had a temper and Mom made a sudden move, she could have been killed."

"Oh my God," Bonnie says. She gives Lily a meaningful look she hopes Mom doesn't catch. Lily nods slowly.

Mom puts a hand on Lily's shoulder. "Well, thankfully that didn't happen." The right side of her face is scraped raw from the concrete. It hurts Lily to look at her. "According to Officer Newhouse," she says, "there's been three or four of these swattings since the beginning of the year."

"But it's the end of the year now," says Lily. "That doesn't feel like a trend to me."

Mom gives her a too-wide smile, her mouth twitching at the corners. There's a cut over her right eye. "Oh, Lily. So exact about everything." She glances at Bonnie. "You two had better get back to work, right?"

"Mom, are you sure you're okay? You're all scraped up. Don't you want to—"

"I'm fine," she says firmly.

"But—"

"I'd be a lot more okay if I knew you and Bonnie were safely ensconced amid all that gorgeous clothing."

Bonnie looks at Mom. "Can you call me later, please?"

Mom peers at her for a long time. "Sure, Bon," Mom says, and Lily's positive she noticed that moment between them. "Lily, can I talk to you in the office for one quick moment before you go?"

Lily nods and heads toward the back of the store, guilt slithering through her, her cheeks reddening from it. Interesting how easy it was to lie to Mom before today—when now, Mom's gaze is burning holes into her back and she can't keep anything from her without melting inside.

Lily opens the door and turns to her mother. "I told Bonnie," she says. "I'm sorry."

Mom exhales. She closes her eyes for a few moments. "It's okay," she says quietly. "I understand."

"Thank you."

Mom opens her eyes, that fresh cut over the right one, the deep scrape on her cheek. She puts both hands on Lily's shoulders and speaks in a whisper. "I think Officer Newhouse might be one of them."

Lily's eyes widen.

"Liz Reese is, definitely. I don't know who else. And Lily . . . I found out . . ." Her voice breaks. Tears spring into her eyes.

"What, Mom?"

She takes several deep breaths, sucking in air and letting it go. "We need to get out of here. Tonight."

"Okay."

"We're going up to Grandpa's. Get Carl to bring you home from work. Ask if he can drive you up there afterward. We can all stay. Grandpa knows. I'll give Carl directions—I know you probably couldn't find it on your own."

"Why don't we all go together?"

"Because I think we should take two different cars," she says. "It's safer that way."

Lily nods slowly. "Okay, Mom. Whatever you say."

Mom pulls Lily to her. She gives her a long, tight hug that feels strange. Final.

"Soon this will be over," Mom says. Mom leaves the office and Lily follows her out. Bonnie and Sara Beth are waiting in the doorway, darkness pressing against the store's one intact window. It's just after five now, a cold, dark night. "Sara Beth, can you help me close up?" Mom says.

Bonnie takes Lily's hand and leads her outside as though she were a little girl. Someone shouts at them, "Everything okay in there?" Both of them say yes without turning around, their heads ducked, coats pulled tight around them as if they're shamed celebs.

Once they're past the green, Lily hears someone calling out her name. She knows the voice. She lets go of Bonnie's hand and whirls around instinctively.

It's Zach Winters. He's right behind her, wearing that long dark coat of his.

"I heard the police were at the store," he says. "What happened?"

Lily stares hard at him. "My mom almost got killed," she says. "That's what happened."

He frowns, his thin face caught in the glow of a streetlamp. "I'm . . . I'm sorry."

"Why?" Lily says. "Did you call them?"

"What?"

"You were out for the day. You knew Mom was at the store. Did you call the cops?"

He stares at Lily. Bonnie calls her name and Lily tells her to go ahead. "I'll catch up with you!" she says.

Zach says, "Why would I call the police?"

Lily bites her lip, all of it closing in on her, each one another rock thrown at her—the cops in the school parking lot; every post on TheYearofTwos, the pictures, the deep-fake videos; the store she helped her dad paint, the books she used to covet, destroyed, desecrated; her mother's face, her worn-out, too-thin body, frail from grief and with a twisted damaged arm; her mom made to lie on her stomach on the sidewalk with Mrs. Reese staring at her, shaking her head and muttering, as though this was all Mom's fault and Lily's fault; these assaults, these pictures taken without their knowledge, the stalking, the waiting, the *watching*.

"Because you're one of them," Lily says.

"What are you talking about?"

"Just admit it," she says. "Liz Reese basically did. One two one two is the day after tomorrow. The cops are in on it. You've thought shitty things about me and my family since fourth grade and there's hundreds or more who agree with you so just come out with it. You hate us. You're watching. You're armed. You want us dead."

Zach gapes at her, Lily's words hanging between them in the cold air. She hadn't intended to say any of that. But really, what does she have to lose? She stands facing him, her back straight. "I know, Zach," she says quietly, condensation pluming out of her mouth. "I *know*."

Zach stares at her for a long time. "I'd never call the cops on your mom," he says. "She's one of the nicest people I've ever met."

"If you like her so much," Lily says, "why did you tell me my whole family is going to hell?"

Zach opens his mouth, then closes it again. "Wow," he says.

Lily gets ready for the big denial. The *What are you talking about? I never said anything like that,* spoken in such a wide-eyed and convincing way as to make Lily think, *Maybe I remembered it wrong. Maybe I was just stoned. Maybe there's something wrong with me . . .*

She steels herself for it, the gaslighting.

"It was fourth grade," Zach says. "I was hoping you'd forgotten."

"You're . . . you admit it?"

He lets out a heavy sigh. "I have some really fucked-up people in my family. Not my mom and dad so much. They at least mean well. But my older brother, my cousin. They told me that stuff about your grandpa and your religion and I guess I thought . . . I don't know. I figured if I acted as mean as them, I could be a different person."

"Different how?"

He shrugs. "Somebody they didn't make fun of. Somebody who wasn't a geek who'd rather read than play sports. Somebody who wasn't . . . small and, you know . . . weird."

"So . . . you don't really believe that stuff?"

"Of course not," he says.

"You don't think my grandpa made a guitar strap out of babies."

"Gross. No. I said *that*?"

Lily looks at Zach, remembering him back then. The shortest, skinniest kid in their class. Almost every day, he'd be in the nurse's office, claiming a stomachache. But Lily knows now it was obviously anxiety. He'd get beat up by girls. By kids younger than him.

"I probably should have talked to you about this a long time ago," Zach says. "Like, when I started working for your parents."

Lily shrugs. "I didn't even remember until yesterday."

Zach holds out his hand. Lily shakes it. "I'm sorry," he says. "Really, really sorry."

"And I'm sorry I assumed things about you," she says. "I guess Carl . . ."

Zach's face grows cold, stony. "Carl."

"You don't like him."

"Remember when I was in the hospital?"

Lily nods. "Encephalitis." She says it purposefully. Meaningfully. Giving him a way out, because it's none of her business why he was there, even if he did try to stab a counselor.

"It wasn't encephalitis," Zach says.

Lily looks at him. "You don't have to—"

"I was at summer camp. I took a whole bottle of allergy pills. I mean, I don't mind people knowing. But my parents. They told everyone it was encephalitis. I guess they figured it's all brain stuff, so it wasn't really a lie." He laughs a little, but it turns into a throat clearing.

"I'm sorry, Zach."

"Don't be. I mean, I did spend nine months in a psych ward. But I got help, you know. I read a heck of a lot of books. I even had a girlfriend there." He smiles.

Lily smiles too.

"And I got away from those assholes at camp who spent every day torturing me and made me want to kill myself in the first place."

Lily's smile drops away.

"One of them was your friend Carl."

She stares at him, remembering how Zach glared at Carl outside the store. The hatred in his eyes. "Carl wouldn't . . ."

He gives Lily a small, sad smile. "It wasn't just him," he says. "He was part of a group."

Lily cringes. Somehow, that makes it worse.

"Maybe he's changed. I don't know," Zach says. "Summer camp feels like a long time ago."

"I think he has."

"That's good," he says. "Anyway, I'm going to go check on your mom. You think she'll be okay with that?"

"I'll let her know you're coming in," Lily says.

"Thanks."

She says a quick goodbye to Zach, texts Mom that he's on his way to the store to see her and heads toward Bonnie's car, Bonnie backing up to meet her halfway. *Carl's changed,* she thinks. *Of course he has. People change every year, every day,* she thinks. *Every second, even, cells are dying off and rearranging themselves and you're becoming someone new. Someone better. Nobody is who they were in high school. At summer camp, especially.*

"Hey?" Bonnie says, once Lily's buckled in. "Looks like you've got something on your mind."

I've changed since high school. I never was a bully, but maybe boys are different. Maybe it was peer pressure. Zach said it himself. Carl was part of a group.

"Just a thing I need to talk to Carl about."

"Is that the blond boy?"

She nods.

"He's seems like a keeper."

Lily looks at Bonnie, who has always been a good judge of character. "You really think so?"

"I do."

"Good," she says quietly. "Because I do too."

Lily texts Carl: Can you pick me up after work and take me home? My Mom has a plan. I can tell you in person.

Carl replies: What time? 6?

Yes. She remembers what mom said. Also, can you pack a bag?

The answer comes back immediately. YES!

Lily smiles.

She thinks about the night ahead of her. An hour more with Bonnie. Then Carl will pick her up, take her home so she can pack an overnight bag and grab her bass and quickly see Mom, then a good hour-and-a-half to two-hour drive in Carl's truck to get to Pearly Gates. There will be plenty of time for her to ask him about Zach, give him the chance to explain why, for a brief period at summer camp, he got sucked into the wrong crowd. After that, they can play games like I Spy and Twenty Questions, search for decent stations on Carl's crappy radio until it all turns to screaming preachers and static and they have to resort to singing "99 Bottles of Beer."

Lily feels a little excited, as though she's planning a vacation rather than an escape. She just hopes Grandpa Nate likes Carl.

TWO days to

One and two and one and two and two and two . . .

And a few things to keep in mind:

Sybil has a bad back and, since the accident, a bum arm. Smokes cigs.

Spawn sees a shrink. Smokes pot.

Big Daddy has a cough that won't quit. Cancer? Maybe.

In short: They may have Satan on their side, but they are not invincible.

> —the Bronze Lord
> WAW WAA WWT

THIRTY-ONE

"Why, Leland?" Nathan asks.

He's asking his would-be killer why because that's what you do when you're seventy-five years old and 140 pounds and there's a man who's thirty-five years younger and a hundred pounds heavier than you pushing you up against a brick wall and holding a box cutter to your throat. If you try to physically fight back, you'll be killed instantly. Since you stupidly left your guns at home, your only chance at survival lies in breaking his train of thought. So that's what you do. You ask why. You engage him in conversation. Give him a chance to brag.

Nathan's not sure where he's heard this—either a martial arts class or a TV show. TV show probably. It doesn't matter.

"Why?" Nathan says it again through chattering teeth. His whole body is shivering. The cold clamps down on his bare fingertips, and though he's wearing heavy socks and hiking boots, his toes are getting frostbitten too. Nathan doesn't want to die in an alleyway behind the Star Lake Post Office in the dead of winter. He doesn't want to be one of those bodies discovered in the trunk of his own car, or stuffed into a crawl space in some postal warehouse months or years from now. Nathan wants to go home, that's all, without being murdered. That isn't asking too much. He wants to go home so he can help his girls.

"I thought you liked my music, Leland," he says, his voice cracking. "I thought we were friends."

"Stop," Leland says.

"Stop what?"

"Stop acting like a normal old man."

"But . . . that's what I am."

"You're not. You're a witch."

Nathan gapes at him. *"What?"*

Leland's forearm presses into Nathan's chest. It's hard to breathe. There's a sting at his throat—the tip of the box cutter, then the tickling warmth of his own blood.

Leland takes a step back. Stares at him.

Nathan feels the urge to cough, but stifles it.

"Why isn't it gold?" he says.

"Huh?"

Leland rubs his dirty stump of an index finger along Nathan's neck and shows him his own blood. Nathan stares at it, thinking of all sorts of awful things. Leland's unsanitized skin. Systematic infection. The type of thing that killed Shira . . . Because that's what it was. And if they'd caught it earlier, if Nathan had allowed them to catch it earlier . . .

"It's red," Leland says. "Your blood. It's supposed to be gold."

Don't be frightened. Focus. "I don't understand."

"You joined a Satanic coven in the seventies and pledged your allegiance to the devil," Leland says. "There, you performed a ritual that transformed your blood into gold. You're the Gold Lord, Nathan Lerner. You should have gold blood."

Nathan stares at him, his mouth very dry, his pulse quick. "Are you serious?"

That was a mistake. Leland presses against his neck. "You must have cast a spell to make it red, like a normal human's."

Nathan takes a breath. "Leland, I know you're a very smart and logical man," he tries. "If I were able to cast magic spells, wouldn't I make myself strong and healthy? Better-looking while I was at it, maybe?" He forces out a laugh, hoping Leland will join him.

He doesn't. "You achieved success with 'Pearly Gates.' Then you asked Satan for a child, and he gave you one, and she was a monster like you. She wrote a book that foretold the end of the world, and it was like a road map. You cast spells to make it happen. You're both evil. Your whole family is evil. Your wife got what she deserved, and your daughter's husband did too. They're both in hell, and the two of you will join them there."

Nathan's muscles tense up, a powerful feeling overtaking him—a rage, uncoiling. *"Don't you dare say that about them,"* he roars. It echoes against the brick walls.

"No one can hear you," Leland says. But to Nathan, that's good news. No one can hear Leland either.

Nathan's rage intensifies, his blood thickening with it. He looks at Leland and he sees Todd McNally and his two friends Lindstrom and Rowley, those little shits pummeling him. Biting him, their teeth in his flesh as he stood there, paralyzed. In Leland's dim eyes, he sees every one of those wolves who drove him into obscurity, who stopped him from playing the music he loves with their hate mail, their threats, who made him warn his talented little girl off writing. These animals with their tiny, hateful brains who are so terrified of creativity, so deeply envious of original thought that they strangle it out of you, then make up some bullshit pious claim about devil worship, just so they can feel better about what they've done.

"Don't try to deny it," Leland says. "I did my research."

Nathan braces himself against the wall, then headbutts Leland. Because of their difference in height, he smashes his forehead into the postman's nose. The crunch of cartilage is sickening, satisfying. Leland howls and stumbles back, blood pouring through his paper mask. He yanks it off, the box cutter slipping out of his hands, clattering somewhere on the pavement.

The rage overtakes Nathan's body, feeding it, giving it power and strength, just like his music used to. *The music you took from me.* He balls his hand into a fist and socks Leland in the solar plexus.

Leland doubles over, then topples to the pavement. Nathan kicks him in the stomach, again and again and again. Leland moans like an animal. He is an animal. He is nothing. *How does it feel, wolf? How does it feel to have your strength robbed from you?*

Nathan spots the box cutter on the pavement. The gleaming bloodred handle. Leland grabs hold of his ankle, but his grip is loose and pathetic. Nathan steps out of it, then stomps Leland's hand, listening to his scream, the music of it . . .

The box cutter's handle is slippery, but after he wipes the blood off on his jeans, he's able to grasp it tightly. He kneels down beside Leland. With his free hand, he takes him by the throat. *To think I trusted you.*

Leland murmurs something. Either a plea for mercy or a threat, Nathan isn't sure. He tries to say it again, but Nathan shushes him. It doesn't matter.

Clearly, this isn't the way Leland imagined things would go down when he took a sick and unarmed old man into a quiet, dark alley. But that's the thing about life: It hardly ever plays out the way you imagine it will.

"You are the most ignorant man I've ever met," Nathan tells Leland, right before he slits his throat. "Let's see if you bleed gold."

—

In Leland's jacket pockets, Nathan finds his smartphone, a burner with a charger, a wallet and a clean handkerchief, which he presses to the wound on his neck. He pockets the burner and the charger, tossing the wallet and the trackable smartphone aside. He also finds a few extra paper masks and takes those too. Carefully, he stands up, his gaze darting around the alley, which isn't an alley so much as a . . . what would you call it? A basement garden? Without plants? It's a bleak, walled-in area where employees can smoke outside without actually leaving the workplace. And it's a perfect square. The only exit is back through the post office.

How the hell am I going to get out of here?

He can't hide the body either. Not by himself. Nathan is physically incapable of moving Leland. And even if he could, there's nothing in this basement garden but a couple of folding chairs and that stupid package

Leland had lured him out here with. Where would Nathan hide him? He can't even cover him up.

I'll turn myself in. It's my only choice.

Nathan has made his decision, and it's giving him a sense of calm. It may be chemical, the adrenaline rush slowly lifting from his body, everything settling back to its usual, frail state. But for whatever reason, he feels more relaxed and clearheaded than he has in a long while.

He'll turn himself in to the police. He has a feeling they'll go easy on him. He's an old man who was senselessly attacked by a crazed postal worker. He killed in self-defense. He'll be fine . . . so long as the first responders aren't in the cabal.

He'll turn himself in, and when the girls come up, they can still stay at his house. Wait out whatever they have to wait out in peace and quiet, away from those prying eyes on their smartphones, in their devices.

Not just the girls. The girls and Carl. *CarlOnGuitar.* Before they drive up, he'll have to ask Lily about him. Just to ease his own mind.

First things first. He takes the burner from his pocket. Taps in 911. As he's doing it, he notices a splash of dried blood on the back of his wrist. He can't figure out whether it's from Leland or himself, and then he sees more of it—a thick spray across the front of his parka, down the length of his jeans, coating the toe of the boot he'd kicked Leland with. He tries running a hand through his own hair. It's sticky to the touch, and he can feel more of it, dried and itchy on his forehead. His eyes sting from it. There's blood on the brick walls, blood pooling beneath Leland's body, the smell of blood everywhere, coppery and stale. Nathan puts on one of Leland's paper masks, but it barely makes a difference. He feels as though he's drowning in it.

Nathan starts to shake, reality setting in. *I could have run out. When Leland was lying on the ground, after I kicked him in the stomach, he wasn't going anywhere. His nose was broken. He was delirious. Babbling. I could have run away then. I could have left through the post office, then out through the front door. I could have shouted that he tried to kill me. "Leland tried to kill me!" No one would have kept me from leaving. They'd have called 911 or taken him to the hospital. I'd be long gone and he'd still be alive.*

But Nathan didn't run. He stayed. And he killed.

Nathan sits down next to the body of the person he just murdered. He closes his eyes, so he won't have to look at the blood.

For a few moments, he's transported back in time, back to 1979, a show at the Palladium. They'd had a packed house, one of the best crowds Prism had ever drawn, and Nathan was in his element, playing the solo from "Pearly Gates," the rhythm filling him, fueling him.

Save me! Some kid in the front row had actually yelled that at Nathan. *Save me!* this pale, pimply kid had screamed, as though he were drowning and maybe he was. Drowning in that sweaty crowd in front of the stage, wasted enough to believe he was going under for real. *Save me!* as though Nathan and this music were this stranger's last, dying hope.

They'd locked eyes, and Nathan had taken his hand from the neck of the bass and made devil horns, just to give the kid a thrill. And the kid had smiled at him. Or was it a grimace? Next thing he knew, they had to stop the show while club management called in an ambulance. But Nathan didn't care. He didn't give a damn about this pimply, sick kid. He was just angry they were stopping the show. Nathan wanted to keep playing. He wanted to play all night, and he was pissed off that this fan and his seizure, or whatever it was, had prevented him from experiencing what could have been the best moment of his life.

Maybe there *is* something off within Nathan, a spark of evil. Something demonic that people like Leland can see because they have it too. No, Nathan isn't a devil worshipper. But maybe this thing within him is worse than devil worship. Worse because it's *real*—this deep, blinding selfishness. *The wolves didn't get to Shira. MRSA did. She'd been gardening and she'd cut herself on a thorn and the cut got infected and you could have saved her. You could have taken her to the hospital earlier, but you didn't. Why? Because you thought the wolves had done it? Yes. Because you distrust modern medicine? Yes. But those weren't the only reasons. You kept her home and tried to cure her yourself because you wanted so desperately to be right.*

Tears trickle down Nathan's cheeks. Close to the surface as ever. *Leland isn't the first person I killed.*

He starts to cry more, when he hears the post office's heavy back door groaning open, a raspy female voice crooning, ". . . one and two and one and two and two and two Big Daddy died for you . . ."

Nathan stops crying. He holds his breath. *I didn't save Shira,* he thinks. *But I will save the girls.*

"Did you do it, babe? Did you remember to video it?" says the voice, which he now recognizes as Leland's tattooed coworker, Bernadette. "I brought my phone so we can go to 7Park and post pics of the body."

Clearly, he was right not to trust her.

Nathan slips the burner back into his pocket, then lies down next to Leland, his heart pumping, thinking of that kid in the Palladium, that face. How he'd seen him in Kennedy baggage claim, and recognized him immediately. *Hey, that's the Save Me kid,* Nathan had thought, before he and his friends tore into him. Before he learned that the kid's name was Todd McNally. *Be more alert this time,* Nathan tells himself, a plan forming in his mind.

—

The thing with people who think you're a Satanic witch: They tend to be frightened of you. And fear, Nathan has learned, is something he can work with.

When Bernadette strolls into the alleyway, phone held out in front of her heavily made-up face, Nathan thinks about a Roger Corman film he saw back in his twenties. Or maybe it was Russ Meyer. Some B movie about devil worshippers. Lots of naked women, which is mostly what he remembers. He thinks about the movie and rises from the ground arms and legs akimbo, teeth bared like fangs. *"Avete omnes Satanam!"*

Bernadette screams, the phone slipping from her hands and landing on the pavement.

"Quiet," Nathan says.

"You . . . you killed him."

"I said quiet. Or the next noise out of you will be your last."

Bernadette's eyes go big as half-dollars. She slaps a hand over her mouth, her head shaking furiously.

Nathan holds out the box cutter as though it were a loaded gun and Bernadette freezes, raises her hands, completely playing into it.

He scoops her phone off the ground. "I assume I can find it on here," he says. "7Park. That is what you said, right? It's something on the internet?"

She nods.

"Listen to me carefully," Nathan says. "I don't want to . . . to sacrifice another person. But trust me, I absolutely will if you don't do what I say."

Bernadette nods again.

"That door over there," he says. "Is there a key for it?"

Another nod.

"The front door too?"

Bernadette waves one of her raised hands, like a kid asking permission to go to the bathroom.

"You may speak."

She does, her voice a squeak. "There's one key for both doors."

"Give me that key."

With one tremulous hand, she makes for her pants pocket.

"I'm watching you," Nathan says, as if he expects Bernadette to be packing heat in her postal uniform. But it has the desired effect. She looks terrified.

Slowly, carefully, she removes something from her pocket, and holds it out—a single key on a brass ring that's shaped like a heart.

Nathan grabs it, then picks up the package, just to make sure it truly isn't something to be concerned over. Sure enough, it's light as can be, and when he shakes it, there's no sound. Empty. He shows the box to Bernadette. "This Leland's handwriting?"

She nods again.

He shakes his head. It's all so disappointing. He drops the package to the ground. He notices his wallet nearby, and scoops it up without taking his eyes off her. "If you scream really loud, somebody should be able to hear you," he tells Bernadette. "But count to one hundred before you do. Or I will come back and kill you."

Bernadette gawks at him as he backs through the door. "But . . ." she says.

He puts a finger to his lips, and she goes silent. Once he makes it into the office area, Nathan uses the key to lock the door behind him. He flicks on the light to the break room, where a little more than an hour ago, Leland had showed him the video of Carl. He sticks Bernadette's phone in the mini fridge, then switches off the light, feeling his way back to the front door.

There's nobody in the post office as Nathan leaves. No cars on the street outside, no one struggling up the sidewalk, pushing against the frigid winds. There are only two cars besides his own parked in the post office lot, most likely belonging to Leland and Bernadette. As he locks the front door and jogs over to Missy, Nathan thinks he might be able to hear Bernadette's screams, but that's all right. It will be a while before anyone else does.

—

Once he's on the road again and out of Star Lake, Nathan finds a safe place to pull over—a convenience store that's closed already, its lights out, not a single car in the lot. Such a sleepy area. Stores like this, closed at 6 P.M.

He kills Missy's headlights, pulls out Leland's burner and taps in Lily's phone number.

Nathan's mind isn't going. He knows his granddaughter's number from memory. That has to count for something.

THIRTY-TWO

Meg pulls into her driveway, her whole body aching. She switches on the dome light and examines her face in the visor mirror: the deep scrape on her cheek, the cut over her right eye, which Sara Beth had insisted on treating with rubbing alcohol. It stings. Meg looks like she's been in a bar fight and feels that way too, given the harshness with which Officer Newhouse had thrown her to the pavement, those words hissed into the back of her neck. *Stay still*, she'd said. As though Meg had a choice.

Later, by way of a weak apology, Newhouse told Meg that three separate callers claimed to have heard shots coming from the Secret Garden. All three said they'd seen a woman in a brown sweater, the owner of the store, holding a gun on her elderly employee.

Three separate callers. All of them aware of who Meg was, what she was wearing and that she was in the store with Sara Beth.

They're everywhere.

Meg turns off the dome light. She had expected to see Carl's truck in the driveway, but it isn't here yet. Her house looks dark and empty and utterly still. She checks the clock on her dashboard. Only six fifteen. Lily gets off at six, but often stays a little later, helping Bonnie to close up. Nothing to worry about, other than this strange feeling of being alone and watched at the same time. At this point, Meg is almost accustomed to it. *Almost.*

Meg turns off her car and gets out, the cold air biting at her wounds. She opens the trunk and grabs the polymer case. With shaking hands, she loads the Glock, the way her father showed her this morning. *This morning. I visited Dad this morning.* It's been the longest day in history. Meg puts the loaded gun back in its case, closes the trunk, then moves back around the car and grabs her purse out of the front seat. She closes the door softly, but when she locks up with her key fob, the beep is much louder than she wants it to be.

In the house across the street, someone starts turning on lights.

"Shit," Meg whispers.

The case clutched in both hands, her purse slung over her shoulder, Meg watches this display. One window brightening, then the next, then the next, followed by the second story, until the whole house is illuminated. She sees a shadow in a second-story window, a lone figure. The silhouette of a man, facing out. Meg opens the case. Removes the Glock. She grabs her keys from her purse and shoves them in her back pocket along with her phone, then backs up, the gun in both hands. She knows the owners of the house across the street, but they're gone for the season. They rent it out as an Airbnb.

The man in the window turns and starts moving, and within a minute, she sees the shadow on the first floor. He's headed for the front door. She raises the gun.

Meg is at her own front door, her back to it, the gun held out in front of her. She's afraid to get the keys from her pocket. Afraid to turn around. She waits. Ten seconds. Twenty. Thirty. The house's front door finally opens.

"Try me," Meg whispers.

The door slams shut. A statement? Or maybe this stranger was just checking the weather outside and saw the crazy woman across the street, aiming a gun at him . . .

She thinks about her neighbors. The Yelp review they're going to get. *Sorry.*

When Meg turns to open her door, though, the toe of her boot nudges something soft. The gun still in her left hand, she yanks her phone from her back pocket. She finds the flashlight. Aims it at her doorstep, a gasp escaping her lips. *I didn't overreact. I'm not wrong to want to protect myself, my home, my child.*

On her welcome mat are three dead sparrows, lined up side by side.

–

She opens the door to her house quickly and double bolts the lock. Then she checks each room in the house. The living room. The kitchen. Every single bedroom and bathroom. The basement. The attic. Each room, turning on the lights, the gun held out in front of her, the slide released and ready to fire. Each time she swings open a door, she gets stronger, less afraid. Angrier. For herself. For her family. For this house she and Justin bought twenty years ago. A fixer-upper they'd furnished with estate sale finds, planning a renovation for when Lily left for college, new windows being just a small part of it. *It will give us something to do in the house,* Justin had told her with a wink, *when we aren't doing other things.*

And now he's gone.

Once she's satisfied the house is empty, Meg heads down to the living room. She sits on the couch Justin bid on and won at an auction in Kingston. Red and gold, with a Southwestern print that made Meg think of a ski lodge they'd stayed at once, their only trip to Colorado. A happy time. She places the gun on the coffee table and sits on this couch. *My couch. My home. My husband. My daughter. My life.*

She thinks of those three birds on her doorstep, the gall of whoever put them there. And her rage boils over. She lets out a shriek that tears at her throat. The sound of it echoes.

–

Moments later, Meg's phone rings. *Neighbors,* she thinks. *Asking if everything's okay.* But who would do that? Who, at this point in the game, would have good enough intentions to check in on Meg and ask why she screamed? The man in the Airbnb? The person who left the dead birds? She glances at the screen. Bonnie.

Meg exhales. "Hi, Bon."

"You said you'd call," Bonnie says. "But I decided not to stand on ceremony."

"I'm sorry," Meg says. "Things have been kind of crazy . . ."

"I know," Bonnie says. "Lily told me."

"Yes, I heard." Her phone dings. She tells Bonnie to hold on a sec and glances at it. It's a text from Lily, verifying the plans for tonight. She texts a quick reply, then gets back to Bonnie. "I just feel so . . . so powerless."

"You aren't, though. You're the toughest person I know. And they sound like idiots."

"Bonnie," she says quietly. "They got Justin."

"What?"

She hadn't meant to say it, especially not over the phone. But now that she has, it's as though a gate has opened, the truth rushing out and into the light. "It wasn't an accident. It was planned. The mechanic is one of them, and he sabotaged my car. The other car on the road—the skinheads who distracted us—they were in on it too. One of them is the son of a religious freak who assaulted my dad forty years ago. And that freak is related by marriage to the mechanic. It spans generations, Bonnie. It runs in families around here like a disease. They . . . they *killed my husband*. And now . . ."

"Oh my God," Bonnie says softly. "Oh my God."

"Please don't tell Lily. I . . . I haven't said anything to her. I . . . I can't figure out *how*."

"You're sure of this."

"Yes."

There's a long silence on the other end of the line. Meg can hear Bonnie's tremulous breath. "I'm going over there," she says finally. "I'm coming to your house."

"No, no. Bonnie," Meg says. "I don't want you to get hurt too."

But Bonnie's ended the call.

—

Ten minutes later, Meg hears tires pulling into her driveway, headlights shining through the thin white draperies she hung herself and now wishes were made of steel. She hears the slam of a car door, footsteps on her walkway. She grabs the gun from the coffee table and moves toward the door. Same as her father did when she showed up at his place this morning. *This morning.*

"Who's there?" Meg shouts.

"Bonnie!"

Meg lets out a massive sigh. She puts the gun back on the coffee table, unlocks the front door and sees her oldest friend standing there in her bright red faux fur. "I . . . I pushed the birds into the bushes," she says. "What the fuck is wrong with these people?"

Meg throws her arms around her, and Bonnie hugs her tightly. "You're smarter than them," Bonnie whispers. "You're stronger." And everything Meg has been thinking solidifies in her mind.

"I'm going to send Lily up to my dad's, with Carl," she tells Bonnie, once she's locked the door and the two of them are sitting on the couch. "But I'm staying here. I'm not going to let them do anything to my home."

Bonnie says nothing for several seconds, her gaze traveling to the coffee table. The loaded gun. "My dad gave me that," Meg says. "He taught me how to use it."

Bonnie smiles. She reaches into her bag and pulls out an ornately sheathed dagger. Meg's eyes widen. She remembers the weapon from Bonnie's father's study, the two of them sneaking in there when they were ten years old, daring each other to open the glass display box, Meg's knees going weak at the touch of it.

Bonnie removes the sheath. The blade gleams. She sets the dagger on the coffee table, next to the gun. "My dad gave me *this*," she says quietly, firmly. "And I'm going to help you fight these fuckers."

THIRTY-THREE

"My mom says it's fine for you to stay with us," Lily tells Carl. They're in the truck, on their way to get gas, when Mom texts her back: Yes. Lily had been anxious to head home and pack a bag but Carl told her he'd once worked a renovation in the Catskills, and he'd noticed driving there and back that gas stations were scarce and tended to close early.

"Sorry, Lily. What did you say? Your mom wants me to drive you up to your grandpa's, right?"

"No, she'd like you to stay up there with us. I mean . . . if you can."

"Really?"

"Yes." Lily laughs. "Why are you so surprised?"

"I dunno. I guess I'm a little nervous. I always am, around people's parents."

"You shouldn't be."

"Really?"

"I think she likes you."

Carl grins.

Lily watches him, his hands on the wheel, calloused and gentle at the same time. She thinks back to what Zach said, and realizes that two things can be true. Carl could have been awful to Zach in summer camp, but he could still be a good person. An honest one, deep down. "Hey," she says. "So, back at the store, after my mom got swatted?"

"Yeah?"

"I talked to Zach Winters. I asked him some questions."

"And?

"He says you bullied him at camp."

She watches Carl's hands on the wheel, the fingers tightening.

Lily swallows hard. "It's okay," she says. "I've gotten involved with friends who made me do things I didn't want to do. I know you're not really a bully, it's just—"

"Why were you talking to him?"

"Excuse me?"

"Why were you talking to Zach Winters, Lily? I told you, he's like . . . unbalanced. He didn't go to that hospital on his own. He had to be forced, and even then . . . I mean . . . Why were you even near him?"

Lily stares at him. The hardness in his eyes. The set of his jaw. *Is he jealous? Of Zach Winters?* For the first time since she's known Carl, she can't figure him out. "Anyway," she says quietly. "I don't think he's one of them."

Carl says nothing. He won't even look at her.

"Is this our first fight?" Lily tries. "Because, um, in case you've forgotten, I'm kinda going through shit right now . . ."

Carl's expression softens, his grip relaxing on the wheel. "I'm sorry, Lily," he says. "I'm just trying to help."

He puts his hand on hers for a few moments and gives it a squeeze. His grip is strong. "I want to save you," he says quietly.

Lily frowns at him. "I, uh . . . I appreciate that. But you know what? I think it would help to think of this as a road trip. You know? And I think you'll like my grandpa. He smokes a ton of weed."

He smiles at her, a normal Carl smile. "He sounds cool," he says.

Lily's phone vibrates. She glances at the screen. It's an unfamiliar number. Probably spam. "You'll love his place too. He's got this sick recording studio, and the whole place is really cool and a little spooky. A renovated honeymoon hotel from, like, the 1920s or something"

Carl grins at her. "It sounds awesome." Then he snickers. "Honeymoon hotel."

She rolls her eyes. *Boys.*

Carl pulls into a gas station and up to one of the pumps, and turns off the truck. "BRB," he says.

"K."

She thinks again about what Carl said. *I want to save you.* It wasn't so much the words themselves, but the way he'd said them. The intensity in his voice. It had made the hairs on the back of Lily's neck stand up, as though some different part of Carl were emerging from a hiding place—the part of Carl that bullied Zach.

I'm being unfair. Lily tries to put herself in Carl's shoes, to imagine what it must feel like for him, starting the day by agreeing to give a girl a ride and ending it at the center of some apocalyptic conspiracy theory. *I'd be acting weird too.* Lily glances out the window. She tries to wave to Carl, but he seems lost in his own thoughts as he works the pump.

Her phone vibrates again, the same unfamiliar number as earlier. She declines the call. But seconds later, the number's back on her screen, the phone humming insistently. "Okay, fine," Lily says. She holds her breath and answers. "Who is this?"

"Lily? Thank God."

Lily lets out her breath. "Grandpa?" she says. "Why are you calling from this number?"

"It's a burner, Lily. It belonged to one of *them.*"

"The wolves?"

"Yes."

"How did you—"

"I need you to write down the number, okay? It's going to be my phone from now on. So answer whenever you see it. Write it down."

"Okay," Lily says.

"You have a pen and paper?"

"Yes." She doesn't feel like explaining "recent calls" on iPhones. She lets him spell out the number that's on her screen.

"You got that written down?" he says.

"Yes."

"Keep it hidden. Show no one this number. And I'd get a burner of your own ASAP. We can't risk talking on any lines that might be compromised."

"What's going on?" Lily says, her pulse quickening. "What's happening?"

"Nothing worth discussing on the lines," he says. "But I do have one question for you."

"Yeah?"

"What's Carl's last name?"

Lily frowns. "Lindstrom. Why?"

There's a long silence on the other line. "He's coming with us. Did Mom tell you? He's with me now."

Grandpa Nate starts to cough, the cough growing into a barking hack.

"Are you okay, Grandpa?"

He's wheezing now.

"Hello?"

"Just you and . . . your mother . . . alone."

"What?"

Grandpa takes a breath, a whistling wheeze. "He can't come with you," he whispers. "Carl can't come. Get away from him. Now."

Lily's heart slams into her rib cage. "What . . ." she says. Grandpa ends the call.

—

"Who were you on the phone with?" Carl says, once he's back behind the wheel.

She thinks about what her grandpa said. *Maybe he's high. Maybe that's it.* "Just my mom," she says.

"Oh. Cool."

"Listen, Carl," she says, "I'm really sorry for everything that's happened today."

"It's not your fault."

"I know, but I feel like I've gotten you caught up in something terrible, without considering your feelings. Your . . . your safety."

"Stop, Lily. I want to help."

"I know. But anyway . . . I think it's best if you just drop me off at my house. I'll call you as soon as I can. And, like, once twelve/twelve is over and everything's back to normal, we can pick up where we left—"

"No."

"What?"

"I told you, Lily. I want to help you."

"I know," she says softly. "And you have, as much as you can. But I've put you in enough danger. It's not fair."

He looks at her. "Did your mom change her mind? Is that it?"

She nods.

"Let me talk to her. I'll put her at ease." He gives her a smile. "She likes me, remember?"

Lily exhales. This is harder than she thought it would be. It's strange too. The more Carl insists on helping her, the less she wants him to. "My mom was pretty firm, Carl," she says. "It isn't you, though. She just thinks it's too dangerous. For you. For us. For everybody."

Carl nods slowly. He says nothing. Doesn't start up the truck. He just stares at her for a long time, looking sort of hurt but also angry. Lily has an urge to open the door and start running.

"Okay, so when I was out there, I noticed two of my tires were low on air," Carl says. "I'm gonna go fill them up."

"When I get back from my grandpa's," Lily tries, "everything will be normal again."

"Sure, Lily." Carl belts himself in for the drive from the gas pumps to the air pumps, which is sort of on-brand for him. And he takes his time unbuckling himself, which strikes Lily as sad, but also selfish. Carl may no longer be going to Grandpa's, but Lily and her mom still need to get there, fast. "I swear I'm not breaking up with you," she says.

"I know."

"So this isn't, like, goodbye forever. If that's what you're thinking."

"I don't think that."

"Okay, because it feels a little like you're stalling and I'm, like, flattered, but—"

"I just need air."

Lily stares at him. His eyes are hard, and his voice sounds deeper somehow.

"Okay," she says quietly.

Carl slams the door to the truck and kneels in front of the left front tire. He attaches the hose and fills it. Lily waits. He'll be done soon and then he'll stop being pissy and take her home.

Lily exhales. Carl moves around to the back of the truck, and as he does, she hears a buzzing. "Carl, your phone!" she says. But he doesn't hear her. She looks around for his phone, but sees that it's plugged into the charger, the screen black.

There's more buzzing, and then Lily sees it. A flashing light, under Carl's seat.

She undoes her seat belt, gets down on her knees and grabs it. It's a burner. The kind of phone you have when you're dealing drugs. Or seeing multiple girls, but pretending you're not. The kind of phone you buy when you have something to hide.

The buzzing stops. Lily casts a quick glance in the rearview, and then she opens the phone, a flip phone. She checks recent calls.

There are a lot of them, especially in the past three days. Lily looks at the numbers. She doesn't recognize any of them at first. And weirdly, none of them have a local area code. Could it be a work thing? *Why would somebody have a burner phone for construction jobs? And why would all the calls on it be nonlocal ones?*

A text comes in. It's from the number that just called.

WE'RE HERE. YOU HAVE HER?

Lily inhales sharply, her whole body suddenly cold, inside and out, as though a switch has been flipped, a thermostat broken. Cold, like she felt after the accident. Cold, like when they loaded Dad onto the stretcher and zipped up the bag. *There has to be a reason for that text. A good reason. A perfectly innocent one. Please. Please.*

She looks at the rearview again, Carl moving to the right rear tire. She goes back to recent calls, and takes a closer look at the phone numbers.

One number appears at least half a dozen times, and she thinks she might know it. "It can't be," she whispers. "I must be remembering it wrong."

Please, please, please, please.

She grabs her own phone and checks recent calls. The one from Grandpa Nate. Looks again at the calls on Carl's burner. Carl's secret fucking phone. It's the same number.

It's a burner, Lily. It belonged to one of them.

Lily feels the driver's side door opening. "What is this . . ." She doesn't get the rest of the sentence out. A hand clamps over her mouth. Carl's strong, calloused hand. His forearm presses against her chest, cutting off her air.

Lily tries to bite his hand, but it's too tight. And then she sees the glint of metal in the other, with a leather hilt. A hunting knife.

"I'm sorry, Lily," Carl says, as he holds the blade to her throat. "I wish it didn't have to be this way."

THIRTY-FOUR

It isn't that unusual a last name. It could be a different Lindstrom than the one who nearly killed me, Nathan thinks, once he's back at his house. *Or if it's the same one, a distant relative. Not a son or a nephew, but . . .* It's a desperate thought and he knows it. Genetics don't lie. CarlOnGuitar looked exactly like Christopher Lindstrom from Kennedy airport. To hear his voice was to hear Lindstrom calling him a dirty heathen. To look into those swamp-green eyes was to feel Christopher Lindstrom sinking his teeth into his forearm. Lindstrom, who was even worse than Todd McNally, because he was bigger, less of a talker. More intent on finishing what he started.

And look at what Carl Lindstrom had done. Videotaping his "Pearly Gates" bass solo with the camera trained on Lily and only Lily. Her name in the title of the video for all the wolves to see. He thinks back to what he'd said to her on the phone this morning. *Don't be mad at your boyfriend. I'm sure he did it with good intentions.* But that was wrong. Nathan was wrong. Carl Lindstrom had done what he did with the worst intentions. And then Leland, that murderous wolf, had shown Nathan the video twelve hours after it was posted. How was a YouTube station run by an unknown eighteen-year-old so instantly available to a forty-year-old postal worker in Star Lake?

He remembers how Leland had smiled at him as he watched Lily play, so eager for his reaction, but clearly for different reasons than Nathan imagined. *How could I be so gullible?*

They're connected, Carl Lindstrom and Leland. Both in the cabal Magnolia told him about. *And now that I've killed one of them . . . well, it's going to change my plans.*

It's okay. Nathan's flexible. The only problem is, he's working on limited energy. Between the coughing jags, which are growing worse, he's managed to shower off all the blood, bandage his neck wound and put on a robe, but now he feels another attack coming on, that terrible burn, like someone's poured battery acid on his lungs. The first hack rips at his insides, and it goes downhill from there, Nathan curled up like a pill bug on the bathroom floor, bombs detonating in his chest one after another after another.

When he's finally able to stop, Nathan's muscles are lax and he feels completely spent. It's as though the illness gave him a reprieve so he could kill Leland, only to roar back again at twice its power. The only thing keeping him going now is his own worst fear.

"Please give me strength," whispers Nathan, who has never been one to pray. "Please let me live long enough to save my family."

He's sitting up now, looking for his second wind so he can dress, pack and wait for the girls to arrive.

With difficulty, he pulls himself to his feet. Every fiber in his body aches, the aftereffects of a fight to the death, the endorphins wearing off. He feels as though he's been hit by a truck, and in a way he has.

"Please give me the strength."

Nathan stops in the kitchen and puts a kettle on, enough water to drink a cup of tea now and make a thermos for later. He pulls a jar of local honey out of the pantry, so he'll remember to add it. His memory hasn't been crackerjack for a while now—he tends to forget most things if he doesn't write them down or isn't looking directly at them.

He walks into his bedroom, changes into a flannel shirt and jeans. Then he takes a duffle bag into the kitchen and starts emptying his cupboards into it—canned vegetables, whole grain bread, a two-pound bag of trail mix. He takes the rice and beans out of the fridge, stuffs it in a Tupperware container and packs that too, along with some silverware and a box of cereal he finds at the back of his pantry, a few months past its expiration date but what the hell? *Who says cereal can expire?* He grabs a few gallon jugs of water out of the pantry as well. They won't fit in the duffel, but he'll throw them in the car. Then he lugs the bag back into his room and stuffs it with heavy sweaters of his that the girls can wear. He can't trust them to dress warmly enough. They have no idea how blisteringly cold it can get up here at night, with no heat.

After he's done with most of the packing, Nathan crouches down and works the combination on the safe beneath his bed to remove the Beretta, as well as his Taurus TX22, which he thinks is simple enough and small enough for Lily to learn how to handle. He decides not to pack the .44 Magnum Nighthawk—it's much too flashy and identifiable for two women on the run. The Ruger too. He never liked that one very much anyway.

Nathan wraps both the Taurus and his loaded Beretta in one of the sweaters, along with a couple of boxes of ammo. As he's standing up, Nathan tastes molten copper, and so he takes a handkerchief out of his nightstand drawer and spits blood into it. *Just long enough to take them on the road, drive them to Wellman's. Make sure they're comfortable and safe and they know what to do.*

Before he killed Leland, it had been his idea to go there too—the ruins of the resort where he spent so many happy summers as a child. Magnolia saw it when she was little. But she probably doesn't remember that there is a livable unit there, well insulated if rustic, with twin beds and a sofa, a clean toilet with a bucket next to it that can be filled with nonpotable water from the faucet near the baseball diamond. Not the Ritz by any stretch, but safe. Hidden. The girls can set up camp there for as long as need be, while Nathan returns home and waits for the something to get him—the fuzz or the wolves or this fucking disease, whichever shows up first.

I won't drag them down with me. I'll never give them up. I can die or face justice knowing I saved them.

He zips up the duffel bag and grabs his parka from the chair before he realizes that it's still caked in Leland's blood. He makes his way to his closet and pulls out a heavy anorak in camo green—a coat bought years ago for a trip to Alaska he'd planned with Shira for their first fall as empty nesters, but wound up getting canceled due to her death. He hasn't worn the coat since then, and when he tries it on, it swallows him.

Through all of this, Nathan makes an effort to stay calm and focused. It's hard, though, to keep himself from thinking about what happened at the post office, or what may have occurred after he left, once Bernadette's screams were finally answered. He can't help but cringe over the story this tattooed Scheherazade will no doubt spin for the police, about some crazy old drugged-out devil worshipper who finally snapped, slaughtering Star Lake's most beloved mailman and locking his poor defenseless ex-girlfriend outside in the cold. (Or is she his current girlfriend? Leland was clearly not the most reliable narrator.) What a tale to tell: a deranged old fool, going postal on a postal worker.

Shouldn't have left a witness.

It was stupid of him not to kill Bernadette. At the very least, he should have injured her enough that she'd be too scared to turn him in. But Nathan could never hurt a woman, even one as noxious as her. What was the line from that pop song that Magnolia used to listen to? *I'm a lover, not a fighter* . . . If he closes his eyes, he can practically hear it, blasting through the tinny speakers of his eleven-year-old daughter's boom box.

Nathan's teakettle whistles. He walks into the kitchen. Since he needs the caffeine, he makes a thermos full of organic green tea, and leaves it on the counter to steep. As he mixes some of the honey into the tea, he thinks about Bernadette again. Screaming into the wind. The cops will find her. It's only a matter of time. But as far as Bernadette and the cops finding Nathan, he figures he's got some wiggle room. When he registered for this PO box, Nathan had yet to renovate the compound, and so he'd used the address of the rental he was staying in at the time, in Bethel. He never bothered changing it with the Star Lake Post Office, which is quite fortunate. As far as he knows, the only places where Pearly Gates' address is connected with his name are the deed to the land and his driver's license.

By the time they track him down at this place the girls should be all set up at Wellman's.

Nathan finishes steeping the tea. Then he walks to the music room and picks up his favorite bass, the one he bought himself when "Pearly Gates" hit the Hot 100. *Reward yourself,* Shira had told him, and he had. It's a 1959 Fender Precision Sunburst. Cost nearly as much as all four years of his SUNY tuition, but Shira didn't complain. *It's beautiful,* she said. *And you deserve it . . .*

Shira said she was overjoyed, because she knew Nathan's goal had been to make the Billboard chart. *Play it in good health,* Shira said, *and with a full and happy heart.*

"Pearly Gates" had stayed on the Hot 100 for two weeks, never making it above 80. But the Fender still turned it into a lasting accomplishment. Shira was right, as usual. After she died, he took the Fender into the home studio of their old house. Played it for weeks, nonstop, barely sleeping or eating. He suffered nerve damage in his fingertips, cubital tunnel that never completely went away. He knew at the time that he was harming himself, but still he kept it up. As though playing the Fender could conjure Shira back. Looking at it closely, Nathan can still see a hint of his blood on the strings.

Tears seep into his eyes. *Focus,* he tells himself. Gently, he places the Fender in its case and closes the latches.

Magnolia once told Nathan that he is more caring and protective toward inanimate objects than he is toward people. He was hurt at the time, but she may have been right. Nathan shuts the door, taking the Fender with him. He's going to give it to Lily.

—

After he's done loading the supplies and the bass into Missy's trunk and placing the car keys on the driver's seat, Nathan returns to his foyer, where he warms himself and sits down and takes several deep breaths. His energy somewhat restored, he's ready to transfer the contents of his bloody parka into the anorak. Once he's done with this final chore, he'll have nothing to do but drink his tea and wait for the girls. He pulls his house keys and sunglasses from the outside pocket, along with a pack of gum, a few guitar picks and a long-forgotten joint. From the inside pocket, he removes Leland's burner, the charger, his own wallet . . .

The black leather wallet feels strange in Nathan's hand. Thicker than he remembers. He holds it up to the light. "Oh God." This wallet is not black. It's dark gray.

He opens the wallet. Leland's wallet. *Must have picked it up by accident,* he thinks. But as he goes through all his other pockets, only to find them empty, the truth envelops him, shrouds him. He can't breathe.

Nathan took Leland's wallet instead of his own. His wallet, which holds his driver's license, Pearly Gates' address printed on it clearly, was left behind in the basement garden with Leland's body. And Bernadette.

"Fuck," Nathan says. "Fuck, fuck, fuck, fuck."

Like a response, Nathan hears a crash in his living room—one of the windows breaking—and then Bernadette's voice, raspy and cruel, calling out his name. "Nathan? Big Daddy? I know you're here."

THIRTY-FIVE

Carl's hunting knife is huge, with a thick black leather hilt and a blade that looks as if it could slice through solid rock. Carl holds it to Lily's throat while speaking to her in the calmest voice, and she's paralyzed by terror— not just from the knife itself, but from the fact that Carl owns it. It makes her stomach drop, the thought of him using this on an animal. "I have to tie you up because you don't quite know yet," Carl says. "But don't worry. I'm going to save your soul. And Lily, you're going to save the world."

Lily's eyes dart around, searching for someone she can signal. There's no one here. The lights are off in the gas station—she could have sworn they were on when they got here, a guy behind the counter with the lottery tickets and cigarettes. But the guy's gone now, or if he's there, he's part of this plan. He's one of them, sitting in the dark, watching.

"Wh . . . where are we going?"

Carl slaps her hard across the face. It stings. "Ask any more questions—I'm supposed to gag you. If you scream, it's worse. Trust me," he says. "I don't make the rules."

Lily says nothing. She doesn't scream. Doesn't move. She breathes deep through her nose until finally, the stinging stops.

He tells her to take off her coat and she does. And then she lets him tie her up with rope he's packed in the cargo bed, a pile of rope that's been sitting there innocently in the same spot as long as they've been hanging out. She's seen it but never questioned it. She just figured, *Don't all contractors use rope?*

Carl binds her hands behind her back, and then he does her legs, tying them together and threading the rope through a metal loop on the floor in front of the passenger's seat. She never thought twice about that loop either, same as she never thought twice about Carl these past few days, posting that video of her on his YouTube channel, insinuating himself into her life, her family, her plan for escape, misdirecting her into thinking Zach was one of *them*—Zach, whom Carl bullied as part of a group. Why had Lily grown so close to him, so quickly? Lily wants to think it was the weed. Carl really did have the most potent, mind-altering weed . . . But it wasn't.

It was the text. Carl starts up the truck and pulls out of the gas station, the rope cutting into her wrists, her thighs, her ankles. *It was that fucking text.*

The text came the morning after the accident. I heard what happened. So sorry about your dad, it said. I don't know what I'd do if that happened to me. But if you need anything, even if it's just someone to talk to, I'm here.

From Carl Lindstrom. That guy from school.

The timing of it got her. Carl was the first of anybody back home to reach out, including her closest friends. It had been in the papers, she was pretty sure . . . But Lily knew how people acted around tragedies like hers. *Maybe she doesn't want to talk. Maybe she wants some time first.* That's what they think. Because it's easier. It's how Lily would have reacted. But here was this guy, this random dude she'd jammed with a few times, who was brave enough to reach out. Lily was still in the hospital, and she hadn't even been able to see her mom yet. She read the text through tears. Read it ten times in a row and responded within seconds: four heart emojis.

Grief turns people into idiots.

—

Carl is talking. He's been talking for probably ten solid minutes, maybe fifteen or twenty. Lily's lost all sense of time since they hit the road, the truck roaring out of town, away from her house, her mom, her life. They're climbing Route 28, and Carl is talking about how this YouTube channel he loves—this "conspiracy expert" named the Lee-Man— listened to "Pearly Gates," read Mom's book and went on a "deep dive" into the "real facts of your family's master plan."

Lily is barely listening. She keeps thinking about her mom. She's called twice since Carl silenced Lily's phone and stuck it near the gearshift. She's seen *MOM* on the screen and wished she could find some way of letting her know what's happened. She feels powerless. Helpless.

"The Lee-Man's channel is fucking brilliant. Much more intense than what we looked at on YearofTwos. I mean, Lily, the Lee-Man has evidence that Jim Jones knew your grandpa. Jim Jones! He even played 'Pearly Gates' at Jonestown. The subliminal messages made them drink the Kool-Aid."

She turns and stares at him.

"What?"

"Nothing."

"Did you know that COVID Patient Zero was reading your mom's book on the plane?"

She wants to laugh at him. To spit on him. She knows he'd kill her if she did. At this point, it almost feels worth it. Going out like that, quickly, without having to endure another minute with Carl. But then she looks at the knife in his pocket and her throat clenches up and her heart starts skittering in her chest again. *No, no, no. I don't want that. I didn't mean it, I didn't* . . . "Carl," she says, interrupting him.

"Yeah?"

"Can I please call my mom?"

"That's a question, Lily."

"I know. I'm sorry. Please. We don't want her looking for us, right? I won't tell her anything. I'll just say we're running late or whatever you want me to—"

"In time," he says.

"What?"

An expression crosses Carl's face, a strange smile. Lily has no idea what it means.

Lily pulls against the ropes, the cold air from outside pressing through the crack in the window, biting her. She looks at Carl. *Can I ask him to turn up the heat, or is that one too many questions?*

He pulls the knife out of his pocket and holds it as he drives. So casually, like someone holding a cigarette. Lily turns toward the passenger's window, wishing the road wasn't so dark, so empty.

"Did you ever think I was in on it, Lily?"

"No." She says it to the window.

"A couple of times, I thought you might be getting suspicious. So I, like, doubled down on the niceness. I've never done anything like this before. I was nervous. I'm glad it worked." He sounds smug. Pleased with himself.

Lily says nothing.

"You know, when I told the Lee-Man that I went to high school with Sybil's daughter, he freaked out. He didn't even believe me at first. He was, like, 'Well, can you get close to her?' And I was, like, 'I can try,' and . . . and he said, 'Try on August twentieth.'"

Lily's stomach drops. Her mouth goes dry, that feeling overtaking her. That deep, pervasive chill. Her ears start to ring. She speaks, and it's like someone else is talking. Someone in a dream. "You knew about the accident. You knew it was going to happen."

Carl's gaze stays plastered to the windshield. "No." He won't look at her. He can't.

"You killed him. You all . . . fucking . . . killed my father."

She starts to shake, tears pouring down her face. Carl opens the glove compartment, Lily hating him, the awful proximity of his skin. He pulls out some tissues and dabs at her face, Lily struggling against the rope. "I didn't have anything to do with it," he says. "I didn't know what was going to happen on the nineteenth, I swear."

Lily just keeps staring at him, her lip trembling, her nose running, more tears spilling from her eyes.

"For what it's worth, I wasn't lying in that text I sent. I really was sorry about what happened to your dad. He was such a nice guy, and I never thought he was in on the whole thing. I care about you too, Lily. A lot."

She turns back to the window. She can't look at him anymore.

"Listen," Carl says softly. "Listen, Lily. I know you aren't going to understand this right away, and I don't expect you to. But just try, okay? When you're going to save the world, Lily, no individual life matters."

Lily presses her forehead against the window. She hates the sound of his voice and tries to shut him out of her mind. She sniffles. He tries to dry her face again but she stays turned away. "You're fucking crazy," she whispers.

"What?" Carl says.

"Nothing. I didn't say anything."

—

Carl doesn't start talking again until they've driven ten more miles. There's a full moon, and Lily has been watching it through the passenger's side window. She can see the face in it. *The man in the moon,* though Lily always thought of the moon as female. Her mom used to read her this book when she was little, a picture book. A smiling lady moon with dimpled cheeks. In the book, the moon likes butter and makes friends with a cow. Lily loved that book. She's trying to remember what it's called when Carl starts talking. It makes her jump.

"We're almost there," he says.

"Where?"

"You'll see." Carl pulls off Route 28 and makes a left on a road called Greenfield. Lily goes over the directions in her head, so she can tell her mom somehow. Text it to her. She wonders if she'll get the chance. She doesn't think so. Carl hasn't blindfolded her. If he thought there was some risk to her seeing where they're going, wouldn't he have done that?

"I think you're basically a good person, Lily," Carl says.

Is she supposed to say thank you? Return the compliment?

"The way I see it, your grandpa and your mom are the real villains, and you're, like, third-generation. You were born into this family. You couldn't help being born."

He makes a turn on another road—Blueberry Hill, it's called. A pretty name. They're in the snowy countryside under a full moon. They pass a barn, an empty field. "You're like Iyanla in *The Prophesy*," he says. "Just like her, really. You've even got opal eyes, like how your mom described her in the book. Did you know that opals used to be used in Satanic practices? I'm thinking it's why Sybil snuck that in."

Why can't he shut up?

"I got to the Nine-and-Tens through the Lee-Man," Carl is saying, "but others have gotten here different ways. We're everywhere, really. You were right about that. And I'm thinking . . . I mean. You read it on the board. You could be like a rock star within the community if you do one thing—"

"My mom's gonna come looking for you," Lily says. "You know that, right?"

"Oh, we're counting on that."

"What?"

Carl looks at her. The truck slows, pulls off the road and stops. Lily looks out the window. They're at a garage called Halloway's. He smiles at Lily. "I'm going to save your soul, Lily. And you're going to save the world." Carl pulls the burner phone out of his pocket and calls a number. "We're here," he says into the mouthpiece.

From behind the garage, headlights flash.

Carl turns to Lily, the knife grasped in his hand. He leans closer, and she shuts her eyes. "Don't worry," he says. "I'm just going to untie your legs so you can come with me."

Lily opens her eyes, aims them at the phone near the gearshift. Her phone. Striped with missed calls from Mom. After he turns off the truck and takes the keys, Carl bends down in front of Lily and frees the rope from the metal loop, the knife never leaving his hand.

Once he's done, he looks up at her. "Don't you want to help save the world, Lily?" he says. "Don't you want to end the plague, just like Princess Iyanla?"

Lily stares at him with cold, flat eyes. "She didn't end the plague."

"What?"

"Iyanla didn't end the plague," she says. "She only slayed the monsters."

His face flushes a little. "Oh, well . . ."

Lily keeps glaring at him, aware of the knife, the unhinged person holding it, yet still she can't help herself. "Didn't you even read the book?"

His jaw tightens. "We're going to stop the world from ending," he says. "And you're going to help us. Whether you like it or not."

He holds the knife to her throat as he lifts her out of the truck. It's freezing outside. Her nose starts to run. But other than that, she doesn't feel it, not really. Carl opens the glove compartment. He removes a roll of duct tape, rips off a piece. "This is just for the video," he says.

Lily's eyes widen. Before she can say anything, he slaps tape over her mouth. He wraps a thick arm around her neck, the point of the hunting knife at her chest, and half leads, half pushes her toward the back of the garage. The headlights flash again.

"My dad knows all about your grandpa, by the way," he says. "Big Daddy put a curse on his best friend at one of his concerts. Gave the poor guy seizures for life. And then, of course, he gets the plague and dies."

They move, their shoes scuffing the gravel, and Lily listens to the scuff, the rhythm. The music of it. She thinks of her grandpa Nate and her mom and the sweet old lady moon from the book she used to read her. She thinks of her dad's smiling face and this cat named Sandy who belonged to the neighbors but would come by their house all the time. She thinks of anything and everything but Carl and where he's leading her.

"I'm telling you, Lily, your grandpa is a really bad man," he says, once they've reached their destination. The headlights. It's a Mazda. A tan Mazda.

Lily stops breathing.

The doors open. Three men get out. The skinheads. They're here.

Lily's breath comes back and she shrieks through the duct tape. She shrieks and shrieks until her throat is raw from it, her nose running, tears streaming down her face. She shrieks until she has no air left, and she feels as though she might die from it.

Carl gives Lily a small, sad smile. And then he holds up Lily's phone, and tapes her.

THIRTY-SIX

It's been half an hour since Lily last texted, saying she and Carl would be back as soon as they got gas, so she could pack her things. Bonnie points out that Carl's made Lily late for work more than once, which is news to Meg. "She's usually so responsible," she says, thinking, *He's probably the reason why she skipped therapy too.*

Bonnie shrugs. "Young love."

"True," Meg says. "But this isn't exactly a normal night. We have to be somewhere—or she does, anyway. And you know . . . they're out there."

Her words are punctuated by the smashing of glass: a rock, flying through an upstairs window. The second of the night. The first time, they hadn't gotten outside in time to see who had done it. But Bonnie's faster now. She grabs her knife and runs for the door, throwing it open and hurrying onto the lawn with a surprising speed. Meg runs behind her. "Who did this?" she hears Bonnie yell. "Show your fucking faces!"

When Meg gets to the door, Bonnie is chasing two figures wearing hoodies, the dagger raised.

Meg catches up to her, the two of them breathing hard, grasping their knees, the breath raking Meg's lungs as she gasps. Down the street, she sees the hoodies stopping briefly, their phones raised, taking footage. "I swear to God," Bonnie says, "if I caught up with them, I would have cut them. I was ready."

"One more day to get through," Meg says. "Then they'll see."

"They won't see," Bonnie says. "Maybe they'll forget. Move on to some other bullshit belief, a new set of people to terrorize. But they won't *see* anything."

The hoodies lower their phones. They reach a car, a couple of blocks away, and get inside. It's a new Range Rover, easily worth twice what Meg and Justin paid for this house. Meg shrugs. "I just know I'll feel better once Lily's on her way to my dad's. Those assholes are one thing. But the people who post on 7Park regularly. The Bronze Lord. The true believers. They're the ones to be afraid of."

"Yep." Bonnie nods, the two of them trudging back into the house, double bolting the door. They return to the couch, the meager spread on the coffee table. The pitcher of water. Two glasses. A plate of crackers and Daiya cheese. Meg's barely touched it. Bonnie tells her so. "You need to eat something."

Meg ignores the comment. She looks at her watch. "I just wish Lily would call me back," she says. "At least tell me where she is. What she's doing."

Bonnie says, "Have you tried checking her Instagram?"

"She's not really one for social media," Meg says. And she isn't, especially after the accident. She looks at her Instagram anyway and proves herself right. Lily hasn't posted anything since March, a selfie in an Ithaca sweatshirt, on the day she made her final decision.

Meg sighs. She calls Lily's phone again, but it goes right to voicemail. She leaves another message. "At least we know she isn't alone," Meg says.

"Right. And that Carl seems pretty strong," Bonnie says. "He'd stick up for her."

Meg looks at Bonnie, their eyes meeting, the same fear in both of them—the nagging, unasked questions.

Flat tire, Meg thinks. *Maybe they got a flat tire, and both their phones died and . . .*

"Maybe your dad has heard from her?" Bonnie asks.

She raises her eyebrows. "That's possible," she says. Meg calls her father's number. It rings four times, and the machine picks up. "Where the hell is my father at seven P.M.?" she whispers, thinking, *At least he didn't take it off the hook again.*

Meg waits for the beep, and takes a breath. "Hi, Dad, it's me," she says. "I don't know if Lily told you, but she and Carl are going up tonight, not tomorrow. She's supposed to come home first, though, and I can't seem to get hold of her. It's been more than an hour. I'm worried. Can you please let me know when and if you hear from her?" She ends the call.

"Where is everybody?" Bonnie says.

Meg replies, "Maybe the world really *is* coming to an end."

Bonnie just looks at her.

"Sorry," Meg says. Not the best attempt at humor, she knows. But she's always been a firm believer in, *If I don't laugh, I'll cry.* Plus, just saying it aloud has given Meg an idea . . .

She grabs her laptop, goes online.

"Are you going to the website?" Bonnie says. "The one Lily told me about?"

Meg nods.

"It sounds horrible."

"It is." She clicks on 7Park, then TheYearofTwos, her heart pounding as she does it, every muscle in her body cringing, contracting, anticipating the information she might find. The pictures; God, the pictures . . . *Please let there be nothing about Lily. Please let her be all right. Please, please . . .*

Meg puts the phone on the coffee table, so that both of them can see the image board. The most recent post is a livestream. She hears two people arguing, but there is no one on-screen. She sees part of a room. The edge of a grandfather clock. It looks familiar. The room looks familiar . . .

The perspective changes, someone lifting the phone. Meg's heart lurches. "Dad," she whispers. "That's Dad's house."

"What's going on?" Bonnie says. A woman's face fills the screen—dyed black hair, turquoise shadow on her lids, winged eyeliner, bright red lipstick. "In case you're just tuning in, I'm Bernadette. You might know me from the Lee-Man's YouTube channel. Sadly, the Lee-Man is no longer with us." She turns the camera on Dad, frail and exhausted-looking. "Big Daddy killed him with his dark magic. And I'm here to get revenge. Maybe save the world in the process."

"Oh my God," Bonnie whispers.

Meg stares at her father's eyes, huge and watery and sad.

"He's been trying to shoot me, but he ran out of bullets."

"Every right to defend my home," Dad says quietly. Meg doesn't think she's ever seen him so tired.

The camera moves to an empty plastic jug on the floor, then back to the made-up woman again. "His home is now covered in turpentine." She holds her nose and winks. "It reeks in here. Right, Big Daddy?"

The view shifts back to her father's pale, wan face, then pulls back to reveal all of him. He's tied to one of his kitchen chairs, his arms behind his back, his legs bound together.

"Is this real?" Bonnie says.

Meg nods, her skin cold, her limbs going numb. She's never felt so powerless.

"This is the devil," says the woman's voice. "He's channeled the devil to end the world. But now I'm going to end him. Even if it means sacrificing my own life to do it. Me and the Lee-Man. Dying to save the human race."

The camera cuts in closer on Dad. He starts to cough, but stops himself. His eyes are bloodshot, and his face shines, sweat or tears. She isn't sure which. "I don't care about dying," he says.

The woman keeps talking, as though he hasn't spoken at all. "In order to save the world, the demon must die a violent death and it must be filmed," she says. "I feel good about this. A little scared. But good."

Dad stares at the camera. "Magnolia," he says quietly. Urgently. "Go visit the Little Mermaid. You'll see it just behind the diamond. A place of safety. Take Missy if she's still around. She has supplies for you girls."

"What is he talking about?" Bonnie whispers.

Meg shakes her head. She knows what he's talking about. But she can't speak. She can't breathe. *I didn't think he was listening to Mom and me. I didn't think he ever listened to me.*

"I hope you're watching this, honey," Dad says. "I know it hurts to see me go. But trust me. I'm okay. I feel good. Better than I've felt in a very long time. I'm going to see Mom. And that makes me . . . so happy."

The camera shifts to Dad's draperies. To a lit match, dropping. A scream escapes Meg's throat, drowning out everything around her, in front of her: the flames on the screen, the woman shrieking, the phone on the floor now, the camera on the ceiling. The flames crawling, consuming it.

Beneath the woman's screams, Meg can hear her father's voice, frail but calm. "The Little Mermaid. She summers there. She'll play Marco Polo with you . . ."

And then nothing but that awful roar.

Bonnie puts her arms around her. "Oh my God, oh my God, Meggie . . ."

Soon, the screen goes black, and the living room goes black too, Meg collapsing on the couch, a wave overtaking her, sucking her in, drowning her . . .

—

Meg is on the couch with her head between her knees, Bonnie next to her on the phone, talking to the Star Lake Fire Department. She's been on with them repeatedly, and from the tone of her voice, the news isn't good this time. Meg opens her bleary eyes. She aims them at the gun on top of the coffee table. The Glock her father taught her how to use this morning. *I could use it on myself,* she thinks.

No. She has Lily to think of. Just like Dad had her to think of. *The Little Mermaid. A place of safety. Just behind the diamond.* She knows what all of that means. Meg and no one else. Dad had sent Meg a message. One that could save her and Lily.

She drinks from the glass of water Bonnie brought her, and listens to her talking on the phone.

"They sent an ambulance," Bonnie says once she hangs up, a false smile on her face that drops away quickly, a mask that won't stay in place.

Meg looks at her, her throat still raw from screaming. "They sent an ambulance for Justin."

Bonnie exhales. She shuts her eyes. "They're both gone," she says softly. "Your dad and that . . . that person. I'm sorry." A tear trickles down her cheek.

Meg puts her arms around Bonnie and hugs her tightly. They stay like that for a long time, Meg thinking of her father's last words, which hadn't been his but her mother's, and her own. *He listened. He remembered.* And he had sounded so calm . . . "Thank you," she says to Bonnie. "Thank you for telling me the truth. I know it was hard."

Once they finally pull apart, Bonnie tells Meg that what doesn't kill you makes you stronger. She says Meg is one of the strongest people she's ever met. That she'll survive this bad time and someday soon, everything will go back to normal.

"Be strong for Lily," Bonnie says. "Lily needs you, Meg."

It's the one thing she says that registers. "Where is she?" Meg asks.

—

Half an hour later, Meg still hasn't heard from Lily.

Around twenty minutes ago, after five more unanswered calls to her daughter, Meg finally buckled and called Charlie Peele. Still too scared to trust the information with a cop (that gee-whiz act of his still feels too good to be true) Meg hadn't mentioned the Nine-and-Tens or what had happened to her father. And so her concern over Lily seemed pretty baseless. Silly, even. *I'm sorry, Mrs. Russo,* Charlie had said, *but Lily's a legal adult. And from what you're saying, she's been missing for . . . um . . . forty-five minutes? I'm afraid there's not much I can do, but I'm sure she'll be back soon.*

Meg had asked him when he'd be able to do anything about Lily, and he told her at least twenty-four hours, maybe more. *That twenty-four-hour rule is bullshit,* Bonnie had said.

I know, Meg replied. *But what can we do about it?* Meg is thinking about Charlie now. What he said about Lily back in the daylight, when Meg's father was still alive and she believed, deep down, that her family had a chance of outrunning this cult. *She'll be famous someday. I'd bet on it.*

"If you want to go out and look for Lily," Bonnie says, "I can hold down the fort here."

"Are you sure?" says Meg, who was just about to ask her if she could do exactly that. Bonnie, who has always been something of a mind reader . . .

Before she can complete the thought, Meg's phone dings. She checks the screen. It's a text from Lily. She lets out a scream.

"Is it from her?" Bonnie says.

Meg nods, her eyes tearing up.

"Finally!"

"Right?"

Meg opens the text. It's in all-caps, which is unlike Lily. WATCH ALONE. SOUND UP. SAY NOTHING. Meg's breath catches in her throat. A video is attached.

"What does she say?" Bonnie asks.

Meg makes herself shrug. "She claims it's . . . uh . . . private," she says, before excusing herself.

"Tell her never to worry us like that again!"

Meg wants to answer, but she can't speak. In the bathroom, she puts in her earbuds, clicks on the video attachment and watches it. The world stops.

THIRTY-SEVEN

"What is it, Meggie? What's happening?"

Meg forces herself to look at her best friend. Then, she makes herself lie to her. "They're at the police station," she says.

"What?"

"They got pulled over and the cops found drugs on Carl." Meg hates saying his name, but she tries not to show it.

"Drugs?"

"Molly," Meg says. "Coke."

Bonnie frowns. "Carl doesn't seem like the type."

"Yeah, well . . . Lily didn't think so either, and she's so embarrassed. She wants me to pick her up, and she wants me to come alone. She . . . she didn't even want me to *tell* you."

Bonnie nods slowly, her dark eyes locking with Meg's. She can sense the lie, Meg knows. The two of them were eight years old when they met. You see each other through all those phases of life, you know when a friend isn't being straight with you. But at the same time, you also know when it's crucial to pretend to believe her.

"I'll stay here," Bonnie says. "You hurry over to the police station. Get your daughter."

Meg glances at the gun on the coffee table. "I'm not taking it," she says. "If you need it, it's there. It's loaded."

"Don't worry about me," Bonnie says. "But can you do me a favor?"

"Yeah?"

"Text me when . . . when everything's okay."

"I will."

Bonnie gives her a strained smile. "Carl sucks, doesn't he?"

"Yes," Meg says. "He really does." She grabs her bag, throws on her coat and heads out the door.

It isn't until Meg is in her car and buckling up that she notices the weight of her own purse in her lap. She checks inside.

The sheathed dagger that once belonged to Bonnie's father is in Meg's handbag. Bonnie must have slipped it in at some point.

Meg starts up the car, plugs the coordinates Carl gave her into her phone. Then she pulls the dagger out of her bag and slides it into her inner coat pocket. It fits perfectly. Invisibly. "Thanks, Bon," she whispers.

—

The video was of Lily, her mouth duct-taped, shrieking, tears running down her face. *If you want to see Lily alive, come here alone. No guns,* Carl said into the camera, as Lily continued screaming in the background. *If you bring anyone with you, your daughter will be killed instantly.* He then trained the camera on his hand, a gleaming knife in his grip. The proof that he meant what he was saying.

God, Meg wants to kill him. She wants to take that knife and slit his throat with it. Cut off every one of his fingers. But instead, she's alone, in her car, following the coordinates Carl sent, claiming he was with three men he described as his brothers-in-arms.

We are watching, Carl had said. Parroting his group's slogan over Lily's screams. *We are armed. We will triumph.*

Meg's on Route 28 now, following the GPS's directions. The farther she drives, the more Meg gets the sense that she knows where she's headed, the closer the dread creeps in, wrapping its bony arms around her, whispering in her ear. *Welcome back,* it hisses as she takes the exit the GPS tells her to take. As she makes that turn on Greenfield Road.

Meg turns right on Blueberry Hill as the phone tells her to, letting it lead her back to Halloway's Garage. She swallows hard, shaking. Soon she's holding back tears.

Do what we say, the text from Carl had read, the one accompanying the coordinates. And Lily won't get hurt.

Meg hangs on to those words, because they're all she has.

—

All the lights are off in the main building, and the ones that would normally be illuminating the large painted sign are off too. And so, as Meg arrives, Halloway's Garage is nothing more than looming shadows on an otherwise desolate road. The tan Mazda is parked in front of the garage, and as she stops her car, its headlights switch on, glaring into her own. A wave of panic crests within her, her heart fluttering, her breathing shallow. There are shadows in the Mazda. *Men. Those men.*

Meg takes a breath. In her mind, she conjures Justin's voice, telling her to calm down and save their daughter. She knows exactly how he'd say it.

You're with me.

Meg cuts the ignition, the panic lifting. *You'll always be with me.* Meg leaves her bag on the front seat and gets out of the car. She steps into the glare of the Mazda's headlights, her hands raised, her phone clutched in the right one, her heart beating against the dagger in her inner coat pocket. "Where is my daughter?" she calls out, the headlights blinding her. "Where is Lily?"

"She's here!" says a man's voice, unnaturally deep, Meg thinks from steroids. "She's going to kill you."

The Mazda's doors open and four of them walk toward her. Trey McNally. His two friends. She can barely see their faces for the shadows, but she'd know them anywhere. The shaved heads. The attitude. As though they have a right to do anything they want. All of them wear head-to-toe camo, which Meg would laugh at if she didn't want to cry, to shriek. Carl limps behind them, a bloody cloth wrapped around his left hand.

Meg looks directly at him and says it again. "Where is Lily?"

This time Carl replies, his voice a pained squeak. "I did it!" He whips the cloth off, shows Meg the bloody stump where his index finger used to be, rivulets trickling down his wrist. "I performed the ritual! You can't hurt me now!"

Meg looks at him, her jaw tightening. "Where is my daughter?"

"She's safe," says the steroid voice. Meg sees his face in the light. It's Trey McNally. "Undamaged."

Meg's stomach turns. "I want to see her. Please."

He shakes his head. Holds up his phone and starts recording her, his idiot friends at his side. "Witness Sybil!" he shouts in that deep, lunkhead voice. "Here to beg for her spawn."

Meg is filled with hatred. Shivering with it, her blood like ice, her veins frozen. She thinks of the woman on the livestream, making similar insane pronouncements before burning Dad's house down and killing them both. She wants to lower her hands. She wants to pull the dagger from her coat and run at them and stab as many of them as she can before she dies too. *Keep it together,* Meg tells herself. *Think of Lily.*

"Your father made my dad have a seizure," McNally says. "Did you know that?"

Meg gapes at him. "Todd McNally nearly beat my father to death. He spent weeks in the hospital."

He doesn't even react. It's as though she's said nothing. "My dad saw Prism in concert. Nathan Lerner put a spell on him. Everybody saw him do it. My dad collapsed. He was never the same after that. He was just a kid. And then he kept having them. For years. The docs said it was psychogenetic, whatever the fuck that was supposed to mean. But he knew what it was. It was Satan's curse."

Meg grits her teeth. She says nothing.

"He survived, though. Until you finished him off, Sybil. You and your plague."

Carl whimpers. "The novocaine's wearing off."

"I want to see my daughter," Meg says. "Now."

Trey grins. He has one gold tooth. It glints in a headlight's beam. "Patience, demon," he says. "We're the ones in control now."

Meg looks at him. The shaved head. The camo. This douchebag, speaking bad B-movie dialogue, cosplaying a soldier. Meg's father is dead. Her husband is dead. She's had enough of this game. She takes a step forward and speaks into the camera. "What do you want? My life for hers? Fine. Do it. But show me she's alive first."

Trey clears his throat. "Patience," he says again, but his eyes give it away—a fast glance to the left, barely noticeable. Meg also glances to the left and sees a truck. Carl's pickup, parked at the edge of the garage. Only the hood is visible, but at this point, she'd know that truck anywhere. Meg turns away and walks toward it.

"What the fuck," Trey McNally says, his deep voice cracking. "Guys, draw your weapons. Speed, take my phone. Get all of this on the livestream."

Meg keeps walking. She hears a shot, then the scramble of footsteps, boots crunching the snow, Trey whispering to the others, *Stop. Not yet. Spawn needs to do it.*

Once she's near the truck, Meg sees a shadow in the driver's seat. A tangle of dark curly hair. "Lily," she breathes. She says it louder. There's no answer.

Meg feels them behind her now, and her pulse races. Lily looks so still. *No, no, no . . .* She shouts her daughter's name again. Pulls open the door and sees her face in the dome light. Duct-taped mouth. Alive. Lily stares straight ahead. She's belted in, her legs tied together, her arms bound behind her back. She turns to Meg. Those shattered eyes. Meg's heart breaks. *What have they done to you?*

Lily whimpers.

"Sh," Meg whispers. "It's okay, honey. It's okay."

Lily's gaze moves up, over Meg's shoulder. She shakes her head furiously, tears filling her eyes.

Meg wants to ask her what's wrong, but then she feels it, the hard fact of a barrel, pressed against the back of her head. She takes a breath. *You're with me.* "It's okay, Lily. I swear. Everything is going to be all right."

"Back up," says one of the skinheads. Speed. The cameraman. "Take three steps back, Sybil."

Meg does as she is told, the gun still pressed to her head, the skinhead moving with her, like a dance. She's aware of Carl and Trey, closing in on Lily, of Speed standing to the right of them, his phone raised, getting it all on tape. "Don't you dare harm her," Meg says.

Trey starts to laugh. With his one good hand, Carl cuts the rope from Lily's legs with a hunting knife. "It hurts," he says to Trey, the wrapped finger against his side. "Is it supposed to hurt this much?"

Trey lifts Lily out of the truck. He stands her on her feet like a life-sized doll. Meg stares at him, at her daughter. He turns to Speed and smiles into the camera. "If the world is to be saved," he says, taking the hunting knife from Carl, "the weaker demon must lift the sword and drive it through the heart of the stronger."

Carl's knees buckle. He drops to the pavement, clutching his hand.

"Jesus, toughen up," Trey says. Carl looks up at Trey, and he splays his left hand in front of Carl's face. Waggles his four fingers, his stump of a thumb. "Look at it. *Look at it.* You see me crying like a fuckin' girl?"

"Put some ice on it later, Carl," says the one behind Meg, the one holding the gun. He says it as though Meg isn't there, and maybe at this moment, she isn't. Slowly, she slides her hand into her inner coat pocket, her fingertips touching the hilt of the dagger as Trey composes himself and moves behind Lily, his movements slithery and obscene. *I'll kill you.* Meg nearly says it, but she stops herself. He's cutting her free. Trey removes the zip ties and takes one of Lily's hands, as Meg crosses her free arm over the one near the dagger, thinking of Justin's tell. His *I-don't-like-you* body language. *You're with me . . .*

Trey McNally wraps Lily's trembling fingers around the hunting knife. "Repent," he whispers. "Stab your demon mother through the heart."

Lily screams. She shakes her head. Trey pulls the duct tape from her mouth, and Lily shrieks. "I won't do it!"

Meg feels the barrel moving from the back of her head, the shooter aiming at Lily. "No!" Meg screams out the word. *"No, Lily! Lily, do it. Please. Save yourself."*

"Save the world," says the skinhead behind her. "Or get a bullet in your head."

Meg's gaze goes to her daughter. To Speed and the phone. To Carl, moaning on the pavement, the blood dripping from his hand. She takes a step forward, her arms still crossed over her chest. "Do it, honey. Kill me. It's okay."

Lily shakes her head.

"Please. I'm asking you. As your mother."

Lily drops her arms.

"Lily, no," Meg whispers.

She hears the skinhead behind her releasing the safety, and it's like the accident all over again, everything in slow motion. Every movement suspended and defined: Speed turning, lifting his phone. Meg rears back, into the chest of the skinhead with the gun and she sees Trey McNally's jaw dropping open, his eyes going huge, like a figure in a dream. And the dagger—Bonnie's jeweled dagger—the glint of the blade as Meg pulls it from her coat, this heavy thing, the hilt tight in her hand, the sheath dropping away, Carl holding his bloody hand on the pavement, groaning.

"Mom! He's coming at you!" Lily shouts.

And Meg no longer feels the way she did on the thruway. She whirls around, slashing at the skinhead's chest, his stomach. The camo blooming red. He drops the gun, screaming. Meg kicks it away. "Run!" she tells Lily.

"No! I'm staying with you!" It comes out not so much a shriek but a war cry. Lily whirls around, plunging the hunting knife into Trey's shoulder. He yelps, staggering back, shock all over his face, his thumb-less hand clasping the bleeding shoulder. Lily scoops up the gun. She stands next to Meg, then in front of her, arms outstretched, knife in one hand, gun in the other. "I can shoot this!" she yells. "I know how! We're both going to kill you if you don't fucking let us go!"

Meg surveys the scene: Trey and his skinhead friend, writhing on the ground, clutching their wounds. Carl, that worthless scumbag, sitting a few feet away from them, cradling his bleeding hand as though it were a baby. Speed drops his phone, both of his hands raised in the air, backing away. He moves into the headlights, and Meg catches a glimpse of his doughy young face, his dull, unquestioning eyes. His bandaged stump of finger . . . . "Give me the gun," she says to Lily.

Meg takes the gun in both hands, and trains it on Speed. She aims at his chest, then his head.

"Please don't," he whispers.

"What's your name?" she asks. "Your real name?"

"Eric," he says. His lip trembles. A tear slides down his cheek.

"Eric what?"

"Henderson."

Eric Henderson from Cleveland. A complete stranger, who, as far as she knows, has no connection even to the beating at Kennedy. Meg starts to laugh. She tries to stop but she can't, the laughter squeezing her from within. She laughs until tears spring from her eyes. *This lunacy. This terrible lunacy.*

"Mom?" Lily says. "Are you okay?"

Meg shakes her head. Tamps down the laughter. "I will be," she says, "once we get away from these pieces of shit."

Still holding the gun on Speed, Meg grabs his phone from the pavement. It's still recording. Still livestreaming. She gives it to Lily. "Film them," she says.

Lily trains the lens on the bleeding Carl and Trey and the other one, writhing and weeping over his wounds, then shifts back to Speed, aka Eric Henderson, who is now out-and-out sobbing. *Shouldn't he be in jail?* Meg thinks. But then she remembers how many of them are in law enforcement. *How right Dad was not to trust police.*

"Film us now, Lily."

Lily holds the phone up, so the lens captures them both. "Those cowards you just saw killed my husband. And tonight, they kidnapped my daughter and me and tried to kill us both," Meg says. "They're murderers. You *all* are. You killed my husband and my father, two innocent, good men. You'll see that soon. December twelfth is going to come and go and there will be no change in the world, no change in your lives. You'll see that you've murdered and tortured and terrorized and stalked my family *for years,* over some idiotic story you read about on the web. Just so you could feel special."

Meg nods at Lily. She turns off the phone and hands it to Meg, who slips it into her coat pocket. With perfect aim, she shoots out the tires on Carl's truck, then the Mazda. Lily gawks at her.

"Grandpa taught me," Meg says.

Carl rocks back and forth on the pavement, grasping his hand and crying. "I'm scared," he moans. "I'm scared."

"About what?" Lily says.

"The . . . the end of the world."

"Jesus," Lily whispers. Meg wings the phone at Carl. It hits him in the chest. "Call yourself an ambulance," she says.

She takes Lily by the hand and moves to her car, holding the gun on them the whole time.

—

Once they're in the car and back on the road and Meg has texted Bonnie that they're both safe, she turns to her daughter, unsure of how to say it.

She doesn't need to, as it turns out. "Grandpa's gone," Lily says quietly. "I know, Mom. They showed me the livestream." She starts to cry. Meg does too and before long the two of them are weeping for Nathan, for his memory, for their powerlessness to help him. Lily tells

Meg that he'd warned her about Carl, "even though I didn't get it," and Meg tells Lily how, only this morning, he taught her how to shoot. "He saved us," Lily says.

"Yep," Meg says. "Him and Bonnie."

"And Dad."

Meg looks at Lily. She puts a hand on hers.

"Keep your eyes on the road, Mom," Lily says.

—

They're quiet for a long time, before Meg tells her daughter the one thing she's pretty sure she hasn't figured out. "Grandpa also gave us a new place to stay."

Lily looks at her. "He did?"

She nods.

"Where?"

Meg smiles a little. "Didn't you hear him on the livestream?" she says. "We're going to see the Little Mermaid. We're staying right behind the diamond."

Lily shakes her head. Obviously, she has no idea what she's talking about. But Meg knows, the language between a parent and child more powerful and effective than she ever imagined—even that between those, like her father and her, who've suffered most of their lives from a failure to communicate.

Dad was telling her about Wellman's. The natatorium. The baseball diamond. A place on the property where they could stay and wait out the twelfth. He was telling Meg to stop by what was left of Pearly Gates and to look in her mother's old car, where he'd probably stashed supplies. And he was telling her he loved her, not to mourn for him, to let him *help* her, for once.

Meg starts to explain this to Lily, but then the car brightens and she sees flashing lights in her rearview. She goes silent. She keeps driving for a short while, the lights blasting into her car until finally, she pulls into the right lane, her heart in her throat, her palms sweating into the wheel. "No, no, no," Meg whispers. "Not now. Not after all we've been through . . ." She holds her breath.

"Mom," Lily whispers. "Help."

But the police car picks up speed and zooms out of sight.

Meg exhales.

"They didn't want us," Lily says. "They don't know us. They just wanted us out of the way."

She starts to laugh. Meg does too. Lily grabs her hand and squeezes it, and the two of them gaze out at the long road ahead of them, Meg feeling something that might be hope.

What can I say? It's the day after one-two-one-two and the world is pretty much the same shitty place it always was. (Oops!) From all the knowledge I have gained throughout this process (and I can't thank you all enough for the insight you have provided) I feel that it's in our best interest to shut down this board and move on while treasuring the experiences we have had here and the friendships that we've made.

Thank you all for your service. Now get out and enjoy life—and stay out of trouble!

Merry Christmas!

—the Bronze Lord
December 13, 2022

EPILOGUE

One Year Later

Lily once heard that the friendships you make at the start of college are based, more than anything else, on fear. You're on your own for the first time, without curfews or parents or the types of restrictions that kept you alive through age eighteen, and so you gravitate toward people who make you feel safe.

She's not sure where she learned this—probably from one of the many how-to-survive-trauma books recommended by Dr. Cody—but she's found it to be true. During her first quarter at Ithaca, she's met some of the most interesting and talented people she's ever known—musicians from all over the world, many as good as or better than she is—and yet her closest friend is Zach Winters. Zach Winters, who, like Mom, is an English major at Cornell. Zach, who, like Lily, once found himself targeted by a group of hateful people, and nearly died from it. Zach, who, like both Lily and Mom, hates Carl Lindstrom with a passion. And since she can talk to Zach about these things, he makes her feel safe.

Lily's thinking about this as she drives home with Zach for winter break, Lily behind the wheel, the two of them venting about Carl, who was charged with kidnapping, conspiracy, attempted murder, accessory to commit murder and a bunch of other crimes Lily can't remember—but who recently copped a plea, resulting in a six-year prison sentence that may end even sooner if he gets paroled.

"At least you didn't have to testify against him," Zach is saying now.

"Who cares?" says Lily, who, along with her mom, has already testified against Liz Reese, Trey McNally, Eric Henderson and their gun-wielding pal Jonathan Fester (yes, that's his real last name), all of them found guilty of similar charges, all serving slightly longer sentences than Carl. "You know me, Zach. I'm on antianxiety meds now. I fear no one."

Zach laughs, but it's more of a polite laugh than anything else. He knows about the nightmares Lily keeps having, despite all the therapy and self-help books and oft-adjusted meds, and the nightly FaceTimes with Mom, just so both of them can be assured that the other's still alive. He knows how much Lily still misses her father, how she sometimes talks to him in the quiet of her dorm room, when her perfectly nice econ major roommate is at the library or out with her boyfriend and she's relatively sure no one can hear her. Zach knows all about that, and he understands, because he too has survived the type of trauma that's inflicted by a group. And even though his suicide attempt failed, Zach, like Lily, will always bear the scars of that trauma, that feeling of helplessness. "You don't have to look at his face," Zach says. "Or that hand of his. You don't have to be in the same room with him, breathing the same air. That's got to count for something."

"I guess," Lily says.

Zach smiles. "That's the spirit."

Lily stares out ahead of her at the thruway, the sign announcing the exit that will take them to Elizabethville. "We're almost there," she says.

"Yep."

The sky is a dense white, as though it can barely contain the snow. It was the same way last year, when Carl showed up at Lily's house and she brought him into the living room, to her open laptop—worried that, by showing him 7Park, she might shock him into leaving her.

"Do you think he was the Bronze Lord?" Zach says.

"Carl? No."

"Why not?"

"Too dumb," Lily says. "He lets other people tell him how to think. Not the other way around."

"What about the YouTuber? The one Carl followed."

"The Lee-Man?"

"Yeah."

"I'd think it was him, or maybe that woman who killed my grandpa, but the Bronze Lord posted after both of them died."

"Good point," he says. "So who? Trey McNally? Liz Reese?"

"Maybe." Lily has another idea, but she doesn't want to tell Zach about it. She doesn't even want to say it out loud . . .

As they reach their exit, though, Lily thinks about this new theory, which sprung into her mind a few nights ago when she and Zach were up late in her dorm room, downing energy drinks while studying for finals. At the time, she'd blamed it on all the caffeine, which makes her jittery and paranoid, and on a story Zach had told her during one of their breaks—something he'd never mentioned before.

Stop thinking about it.

"Stop thinking about what?" Zach says.

Lily hadn't even realized she'd said it out loud.

"Huh? Oh . . . Driving. I don't want to think about driving. It still makes me nervous."

Zach gives her one of those looks she doesn't like, as though she's the subject of a critical essay he's writing. "Don't worry," he says finally. "You're doing great."

—

"Surprise!"

Lily's heart pounds. She steps back, practically falling onto Zach, who takes her by an elbow, supporting her, always supporting her, as her mom steps forward. "It's just a few of us," Mom says as she pulls Lily into a hug, warm and tight and comforting. "The big surprise is the vegan cake. I baked it myself. We didn't mean to scare you."

Lily's breathing slows, her pulse settling back to normal. It feels good to hug Mom again. And she's right. There really are only a few people at Lily's house: Mom, Zach's parents, Bonnie and Sara Beth. Lily's still a little annoyed about it, though. "You didn't have to shout 'Surprise,'" she says quietly.

"I'm sorry," Mom says.

"It's okay." Lily remembers what Dr. Cody told her during one of their Zoom sessions: Trauma is a heavy curtain. It lifts slower than you want it to, and it drops from time to time.

Once they finally separate, Lily looks around at everyone and inhales the smell of the Christmas tree her mom's bought but hasn't yet decorated. (*I'm waiting for you,* she'd told her during their last FaceTime.) She notices how wonderfully warm it is in this drafty house, thanks to the new insulated windows, and how happy everyone is to see her. It feels good to be home, which is more surprising to Lily than anything, even the concept of Mom baking a cake. Slowly but surely, the curtain is lifting.

"Oh . . ." Mom says, tearing up a little, not at the sight of Lily, but at the case in her hand—Grandpa Nate's bass. When they were staying at the bungalow at Wellman's, Lily played it for her mom every night, their one form of entertainment. She played the "Pearly Gates" solo, and even unamped, it felt as though Grandpa was there with them. "You brought the bass home," Mom says.

"I bring it everywhere."

They all go into the kitchen, which Mom has recently redone with some of their settlement money. There's a new chef's oven, a Sub-Zero refrigerator, sparkling tile floors. Everyone removes their shoes before entering, Sara Beth moving to the refrigerator to take out the cake. They gasp when she turns around with it—snowy-white icing, *Welcome Home, Zach and Lily* piped in red and green on top.

"Nice job, Meggie," Bonnie says.

"So festive," Zach's mom chimes in.

"It's beautiful," Lily says.

"Well, I'd be remiss if I didn't tell everyone that Sara Beth decorated it."

"Helped," Sara Beth says. "Magnolia did ninety-nine percent of the work."

Sara Beth places two candles on top of the cake. Bonnie pulls Lily into a hug and leads her to the head of the table, next to Zach. Mom takes a book of matches out of her pocket. She lights the candles, one for each of them.

"What are you going to wish for?" Zach says, and again, Lily finds herself recalling what he'd shared with her when they were studying, about how when they were outside smoking cigarettes the day the store got vandalized, Sara Beth had told him that, back in the seventies when she was living in New York City, she'd thought about working in law enforcement. Zach had never seen 7Park. He'd never read the Bronze Lord's posts, which have since been taken down, along with the entire image board, the site itself suspended from activity.

And so, when Sara Beth had told him about the rumors back then—of "a secret network of Satanic covens" in New York City, and how she'd thought herself perfect to go "under deep cover" to bring them down—he hadn't thought much of it. Just small talk, from an eccentric old lady who, at the time, had been trying to distract him out of a panic attack.

But Lily had. She'd thought about how the Bronze Lord was probably someone who went way back with her family and still saw them today, who knew about her mother's bad back and arm and her grandfather's cough. Who knew she smoked pot (and Mom smoked cigs? Really?).

What if Sara Beth sees herself as being under deep cover? What if she's seen herself that way for the past forty years? During the study session, Lily had banished the idea from her mind. Sara Beth was Mom's godmother, after all. She'd comforted her through her mother's death and Dad's death, and then the death of Mom's father, whom she seemed to have loved. She'd celebrated the release of Mom's book at fifteen, she'd baked Mom and Dad's wedding cake and she'd helped run the bookstore, basically for a lifetime. Lily understood that ideas like these—paranoid thoughts that crop up after two Monsters in the middle of a stressful, sleep-deprived night—are not to be taken seriously.

On the other hand, Lily has known Sara Beth her whole life, and during that entire time, through all those steamy summers, she's never once seen the woman in open-toed shoes.

As Mom finishes lighting the candles, Lily's gaze travels down, to Sara Beth's hippie skirt, to her skinny legs, to her thick, comfy-looking, perfectly opaque socks . . .

Zach turns to her. "What are you going to wish for?" he says.

Lily answers quickly. "Peace of mind," she says. Then she closes her eyes, takes a deep breath and blows out her candle.

ACKNOWLEDGMENTS

Big thanks to my terrific agent, Deborah Schneider, who sold my first book twenty years ago. (!!!) I hate to age us, Deborah, but Happy Platinum Anniversary! Sending gratitude also to the amazing Brian Lipson—so happy we are working together. I am a very fortunate author to have worked with the brilliant Danielle Dieterich on this book—to say I'm grateful for her guidance would be a huge understatement. Thanks also to Grace Vainisi, to my longtime editor and friend Lyssa Keusch, and to the fabulous Carrie Feron.

It isn't every writer who is lucky enough to have a BFF like James Conrad, co-owner of the world's greatest bookstore, The Golden Notebook in Woodstock, NY. Thank you, James, for your bookseller knowledge and for like a billion other things.

I'm also so thankful to my family of friends—Chas Cerulli, Paul Leone, Cindy Chastain, Kip Voytek and the aforementioned James for their support, as well as my dear group of writer friends for helping me keep my sanity. You all know who you are.

As ever, I'm grateful to my wonderful mom, Beverly L. Sloane, for her love and encouragement and to Marilyn Gaylin, who continues to make me feel like the world's luckiest daughter-in-law.

Last but not least, thank you Mike and Marissa for pretty much everything. I love you guys so much.

ABOUT THE AUTHOR

Alison Gaylin is the Edgar and Shamus Award–winning author of fourteen books. A *USA Today* and internationally bestselling author, she lives with her husband in New York's Hudson Valley.